Praise for
Once a Queen

"*Once a Queen* is reminiscent of beautiful books of magic written in the past, but it's also a fresh, delightful new tale for our wonder-hungry era. With a rich sense of place, vivid characters, a page-turning plot, and a redemptive theme about the healing of generational wounds, Sarah Arthur has created a story that lingers in the memory and shapes the soul long after reading the last page."

—MITALI PERKINS, National Book Award nominee and author of *You Bring the Distant Near, Rickshaw Girl,* and *Holy Night and Little Star*

"Readers of Lewis and L'Engle, prepare to be enchanted. This is a captivating novel that will make you want to revisit the fantasy stories of your childhood."

—SARAH MACKENZIE, author of *The Read-Aloud Family*

"I discovered some of my favorite books when I was young and my family lived in a farmhouse—I would read long into the night under my blankets, flashlight in hand. Well, as soon as I started reading Sarah Arthur's book *Once a Queen,* I felt like that little kid again and I simply didn't want to stop reading. The detailed setting, the memorable characters, the mysterious storyline—everything comes together to create a generational book."

—SHAWN SMUCKER, author of *The Day the Angels Fell*

"*Once a Queen* is written in sumptuous language that makes this poet's heart sing. The magic here is palpable as Arthur deftly ferries readers from one world to another and back again with a wave of her pen. Best of all is the tenacity of hope woven throughout this tantalizing coming-of-age tale of a young girl bravely exploring her family's painful secret past in search of healing for them all in the present. This may be a fantasy, but it many ways it is all too real."

—NIKKI GRIMES, *New York Times* bestselling author
of *Garvey's Choice* and *Garvey in the Dark*

"*Once A Queen* is Sarah Arthur's love letter to great children's literature. Throughout this book, beginning with the title, one sees her great love for classic writers such as C. S. Lewis, J. R. R. Tolkien, and E. Nesbit. However, this book is no simplistic homage. Within these pages, Sarah Arthur tells her own unique tale, full of intrigue and wonder, which is sure to enchant the imagination of a new generation of young adults."

—DAVID BATES, co-host of the
C. S. Lewis–themed podcast *Pints with Jack*

Once a
Queen

Once a Queen

 A NOVEL

SARAH ARTHUR

WATERBROOK

Copyright © 2024 by Sarah Arthur
Map copyright © 2024 by Luke Daab

A WaterBrook Trade Paperback Original

Published in the United States by WaterBrook, an imprint of
Random House, a division of Penguin Random House LLC.

WATERBROOK and colophon are registered trademarks of
Penguin Random House LLC.

Excerpt from *Once a Crown* by Sarah Arthur copyright © 2024 by Sarah Arthur.

LIBRARY OF CONGRESS CATALOGING-IN-PUBLICATION DATA
Names: Arthur, Sarah, author.
Title: Once a queen / Sarah Arthur.
Description: First edition. | Colorado Springs: WaterBrook, [2024]
Identifiers: LCCN 2022039065 | ISBN 9780593194454 (trade paperback) |
ISBN 9780593194461 (ebook)
Subjects: CYAC: Fantasy. | Family life—Fiction. | Secrets—Fiction. |
Grandmothers—Fiction. | LCGFT: Novels. | Fantasy fiction.
Classification: LCC PZ7.1.A7855 On 2023 | DDC [Fic]—dc23
LC record available at https://lccn.loc.gov/2022039065

Printed in the United States of America on acid-free paper

waterbrookmultnomah.com

2   4   6   8   9   7   5   3   1

Interior art credit: wirakorn, kozyrina © Adobe Stock Photos

Book design by Sara Bereta

For Tom, Micah, and Sam:
You are the best magic.

Author's Note

The events in this story are fictional except the British rail crash of October 8, 1952. Three trains collided at Harrow and Wealdstone Station in northwest London, leaving 112 dead and 340 injured—to this day, the deadliest peacetime rail crash in the nation's history.

Likewise, all the characters are fictional, but Professor Kinchurch is based (very loosely) on two historical figures: Constance Savery and Dorothy L. Sayers, two of the first women scholars to receive degrees from Oxford University in 1920. Both were prolific writers.

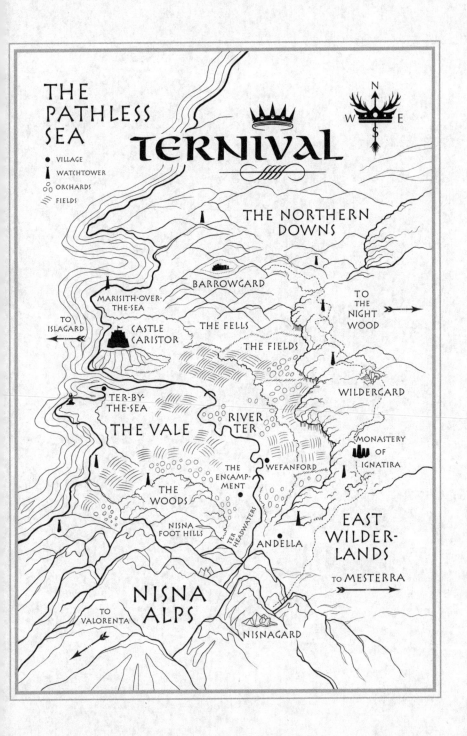

PART I

When you are young so many things are difficult to believe, and yet the dullest people will tell you that they are true—such things, for instance, as that the earth goes round the sun, and that it is not flat but round. But the things that seem really likely, like fairy-tales and magic, are, so say the grown-ups, not true at all. Yet they are so easy to believe, especially when you see them happening.

—*The Enchanted Castle* by E. NESBIT, 1907

The tales of Mesterra—of its inhabitants and visitors, both good and evil; some who came and went from other worlds; some who came and stayed—are full-told in *The Writ of Queens*. Few have read it, however, for it languishes in an obscure library in Tellus. If you are very lucky, you might stumble upon it and read the stories for yourself.

But here, in the tales of Ternival, we shall follow the stories as yet untold.

—*Ternival: Selected Tales* by A. H. W. CLIFTON, 1940

Chapter

1

I n all the old stories, in those fairy tales I still half believed, this was how it happened. Ordinary kids were visiting relatives, maybe. Or stuck at boarding school. Alone. Uncertain. Yearning for adventure. And before long, adventure came to them. They took a wrong turn, were chased away from everything familiar— and suddenly a door opened to another world.

That summer, at age fourteen, I was too old to believe anymore, of course. But the ache, the yearning, was still there.

It never leaves us, really. The question is whether it will become our truest hope or deepest wound.

Or both.

༺ ༻

JULY 1995

"Whatever you do," Mum said as the car swept toward my grand-mother's estate, "don't mention your father."

It'd been raining ever since Grandmother's chauffeur, Paxton, had picked us up from the airport. Gray suburbs had eventually given way to crooked villages, then to muddy farms and pasture-lands bordered by dripping hedgerows. Ahead loomed a range of mist-bound hills, moody and mysterious. Like we'd fallen into a fairy tale. Grim but thoroughly enchanting.

I tore my gaze from the window. "Don't mention Dad?" I repeated. "Why not?"

Mum sat rigidly in the back seat next to me, fiddling with the clasp of her handbag. After our long flight, her librarian tweeds were crumpled, her chin-length brown hair disheveled, her small, fine-boned face pale and tense. "Just don't," she said. "Actually, pause, in general, before you speak. Blathering is a habit your grand-mother never could stand."

"I don't blather."

She exhaled. "Nosiness, then."

"I'm not nosy." This wasn't strictly true.

"Eva, dear, you're lovely. But she doesn't know that yet."

I held my tongue. I could practice not being nosy, all right. Never mind that my grandmother and I were perfect strangers. Never mind that, until now, there'd been no transatlantic trips between England and Connecticut in all my fourteen years. No phone calls. No birth-day cards. And no explanations, despite my many questions.

Mum appraised my ginger-blond curls with another sigh. "It will have to do," she murmured to herself. "If only we could find your *comb* somewhere . . ."

Paxton's glance in the rearview mirror met mine for a second. Silent and morose, like a heron, the old chauffeur hadn't said more than five sentences since we'd left the airport. Those eyes held se-crets, I thought. He knew something.

Most visitors bound for the Wolvern Hills would've taken a train, which normally was all my parents could afford. But, I was told, we don't ride trains to meet my grandmother. No explanation for that either—we just don't. Instead, Paxton had met us at Heathrow and loaded our luggage into "the Bentley," as Mum called it. Now for the past few hours, we'd been winding our way toward my grandmother's estate of Carrick Hall.

I tried to act as though all this was perfectly ordinary. Riding in an actual luxury car driven by an actual chauffeur to an actual English manor house owned by my actual grandmother. As one does. But a bottled-up shriek of excitement bubbled just below the surface.

"There's the village," Mum said, her voice strained. "Won't be long now."

The car had begun to climb toward a cluster of terraced stone buildings. I took this to be Upper Wolvern, the tiny village in the West Midlands near where Mum had grown up. We drove over a bridge spanning a chattering stream and onto the narrow high street lined with picturesque shops and cottages. Despite the gloom, flower beds and window boxes exploded with color.

The Bentley climbed up and up, past a half-timbered pub and around a bend lined with stone walls. At a roundabout with a giant boulder in the center, a road branched off to the right, next to a sign that read Wolvern College, est. 1865. The main road continued to the left, but we headed straight onto a narrow lane.

The lane climbed past a rugged church surrounded by blackened, leaning headstones, all of which looked hundreds of years old. Beyond the churchyard ran a high stone wall just as ancient. A stout gatehouse was built into the wall, and beside it, a broad archway opened to a winding drive.

Somewhere down that drive lay Carrick Hall. My mother's childhood home, the storied manor house at the foot of the Wolvern Hills. What little I knew had been pieced together over the years from Mum's rare descriptions, few of them happy. Forty-two rooms, many of them shrouded or empty or locked. A strange landscape of sculpted yews, known as topiaries, which drew tourists from all over the world. Grandfather Torstane, famous art collector, long dead. And Grandmother, a great beauty, all alone save for a handful of staff.

And my mother, Gwendolyn, their only child, gone for twenty years.

Which baffled me. Why leave such a fascinating place? Why abandon such an intriguing family? When questioned, Mum always demurred: "I'll explain someday." Her reticence only made the mystery more tantalizing, my curiosity more insatiable.

But now, I hoped, I'd finally learn everything.

"Ready?" Mum whispered. She seemed a hundred times more nervous than I was.

I took her hand. "Are *you?*"

She squeezed my hand and gazed straight ahead.

℘ ℘

Paxton maneuvered the Bentley through the archway. We now followed the course of a stream through a narrow valley of pasturelands and woodlands, ascending all the time. The fog thickened.

We passed an orchard, mist drifting between the trees. A figure emerged, pushing a wheelbarrow: a boy not much older than me. He was lean and black-haired, pale features almost elfin. He nodded at the car as Paxton lifted a hand.

"He *must* be a Stokes," Mum said, looking back.

Paxton nodded. "Aye, that's Frankie Addison. Holly's eldest. Helps his grandfather Stokes with the gardens after school."

"My word," she said, facing forward. "I keep waiting for news that old Stokes has retired, but he never does."

"Stays on for tradition's sake." Unlike *some* people, Paxton's tone suggested. But Mum, if she noticed, ignored it.

"And the boy," Mum continued. "Eldest of five, I believe?"

"Aye, madam. Holly's got her hands full, what with helping daily at the Hall and her Jim gone driving lorries."

"Is he?" Mum said, frowning.

"Not enough work in the Wolverns."

She looked away and pressed her lips together.

"After school?" I whispered to Mum. "Don't kids get the summers off here?"

"What?" she said distractedly. "Oh. Not till later. Schools run on trimesters here, you see—and summer term lasts through the end of July."

The trees cleared, and Carrick Hall rose from the valley like an old gray dragon. Through the fog I could make out a sprawling manor house of high walls and peaked roofs surmounted by a square central tower. Still higher behind it rose those stark, empty hills, half-veiled by swirling clouds. My bottled-up excitement threatened to burst.

As we swept around a circular drive, an enormous green figure loomed out of the mist: a larger-than-life topiary of a snarling wolf. Next to him crouched what appeared to be a gargoyle, expertly sculpted from living greenery. Other fantastical figures now came into view: ogres and dragons, centaurs and sprites, scattered around the grounds, emerging from flower beds and hedgerows. A bizarre menagerie.

"You weren't kidding about the topiaries," I murmured.

"I wasn't kidding about anything," Mum said.

I glanced upward as the car drew alongside a flight of steps. Near the great front doors stood what looked like a stone statue of a stately older woman in gray—beautiful, with tragic eyes.

The car stopped. We climbed out. The figure stared at me, one hand clutching its chest. Then it gasped raggedly and looked at Mum.

The statue of flesh and blood was my grandmother—and, for a moment, she thought I was the living dead.

"Hullo, Mother," my own mum said pleasantly. "Paxton made good time, I think. Tea ready?"

Once upon the Warp of Time, Magister the World-Weaver fashioned a flat world. A vast sea spread across it from edge to edge in every direction, and in its center rose a wide landmass of high mountains and deep woodlands, moors and deserts, fens and dales.

Rich was this land, vibrant and lovely.

Magister the World-Weaver then brought forth animals to roam the land, birds to soar the skies, and sea-beasts to ply the waters. So, too, did he make strange creatures, which, in other worlds, are the stuff of legend. Dryads and dwarves, satyrs and centaurs, and wise animals of every kind . . . all woven into being and called to make their home in that fresh new world.

Mesterra, Magister called it. For the land seemed suspended in all the vast blueness between sea and sky like a sparkling jewel.

—*Ternival: Selected Tales* by A. H. W. CLIFTON

Chapter

2

Only now do I understand what a shock I must've given Grandmother, stepping out of the past like that. Mum had sent her my school pictures over the years, but that summer I was fourteen, choppy curls awry, wearing the same expression of curiosity and expectation—and, let's be honest, nosiness—as another girl Grandmother had once loved, many years ago.

But I knew none of that yet, of course.

As I climbed the steps to meet her that July day, Grandmother seemed to pull herself together. She exhaled slowly and managed a wry half smile.

"Paxton will bring your things," she said. Her voice was deeper than I expected, cool and controlled. "And this must be Eva."

"Hello," I said. My own voice quavered with nervousness. I wouldn't blather. I wouldn't.

She reached out a hand like the Queen. Was I supposed to kiss it or curtsy or something? Or hug her, like other people hugged their grandparents?

No, this was a handshake. Reserved, impersonal.

"Well," she said. "Shall we?" She turned and strode down a richly paneled entrance hall toward a grand staircase. Mum and I followed.

The hall was cold and high-ceilinged, with numerous closed doors on either side. Its dark, heavy furnishings seemed designed for giant kings: a massive marble-topped table, a throne-like chair, a grandfather clock. Overhead, a huge chandelier fashioned of deer antlers did little to illuminate anything. The only natural light came from a set of narrow windows, high in the landing at the top of the stairs.

I shivered—from nervousness or cold or excitement, maybe all three.

Grandmother walked swiftly. Her height was startling. She was a head taller than Mum, at least. Her silvery hair had been swept up into a miraculous whorl, making her appear even taller, and I could tell it was long—long enough to reach below her waist. She moved, despite her age, with the confidence of an athlete.

I glanced at Mum, who'd shrunk into herself like a wary mouse. All grays and browns, she might've disappeared into the paneling. I looked away, embarrassed.

Before we reached the staircase, Grandmother turned to the right and led us into a surprisingly bright drawing room furnished in eggshell blue, with floor-to-ceiling windows and comfortable seating before a roaring fire.

"I imagine you're tired," Grandmother said, motioning for us to sit. "Mrs. Fealston will bring the tea." She lowered herself effortlessly into a cushioned chair and brushed her skirt with slender ringed fingers.

The three of us sat silently for an awkward minute. "The gardens look well," Mum finally said. I followed her gaze toward the far end of the drawing room, where immense French doors overlooked a veranda leading to formal gardens. Topiaries dotted the landscape there, too, among flowering shrubs and hedges. A long, lush lawn ended at a domed pavilion, beyond which rose a line of trees—and above that, the hills.

"Paxton says Stokes is still going strong," Mum continued.

"Yes, he's here most days, puttering about. Comes in from the village."

"Must be eighty if he's a day. Mrs. Fealston, too, for that matter."

"Ninety, I think," said Grandmother grimly.

Just then, footsteps sounded outside the door. "Ah, there she is!" Mum exclaimed. She rose, eyes sparkling.

Though my mother had shared scant details about anyone else at Carrick Hall, I'd heard plenty about the longtime housekeeper, Ivy Fealston. She'd been Mum's beloved nursemaid, long ago.

A very old woman entered, trundling a tea trolley. Small and alert, like a wizened fairy godmother, she wore a plain brown dress and cream-colored apron, her white hair pulled back in a bun. As Mum stepped forward, the old woman's face crinkled into a smile.

"Mrs. Fealston!" Mum said, taking her hand.

"Ah, Mrs. Joyce! So good to see you at last."

"And this is Eva, obviously."

Mrs. Fealston's intelligent gaze settled on me. She froze in place, taking in my summer-tanned cheeks, my unruly hair, my eagerness. Then she released a long sigh, like a prisoner glimpsing sunshine for the first time in years. I resisted the urge to jump up and hug her. She seemed eminently huggable—unlike Grandmother.

"Eva is eager to see the house, of course," Mum continued, "but we wouldn't miss your tea for the world."

Mrs. Fealston's expression became all business. "And you're tired, no doubt. I can take Eva round the house tomorrow, after you've both had a good rest. Shall I pour?"

"Allow me," Mum said. "It's been a couple of decades, but I think I can still manage an English teapot."

Mrs. Fealston nodded and left, discreetly closing the door behind her.

"But—" I began.

"She won't stay, even if we ask," Mum said, sitting back down and reaching for the tea trolley. "This is an English manor house, you see. It simply isn't done."

Either Grandmother didn't catch Mum's note of sarcasm or chose to ignore it. "Mrs. Fealston feels her domain is the kitchen," Grandmother said, studying her hands. "And I don't interfere. It's a very old way of life, and not common anymore. But she'd welcome you there, Eva, I'm sure."

"Where *is* the kitchen?" My voice cracked with tiredness.

"Mrs. Fealston will show you everything tomorrow," Mum said firmly. She turned to Grandmother. "Will there be a coach today?"

"Not with the fog. Tourists will keep to the Cotswolds, I expect."

"Well, that's a relief."

According to Mum, Carrick Hall was a popular destination for tour groups, thanks to the strange topiaries and my late grandfather's art collection. And Mrs. Fealston was known as an excellent guide. But Mum herself had never liked the busloads of day-trippers that roamed the grounds all summer. We were to vanish whenever they arrived, keeping out of sight until they left. "A necessary evil," Mum called them.

As we drank our tea by the fire, Connecticut seemed worlds away. By now my school friends had scattered to sleepaway camps all around New England. The university campus where Dad taught as an adjunct professor was mostly empty. I pictured him in his research cubicle, bearded face lit blue by the computer screen, forgetting to eat, wearing the same sweats day after day.

I tried to envision him in this drawing room—and failed.

"Your things are in storage, I suppose," Grandmother said.

"They are," Mum replied. "Packing up didn't take long. We've done this plenty of times, haven't we, Eva?"

"But you two will stay as long as possible, of course," Grandmother said. "No rush to return until you hear about . . . until things are arranged." It struck me that they were speaking of my father without speaking of my father.

Mum looked squarely at Grandmother. "Robert is quite the best candidate for the position, actually. I imagine we'll hear soon." So much for not mentioning Dad at all.

"Even if *you* must leave, Gwendolyn, Eva can stay as long as she likes." Grandmother turned to me. "Your mother told you that you're welcome here for the rest of the summer, yes? If not longer?"

"Longer?" I echoed, glancing at Mum.

"This moving about all the time," Grandmother said imperiously, "can't be good for a young person's development. How on earth do you make friends? I've said numerous times that you should finish your education here at Wolvern, stay at one school for the duration. But of course, your mother *would* insist otherwise."

I squirmed and glanced at Mum again. Her mouth was pressed into a firm line. Truth was, we'd bounced from apartment to apartment my whole life, following the path of Dad's academic career. This July, however, we hadn't renewed our lease. Dad was close to securing a tenure-track position with Whitby College in Chicago, and it didn't make sense to settle anywhere else until we knew for certain. So, while he'd arranged to stay with a colleague in New Haven, to my astonishment Mum had announced that she and I would spend a few weeks with Grandmother. In England. At last.

But Grandmother was right. Moving so frequently *had* been difficult. Pack up. Start over. Walk into a new classroom full of strangers. Decide whether to make any effort, since the next thing was another goodbye. Nowhere had ever really felt like home—except the vague dream of Carrick Hall.

And now here I was. In my grandmother's presence, gazing at her porcelain-perfect face, her glamorous sweep of silvery hair, her exquisite poise. My imagination had built her up into a kind of empress—and so far, she didn't disappoint. I'd never met anyone so satisfyingly, unnervingly *regal*.

Plus, Carrick Hall was just as spectacular as I'd always imagined. More, even. And if Mum agreed, I might get to stay longer than planned.

Mum scowled at the fire, mulish. Grandmother looked everywhere but at me. As the awkward silence stretched on and on, the gilded ceiling seemed to press down on us, like the lid of a cage.

I couldn't decide if I wanted to stay or escape.

To steward his new world of Mesterra, Magister called a people from another world altogether.

That world was Tellus, which he had woven already on the Warp of Time. He had patterned its people after his own likeness, and thus were they well-familiar with the virtues of Inspiria, his eternal palace in the mountains beyond all worlds. And likewise would they recognize all manner of evil—yea, even within themselves—for against such forces did they daily do battle.

The Children of Tellus, Magister called this people. But in our own world they are called *humans,* for they are of the earth.

So Magister lifted a silver horn to his lips, sounded a mighty blast, and called forth a company of humans from Tellus, who arrived in Mesterra as if by magic.

A humble gardener and her husband appeared, blinking and bewildered in the fair light of that new world. And with them came a bookish, bespectacled girl named Augusta, on whose family estate the gardener and her husband had been working. And also another girl, Augusta's neighbor Maggie, who'd just torn her pinafore whilst climbing trees. Plus Augusta's governess, who'd been complaining to the gardener about the lettuces. And with them came a very wet dog.

This was rather more visitors than Magister needed, but his call was strong, and they'd been standing together in the garden when it came.

Chapter

3

After tea with Grandmother, Mrs. Fealston led me up the grand staircase. For such an elderly person, she moved at a terrific pace, her low heels click-click-clicking with military precision as if she couldn't whisk me away from Grandmother fast enough. Once we reached the second floor, I caught glimpses of museum-quality paintings, suits of armor, and vast tapestries flashing past—as though from a high-speed train.

"Your grandmother's rooms." Without pausing, she gestured toward a gilded hallway. I understood it to be off-limits. But I could barely glance at it before we kept climbing, up and up. By the time we arrived at the fourth floor, I could hardly catch my breath.

We came to a sudden halt. She flung open a small, ornate wooden door to our left and stepped inside. "This was your mum's room when she was a girl," Mrs. Fealston announced, only slightly winded. "I see Paxton's brought your things."

I took a deep breath and followed. My jaw dropped. The room

was bigger than our entire apartment in New Haven. A blue vaulted ceiling soared overhead, painted with white blossoms and dancing dryads. To the left stood a high canopied bed accessed by a small flight of steps. To the right was a gigantic wardrobe next to a bookcase loaded with books. On the far wall, a marble fireplace was flanked by two stiff chairs, which stood at polite angles as if ignoring my cheap luggage by the bed.

After all our years in student housing and tiny apartments, I couldn't picture Mum in such a huge space, surrounded by glamorous furnishings.

"It's a strange house," Mrs. Fealston said cryptically, "but you'll make yourself at home here soon enough. Rest now. It'll be a few hours till supper. We'll take a proper tour tomorrow." Then she left, closing the door firmly behind her. She hadn't locked me in, exactly, but the expectation was clear: Stay put until called for.

I tried to steady my breathing. Was I really supposed to just hang out here all afternoon, like this was some sort of ordinary hotel? It wasn't fair. But perhaps Mum had warned her about my nosiness. Which wasn't fair either. Well, okay, then. If I couldn't be nosy out there, I'd be nosy in here.

I turned and studied the antique wardrobe. It stood at least nine feet high, as if designed for giants. A person could easily climb inside and disappear.

Not really, of course. I smiled faintly, remembering how many times I'd knocked on the backs of closets and cupboards as a child, imagining I was Lucy Pevensie looking for Narnia, or Amabel from E. Nesbit's *The Magic World*. It'd taken me an embarrassingly long time to accept that there were no portals to other realms. No magic wardrobes or jewels, tapestries or train platforms.

But magic still clung to the memory of the stories—or perhaps I still clung to the magic. The very walls of this place turned me into a believing kid again.

I took a step closer. Then I twisted the handle and swung the door open.

Empty. The back of the wardrobe stared me in the face.

I pressed my hands against the solid wood panels that lined the inside. Nothing happened, of course. I stood there foolishly for a moment. Then I made a half-hearted attempt at unpacking my things onto the shelves, as if that's what I'd intended all along.

Well, that was done. It'd taken all of five minutes.

I eyed the closed bedroom door. Maybe one quick foray into the hallway? But no, best not earn Mrs. Fealston's distrust.

Instead, I wandered over to the bookcase and pulled a slim volume from the middle shelf. It was *The Little White Horse* by Elizabeth Goudge—one of my favorites. I opened the front cover. Scrawled across the title page was familiar handwriting: *Gwendolyn Lucinda Torstane,* my mother's maiden name. These had been *her* books, of course. I ran my finger along the well-worn spines. George MacDonald. Frances Hodgson Burnett. J. R. R. Tolkien. E. Nesbit. C. S. Lewis. Mary Norton. Lord Dunsany. Madeleine L'Engle. Beloved authors, Mum's and mine.

But one book was missing. None of the shelves contained my absolute favorite, a collection called *Ternival: Selected Tales* by A. H. W. Clifton.

Its absence surprised me. Mum had whispered the tales to me as bedtime stories before I could read—stories about Augusta and her best friend, Maggie, who'd been among the first to stumble from our world into the magical realm of Mesterra. And about Andella the Archeress, who'd slain the foul wolf of the Wilderlands when the Vale of Ter was discovered beyond Mesterra's westernmost boundaries. And about the sisters Flora and Annabel and their cousin Claris, who'd fought fell enemies, danced with dryads, and become queens of Ternival after the Battle of Marisith-over-the-Sea.

It was the rare classmate who'd ever heard of Ternival, much less adored it as much as I did. The book hadn't been a smash hit when it was first published during World War II. The writing was curiously choppy in places. Plus, the collection was incomplete, as if Clifton had intended to write a sequel but never got around to it. But to me it felt so *real*. As if Clifton hadn't merely *invented* Ternival but had *been* there. In person.

I couldn't always tell if the main characters were heroic or selfish. But they'd returned to our world changed. Nobler. Humbler. Braver. Like I wanted to be.

Anyway, Mum herself had first heard the tales from Mrs. Fealston, by firelight, in the nursery of this very house. When I'd gotten older, my parents had bought me a copy at the library's used book sale, and I'd run around the apartment, shrieking with excitement, till the building manager knocked irritably on the door. Even my father kept several copies of his own, bookmarked and tabbed with bright sticky notes, which he was constantly losing and finding again.

In my mind, Ternival and my family were inseparable. So why wasn't the book here, on my mother's shelves?

Restless, I went over to the windows.

From this height the hills appeared closer, higher, even more formidable. Below and to the left was what Mum had called the kitchen garden, planted with a green profusion of vegetables and herbs—a friendly kind of place, sheltered by a high stone wall from the rest of the estate. Against one end leaned a toolshed half-buried by a flowering vine, and beyond the kitchen garden was a cluster of crumbling outbuildings: stables, barns, a dovecote.

Directly below me were the formal gardens I'd seen from the drawing room. To the right was yet another garden, this one entirely enclosed by high hedges, like a secret green jewel. It had no obvious entrance, and nothing was on its lush lawn except a rectangular reflection pool, in the middle of which stood a statue, what looked like a smallish young woman facing away from the house.

Something about her intrigued me, even from this distance. Maybe it was the joyfulness of her posture. Or perhaps it was her golden hue—so unlike the muted grays and greens of the rest of the landscape. She practically glowed.

That did it. I *had* to see her face. Right now. Forget what Mrs. Fealston said.

I peeked into the hallway.

No one. This was my chance.

A nearby passage, almost hidden by a large potted fern, made the perfect escape. I followed it to a series of back stairwells and landings. Some led to ornate hallways with locked doors and dead ends, others to long passages lined with empty rooms or to shuttered spaces full of shrouded furnishings. I kept wandering, always downward, and soon became lost altogether.

Finally, in what felt like a subterranean tunnel, a brief flight of stone steps led up to a heavy wooden door that looked as if it hadn't been opened for decades. Beyond it I could hear a faint hammering.

I tried the door, which didn't budge. Mustering all my strength, I threw my shoulder against the weathered wood and crashed into open air.

The company from Tellus looked around in confusion, as if they had found themselves in a very bright, very strange dream. The dog, who belonged to Augusta, sniffed cautiously, barked once, and began leaping about in a frenzy of excitement. Never had any hound of Tellus smelled a world so delicious as Mesterra on the day of its dawning.

"Welcome, Children of Tellus," said Magister to his guests.

"Where are we, sir?" said Augusta.

Then forthwith did Magister explain about Mesterra, how he had woven it just that morning and how, moreover, he had called the gardener and her husband thither to help steward it, if they chose. But the rest of the company, said he, were there only for a short while, to bear witness to this great honor. Except the dog, who had taken off joyfully after a Mesterran rabbit.

Chapter

4

I plowed straight into the boy from the orchard. He'd been poised in the kitchen garden like a blacksmith, hammer in mid-swing. But now he stumbled back, elfin eyebrows arched in surprise, as I awkwardly grabbed his arm to keep from falling. The hammer missed my shoulder by inches.

The boy pushed away with a sharp exclamation. Whatever he said was definitely English, but unlike any English I'd ever heard.

I gasped. "I'm so sorry!"

He attempted a slight bow that was more of a nod. "Sorry, miss. Er . . ."

"No, no," I said, "*I'm* sorry."

"My fault, really." His words were now crisp and clear. Observing me warily, his eyes were dark as fresh-turned earth, with a stab of light in each center. Freckles like nutmeg were sprinkled across his face. "Sorry to've disturbed you, miss."

I hunted for a phrase that sounded appropriately English. "Not at all. I mean, you didn't disturb me. Totally fine. Carry on." The whole thing was absurd. *I'd* blundered into *him*. But he didn't crack a smile. "I'm Eva. Joyce. My grandmother is Mrs. Torstane. And my mum is . . ." I trailed off, realizing he probably knew all this already. Who else would I be?

He nodded again. "Frankie Addison, miss. My mum is a daily here at the Hall. And my grandad, Stokes, is the gardener."

"Yeah, I know. I mean, Paxton told us as we drove in." I paused with embarrassment, then said in a rush, "Please, Frankie, call me Eva. Just Eva. That's what everyone calls me at home."

He shifted uncomfortably. "Oh . . . er . . . right."

"So," I plunged on, "Mrs. Fealston told me to rest till supper. But from my room, I could see . . . there's a garden . . . a statue of a girl . . ."

His eyes lit up. "Oh? You mean, by the reflection pool?"

"Yes, that's the one. But I'm all turned around."

"The entrance is hidden anyway," he said. Then, as I hesitated, he added, "Here. Allow me." He headed down a path along the wall and disappeared through an archway. I followed.

Frankie said nothing as we emerged into the formal gardens. Mist clung to the flower beds and drifted among the sculpted greenery, as if someone had turned on a fog machine. Up close the figures were much larger than I expected, life-size or bigger. We passed a rearing centaur—half man, half horse. Beyond that, a dark green oversized rabbit on its hind legs peeked from behind a flowering shrub. As we passed a flight of steps leading up to a veranda, I recoiled at the sight of a mastiff, far bigger and fiercer than a regular guard dog.

"Mum mentioned there'd be topiaries," I ventured, "but I'd no idea there were so *many*. Who takes care of them?"

"Grandfather, of course." He seemed surprised and even annoyed, as if my ignorance was insulting. "It's his job. He's done it for years and years."

It felt weird to speak of the estate with a stranger who knew the place better than I did. How long had Frankie lived in Upper Wolvern—his whole life?

"They're creepy," I confessed.

Frankie snorted. "Yeah. But the tourists love them. It's the main reason they come."

"Which one is your favorite?"

He stopped and turned so abruptly that I nearly ran into him. For a long moment he studied me, brow furrowed, as if assessing whether I could be trusted. Then he pointed toward a light green topiary nearby, a willowy woman in a flowing tunic. Her long hair fell, mingling with her dress, till it wound around her feet like the roots of a tree.

"There," he said. "Grandad calls her a dryad."

"Oh, like the dryads in the old fairy tales!" I exclaimed without thinking. "Like the trees in Ternival that take human shape and dance!"

Frankie studied me again. "You know those stories? About Ternival?"

I gave a short laugh. "I used to believe they were true, actually." The confession came out of nowhere, and instantly I blushed. "I mean, when I was really little. Like how kids believe in the tooth fairy and stuff . . ."

I expected him to laugh, but instead, his voice was low, earnest. "Well, when you see the dryad up close, you might change your mind."

I blinked in surprise. Frankie's gaze never wavered, as if there were many more things he wanted to tell me, a hundred thousand stories, each better than the last. But again, the wariness, like he wondered if I was laughing at him. The points of light in his eyes unnerved me, and I looked away.

He turned and kept going. As we neared the high hedge, it became clear that it was impassable. If I hadn't already glimpsed the secret garden from my tower, I never would've known it was there. Frankie ran his hands along the greenery till he found a low, hidden break in the branches, and we crawled through, twigs scraping my clothes and tugging my hair.

Ah! Here it was, the green jewel of a secret garden. Stillness lay over the reflection pool like it'd fallen under a spell. And in the middle of the pool, as if standing on the water itself, rose the statue.

"There she is," Frankie said.

I took a step nearer, and another, and another, till I stood at the pool's edge. I could see her face now. And it was so familiar, I might've been staring into a looking glass.

She was me.

✤ ✤

The unruly curls, the pert nose, the way the eyebrows seemed to float above wide-set eyes . . . it was a face I knew by heart. Yet the body curved like that of a grown woman: fuller than my own, less gawky. And the clothes were old-fashioned, as if she'd just stepped out of a vintage ad from the 1950s. Her stone face gazed toward the empty hills and smiled, like she knew some great secret too wonderful and joyous to share. I wanted, more than anything, to know that secret.

But the whole scene didn't make sense. How did anyone in England know what I looked like—not just in school pictures, but in person? And the statue had the worn, lichen-speckled appearance of stone that'd been here for decades, longer than I'd been alive.

"I-I don't understand," I sputtered. "This looks really . . . *old*."

"Your grandfather commissioned it after she died."

"After *who* died?"

He swung to face me, astonished. "You mean, your mum never told you?"

"Never told me?"

"About your grandmother's sister?" His voice seemed suddenly too loud in that quiet space.

"Er . . ."

He stared at me, unmoving as a statue himself, his expression almost angry. Then he turned and began marching back the way we'd come.

"Hold on!" I called after him. "My grandmother had a sister? What happened?"

"Not my story to tell," he said as I scurried to catch up. "I'd best get back. They'll be expecting me for supper."

I struggled through the hedge and followed him across the formal gardens. There had to be a way to get him to talk. I couldn't bear to enter a house full of adults and shut down this conversation just as things got interesting.

But I needn't have worried. As soon as Frankie banged through the door from the kitchen garden, he blurted out, "She doesn't know. They haven't told her *anything*."

Then did Magister invite the gardener and her husband to forsake Tellus and make their home in Mesterra, to govern it with mercy and justice, to steward its riches, and to care for its citizens. And the couple, who were tired of working land they didn't even own, agreed. After all, it wasn't their fault about the lettuces.

And the citizens of Mesterra, for their part, pledged fealty with a good will, and all present hailed the gardener as the First Queen—all except the governess, who found the proceedings in poor taste. And the dog, who'd never obeyed to begin with.

That very hour the First Queen was crowned with a gleaming circlet woven of silver strands still warm from the fires that had forged Mesterra's mountains. It was a crown of great power, which could protect Mesterra from its enemies, from generation to generation.

Magister imbued the crown with six newborn gems cunningly shaped like the golden pears of Inspiria. And the gems, it was said, glowed and sang.

Chapter

5

Compared to the chilly gardens, the large, low-ceilinged kitchen bustled with warmth and life. Mrs. Fealston stirred a pot of something savory on an oversized range. An old man with a steaming cup sat at a rustic table that ran the length of the room. At the far end of the table, a dark-haired woman folded linens, her wan, freckled face an older, female version of Frankie. None of them noticed me.

Mrs. Fealston looked hard at Frankie. "What happened?"

"She saw the secret garden," he said, plopping down on a stool at the table. "And the queen. But she doesn't know who she is."

"You mean, who she *was*," said the dark-haired woman. She was clearly Frankie's mother, Holly Addison. And the old man was his grandfather, Stokes. The gardener's creased face and gnarled hands indicated he was every bit as old as Grandmother had said, if not older. But there was something solid about him, like the hills. Weathered but unshaken.

"Who she *was*?" I echoed.

The grown-ups turned, startled. Old Stokes lumbered to his feet.

"Miss Joyce," said Frankie's mother with a curt nod.

"No, please," I protested, "call me Eva. Just Eva."

They glanced at one another uncomfortably.

"Very well, Miss—Eva," Mrs. Fealston said. "This is Frankie's mum, Mrs. Addison. She's a daily here at the Hall. And this is his grandfather, Mr. Stokes, the gardener."

The old man nodded, still standing.

Frankie's mother stared at me for a long moment, then gave a short, mirthless laugh. "Well," she said, shaking out a dishcloth with a loud, almost indignant snap, "till I saw her with my own eyes, I wouldn't have believed it."

"Hush now, Holly," growled Stokes, sitting back down heavily.

I moved to the table and pulled up a stool next to Frankie. "Why did you call her a queen?" I asked him. "The statue, I mean."

Mrs. Addison rolled her eyes and shook out another dishcloth. "Here we go."

"Well—" Frankie replied, but Mrs. Fealston cut him off.

"She should hear all this first from her mum, not from you."

"But—" I began.

"These are questions for your mum, love," Mrs. Fealston reiterated firmly.

Mrs. Addison scoffed. "As if Gwen—as if Mrs. Joyce—will tell her now, after all these years! She never believed it herself, not really. And she still doesn't, I bet."

"Just because you don't believe it either doesn't make it untrue, Mum," Frankie said.

Mrs. Fealston set two bowls of steaming soup on the table before us.

"Believe what?" I asked.

"Eat up, now," Mrs. Fealston said.

At the smell of that soup, after all my hours of traveling and taking partial meals on little sleep, I was suddenly ravenous. I dug in. The soup was cabbagey and creamy, flavored with sage, and thick with chunks of ham and potato—to this day, the best soup I've ever tasted. Silence followed, punctuated by the snap of Mrs. Addison's linens and the scraping of silverware.

My mind buzzed. I had *so* many questions to ask these people, these strangers who seemed to speak in code. I was beginning to think they knew me better than I knew myself.

But before I could speak up again, Stokes said to Frankie, "Weather should hold, lad. We can start planting the cultivars tomorrow."

"I wheeled the pots to the orchard already," Frankie told him. "Thought I'd get a head start. I can help you plant a few trees before sundown, if you like."

"Not today, you won't," his mother interjected. "Chores here first. And then I need you back home with the little ones while I clean up supper."

Frankie shrugged. "Tomorrow, then."

"After breakfast," Stokes agreed, "we'll get the cultivars in the ground."

Something in me didn't want to be left out of this new circle. Maybe I was tired or lonely, or both.

"I'll help too," I said—as if I had any idea what a cultivar was.

There was a startled pause. "Well," said Mrs. Fealston triumphantly. She turned to Frankie's mother. "You can't complain she puts on airs now, can you? Like her mum, she is."

"Mrs. Torstane wouldn't approve," said Mrs. Addison with a

sniff. Then her face softened. "But I'm sure Dad will be glad of the help." She picked up the basket and headed into a passageway that led to a flight of stairs.

"Off you go," Mrs. Fealston said to me. "Holly will take you up to the dining room. We'll bring supper shortly for you and your mum—not that you'll need much now."

"What about Grandmother?" I asked. "Will she join us for supper?"

"Oh, she might. Or she might not."

I half waved goodbye to the others, feeling like I'd just been kicked out of their private space, and followed Frankie's mother up the twisting staircase.

We arrived in a narrow, unadorned passageway on the backside of what turned out to be the formal dining room. The door between them opened silently, like a secret entrance. In fact, from the dining room side, the doorway blended into the paneling almost completely. Mrs. Addison entered, put down the basket, and began to set the long, gleaming table for supper.

I hovered uncertainly, wondering whether I should go up to my room or see if Mum was awake. I felt so . . . intrusive.

"Can I help?" I finally asked.

"Almost done now, Miss—" Mrs. Addison began without looking up, then stopped herself. "It's only just the two of you. Well, three, if Mrs. Torstane has a mind to."

The room was long and ornate, furnished chiefly by the dining table flanked by matching sideboards. More than a dozen high-backed chairs lined either side. At one end of the room, a bank of windows overlooked the circle drive, while at the other end, fire crackled in a massive marble fireplace. Over this hung a vast framed tapestry of a hunting scene in which a pack of gray dogs, noses high and tails aloft, chased a large white stag with towering antlers. The stag gazed out of the frame with fraught dignity, as if longing to speak.

I swung around. "Is there some reason why we can't just eat in the kitchen, like Stokes and Frankie? This seems so . . . so . . . fancy. And a lot more work for you."

"This is where Mrs. Torstane dines." Every time Frankie's mother said *Mrs. Torstane,* her lips curled like she tasted something sour. "But it's kind of you to think of it." She looked me full in the eye. "Whatever the others say, I see your mum in you, more than anything. Things haven't been the same here since she left."

After grabbing the empty basket, she disappeared back through the hidden doorway.

I stood alone, feeling as though I'd been left holding a pile of jumbled puzzle pieces. I thought back through the many times I'd plied my mum with questions over the years. Were there other relatives in England besides Grandmother? *Not really,* Mum always said. *No one close.* Yet now that I'd met the staff, it seemed plain there were indeed other relatives—or had been.

I spun out of the dining room toward the grand staircase in search of Mum. But then I skidded to a halt.

On the bottom step stood my grandmother.

Then did Magister gather the whole company he had summoned from Tellus—except the dog (who'd exhausted itself digging for moles).

"Listen well, O First Queen of Mesterra," said Magister to the gardener. "Guard the crown that adorns thy brow, for through it shall thy power be established and thy peoples know peace. Suffer it not to fall into the hands of they that would use it ill, for its power might be turned against thee.

"Be warned, O Queen. Should such danger threaten thee, sunder the gems from the crown and bury them, that their power might be diminished, their music muted, and their whereabouts unknown, lest they draw unto themselves enemies of fell purpose.

"Yea, be warned: These are gems of great power, for they were fashioned on the day of Mesterra's dawning. Ever will they seek to return to the crown—and likewise will the crown call to them. Touch the gems at thy peril, for they might bear thee where thou dost not wish to go.

"But take heart," Magister added more gently. "Should such a fate befall thee, all is not lost. Many generations hence, in an hour of great peril and doom, Children of Tellus will once again appear in this world, and the crown shall be restored. And then shall all the lands know peace."

Chapter

6

"Hullo, there," Grandmother said. In the dim light from the chandelier, she seemed to glow. She wore a sea-blue tunic and an elegant shawl embroidered in purples and greens, which glittered with golden flecks. Her wrists and fingers sparkled with jewels; her soft hair glistened.

"You're so pretty!" I blurted.

She smiled. Like a bright wave breaking on a summer sea, her spontaneous smile is something I'll never forget. It's the kind that shatters hearts. It prompts people to pledge undying fealty. It raises kingdoms and brings them down. And in that moment, I wanted nothing more than to be its cause forever and ever.

"Thank you," she said, descending the final step. "I often change for supper, you see. It's how your grandfather liked to do things."

I glanced at my own crumpled travel clothes, puckered with pulls from the hedge and flecked with bits of leaves. A flush of embarrassment washed up my neck.

"I was just headed up to change too," I lied.

She appraised my outfit, her smile now gently amused. "Nonsense. You're quite acceptable. Especially after such a long trip."

I flushed again. I wasn't immune to fashion. While my parents preferred to remain at home in pajamas, two brains immersed in books, it was just their luck to have birthed a daughter with a mind for design, a flair for color, and a passion for wearable art. I'd brought all my favorite outfits this summer, overpacking to the point of absurdity. And now, for the first time in my life, I'd met a grown-up who just might appreciate it.

"I brought a dress that color," I said, indicating her blue tunic, "with one of those old-fashioned Peter Pan collars. I found it at a vintage shop in New Haven. But it looks almost new and fits me great—I mean, perfectly."

Her eyebrows arched. "Oh? I'd like to see that."

"Really? I have a bunch more too. I could go get them and bring them down for you to see. But they need ironing."

"Please, don't trouble to run all the way up there," she said. But at my crestfallen expression, she glanced at the grandfather clock nearby. "Well, it's not yet time for supper. Shall we go up and see them together?"

Was this really happening? Was my stately grandmother offering to do something frivolous? Knowing what I do now about her practiced reserve, I'm even more astonished. Perhaps she, too, had had no one with whom to enjoy beauty, not for years and years.

She led the way, gliding confidently up the grand staircase as if age meant nothing. At the second floor she turned in a different direction than Mrs. Fealston had brought me earlier, cutting through a long open space adjacent to her own wing.

It was a gallery of portraits. Painting upon painting of grim men in Victorian dress, bored men in top hats and furs, determined men in uniform from every era of the past two hundred years. Women, too, in their shining curls and voluminous skirts, and children holding fruit. My ancestors.

I slowed my pace.

Grandmother glanced over her shoulder at me. "Haven't you seen the gallery?"

When I shook my head, she gave a short laugh. "Ah yes. I imagine Mrs. Fealston wanted to do everything properly later, like one of her tours. Well, we don't have much time before supper, but at least I can show you this." She led the way to the largest of the portraits, which anchored the others as the centerpiece.

A brooding young man with wavy blond hair gazed out from the painting. He was dressed in a short-sleeved white shirt tucked into high white trousers, and he held a longbow in one hand. Leather braces adorned his wrists while a quiver of arrows hung from a belt at his waist. He had my mother's eyes.

"Your grandfather was a fine archer," Grandmother said, "especially with a longbow. This was shortly after we were married in 1953. Back when he was president of the Wolvern Archery Club."

It was an ominous scene. In the background stood Carrick Hall, gray and eerie as if awaiting a storm. And in the darkened woods beside it, a glimmering creature, a great white stag like the one in the tapestry downstairs. The young man's expression held both fear and determination, as if he didn't want to hunt the stag but was duty bound to destroy it.

"Mum says he was kind," I ventured. Mum had told me little else about him, in fact, other than that he'd died before I was born. The topic always seemed fraught with a tension I didn't understand.

"He was."

I could read nothing from Grandmother's expression. She kept walking. I followed her out of the gallery and up the stairs toward my tower room, feeling slightly chilled. Had she loved him, or hadn't she? Did she miss him, or didn't she?

Grandmother took a few steps into my room and then hesitated, twisting away from the view of the gardens and the statue below.

"Here it is," I said. I grabbed the blue dress with the Peter Pan collar from the wardrobe.

"Yes, that's a classic!" she exclaimed. She stepped forward admiringly. "Look at the fitted bodice and the braiding. Probably 1958, '59."

I pulled another dress from the wardrobe, a floral Laura Ashley with a scalloped hem that I'd scored at a garage sale. She took it and held it up. "Oh, this is lovely! Not vintage, but just perfect. Look at the hemline!"

We examined dress after dress, holding them up to the light, pressing them against my shoulders to gauge the length. I blathered on about where I'd found them and what shoes I planned to wear and what else matched. Apparently she didn't mind when people blathered—as long as it was about fashion.

"I don't have a cardigan for this one," I said of the blue dress. "I thought I'd look in the shops while I'm here."

"You will," Grandmother said, holding it up against me with an appraising eye, "because I'll take you." She said it with such authority that I wondered if she'd already planned an outing. "Would a trip to Hereford tomorrow be too soon after your travels? Or maybe Worcester? I could ask Paxton to bring the Bentley around after breakfast, if you like."

No, I realized: She was planning this on the spot because she knew I'd like it. And because she wanted to spend more time with me. My lungs expanded with the sheer thrill of spending a whole morning—a whole day, even—with this glorious grandmother. "Can we?"

"Of course. And wear the blue dress tomorrow." She then began unwinding her shawl. "It will go perfectly with this." She lifted the shawl, its swirls of purple and green shimmering, and placed it around my shoulders.

"Really? You want me to wear this?" I couldn't keep my hands off the silkiness of it, the golden flecks lighting up under my fingers like fireflies.

"Not just to wear. To keep."

Just then, Mum appeared, so obviously startled at the sight of dresses scattered everywhere, the shawl around my shoulders, her mother and daughter smiling, that she nearly collided with the doorframe.

"Mrs. Fealston has announced supper," Mum said, avoiding our eyes.

We followed her down the stairs in awkward silence.

Once in the dining room, Grandmother seated herself at the head of the long table, Mum to her right and me to her left. I was grateful for the presence of Mrs. Fealston, who insisted on serving us from a sideboard before leaving us to ourselves.

As we ate, a chilly draft crept along the floor. Mum's sullen silence persisted throughout the meal—but Grandmother seemed oblivious. She spoke blandly of the weather, the gardens, the headlines. She made no mention of our planned trip till the very end, when we'd already risen to leave.

"Oh, Gwendolyn, dear," she said offhandedly, "Eva and I plan to visit the shops in Worcester tomorrow. Care to join us?"

As before, Mum pressed her lips into a hard line. "Mrs. Fealston was planning to show Eva the estate," she objected, her tone flat.

"Oh, I'm sure it can wait. I imagine there are any number of new bookshops in Worcester now. We could split up and meet back at that little café near the cathedral."

In the brief silence that followed, I sensed a battle was being waged. Some sort of challenge had been thrown down—one freighted with many past challenges.

Finally my mother capitulated. "Very well," she said. "What time?"

"After breakfast," Grandmother replied. "Good night, then."

Grandmother's gaze met mine for a moment, then fell on my wayward curls. With a suddenness that seemed to quench all light in the room, her face drained of color, and she left.

❦❧

I couldn't sleep. It was only my first night in England, after all, and midnight felt like early evening to me. I'd just decided to grab a book from the bookcase when the clouds rolled aside and a brilliant moon blazed through my tower windows.

I flew toward the glass, drawn like a moth to the marvelous light. Was it bigger and brighter than a normal moon? Yes, it had to be. It lit the formal gardens with silvery magic. A curtain had gone up, some veil had been drawn aside, as if all the world's myths could be told on this one fantastical stage. Anyone viewing it would expect to see impossible things.

And I did.

A lady stepped through the archway from the kitchen garden, pacing like a sleepwalker. Face obscured by shadow, she wore a flowing white garment that trailed behind her. Her lustrous hair rippled down, down, nearly to her bare feet. For a moment I thought the dryad herself had awakened and uprooted herself to roam the earth.

The lady glided across the lawn in the direction of the secret garden, pausing periodically as if seeking something she'd lost. She'd almost reached the hedge that hid the reflection pool when another movement caught my eye.

Following slowly, as if to not disturb her, came an enormous white stag.

Its antlers towered like the branches of an ancient tree, higher than the garden walls, glittering with moonlight. Its massive neck and torso rippled with power. Yet it moved with such gentleness and grace that it must've made no sound, for the lady seemed unaware of its presence.

The great stag followed her silently, a protective rear guard, until she turned away from the house and vanished into shadow. The creature followed. I watched until it, too, disappeared into darkness.

Magister then bade Augusta and Maggie and the governess to stand in a circle. At his signal, they were to clasp hands and not let go until they found themselves again in Tellus.

So the three of them clasped hands, as Magister had bidden them. And as soon as their hands touched, a mighty music rushed through their bodies like the roar of a waterfall. Mesterra swirled and vanished, and they felt themselves falling through what looked like a tunnel of twisting threads.

Then did their feet land on solid earth. The swirling ceased, and they found themselves back in the garden on Augusta's family estate just before teatime.

Only then did they realize that they'd left behind the dog.

Chapter

7

When I awoke the next morning, I lay in bed for a groggy moment, blinking up at the canopy. The last I remembered, I'd been standing at the windows, drenched in moonlight, watching strange things unfold in the gardens below. How had I returned to bed? What had happened to the lady? And the stag?

I flung back the covers, stumbled down the little flight of steps, and rushed to the windows. The only thing moving in the gardens below was a rabbit, nibbling languidly on a flowering shrub in the morning gloom. No lady. No stag. Nothing out of the ordinary. Just my second gray day in the Wolvern Hills.

I pressed my forehead against the glass. It'd been a dream—right? Probably just some jumbled nonsense prompted by the estate's strange topiaries, the dining room tapestry, my grandfather's portrait, and jet lag. I tried to shake it off.

Then I remembered: Today I'd be shopping with Grandmother.

With a yelp of dismay, I dashed down the hall to the bathroom and hopped in the shower.

I'll never forget the scene I glimpsed through the kitchen doorway when I finally arrived downstairs. Mrs. Fealston was pouring coffee for Stokes at the table like he was royalty. Frankie sat next to him, chatting affectionately. Mrs. Addison was washing a skillet in the sink, humming. All four of them looked relaxed and cheerful in their own private space.

Then Mrs. Fealston spotted me. "Good morning, my dear."

The peaceful mood broke. Frankie scrambled to his feet. Stokes rose and nodded at me. Mrs. Addison turned, took one look at my smart blue dress and shawl, and resumed washing dishes with a sniff of disapproval.

"We hear you're to visit Worcester today," Mrs. Fealston said.

"I'm really sorry," I said. "Honestly. I *wanted* to help in the gardens today. And to take your tour, Mrs. Fealston." My words felt miserably inadequate. "Grandmother just . . . just *decided,* and I couldn't say no."

"We understand, dear." Mrs. Fealston gave me a gentle smile. "One doesn't want to upset her."

"Maybe tomorrow?"

"It'll have to wait till Monday. On Sundays we worship, and then we rest." She spoke as if these were principles on which the earth was established.

Stokes and Frankie took their seats. "Aye," Stokes said in his gravelly voice. "Monday will do." He looked at Frankie, who studied the table. "Best finish up breakfast, lad. We can plant the cultivars today, and then there'll be plenty of beets to harvest on Monday." Stokes glanced at me with what might've been a wink.

I wished Frankie would acknowledge me. I wanted to convey a wordless apology, the promise that I didn't, as a rule, like to break promises. For some reason his good opinion mattered. All their opinions mattered.

"Run along, love," Mrs. Fealston said. "Paxton will bring the Bentley around soon. You won't want to keep your grandmother waiting."

I left the kitchen, feeling like I'd let everyone down.

"Moles've been at it again," came Stokes's voice as I started up the twisting staircase out of view. I paused partway, not intending to eavesdrop but feeling torn between two worlds. Down here was the everyday world of ordinary people. Up there, a completely different one of finery and formality. I wanted to belong to both, but I felt like an intruder everywhere.

"What you wouldn't give for a pair of magic moles to lend a hand with those cultivars!" Mrs. Fealston's voice wafted up the stairs. "You could plant two whole rows by sundown."

I gripped the handrail. Had she said *magic moles*? Like in Ternival? The kind that are talkative and helpful?

"Magic moles, now," Stokes agreed, unperturbed. "Those chaps will dig where you ask them. If you ask kindly."

Mrs. Addison groaned. "Oh, for pity's sake."

"Not to worry, Grandad," Frankie said. "We'll get it done. You might not have magic moles, but you've got me."

I looked around wildly, wondering if this was some kind of trick. They spoke as if such creatures were the most natural topic in the world. As if such things were *true* rather than the stuff of fairy tales.

Were these people crazy? Or, as Mum would say, *mad*? Mad as hatters, the whole lot?

I began tiptoeing up the stairs. I didn't want to be caught eavesdropping—and laughed at if they were joking. Yet my heart pulsed with something like hope. What if . . .

No, it was impossible.

But . . . what if?

ᚷ ᚨ

After breakfast in the dining room, where Mum and I ate alone, Paxton pulled the car up to the front doors. We waited in the Bentley for what felt like an age. Paxton drummed his fingers on the wheel while Mum, in the back seat beside me, began sighing at intervals. By the time Grandmother joined us, resplendent in a petal-pink cashmere ensemble, Mum's lips once again were set in their familiar grim line.

Grandmother, for her part, smiled at the sight of her shawl around my shoulders before climbing into the back seat next to us. "Shall we?"

As we left for Worcester under rolling clouds, Grandmother kept up a light, rambling commentary.

"That's the way to Lower Wolvern," she told me at the roundabout, pointing right. "Much larger than Upper Wolvern, of course. We can walk there when the weather's fine." We continued straight onto High Street in Upper Wolvern, past the shops, and across the bridge. "The stream comes down from the hills behind Carrick Hall," she said. "Runs all the way to the River Severn, and from there to the Channel. I'll take you there one day."

Just beyond the village, Grandmother pointed left, down a long, straight drive toward a massive pillared mansion set against the backdrop of the rugged hills. "Wolvern Court," she said, "summer residence of Lord Edward Heapworth. Old family friend. I imagine he's staying in London at present, but he usually returns with his family by midsummer. We'll be sure to introduce you."

Mum snorted sharply beside me—whether in frustration or amusement, I couldn't tell.

At one point we slowed to let a flock of sheep cross the road while Paxton again drummed his fingers on the wheel. I bit my lip to keep from squealing. Sometimes England was just so . . . *English*.

As we continued to Worcester, Grandmother spoke of shopping, what we might find in the city, and whether the shops were similar to those in the States.

"I brought a little spending money," I said.

"No need. You're my guest today. We'll buy whatever you wish."

I grinned like a fool. Grandmother was turning out to be even more amazing than I could've imagined. But one glimpse of my mother's face—jaw clenched, cheeks blotchy with anger—and I felt a stab of annoyance. Why couldn't Mum simply enjoy herself?

That very day did the First Queen of Mesterra begin her brief but glorious reign, governing with humility, wisdom, and joy, as Magister had bidden her. And great was her renown among the creatures of that world.

She and her husband built a modest house of stone: their own house, on their own land. And they cleared plots for gardens and planted orchards from cultivars that Magister himself had given them, which he had brought thither from the groves of Inspiria.

And ever after were Mesterra's pear trees prized by the people of that land and planted in new realms they discovered by and by. It was said that the scent of those pears was the harbinger of home and, if ever you had wandered far and wide, by that scent would you know that you neared your journey's end.

Chapter

8

When we arrived in Worcester, Mum left us to hunt for her favorite old bookshops—we'd meet her later for lunch. Grandmother, meanwhile, led the way down Friar Street toward the fashionable boutiques.

At the first shop, a smartly dressed attendant recognized Grandmother immediately and ensconced me in a dressing room, where I was to try on some "suitable summer attire for a country estate." Six outfits later, we went to the counter.

I expected Grandmother to select just one outfit. But no. She purchased them all. *All*. The total came to hundreds of pounds.

My stomach dropped. After a lifetime of shopping at thrift stores, I knew what my mother would say. It was extravagant, ridiculous. Selfish, even.

Slowly I followed Grandmother out the door. A fleet of shopgirls trailed behind us and handed the bags to Paxton, who waited at the curb with the Bentley. As I made to climb back into the car, Grandmother gestured to me.

"Come, Eva, dear. There's more."

And so it continued, shop after shop. After the first hour, every store began to look the same. The world seemed full of dresses and shoes, handbags and jewelry, more than I could possibly wear during my few short weeks in England. When we finally stepped into a boutique that exclusively sold luggage, where Grandmother picked out a matching set of designer suitcases for me to keep, my energy had burned too low to hide my growing unease.

"No . . . please," I protested. "Isn't this just too much? Something simple is fine, really."

"Nonsense. You need a good set of luggage for traveling, and this will last your whole life."

"But I almost never travel." I was too tired to finesse my words. "Mum says we can't afford it."

"Don't be silly. You'll most certainly be traveling." She motioned for the shopgirl to take the luggage out to Paxton. "You can count on visiting me again. Very soon."

I followed Grandmother to the Bentley, battling a welter of emotions. Every daydream I'd ever had about this mysterious woman paled in comparison with the real, living person. Why had Mum kept me away from England for so long? Grandmother and I obviously got along just fine. Plus, Grandmother easily could cover my airfare. So what was the problem?

By the time we met up with Mum for lunch, I was exhausted. And vaguely angry. I couldn't shake the feeling that Mum had misled me all these years, that somehow Grandmother and I had been kept apart unjustly, all because of Mum's sheer stubbornness.

When we returned to the car, Paxton was rearranging the shopping bags in the overflowing trunk. Mum stiffened as we drew near.

"Making up for lost time, I see," she sniped, her cheeks growing blotchy again. She yanked open the front passenger door and climbed in before Grandmother had the chance to respond.

I glanced at Grandmother, who seemed unfazed. Paxton opened the back door for her to climb in, then did the same for me, his expression blank.

No one spoke on the long, awkward ride back.

Upon our arrival at the Hall, I flopped onto my bed while Paxton unloaded the mountain of bags into my room. He glanced at me morosely, then shut the door.

Grandmother never appeared for supper. Mum and I ate in near silence as the gray clouds outside ushered in a long, gloomy dusk. It matched my mood exactly. Why did it feel as though—no matter what I said or did—I was bound to disappoint . . . everyone?

ᘓ ᘔ

Once again, I couldn't fall asleep. What I'd seen the night before had been just a dream, I told myself. But it was worth waiting to see if it might happen again. And if nothing happened, I might as well read myself to sleep.

I grabbed E. Nesbit's *The Enchanted Castle* from the bookcase and pulled a chair over to the windows. But I didn't need the book.

As before, the moon rose. It sailed above the Wolvern Hills like a silver sun, a beacon blazing through my windows. Yes, it really was brighter than an ordinary moon—I was sure of it. And the garden below, with its bizarre topiaries, really was the sort of place where anything might happen.

And sure enough, something did.

Through the archway from the kitchen garden came the lady. Her long hair hung free and silvery in the moonlight, obscuring her face. Her white gown trailed on the grass as she paced toward the secret garden. Now and then she'd pause and turn, as if looking for someone, but continued always in a direct line toward the hedge. As if she could sense the presence of the statue on the other side. As if somehow she knew the girl was there but couldn't reach her.

Then the lighting in the garden intensified, as though another moon were about to rise. Through the archway stepped the great stag. Its massive body glimmered. From its mighty antlers strands of light seemed to twist up and away, spinning into the sky like the aurora borealis. Who needed a moon? The stag *was* the light.

It followed the lady slowly, almost patiently. When she reached the high hedge, she paused there, as if uncertain why she couldn't find her way in. Then she lifted her face to the moon.

It was my grandmother.

Augusta and her neighbor Maggie, upon their return to Tellus, pledged never to tell another living soul of all that had transpired. For they knew that grown-ups, in particular, would not believe them, and they did not wish to throw their pearls before swine, as the saying goes. But many years later, when they were wiser, they told the stories to children.

And the governess, who thought she'd been dreaming, went straight to the estate's housekeeper and complained about how the gardener had gone off without giving notice.

As for the dog (whose fault it was about the lettuces), he eventually settled down in his new world, learnt the art of speech, and became a respectable hound. He married a Mesterran beagle with soft ears, and from them came all the generations of royal hunters and guardian mastiffs that ever chased rabbits in Mesterra.

Chapter

9

Mum and I stood near my tower windows the next morning, drinking in the sunshine. The Wolverns had never looked more beautiful. Down below, in the secret garden, the pool mirrored the blue sky perfectly. The statue of the young woman sparkled from head to toe with dew that looked like diamonds.

I wondered if now, at last, I could ask Mum all my burning questions—and tell her what I'd seen. But could I trust my own story?

Earlier that morning I'd awakened, once again restored to my bed, with no memory of leaving my spot at the windows or climbing back under the covers. I'd opened my eyes at dawn and lain there, bewildered, as outside my windows shone a real, solid, sunlit world. As if nothing strange had happened the night before. Yet hadn't I seen the stag again? And Grandmother?

Now Mum was helping zip up the back of a new dress for church.

I'd been worried about wearing it, fearing her disapproval. But she seemed more cheerful today, chattering away about the gorgeous weather, as if determined to shake off yesterday's awkwardness. But I couldn't shake it.

We went downstairs to where Mrs. Fealston waited by the front doors.

"Where's Grandmother?" I asked.

"Ah . . . she won't be joining us," Mrs. Fealston replied. "Not today."

"Not ever," Mum corrected her.

"One never knows," the housekeeper said mildly, opening the doors and following us down the steps. "Mustn't push her, you know. Let her join in her own time, her own way."

I felt deflated. Mrs. Fealston had spoken so declaratively about the importance of worship in the rhythm of Carrick Hall that I'd assumed Grandmother would participate. And here I'd risked Mum's disapproval by wearing one of my new dresses, because I knew Grandmother would like it.

"Are you sure you don't want me to ring Paxton?" Mum asked Mrs. Fealston as we started down the drive. "It's a long walk."

"Nonsense." Mrs. Fealston flourished a large unopened umbrella that she used as a cane. "Just wait till you see me when the coaches arrive. I tromp about all day. Good for a body to keep active."

"Right." Mum grinned. "I want to be just like you when I grow up."

Mrs. Fealston laughed. Their happiness was infectious—Mum practically skipped down the drive. Was it because we were leaving Carrick Hall? Because Grandmother wasn't around? Or was it the sunshine that ignited every drop of dew till the flowers and trees sparkled like gems?

As we walked, Mrs. Fealston assumed her role as tour guide.

"The estate's prized pear trees," Mrs. Fealston said, pointing her umbrella at the orchard where we'd first seen Frankie. "Planted at the turn of the century by Stokes's aunt and uncle. Masterful gardeners, they were. Designed the topiaries too." She pointed to the other side of the drive, where rooftops rose above a distant grove. "And there's Wolvern College. Just past that old grove is a tall fence. It's the dividing line between the college and the estate."

"In England, *college* can mean 'secondary school,' like high school," Mum explained to me. "And this one has boarders as well as day pupils." She turned to Mrs. Fealston. "Didn't Stokes work over there before coming to Carrick Hall? He was from Lower Wolvern originally, I believe."

"Oh yes. We grew up together. Then he got married and moved to London for a time. After the war began, he and his wife moved back to the Wolverns—the war office wouldn't take him, you see: bad heart. But he could watch for enemy planes by night, up in the hills. And by day he worked as a groundskeeper at the school."

"And then, after the war, they hired Stokes here," Mum mused. "I wonder why he left the school?"

Mrs. Fealston sniffed. "Used to be a miserable sort of place, till the administration changed."

"Used to be," Mum echoed with amusement. "You mean, fifty years ago."

"Fifty years is young in this country," Mrs. Fealston quipped.

Mum laughed. She strode ahead and turned to face us, as if wanting to seal the moment with a mental snapshot. She drew in her breath. "Oh, darlings—look!"

We turned. At the end of the drive stood Carrick Hall, transformed by sunlight from an old gray dragon into a winged creature of sparkling beauty, as if released from a century-long spell. And above it, beyond the hilltops, even more fantastically lit than the house itself, soared a towering edifice of golden clouds, turreted like a fairy palace from beyond the walls of this world.

Unbidden joy sprang up in me, a gladness so close to sorrow that tears burned my eyes.

"There," said the housekeeper with satisfaction. "There it is." As if she, too, saw a palace rising majestically above the Hall—and not for the first time.

"Best keep going if we don't want to be late," Mum said behind me.

The spell was broken. We turned reluctantly and continued down the drive.

Just past the outer wall stood the church with its square Norman tower and moss-covered roof. A flock of villagers milled about the front doors. I hesitated. It was my first encounter with a group of locals. Would they treat me the way the Hall staff did? Like I was intruding on their space?

I glanced back up the drive. The clouds had shifted and become no more than clouds again.

"I need to steal Eva for a moment," Mum said to Mrs. Fealston before we reached the church doors. "We'll meet you shortly."

She led me around the back of the building to a cluster of gravestones, one of which stood tall above the others. Carved into the impressive stone pillar was our family name, TORSTANE. And at its base, the name *Richard Ellsworth*. My grandfather.

Mum crouched. "He was so kind," she said, brushing leaves off the lettering. "We'll bring flowers later." Then she stood and gazed up at a pair of swallows looping through the cloudless sky. "He would've loved this day. He would've loved you."

In the past, whenever Mum spoke of Grandfather, her tone had been reverent rather than affectionate. But now I pictured the handsome young man in the gallery portrait, his grip on the longbow, his determined face. Her daddy.

I missed my own dad suddenly. Our small family had never been apart more than a few days at a time. Yet he'd be waiting for us when we returned. He'd glance up from his computer, give me a kiss on the cheek, and ask how my trip had gone. But Mum would never see her daddy again.

I took her hand. We stood, watching the swallows, till the church bells began to peal.

It might be assumed that all lived happily ever after. But one warm twilight in midsummer, as the moon rose, Augusta and Maggie spotted a huge silvery stag in the woods. Their hearts leapt within them, and they made haste to follow it. Before long they entered a clearing where they stopped in amazement, for the trees were dancing around the stag.

Suddenly two human figures stepped into the clearing. The stag vanished, the trees froze in place, and Maggie exclaimed, "Your Majesty!"

For it was the First Queen of Mesterra, the gardener, back again. And with her was her husband. They seemed dazed, as if they'd just stepped from one strange dream into another.

No one ever learnt why they'd returned—though it seemed to have something to do with the crown, a sorceress, and a great battle. They were safely restored to Tellus, but not without tears.

Augusta's parents welcomed them back to their previous jobs, for good help was hard to come by. The gardener, for her part, turned her grief into the crafting of topiaries that reminded her of Mesterra. And her husband planted pear trees from a few cuttings he'd somehow carried between worlds. From the wood he carved lovely pieces that graced Augusta's family estate.

Never again would the First Queen return to Mesterra. But her heart longed for it every hour to the end of her days.

Chapter

10

The clanging of the church bells sent a charge of excitement through me. My introverted parents had been regular—if not particularly involved—churchgoers throughout my upbringing. But whenever we went, it was never to such a loud, joyful summons.

Mum and I made our way toward the open front doors with the rest of the crowd. Holly Addison stood nearby, holding a sturdy baby on one hip. Her other hand gripped a scowling, sniffling boy of about seven. Next to them stood Frankie in a simple shirt and bow tie, hair combed carefully to the side. His hands rested on the shoulders of a waiflike girl who looked maybe four years old, Frankie's spitting image—except she was even more elfin, with straight black hair tucked behind ears I could've sworn were pointed. She stared at me with large earth-brown eyes.

"Here, Tilly, take Georgie," Mrs. Addison was saying to yet another child, a tallish girl of about nine with luxurious long brown hair. Tilly took the baby as Mrs. Addison doubled her grip on the middle boy and hissed something in his bright red ears. He ceased scowling at once but kept shuddering with suppressed sobs.

"There, now, Jack," Mrs. Fealston said quietly, taking his hand. This seemed to calm him.

Mrs. Addison smiled at Mum. "Lovely to see you, Mrs. Joyce!" I'd never seen Frankie's mother smile before.

"Oh, do stop with the formalities." Mum reached forward to give Mrs. Addison a hug. This was a meeting of old friends, I realized. Had they grown up together? But of course they had. The village wasn't large. What other playmates would there have been for an only child like my mother?

"Well, here's my brood," Mrs. Addison announced. "This is Frankie, of course. And Matilde, my oldest girl. We call her Tilly. And Baby Georgie." The baby in Tilly's arms grabbed a fistful of her long hair, which Tilly attempted to free with a flustered giggle. "Then Jack, my middle child," Mrs. Addison said of the sniffling little boy. "Hush, now, there's a good lad. And my youngest girl, Elspeth."

Again the littlest girl stared at me like I was the queen.

"My Jim wishes he could be here too," Mrs. Addison added, "but he drove full loads twice to Edinburgh this week, and he's worn out. Dad's already seated inside."

A single bell in the church tower began to toll.

Mrs. Fealston ushered all of us inside. "You two should sit up front in the family pew," she whispered to my mother. "The villagers never sit there, out of respect, so it's been empty for years and years."

"Bother the pew!" Mum said. "They can keep their formalities." She marched instead to where old Stokes sat halfway down the left side, the rest of us on her heels. The church wasn't crowded, but by the time we'd all crushed ourselves into pews, it felt packed. In the shuffle I somehow found myself seated between Tilly and Frankie, our shoulders pressed unceremoniously together.

As I shifted position, my hand accidentally brushed Frankie's. We both started as if we'd been pinched. Warmth crept up my neck, and I hunted nervously for some topic to deflect the awkwardness.

"What did Mrs. Fealston mean the other day," I whispered, "by 'magic moles'?"

His eyes remained fixed on the carved wooden screen behind the altar. "Heard that, did you?"

"You and Stokes seemed to know all about it. Were you just teasing?"

"Don't be daft."

"So . . . you mean . . . you really believe . . ."

With an abrupt wheeze, the organ processional started, and we all rose to our feet, prayer books in hand. Singing began, and Frankie joined in, his voice surprisingly clear and robust. "All people that on earth do dwell," he belted out, like it was the national anthem. I tried to follow along but soon gave up.

We sat back down, with much shuffling of prayer books and bumping of shoulders. While someone up front began sharing parish announcements, I leaned toward Frankie again. "You mean, you really believe in all those old stories?" I whispered. "About other worlds beyond ours?"

"And why not?" He looked me full in the face. Something about his expression reminded me of the stag in the tapestry above the dining room fireplace. Bold, a little desperate, yet full of dignity. Behind us, his mother cleared her throat in warning.

There was a long prayer, then more singing, and I began to lose track of how many times we stood and sat back down. But I couldn't concentrate. Was Frankie serious? Other worlds. Like Ternival.

I felt dizzy suddenly, as if the spinning earth had shifted slightly off course. I thought of the golden palace above Carrick Hall and of the great stag following Grandmother silently across the lawn. I thought of Grandmother's face in the moonlight—and shivered.

Baby Georgie had fallen asleep on his mother's lap. But Jack and Elspeth, farther down the pew behind us, were growing restless. Mrs. Fealston did her best, plying them with lollipops and pens for drawing on scraps of paper. But finally, in the very middle of the homily, the little girl's voice rang out.

"I want to see the queen." Elspeth spoke as clearly as one of the smaller bells from the tower. Every soul in the sanctuary could hear her.

I glanced at Frankie. He pretended to study the carved screen, his face paler than ever. There was shushing and shuffling behind us, but the child was determined.

"I want to see the *queen*."

"Elspeth means *you*," Tilly whispered.

"What?"

"My sister thinks you're a queen. Like the statue."

I looked over my left shoulder. Elspeth sat at the end of the pew, near the side aisle. I couldn't catch her eye. Maybe if she could *see* me, at least, she'd be content?

"But I want to see the queen!" Her voice had risen to a wail.

Mrs. Fealston stood grimly and began exiting the pew, gripping Elspeth's hand. I stood also and slipped along my row, trying not to mash people's feet on my way out. By the time I reached the side aisle, Mrs. Fealston and Elspeth were exiting the open doors. I didn't dare run to catch up till I'd reached the doors myself.

I dashed out into the sunshine. The two of them were well beyond me now, making their way through the churchyard. Then up ahead of them, I saw my grandmother emerging from the cluster of gravestones. She held a large empty vase in her arms. Even from that distance, I could tell she'd dressed with care: a white linen skirt and matching jacket, her marvelous hair wreathing her head like a crown. She didn't notice us but instead began to walk back toward Carrick Hall.

Elspeth yanked her hand from Mrs. Fealston's. "There she is!" the girl cried and began to run toward my grandmother.

"Elspeth!" called Mrs. Fealston. "Come back at once!"

Grandmother turned at the sound of voices. The child ran till she reached her, then dropped a tottering curtsy. "Your Majesty."

One look at Grandmother's face—hard and white as marble—and I began to run toward her too. Something was very, very wrong.

I didn't know why, but I had to stop Elspeth from saying more. But I was too late.

"Tell me about that other world, Your Majesty, about the dryads and giants," the girl blathered. "Were the giants *very* bad? And the great stag, was it—"

"Enough," came Grandmother's voice, cold as stone.

I reached Elspeth at that moment, my heart in my throat. Mrs. Fealston came scurrying up behind us.

"What have you told her?" Grandmother demanded of Mrs. Fealston. Somehow I knew she didn't mean Elspeth. She meant me.

The housekeeper held Grandmother's gaze. "She's seen the statue, madam. Of course, she's curious."

Elspeth finally seemed to understand that something uncomfortable was happening. She hid behind me, thin hands grasping my waist. She felt as light as a fairy.

"There will be no more of this." Grandmother's tone held a strange violence that frightened me. I couldn't bear to see her lovely face so transfigured with anger. As she turned and stalked toward the gatehouse, I pulled myself away from Elspeth and ran after her.

"Wait, Grandmother!" I caught up and kept pace. "No one has told me anything. Really. I've been dying to know, and they keep telling me to ask Mum. And anyway"—I attempted a light laugh— "I'm sure it's all in fun. They don't mean it."

Grandmother halted and fixed her cold eyes on mine. Her height made her seem unassailable. Her white outfit, rather than blazing in the sunshine, seemed to drain the light from everything around it, as if we stood under overcast skies on a field of endless snow. The tall vase in her arms could've been a scepter. Or a wand.

"They're mad," she said, her voice thick with fury. "At their age, still believing in fairy tales! And you're old enough to know better. There are no dryads, no giants, no great stag. *There are no other worlds.*"

"But . . ."

"Go back to your mother," she commanded, turning and striding away. "And *never* speak to me of this again."

Then at last did Magister withdraw to his palace of Inspiria, high in the mountains beyond the edges of all worlds.

And ever after, it was said, on clear days you might catch glimpses of the palace rising above the clouds: now near, now far, betimes almost invisible, but never departed.

Likewise, betimes did the silver horn of Magister sound upon the wind and the smell of Inspiria's orchards waft across the air.

Best of all, if you were very lucky, a door might open between worlds, and you might step across the border into Inspiria itself.

Chapter

11

I stood frozen to the spot. Something in me was dying, the last secret hope that beyond our world shines another realm, the source of all the best stories that have ever been told.

Then warm hands touched my arms. A kind voice reached my ears, and a steady presence, stable like the glad earth, guided me gently back to the Hall. Soon I found myself seated next to Mrs. Fealston at the long kitchen table. She said nothing, merely let me sit, silent and sad.

"What just happened?" I finally managed to ask. "Why was she so upset?"

Mrs. Fealston sighed. "Ah, my dear, the human heart is a strange thing."

"But what's so bad about believing in things beyond this world? I mean, I know we're supposed to outgrow fairy tales and all that. But . . ."

"Are we?" Mrs. Fealston's intelligent eyes fastened on mine.

"W-what do you mean? Are you saying you've seen . . . things?" I didn't dare say more. Not about the stag, or about Grandmother roaming the gardens at night. Not yet.

Mrs. Fealston seemed unperturbed. "Indeed I have. Seen some things in my time. And Stokes—he's seen even more. It runs in his family, you might say, to glimpse what lies beyond this world."

Hope flickered again, a coal coaxed to life. Before the flame could die, I named my secret wish, my deepest longing, there at that ordinary table, its scarred wood solid beneath my hands.

"You mean, there *are* other worlds?" I whispered. "It's all true?"

"Of course it's true! Nothing truer. But we can't force these things, you know. Doors to other worlds will open. Or they won't."

She couldn't be serious. Grown-ups never talked like this. Never. Yet here, in the space of two days, I'd heard more than one of them matter-of-factly assert impossible things.

But not Grandmother.

"Your grandmother loves you," Mrs. Fealston said sternly, as if reading my mind. "It's love and fear that do such things to a person. And grief that twists the human soul. You'll learn this, sadly. But your grandmother wouldn't lose you for the world. Not for *any* world. You'll see. She'll come around. Give her time."

A kettle on the range began to wail. Mrs. Fealston stood to turn off the burner, then poured hot water into a teapot. The simple ceremony of this elderly woman—older than anyone I'd ever known, performing a task so normal yet so timeless—broke through my sadness and confusion. Grandmother might be upset with me for reasons I didn't understand, but ordinary goodness remained. Simple pleasures. Human kindness. Sunlight.

Emboldened, I said, "I've seen things too."

"What's that, love?" She spoke as though humoring Elspeth.

"A great stag."

She gasped and nearly dropped the teapot. "A *what*?"

"From my bedroom windows, walking in the gardens. For the past two nights."

Mrs. Fealston stared at me. "This is no joking matter, child. You're certain?"

"I . . . I think so." My voice wobbled. "It's enormous, bigger than any creature I've ever seen. And it glows like the moon."

Mrs. Fealston set the teapot down with a thump, then collapsed onto a stool. "Yes, yes, that's him," she whispered. "But it's been years since he's made an appearance at Carrick Hall. This can only mean . . ." She shot me a piercing look. "And that's not all you've seen. Is it?"

"No," I admitted. "I've also seen . . . Grandmother. Roaming the gardens like she's in a trance. She seems . . . lost."

"Oh, my dear." She closed her eyes briefly, as if I'd just relayed the worst possible news. "Does your mother know?"

"No. I wasn't sure what to tell her. It just feels like a dream."

"It is no dream. But you mustn't tell your mother—I'll do that myself, when the time is right. Your grandmother hasn't had an episode like this in years, not since Gwendolyn left. It must be the shock of seeing you . . ." Mrs. Fealston rambled, as if to herself. "And here I'd assured Gwendolyn that everything was sorted now, that it was safe to return. But this . . ."

"You mean, Mum knows about Grandmother's . . . episodes?"

"Oh yes. Everyone at Carrick Hall knows." Then she looked at me sternly. "Promise me, child."

"Promise what?"

"That you'll say nothing to your grandmother about this."

"But I don't un—"

"I'd hoped her mind had begun to heal, after all these years, but this is a setback, and no mistake. She isn't herself in those moments, do you understand? Any interference could make things worse. You must *not* engage her when she roams the gardens at night. Am I quite clear?"

"But what's wrong with her? What happened?"

Just then, Mum entered the kitchen, holding Mrs. Fealston's umbrella. "You left this behind," Mum told her. "Everything all right? Elspeth won't stop crying. Told Holly something about a witch casting a spell."

"A run-in with Mrs. Torstane, is all," Mrs. Fealston replied, recovering her usual composure. "The little child was confused, and Eva got caught in the middle."

I frowned. That wasn't exactly true. Mrs. Fealston had deliberately left out, well, everything.

"But Mrs. Torstane will come around," Mrs. Fealston added. "She always does."

"Does she?" Mum didn't try to hide her skepticism. "In any case, it's glorious out there. Shall we take lunch in the garden?"

While sunshine poured down and birds hopped between vegetable rows, Mum and I spread a tartan cloth on a small table by the kitchen stoop. We set out the silverware and willowware, gathered three unmatched chairs from various parts of the kitchen, and poured milk into a flowered pitcher. Mrs. Fealston produced ham, hard-boiled eggs, tea, and fresh bread and butter. We sat down as if to a feast made for queens.

My brain still buzzed with everything that had just happened. Even more puzzle pieces had been thrown into the jumbled pile, and rather than adding clarity to the picture, they seemed to make it more muddled than ever. I couldn't ask Mum about Grandmother and the stag, for one thing—that topic was off-limits. At the same time, Mrs. Fealston had insisted there were things I needed to learn from Mum, not from Frankie or anyone else.

"Mum," I said between bites, "Frankie said a bunch of stuff about the statue in the secret garden, before he realized I didn't know what he was talking about. Who was she?"

Mum paused with a forkful of ham halfway to her mouth.

"He said something about Grandmother having a sister . . . who died?" I stopped myself before I added, *And he called her a queen, just like Elspeth called Grandmother.* But one thing at a time.

Mum glanced at Mrs. Fealston for help, but the housekeeper seemed absorbed in pouring the tea.

"Yes, your grandmother had a younger sister," Mum admitted. "But she died long ago, before I was born."

"Really? She must've been young, right?"

Again Mum looked at Mrs. Fealston, who busily folded and re-folded a tea towel.

"Yes, early twenties," Mum said.

"How'd she die?"

As Mum hesitated, Mrs. Fealston said, "You'll have to tell her eventually, my dear."

Mum threw her hands in the air. "Thick as thieves already, are you? Fine. We'll go to Cambridge on Tuesday. Does that satisfy?"

I blinked. "What's in Cambridge?"

"My great-aunt Bertie," Mum snapped and left the table.

As she went inside, slamming the door behind her, I looked in bewilderment at Mrs. Fealston. "Who is Great-Aunt Bertie?"

"Excepting your grandmother," said Mrs. Fealston with a sad sigh, "she's the unhappiest woman in England."

When the inhabitants of Mesterra grew numerous and prosperous, they began to populate nearby realms. And other Children of Tellus were drawn thither through portals unknown. One of their descendants—the youngest son of Queen Ternivia the Vigilant— sought to establish a new realm far beyond the West Wilderlands, in regions uncharted by any map found in his mother's court.

He was called Wefan the Wanderer, named for Mesterra's brightest planet. And the land he found was the Vale of Ter.

Or Ternival, as it is known today.

Chapter

12

Nighttime again. And either my body still hadn't adjusted to the time difference, or I was too keyed up after the day's events to settle down.

Mrs. Fealston had insisted that what I'd seen by night was real. Yet she'd also warned me against interfering. But there was nothing to stop me from keeping watch from my windows again.

Sure enough, up came the moon beyond the hills. And sure enough, through the archway stepped my grandmother.

Her face in the moonlight was no longer transfigured with rage, like it had been in the churchyard. Now it just looked forlorn. Sad enough to break my heart.

I launched out of the room. Quiet as a cat, I plunged down staircase after staircase, the carpets chilly against my bare feet. The final step landed me in the side passageway off the dining room, and I slipped through the hidden door. Everything was dim with shadows.

There was just enough light to make my way through the dining room without crashing into anything. Yet something about the air felt different, as if a huge creature had just released a long sigh. Was it a draft from the chimney? I glanced at the fireplace.

Above the mantel, the stag in the tapestry was . . . gone.

Just then, the room plunged into darkness.

A cloud had passed over the moon. I groped my way to the entrance hall and from there to the drawing room just as the moon emerged again. Now I knew why the air felt different. The French doors stood wide open to the veranda and the gardens below, moonlight flooding the room.

I paused, heart pounding. Then I ran through the drawing room and down the veranda steps into the formal gardens, bare feet slipping on the wet stones. I reached the dryad topiary and then ducked into the shadow of another large shrub. In the silver light I felt too exposed, like an actress who has stepped onstage at the wrong cue. But in the shadows I could breathe. And decide what to do next.

Grandmother must've taken a different route than on previous nights, for I'd lost track of her. Not far from me stood the dryad, motionless. Dew drenched her tiny leaves like tears. Frankie was right: Up close she seemed practically alive.

"Dearest!" came a voice, wistful and sad, wavering on the calm air.

Several yards away, Grandmother was walking toward the hedge with her back to me, unaware of my presence. When she reached the hedge, she lifted her hands as if trying to find a way inside.

"My dearest," she pleaded, "do come back. Please, please."

A small figure came hurrying down the pathway from the veranda. It was Mrs. Fealston, dressed in a robe and slippers. I pushed deeper into the shadows and tried to keep perfectly still.

Grandmother, oblivious, continued to run her hands along the hedge as if searching for an opening. "Oh, let me in!" she cried. "Oh, my dear, do not shut the door. Here I am. Canst thou not see me? Do let me in."

"Come now, Your Majesty," came Mrs. Fealston's steady voice. "Such a lovely night, indeed. But I fear you are weary. Shall we retire?"

Grandmother turned slowly, as if trying to remember something. She didn't seem surprised by the sight of Mrs. Fealston, nor by Mrs. Fealston's calling her *Your Majesty*. Yet confusion warred with grief on her face.

"A fire is lit in Your Majesty's chambers," Mrs. Fealston said. "Do come in where it is warm and dry."

"But . . . but where are my kinspeople?" pleaded Grandmother. "If I could but find the door! Lost, lost, all lost."

"Not lost, Your Majesty," Mrs. Fealston said calmly. "Merely hidden, like stars that've set below the hills. You can send forth scouts at dawn."

By now the housekeeper had looped a gentle hand through Grandmother's arm and begun to lead her back up the steps.

"Not lost," Grandmother repeated, her voice thin with exhaustion.

"Just so."

"Merely hidden."

"Indeed, Your Majesty. Like the stars."

As the two entered the house, I waited in the shadows, trying to calm my breathing.

What had just happened? Grandmother was definitely not herself. Her speech was so strange—downright Shakespearean. And Mrs. Fealston had played along. *Your Majesty,* she'd said. Just like

Elspeth. But this time Grandmother hadn't minded. She seemed to take it as a matter of course. Like they'd had this conversation many times.

I began to shiver. Part of me wanted to stay out here and search for the stag. Perhaps at night it somehow broke loose from the tapestry to roam the earth? Or perhaps it came alive whenever the moon was high, or whenever Grandmother wandered alone, or both? And where was the stag now?

But I was getting colder and colder just standing there barefoot. And anyway, this whole episode had been a near miss. If Mrs. Fealston were to catch me, I wasn't sure what she'd do—probably out me to my mother.

No, too risky.

I sneaked through the French doors and back upstairs to my room.

Before Prince Wefan set off for new lands, his mother, Queen Ternivia of Mesterra, gave him the crown that had once belonged to the First Queen.

The crown had been passed down from generation to generation by the sovereigns of Mesterra, for its chief virtue was to protect the wearer, the land, and the peoples from their enemies. Over time, the crown had cooled and its gems had lost some of their gleam, but ever afterward the circlet had retained some of its original power.

Indeed, it was said that if you were very, very quiet, you could hear the gems faintly singing.

But at some point in the crown's long history, the gems had been sundered from it and somehow lost. By the time of Queen Ternivia, the crown's settings had remained empty for many generations—and thus the circlet's power had diminished more than ever. Even so, Queen Ternivia relinquished the crown to her son, to offer what protection it could in whatever new realm the prince might find.

Chapter

13

"How'd you sleep, my dear?" Mrs. Fealston popped into the dining room the next morning as Mum and I were finishing breakfast.

It was a trick question, of course, meant to gauge whether or not I'd witnessed anything in the gardens last night. But no *way* would I admit to disobeying her.

"Oh, just fine." I lifted my linen napkin to wipe my mouth. I hoped it'd hide the blush of shame that always arose when I lied. "I must be adjusting to the time difference."

"Wish I could say the same," Mum complained. She took a sip of coffee. "I've been up for hours every night, roaming like a ghost."

Mrs. Fealston glanced at me in alarm.

The whole situation felt like I'd parachuted into a minefield. Grandmother hadn't made an appearance at meals—or anywhere else except the gardens during the night—since our awful encounter in the churchyard on the previous morning. But just knowing she was somewhere in the house made my stomach churn. How would she react to me now? What would we say to each other? And meanwhile, I'd been warned against speaking to Mum about Grandmother's nighttime episodes. But neither could I admit to Mrs. Fealston what I'd been up to last night.

So now, a mere four days into my visit to England, I was compelled to keep secrets from the very people I'd hoped to *learn* secrets from. There was no safe footing anywhere. Except maybe with Frankie. But he wouldn't be around till after school.

"I was wondering if Eva might like for me to take her around the estate this morning, finally," said Mrs. Fealston. "The rain will keep the tourists away for now. Unless you two had plans?"

"How kind. Thank you!" said Mum. "We've no plans, have we, Eva?"

"I'm supposed to help Frankie and Stokes in the kitchen garden after school," I replied. I tried not to sound testy about my schedule always being decided for me.

"Oh, that won't be for hours," Mum said with a dismissive wave. "Not till teatime, at least. Plenty of time for both." She seemed a little too eager to be rid of me.

Mrs. Fealston and I agreed to meet at my tower bedroom and work our way down from there.

"In fact," said Mrs. Fealston when she arrived, puffing slightly, "it's most appropriate to start here, as it's the oldest section of the house. Part of the original medieval tower, you see. The rest was built in stages around it."

We made our way down from the tower to the third-story rooms, most of them empty. Mrs. Fealston settled into a special cadence, which I began to think of as her tour guide voice. Here were the chambers for the lesser guests, each with its own fireplace. Here was the dumbwaiter, which wasn't installed until 1890. Here was the old nursery, which Mrs. Fealston described dispassionately—as if she herself hadn't spent hours here, years ago, entertaining a small child named Gwendolyn.

The second story featured the music room and ballroom, the billiards room and study, all designed by some eighteenth-century earl. Plus a spectacular view up the long drive. I kept silent, not wanting to admit I'd seen much of this before. I hoped Mrs. Fealston would unlock the many locked rooms, but she didn't. Nor did she lift the shrouds from the covered furnishings in the long, lonely rooms to show what was underneath.

Once again she steered clear of the wing containing Grandmother's private rooms and instead took me into the portrait gallery.

"Grandmother showed me these already," I finally felt free to say. "Especially this one, the portrait of Grandfather."

"Ah! Yes, a wonderful piece. He was such a kind young man. A bit spoiled, perhaps, but not pretentious—war service had seen to that. I liked him at once."

We stood before the painting for a long time. Grandfather's anxious eyes stared back at us, the white stag glimmering eerily against the dark woods behind him.

"Did he . . . did he know about the stag?" I asked in a low voice. "And Grandmother's episodes?"

Mrs. Fealston sighed sadly. "Alas, yes. Your grandfather knew. It was his one great heartache. That's why he brought me back on staff, of course. This was before Gwendolyn was born, you see. I was hired to care for your grandmother. To make sure no harm came to her. And that's why he hated that stag. He didn't understand it was here to protect her."

"Protect her? From what?"

Mrs. Fealston blinked at me, then shook her head as if to clear it. She turned and began walking rapidly again. "Now, if you'll follow me . . ."

Frustrated, I followed Mrs. Fealston down the grand staircase to the entrance hall. I'd been so close. She'd almost revealed something vital—I just knew it. Perhaps if I was very patient and listened more than I talked, she'd slip up again.

"And here," Mrs. Fealston announced in the dining room, pausing under the framed tapestry over the fireplace, "is one of the finest pieces at Carrick Hall. Medieval tapestry, probably fifteenth century, made from silk, wool, and bits of gold and silver thread. The dye colors came from plants—madder, woad, and weld—and it was crafted by unknown weavers over many months. One square inch would've taken a master weaver more than an hour."

She moved closer and motioned toward the intricately carved frame.

"By the mid-twentieth century, the edges—or selvedges, as they're called—had begun to fray. So to protect it from unraveling, it was framed. In fact, the frame itself is one of the most remarkable things about the whole piece. It was carved of pear wood from the rare variety of tree found only here, at Carrick Hall. Indeed, just a handful of other such pieces exist in all of England."

She ticked the items off on her fingers.

"Another large frame, whereabouts unknown. A third much smaller frame, which was given away long ago. And the occasional unique pieces, such as inlaid boxes, which turn up now and then at auction. All known by this." She pointed to the corner of the frame, where a carven crown encircled the trunk of a delicate tree.

"The artist's signature," I said, leaning in.

"Yes. Quite so." She glanced at me with a faint smile. "A pear tree and coronet. If the Torstanes had a family crest, this would be it." Then she led the way back out into the entrance hall.

"We'll skip the drawing room for now," she said. "It's your grandmother's favorite room, and I'd hate to disturb her."

Something about the gray morning light, filtering dimly from those high windows on the landing, gave the whole entrance hall a wintry atmosphere. What fun it must be to decorate this place for Christmas! Unlike the tiny college apartments I'd grown up in.

"This must be so lovely during the holidays," I said. "I can just picture that great banister draped with pine branches, the chandelier hung with mistletoe . . ."

There was a brief pause. "I've never known your grandmother to decorate the Hall for Christmas," Mrs. Fealston said stiffly. "Now, if you'll follow me . . ."

Next to the drawing room was a closed door that I hadn't yet entered. "The library," Mrs. Fealston said and pushed open the door. But before I had the chance to look around, a gasp near the ceiling made us both jump. We glanced up to see my mother balanced precariously atop a wheeled ladder.

"Good heavens!" Mrs. Fealston exclaimed.

Mum exhaled. "My word, but you startled me. I thought you'd already toured through here." She hastily made her way down the ladder.

"Whatever were you doing up there, my dear?" Mrs. Fealston asked.

"Oh, just looking for something I lost track of years ago. Are you expecting day-trippers today?"

"If the rain lets up—probably after lunch."

Mrs. Fealston switched on more lights. Books by the hundreds surrounded us: old books, leather books, newer books, books in

glass-fronted cases, huge open books on stands, almanacs and jour-
nals, shelves upon shelves ascending to a high timbered ceiling.
Wheeled ladders stood at intervals, reaching shelves far above our
heads.

Before Mrs. Fealston could resume the tour, the door opened
and Paxton's long, gloomy face peeked in.

"Tour coaches just arrived," Paxton announced in a tone of
doom. He might as well have said, *We've been invaded by locusts* or
The bubonic plague has come.

"Oh, bother," said Mum.

"Well, the rest of the house will have to wait, Eva, dear," said
Mrs. Fealston. "Run along now. You'll want to stick close to your
mum—she knows what to do."

"Hide in the kitchen," Mum said bitterly. "That's what we do.
Otherwise the tourists will gawk at us like we're zoo animals."

"An inconvenience, I know," said Mrs. Fealston. "But it's good
business."

She walked toward one of the bookcases and gave the corner a
tug. The bookcase swung out, away from the wall, revealing yet
another hidden passageway like the servants' entrance to the dining
room. As I followed her and Mum through the doorway toward a
twisting staircase, I glanced back at the library.

What had Mum been looking for?

Legend claimed that, generations before the reign of Queen Ternivia, the crown's gems had been removed during a battle against a raiding army of ogres so that the stones could be preserved should the circlet be taken. And in the smoke and confusion, before the hard-won victory, the gems were lost.

Another legend told of how the gems had been stolen and sold to a merchant caravan from Valorenta. The merchants, unaware of the gems' true power, carried the treasures across the desert into the mighty Nisna Alps, where the gems proved dangerous and were thrown into an ancient mine.

Thus did a prophecy arise, that one day the gems would be found and the crown's settings restored. And on that day the circlet would become a thing of inestimable power, for the gems would have grown in strength during their long concealment. Once restored to the crown, they would render the wearer safe from her enemies and secure her borders in peace.

Many brave young women and men did seek their fortunes, and their sovereigns' favor, by hunting far and wide for the lost gems.

Yet to no avail.

Chapter

14

After teatime, I set out to find Frankie in the kitchen garden—where, Mrs. Fealston said, he'd turn up after school. I knew nothing about gardening, of course, thanks to a lifetime of apartment dwelling. But I was determined not to "put on airs," whatever that meant. And to make good on my promise to help.

Plus, Frankie was the only one I could talk to about Grandmother and the stag.

I followed the path through the kitchen garden, between the neat rows of lettuces and cabbages and climbing peas. As I approached the toolshed, I heard voices, the gardener's low rumble and Frankie's lighter, affectionate tone. And then I saw them, sitting comfortably shoulder to shoulder on the bench outside the shed.

Sudden jealousy gripped me. It wasn't fair that other kids got to know their grandparents like this, to become close to them, while I didn't. My dad's parents had been fairly old when he was born, and they died shortly after he graduated from high school. He was an only child like me and Mum, so I'd grown up without any extended family at all. But here in Upper Wolvern, Frankie was surrounded by family who loved him. They'd watched him grow up, knew all his quirks and foibles. Unlike me, he could sit on a garden bench after school and talk with a grandparent about his day—and be accepted for who he was.

I knew it was petty. But in that moment I decided not to tell him about Grandmother and the stag. Frankie could have his private family moments, and I'd have mine—bizarre as they were.

Frankie looked up with a crooked grin, as if Stokes had just said something amusing. "Hullo, Eva. Ready to dig up beets?"

He led me into the toolshed, where we found trowels and gardening gloves. Then we knelt next to a row of dark green plants, and Frankie demonstrated what to do. A deft plunge and twist of the trowel, a gentle tug on the greens, and out popped a beet from the soil.

"I've never eaten a beet in my life," I admitted.

"I like them pickled." He dug into the soil with gusto. "With a hard-boiled egg. Makes all this worthwhile, somehow."

We worked for a while in silence, the warm sun on our backs, birdsong in the air. Now that I'd decided not to tell him about Grandmother and the stag, I couldn't think of anything else to talk about. But then I remembered what Mrs. Fealston had said about Stokes, that it ran in his family to glimpse what lies beyond this world. Certainly Frankie would know what she meant. But I decided to ease in with a different topic.

"Mum says we're going to Cambridge tomorrow. We'll be gone for a few days."

"Ah," he said, as if a trip to Cambridge made perfect sense. "That's where your parents met. At university."

It was unnerving, really, how much he knew about my family.

"Mrs. Fealston says your father is writing a book," he continued, "about Professor Kinchurch."

I looked at Frankie in surprise. Very few people knew anything about my dad's research. Even I didn't know much about it. Some boring theory about one of the first female scholars to receive a degree from Oxford, a long-dead theologian named Kinchurch. Dad had been working on this theory for so long that Kinchurch— whom we simply called "the Professor"—had become almost like a fourth member of the family. And now, at long last, a publisher had expressed interest in Dad's research, which consumed his every waking hour.

"Why didn't your father come to England with you?" Frankie asked.

I shrugged. "He says he's got the last bit of writing to finish up. It's all about the footnotes right now, apparently. Pages and pages of footnotes." The sun blazed on my shoulders. I rocked back on my heels, wiping my forehead with a dirty glove. "Then we'll load up the moving truck."

"You're moving? Where?"

"Not sure yet. But Whitby College in Chicago will probably hire him for a tenure-track position."

Stokes shuffled out of the toolshed and lowered himself onto the bench in the sunshine. He appeared to be engrossed in repairing a rake, but I suspected he was listening.

"So what will you do in Cambridge?" Frankie asked.

"Mum wants me to meet someone she calls her great-aunt Bertie."

"Oh!" he exclaimed, twisting to face me. "So she told you!"

"Told me?"

Stokes coughed.

Frankie hesitated. "Well . . . just that you . . . have other family. In England."

I could tell he had more to say, but the watchful presence of Stokes held him back. *She should hear all this first from her mum, not from you,* Mrs. Fealston had warned. Frankie was so darned *obedient.*

"Cambridge is where I'll study one day," he announced after a moment. "I'm going to be a theologian. Like Kinchurch."

Since most of my classmates back in the States aspired to attend Yale or Harvard or Boston College, this didn't faze me. I was unaware that—in England, at least—the sons of lorry drivers don't generally become theologians.

"Well, when I write *my* groundbreaking theory," I told him, "I'm going to finish quickly and be done with it. I can't tell you how many times I've wanted to take my dad's computer and throw it out the window."

Frankie snorted. Stokes's rumble of amusement proved that he was indeed eavesdropping.

I kept digging. There was something satisfying about the heft of earth under the trowel, the way the beetroots popped from the soil as I pulled them up. The warmth, the birdsong, Stokes's sturdy presence, Frankie's earnest face—it was all good.

I plunged my trowel into the dirt and felt it scrape against something solid.

Frankie glanced my way. "Probably a big stone."

I pushed into the dirt from a different angle, but again the scrape and a hollow clunk. Frankie set down his trowel and rocked back on his heels to watch. Stokes, too, had stopped what he was doing. I began digging in earnest.

Something began to emerge from the dirt, something made of wood.

"It's a box," I said, setting the trowel aside and scraping with my hands. Soon I was able to get my fingers under it and lift it from the soil. It was about the size of a pencil box, dark and delicately carved, with a jagged slash across the lid. I brushed the dirt from the carvings with my gloved fingers. On one corner of the lid was the same tree and crown as on the tapestry frame.

"Oh!" I breathed. I glanced at Frankie. His face had grown so pale it was almost translucent.

"Locked?" Stokes asked from the bench.

I turned the box around in my hands. Yes, there was a clasp, but so caked with dirt it wouldn't budge.

Frankie leaped to his feet. "Let's break it open!"

I scrambled up and followed him into the vine-shadowed toolshed. He grabbed a small screwdriver and a hammer, and with a sharp tap-tap, the clasp came apart. Carefully I lifted the lid.

A faint ringing filled our ears, as if we'd opened a music box. Several bright things like diamonds flashed against a lining of dark velvet. But I didn't get a better look.

Stokes appeared suddenly and slammed the lid shut.

"Belongs to your grandmother," he growled, yanking the box away. "Best not meddle."

Then he strode out of the shed and headed toward the house faster than I'd ever seen him move.

Queen Ternivia of Mesterra, knowing that her son's departure was imminent and his future uncertain, embraced Prince Wefan for the last time. He hid the crown she had given him in his leathern satchel, to save for such time as he had need.

Then Wefan gathered a company of true-hearted subjects: dwarves to mine and moles to delve; centaurs to counsel and falcons to scout; hounds to guard and dryads to wake their fellow trees to life. All pledged fealty to the prince and loyalty to one another, and all prepared to forsake their homes for new lands.

Finally the prince bade farewell to his mother and father and set forth.

Chapter

15

Frankie grabbed both my gloved hands. "Did you see them?" he hissed, the points of light in his eyes blazing. "Do you know what they were?"

"I saw—"

"Those bright things in the box—they were the gems! I always knew they'd turn up somehow." I'd never seen his face so alive.

"The gems?" I echoed. "What gems?"

He dropped my hands and began pacing. "Remember? In the tales of Ternival, remember the gems from the crown?"

I felt suddenly panicky. Maybe Frankie *was* mad. Yet . . . hadn't I seen the stag with my own eyes? Weren't the gems almost . . . singing?

"You're not serious," I said—which was ridiculous. This kid was nothing if not serious.

He stopped and stared at me. "One hundred percent."

"But how do you know it isn't just someone's old jewelry box?

The kind that plays music when you open the lid? Anyone could've buried something like that."

"No, didn't you see? They weren't ordinary gems." He began pacing again. "They . . . shimmered and pulsed, like they were singing. That's why Grandad had to take them. They're dangerous. They're *magic*."

"Wait, Frankie. Back up. This means . . . you're saying . . . you mean, the stories are *true*?"

Once again he halted. "Of course they're true! Nothing truer."

He sounded just like Mrs. Fealston. But somehow, coming from Frankie, the words seemed even more plausible. Like he didn't just believe in fairy tales in general, on principle: Instead, he believed in *Ternival*. That Ternival was *real*.

"And that's why," Frankie rattled on, "whenever I've had the chance, I've been hunting for the gems all over this place. And the box was right here the whole time!"

"So . . . if the gems are real," I said slowly, "then does that mean portals for getting into other worlds are real too? Like tunnels. And magic paintings. And doors that open when they didn't open before?"

"Exactly! And wardrobes and railway platforms. And amulets and magic carpets, for all we know. Anyway, I've always suspected that those things haven't gone away. They're still here, in our world. But they've been lost. They've been hidden or forgotten or misplaced among ordinary things."

"And you think we can find them?"

"We just found some, didn't we?"

"Okay, but how did the box end up *here*? In my grandmother's garden?"

"You really don't know?"

I shook my head.

He paused. "Mrs. Fealston says it's not my story to tell. That you need to hear it first from your mum."

"I know, I know," I said irritably. "But if my mum doesn't believe, then *she'll* never tell me."

Frankie frowned, wavering. "Not my story."

"Fine. So tell me *your* story."

"Can I trust you to keep a secret?"

"Seriously? All this time I've been waiting for anyone around here—*anyone*—to trust me with secrets."

Frankie peered through the doorway, then turned back to me. "Right," he whispered. "Long ago, before Grandad was born, his aunt and uncle vanished right out of this world. One moment, they were working, going about an ordinary day . . . and the next, they were gone, just like that."

"An ordinary day." I leveled my gaze at Frankie, hoping he would break under pressure and explain more. But nope. "So how do you know they didn't just die? Got murdered or something?"

"Because eventually they came back. But not before . . ."

"Not before?"

There it was again, that noble expression on his face. Like the stag. Frankie drew himself up to his full height. "Not before Grandad's aunt was crowned queen. Of that other world."

I couldn't speak. Before me stood a boy—a young man, really—who believed, in the depths of his soul, that he was kin to royalty.

My own grandmother came to mind, wandering the gardens at night, acting as though it was perfectly normal to be called *Your Majesty*. What if . . .

"And my grandmother? Was she . . ."

He folded his arms and gave me a look so stubborn, I wanted to shake him.

"Frankie, just tell me!"

"I can't. But I *can* tell you one thing. It's just a guess, really, about your great-aunt Bertie. Grandad seems to think she owns something that once belonged here, at Carrick Hall."

"Like what?"

"Something special."

"You mean something magical, like the box of gems?"

"Yes. Maybe. I'm not sure."

"Well, that's helpful," I said sarcastically. "And while I'm in Cambridge, I'm supposed to look for this unidentified magical object?"

He shrugged. "Worth a try."

"Fine. And *you* should try to find out what Stokes did with the box."

Frankie pulled back, suddenly cautious. "Er, I don't know. I mean, he said it's best not to meddle."

This was the annoying side of Frankie. The obedient, rule-following side. "But what if he's wrong? What if they're all wrong?"

"But if they're wrong about this," he countered, "how can we be sure they're right about everything else?"

It was a fair point. At the same time, we couldn't just give up. "But if they're right, those gems might be the key to *everything*, Frankie. I think you should try to find them anyway."

He clammed up mutinously.

"C'mon," I wheedled. "It's not really meddling. Not if it's my own grandmother's estate."

"Easy for *you* to say," he retorted. "*You* might be able to sneak around doing whatever you like, but I can't. Everyone walks on eggshells around here, trying not to upset your grandmother. If I mess this up, my family could get sacked."

This was a new thought. If Grandmother flew into another cold rage, the stakes for Frankie—for all of them: the Addisons, Stokes, even Mrs. Fealston—were far, far higher than for me.

All my excitement evaporated. "Oh, right," I said awkwardly. "Sorry."

"So if we do anything, it's got to be after you return from Cambridge. And super secretly. Like we're spies."

"Sure." But part of me still chafed at the idea. After all, the gems belonged to *my* family. *I'd* been the one to find them. Maybe when I got back, I could search without him.

A tiny doubt crept in. Pursuing the gems behind his back—not to mention, hiding the fact that I'd seen the stag—might not make me a very good friend.

But I pushed the doubt aside.

For many long months the company wandered up hill and down dale, deep into the West Wilderlands. But denser grew the forests, and harder the way, till forward marches proved impossible. Even the falcons could see nothing beyond the trees that ran in all directions. So the company turned toward the Nisna Alps and began their ascent to see from the heights what lay still farther west.

After many terrible trials, including an avalanche that forever blocked their way back to their homeland, the company at last descended from a steep mountain pass into a lush, wooded valley. There they found a river of pure water that flowed from the mountains, and along the river was a fair land they could clear for farming. The valley boasted game and fish, timber and stone, in abundance.

And on that first cloudless night, beneath a sky full of unfamiliar stars, they encamped in an open field by the laughing river. And great was their rejoicing, for they had found safe passage and a good land.

The prince called the River Ter after his mother, Ternivia, and named this new land the Vale of Ter—or Ternival. And the company lauded him as their sovereign.

Chapter

16

That night was so dark I couldn't see anything from my tower windows. Would Grandmother appear without the moon? Would the stag? After briefly waiting and wondering, I pulled a sweatshirt over my pajamas and crept downstairs barefoot, determined to camp out in the dining room. If the stag in the tapestry moved or vanished, I'd notice. If Grandmother came down the grand staircase, I'd notice her too.

But either I'd finally adjusted to the time difference, or the excitement of finding the gems had worn me out. The next thing I knew, the grandfather clock in the entrance hall was striking half past midnight, and moonlight now blazed through the dining room windows. I'd fallen asleep with my head on my arms on the table. I sat up quickly.

Once again, the stag in the tapestry was gone.

I stumbled out of the room, through the hall, and into the drawing room. This time the French doors were closed, but I didn't pause to wonder what this meant. Instead, I threw the doors open and bolted down the veranda steps.

Clouds drifted across the face of the moon, and the gardens grew darker and darker. But just when I thought the light would fail altogether, something began to glow from inside the secret garden, like someone had lit a fire. Not of orange and red flames, but of silver starlight. A bonfire made of galaxies.

I dashed for the hedge and began hunting for the break in the branches. By the time I finally found it, less by sight than by sheer luck, I'd never been so cold and wet. Climbing inside was a messy scramble, and I tore my pajamas across the knee. But soon I stumbled through.

Then I dropped to the ground. Call it kneeling, if you like. Or rather, cowering in fear and awe. In the middle of the garden stood the great stag, glowing as though the moon had fallen to earth. He towered like a sentinel, antlers higher than the hedge, points sparkling against the span of stars. Around him the air seemed to ripple with spun threads, as if the tapestry had come alive, the entire landscape a patterned story into which he and I and every other living thing were woven.

The stag gazed at me for what felt like a full turn of the earth. I wished he would speak. I trembled with terror that he might. I wanted to ask him everything. Yet a great calm flowed from him, a stillness so complete that it silenced all my racing thoughts.

Somehow I understood. The very fact of his presence, there in the cool of the garden, was in so many ways the answer. He was not of this world. He'd come here from a place beyond anywhere I could imagine.

And I knew something else too.

I believed.

All of it. Every story. I'd always believed, ever since I was a little girl. I'd never really stopped. And now I was seeing proof with my own eyes.

At long last the stag turned and made for the opposite hedge. The branches pulled aside as if by magic, and he glanced back at me before stepping lightly through.

There was no going back now.

The opening in the hedge revealed a narrow track retreating into a deep wood. Ahead of me walked the stag, dappled now in shifting shadows but still glimmering like a star. The amount of ground he could cover with each stride was astounding. I trotted to keep up. The rocks and sticks digging into my bare feet were the only things that convinced me I wasn't dreaming. No sound broke the still air, no humming engine or barking dog. We moved forward like two ships sailing on a silent sea.

The track began to climb as the trees thinned, and soon we came upon walled lawns and unfamiliar outbuildings, ghostly in the moonlight. Eventually those gave way to a line of dense shrubs on our right, and on our left, a high wall shielded whatever lay on the other side.

The stag stopped. Next to him was a low, arched wooden door in the wall.

Suddenly there came a mighty rending, wood scraping against stone. The door opened, and light stabbed through the doorway, transfiguring the creature from silver to gold.

A glorious scent like ripened pears rippled toward me on a warm breeze. Through the open archway, sunlight streamed from a deep blue sky. Tawny fields, bordered by trees loaded with golden fruit, stretched on and on to distant foothills. Beyond the foothills rose a line of mountains, and atop one of the peaks soared the palace that

I'd seen in the clouds—except it was no longer made of air but of glowing stone that held its own light.

I'd thought I could believe anything. But I wasn't prepared for this. Was I glimpsing Inspiria? Was that the palace of Magister, high in the mountains beyond all worlds?

The sound of a distant horn, high and piercing, echoed from the palace. My heart leaped. If I could've run toward the sound—and not stopped running till I found the one who made it—I would've done so to the last age of the world. But awe of the stag held me back. Slowly, majestically, he lowered his antlers and stepped through.

The sunlight vanished. The stag, the fields, the trees, the mountains—all were gone. The door was shut. Once again, I stood alone and shivering under the stars.

I tried the door. It was locked.

I choked out a sob. "Lost!"

But even as I said it, I knew it wasn't true.

Not lost. Merely hidden.

Like the box of gems that Stokes had whisked away somewhere. Like whatever secrets Aunt Bertie's house might hold. Like all the missing portals between this and other worlds.

Still out there, waiting to be found.

PART 2

Amabel . . . took up the [railway timetable] again to look for Whitby, where her godmother lived. And it was then that she saw the extraordinary name "Whereyouwantogoto." This was odd—but the name of the station from which it started was still more extraordinary, for it was not Euston or Cannon Street or Marylebone.

The name of the station was "Bigwardrobeinspareroom." And below this name, really quite unusual for a station, Amabel read in small letters:

"Single fares strictly forbidden. Return tickets No Class Nuppence. Trains leave Bigwardrobeinspareroom all the time."

And under that in still smaller letters—

"You had better go now."

What would you have done? Rubbed your eyes and thought you were dreaming? Well, if you had, nothing more would have happened. Nothing ever does when you behave like that. Amabel was wiser. She went straight to the Big Wardrobe and turned its glass handle.

—"The Aunt and Amabel" in *The Magic World*
by E. Nesbit, 1912

Chapter

17

"Fog again," Grandmother said, gazing through the dining room windows.

I'd come downstairs that morning dressed in one of my favorite new outfits: a light green shift with a flowing linen skirt, a Venetian glass pendant at my throat. It felt like something a princess would wear for a seaside holiday. Plus, it hid the long scrape across my knee, proof that my nighttime adventures had been real.

All of it—the radiance of the stag, the scent of fruit, the sound of the horn, the sunshine beyond the door—lingered like an ache in my heart. But once again, I had no memory of how I'd returned to bed.

Now I sat eating toast at the gleaming table as if nothing impossible had happened. But something had changed. Something in me.

"Did Mrs. Fealston tell you?" Mum said to Grandmother from her place at the table. "Eva and I have decided to visit Cambridge."

"Oh? Whatever for?" Grandmother seemed to be making a studied effort of not looking at me.

"To see Great-Aunt Bertie. I haven't been there since . . . Well, it's been too long."

Grandmother poured herself some coffee at the sideboard and sat down. "Yes, well, the years haven't been kind to Bertie, I'm afraid. Though her mind is sharp as ever."

"That's what Mrs. Fealston says. And still in the same old house, apparently. The place hasn't changed much, I suppose?"

"No, unfortunately," Grandmother said with a small shudder. Then she set down her cup and looked at Mum. "You mean, you're going today?"

"That's the idea."

"But you've only just arrived! And anyway, I'm not sure I can spare Paxton. I have . . . plans."

Watching the two of them over my toast and marmalade, I half suspected Grandmother had invented her "plans" on the spot. Two flushed circles appeared under her high cheekbones.

"I was intending to drive us myself," Mum said.

Grandmother stared at her in blank astonishment. "The two of you, alone? But, Gwendolyn, it's several hours. And you can't drive."

"Nonsense. Of course I can. What else do you think we do in the States?" Mum's tone remained light and teasing, but there was that edge again. "We'll take my old Mercedes. Paxton says it's sound as a bell—he tuned it up yesterday, in fact. And we'll be back by teatime on Friday."

Escape. That's what it felt like to leave Carrick Hall. Mum, in particular, behaved like a schoolgirl on holiday. As we left the Wolverns behind, she sang all the silliest songs she'd taught me as a child—to which I responded with epic eye rolls from the passenger seat. She insisted we play the alphabet game ("I'm going to Cambridge, and I'm taking a _____"), although, in our nerdy family, none of the words could be fewer than five syllables. I almost won, but there was no beating Mum in this mood.

Since we'd arrived in England, a rift had grown between us. Mostly due to her fraught relationship with Grandmother. Every topic I wanted to discuss felt off-limits. Now, in our first real stretch of time alone together, our usual camaraderie returned. This was the Mum I knew.

As we approached Cambridge, she grew even more giddy. "Oooh, you can see the spires, Eva!" And then, "Hmm, that museum is new." And, "There's the pub where your father and I had our first date." Finally she pulled into a small parking lot off a side street, and we got out.

University campuses were nothing new to me, of course. But I'd never seen anything like Cambridge at the height of summer. Ivied halls, ancient spires, arched bridges, vaulted chapels, vast libraries, faculty in their academic robes, museums and galleries and gardens along the River Cam . . . No wonder Mum loved it.

As she strode happily down the sidewalks, she seemed to have shed about twenty years. She'd become a young college student again. In love with academia, in love with my dad, in love with life. It took my breath away.

What had happened between then and now? Something had closed her off, shut her down, made her pull into herself like a mouse into its hole. Even beneath her excitement was a sadness that wouldn't go away.

We stayed overnight at a modest guesthouse off a large green within walking distance of her alma mater, Clare College. The next morning, before leaving for Aunt Bertie's, we drove past some of the oldest colleges, eventually ending up at a row of quaint shops off another side street.

"Warren's," Mum said with a smile as we got out of the car. "The bookshop where your dad and I met."

I peered through the bow window. For years my parents had told me about this place, with its quirky displays and crowded shelves, its dust and cobwebs and quiet. Somewhere down one of those aisles, during Mum's first term at Clare, my parents had collided spectacularly. Mum dropped all her books, of course. Dad helped her retrieve them, of course. And that was the beginning of everything. Geekiest romance ever.

"Hasn't changed much, I see," Mum said, still smiling. "It's come under new ownership in the last year or so: family by the name of Rastegar, from Iran. We've continued to order books from them. For your father's research."

She pushed the door open, and a bell rang faintly as we entered.

"Good dawning to thee, friend," called a hearty voice from a back room. "Be right with you."

We wandered the aisles. Every shelf was scrupulously labeled in minuscule, elegant handwriting. Looking closer, I realized the labels were a detailed catalog of seemingly unrelated minutiae. *Medieval Persian Recipes* shared a bookcase with *Edwardian Cabbies of Greater London,* while *Experimental Preparatory Schools* flowed into *Pear Varieties of Herefordshire.* I felt like I'd been invited to play a trivia game in which all you're given are the answers, not the questions.

"Still the same!" Mum whispered with delight.

"But how is it organized? Definitely not the Dewey decimal system."

"That's why it was originally called 'The Warrens.' It's a veritable rabbit warren. Once you start chasing a category, you find yourself falling down and down into Wonderland."

"I greet your honors," said the voice, closer now. "And how may I help you?"

Behind the front counter, a short, balding, bespectacled man observed us with interest.

"We're just browsing," Mum said with her usual shyness. Then she seemed to change her mind and approached the counter. "Mr. Rastegar?"

The shopkeeper nodded. "At your service."

Mum extended her hand. "Pleasure to finally meet you, sir. I'm Gwendolyn Joyce. You might remember my husband, Robert? We often order books from you, for shipment to Connecticut."

Mr. Rastegar suddenly smiled and pumped her hand. "Good now, some excellent fortune! Welcome, Mrs. Joyce, best of customers, all the way from America."

"Well, gracious!" Mum said, flushing pink. "How kind. And this is my daughter, Eva."

A curtain toward the back of the store twitched aside, and a cautious face peered out.

"Mrs. Rastegar!" Mr. Rastegar waved toward the curtain. "Come meet our stalwart customer, Mrs. Gwendolyn Joyce, and her incomparable daughter. We are well met."

A petite older woman, even smaller than Mrs. Fealston, slipped through the curtain. She carried a tray laden with pastries, which she set on the counter. Then she shook hands all around.

"Good cheer, ladies," said her husband, gesturing toward the tray. It was piled high with perfectly shaped cream puffs. "Now turn we towards your comforts. My wife is the best baker in Cambridgeshire."

"Please," said his wife, smiling, "eat."

"Oh! Lovely. Thank you."

We each took a cream puff. I'm not sure what I was expecting—something yummy, certainly—but nothing like the explosion of deliciousness that was one of Mrs. Rastegar's pastries.

"Gracious!" Mum said again.

"It's the best thing I've ever had," I said, and meant it.

"Small miracles, yes?" said Mr. Rastegar. "Now. What brings you to this side of the pond, as they say?"

Mum swallowed and brushed a crumb from her cheek. "Well, you see, my mother still lives in the West Midlands, so we're staying with her for a few weeks—my husband is interviewing for faculty positions in the States. But I have a great-aunt in Cambridge. So we're stopping in to see her."

"Quite right, quite right. And how fares Professor Joyce and his research? I am always sure to make note, as he requested, of anything by Clifton. To help prove his theory, yes?"

"Clifton?" I interjected. "You mean, Kinchurch." I looked at Mum.

"Oh, er . . ." Mum seemed suddenly flustered.

"Exactly," Mr. Rastegar said to me with a wink. "It will all come clear one day, I am certain. A finer scholar than your father, I have yet to meet."

Just then, the door from the street opened and a voice called, "Is that you, Gwenny?"

In the weeks that followed their discovery of the vale, Wefan and his company set out to explore it.

To the south rose the foothills of the Nisna Alps, from which they had come, high and formidable. From those lonely peaks flowed the River Ter, cold as snow, coursing down the valley. To the east lay the impassable forests of the Wilderlands, across which was their homeland, many leagues distant. To the north ran a range of downs, windswept and bare, surrounded by lowlands treacherous with fens and fogs.

And finally, the company followed the river westward to where it emptied into an uncharted sea. The chilly coastline stretched from north to south, with shale beaches buttressed by lofty cliffs. *The Pathless Sea,* they called it, for of its reaches they knew naught. And as yet, they had no ships.

Eventually the small clearing on the River Ter became the village of Wefanford and then a cluster of villages along the valley. And their settlements spread northward to the downs, westward along the river to the shores of the Pathless, and southward into the wooded foothills of the Nisnas toward the headwaters of the Ter. But to the forests of the East Wilderlands they dared not go, save to hunt, and it remained a trackless waste.

Chapter

18

Into the bookshop strode one of the most elegant men I'd ever seen. Tall, tanned, impeccably dressed in breezy linens, he approached Mum with an enormous toothy smile. "By Jove, it is you!"

Mum flushed deeply and dropped a small curtsy. "Lord Edward!"

"Don't be ridiculous," the man said. "Just plain old Edward to you. Always have been, always will be. And who is this?" He flashed his smile at me. I felt my neck grow warm.

"This is Eva, my daughter. Eva, meet Lord Edward Heapworth. Friend of the family."

I froze, uncertain whether to curtsy or what. Lord Edward shook my hand with mock solemnity. "That's it. You've got the right idea. None of this curtsying business."

"What on earth brings you to Cambridge, Edward? Mother seemed to think you were still in London."

"Ah, my fame precedes me! Yes, well, as it happens, I rang up your mum this morning because I'd heard you were back in England at last. And dear old Mrs. T. told me you were coming here to see Bertie. But also, as it happens, Eddie, my oldest, is at Magdalene."

He pronounced it "maudlin," which at first made me wonder why his son Eddie was sad. But no, Lord Edward meant Magdalene College here in Cambridge.

"Anyway, I'd a feeling you might stop by Warren's—saw your Mercedes outside just now, in fact. What luck, eh?"

He then turned to the Rastegars.

"Splendid to see you, Mr. and Mrs. Rastegar!"

"We are well met, my lord," said the shopkeeper. "How does my good Lord Edward?"

"Please," said Mrs. Rastegar, pushing the plate of cream puffs in his direction.

Lord Edward popped an entire pastry into his mouth and closed his eyes. "Heaven. Absolute heaven. You've outdone yourself, Mrs. Rastegar. Thank you! Now, don't forget what I've said about setting up shop in Upper Wolvern someday. Bookshop and tea shop together, eh? Consider me your first investor." He turned to Mum and me with a flourish. "What you may not know, dear ladies, is that Mr. Rastegar is actually *Professor* Rastegar—and he was once Iran's foremost expert on Shakespeare."

"A plague on both your houses!" said the professor, beaming.

"*Hamlet!*" crowed Lord Edward.

"*Romeo and Juliet,*" said the other three grown-ups in unison.

"Right you are," Heapworth said cheerfully. "I *knew* it was one of the tragedies, eh? Here, Gwenny: I'm starving. What d'you say we all grab a bite at the pub next door? My treat. How about it, Professor?"

"We thank your grace," said the shopkeeper, "but alas, we must keep the shop."

Lord Edward smacked his forehead. "But of course. Silly me. Cheerio!"

"Take pains," Professor Rastegar said, "be perfect, adieu!"

Before Mum could protest, Lord Edward Heapworth swept us out the door. In short order, we were seated at a corner table in the pub, where he breezily ordered a round of fish-and-chips—including a batch to be sent next door for the Rastegars. He never once asked what we wanted, but somehow that didn't seem to matter. Mum leaned back in her seat and exhaled.

"Ah, jolly good," said Heapworth as he returned from the counter with our drinks. "London is much too posh—and dirty and *hot*. So, Gwenny, tell me everything."

Mum laughed. "What's there to tell? I went off to America, like I said I would. Finished my degrees, like I said I would. And married Robert Joyce—"

"Like you said you would," he interrupted, grinning.

"And Robert finished *his* degrees—in fact, he'll be tenured faculty soon. And we had Eva. But I'll let her tell you about herself."

I blushed and stammered something about liking school and the swim team and England. All the while, Heapworth rested his chin in his hands and nodded like I was the most interesting person in the world.

"All of that is wonderful," he said to me, "but can we discuss this simply gorgeous outfit of yours? You know that color exactly suits your eyes, of course. But the pattern on that Venetian glass is too stunning for words." He turned to my mother. "Gwendolyn Joyce, how on earth did you manage such a fashionable daughter?"

Mum laughed again. I was both flattered and unnerved by this curiously attentive yet inattentive man.

"Your turn, Edward," Mum said. "How are your children? Three, I think?"

"Yes, heaven help me: two boys and a girl. They're just terrible, terrible. Eddie is spectacular at everything. Puts me to shame. The youngest, Aurora, is dazzling everyone at primary school. And the middle one, Charlie, is slogging his way through prep school. Might not make it, either, unless old Dad here smooths things over with the head."

"That bad, is it?" Mum said mischievously. "Charlie sounds rather like you, I'd say."

"Too true, alas. I've thought about sending him to Wolvern instead—if they'll let him in. But can you imagine? Lord Edward Heapworth's son, from Wolvern Court, at Wolvern College?"

"In the Wolvern Hills," Mum added.

He groaned. "The poor head wouldn't know which way was up."

"Oh, he'd manage, I'm sure. Especially if there was money involved."

Heapworth roared with laughter. "You know, I've missed that about you, Gwenny. Absolutely forthright. You've been away far too long."

"And your wife?" Mum quickly changed the subject. "Is she with you?"

"My wife? You mean Vicky or Liz?" At Mum's confused expression, he grinned again. "Sorry, Gwenny—the look on your face! No, Vicky and I divorced—long, boring story—and then I married Liz. We lasted about a year. No partner at present."

"What about the art scene, Edward? I imagine you've got a number of clients."

"Oh, is that what they're called? Clients? Yes, I suppose. It's ridiculous sport, but some of those tapestries auction for millions, you know."

Mum turned to me. "Lord Edward knows more about medieval tapestries than anyone you'll ever meet."

He shook his head. "Ah, you flatter me, my dear. Look, I'm blushing. But yes, I'm up to my neck in the auction scene. Which reminds me: I'd love to have a look around your mother's pile sometime—still some very fine works there, I imagine."

"You're right. Although she's decided to sell a few."

"Shame," he said. "Not the tapestry of the hunting scene in the dining room, I hope."

"No, that's still there. It's a fixture of the tour."

"Oh, good show. And please tell me she's kept that other framed tapestry, the one with the dryads? Even as a child I knew there was something special about it."

I was suddenly on high alert. Dryads?

Lord Edward turned to me. "We used to pretend, as kids, that the tapestry came alive, you know—like in the fairy tales. We'd try to climb through it." He winked.

"Alas, Edward," Mum said, ignoring him, "Father sold it when I was maybe thirteen, fourteen, don't you remember? Mother couldn't stand the thing."

"Shame," he repeated and pursed his lips.

Before I could form a coherent question, our food arrived. Heapworth sniffed luxuriously, flourished his silverware, and cut into his fried fish with a fork and knife. I'd never seen anyone but Mum eat fried food with utensils.

Mum's expression now looked strained, as if the topic of the tapestry had unsettled her—or maybe it was all this socializing. She ate quickly and soon said, "Well, I suppose we should be heading to Bertie's. Her housekeeper must wonder if we've gotten lost. *So* kind of you to treat us to lunch, Edward. Do ring us up when you're back in the Wolverns, will you?"

"I'd be mad if I didn't."

"You're mad anyway," she said with a smile and rose from her seat. He laughed loudly and stood to bid Mum farewell with a kiss on both cheeks. He pumped my hand, opened the pub door for us, and waved us off down the street.

When we climbed back into the car, I finally found my voice. "Okay, I can't stand it anymore. I *have* to know. What's all this about a tapestry of dryads? And what did Professor Rastegar mean about Clifton? And who the heck *was* that guy—your old boyfriend or something?"

She sighed with exasperation. "I'd rather not ruin this afternoon by dredging up the past, darling."

"I'm not the one dredging up the past!" My voice rose. "The past is dredging up itself. And there's nothing you can do to stop it. So you can either tell me, or I'll pester other people till I find out."

Mum returned my glare. "Well, then, you can pester other people. Because in about ten minutes I'll have Aunt Bertie to deal with, and that's about all I can handle at the moment."

She put the car in gear, and we peeled off down the street.

At the founding of Ternival, Wefan the Wanderer married the stalwart archeress Andella, whose mastery with a bow was unmatched from the Nisna Alps to the shores of the Pathless. And their children grew up swift of foot, strong of arm, and wise in the ways of all woodland things. Their descendants ruled Ternival with humble mien, good grace, gentle hands, and large hearts, as their ancestors had ruled Mesterra. And long was Andella remembered amongst the people.

For it was in those early days of Ternival that Andella first saw the stag.

Chapter

19

By the time we arrived at Aunt Bertie's house, the sky had clouded over, and the air was damp and chilly. The long block of midcentury brick homes seemed abandoned, their bland façades unfriendly.

As we approached the door, Mum turned to me. "Right," she said quickly, as if wanting to get the whole thing over with. "I should probably warn you that Aunt Bertie . . . Well, first of all, she's a sickly old woman and disagreeable most of the time. But behind all that, she's a very sad woman, and lonely. Her only child—Grandmother's cousin, you see—died as a young woman. It'll do her a world of good to see us, especially you. So you'll be sweet, won't you? No matter how peevish she is?"

I nodded, putting on my sweetest expression. Mum rang the bell.

The door soon opened, and a scowling housekeeper peered out.

"Oh, Mrs. Joyce—thank heaven! You're here not a moment too soon. She's in one of her *moods*." The housekeeper glanced at me. "Not to worry, ducky. She won't eat you."

The housekeeper led the way down the hall. It was an odd home, bereft of comforts and decidedly ugly. She led us into the sitting room, where a thin elderly woman sat on a hard plastic chair. The old woman's face was pinched and hollow. A sack-like shawl covered her bony shoulders, no doubt because all the windows stood wide open. Her hair had been dyed an alarming burnt orange in startling contrast to her turquoise-blue eyes, which stared at me almost greedily.

"Well, I never!" the old woman rasped. "The child is as like her as two peas in a pod. And what does your mother think of *that*?" Then she laughed, a dry croaking that turned into a hacking cough.

"Hullo, Aunt Bertie," Mum said, then stepped forward and gave her a peck on the cheek. "This is Eva, of course." She offered a cushion for Bertie's back, which the old bird waved away irritably.

"Tea?" Bertie croaked.

The tea service waited on a nearby cart, accompanied by round biscuits that looked like dried-up sponges. Mum briskly picked up the teapot before Aunt Bertie could reach it and proceeded to pour.

"And why isn't that husband of yours with you?" Aunt Bertie demanded.

"He's back in New Haven, finishing up some research."

"What research, exactly?"

"Oh, you know," Mum said vaguely.

Aunt Bertie's eyes glinted. "Don't tell me Robert is still obsessed with that Kinchurch woman."

"Er, actually, yes."

"Thought so. Ha! Any female who fancied herself a theologian should've been run right out of university. And then to write fairy tales too—"

"Fairy tales!" I blurted. "But—"

"Kinchurch was actually quite brilliant," Mum interrupted in that clipped tone she reserved for her elders in England.

Bertie sneered. "Brilliant, maybe. And dangerous. I wish she'd never crossed paths with our family."

"But the girls were all fully grown by then, able to make their own decisions."

"No, no. You weren't there, Gwendolyn. You didn't see what I did. That woman was unnatural." Aunt Bertie's nervous eyes grew brighter. "It was *her* fault they were in London that day. She used to gather them together in secret, like some sort of cult. My daughter never told me, but I knew what they were doing. Your grandmother knew too. We tried to stop them!" Years of grief and anger seemed to erupt from the old woman like wasps from a nest. "Repeat the vow, drink the poison, ride the train—what's the difference? That morning, that awful morning . . ."

Mum turned to me with a forced smile. "Eva, would you like to see the garden? Aunt Bertie has lovely topiaries."

"Not anymore," Aunt Bertie snapped. "They were my girl's. I tried to keep them up, but I can't now." She looked at me sharply. "Wander wherever you like. Just don't mess about upstairs."

I didn't know which was worse: listening to the rants of a bitter old woman or missing out on family secrets.

"Run along now," Mum said. This was a command. I slipped into the hallway.

To my left, a small dining room smelled of spoiled milk, which turned my stomach. To the right was what looked like a study full of old books, which had potential—but upon closer inspection, they proved to be of the encyclopedic variety, dry and boring. Down the hallway, the housekeeper was banging pans in the kitchen. She didn't strike me as the kind of person who tolerated being disturbed.

I glanced up the stairs. Cold air flowed from open windows somewhere above, and I could hear birds outside, twittering in the gloom.

There was no one to stop me.

I took the stairs two at a time. A damp chill wafted through an open window on the landing. Four more steps, and I was in a narrow hallway with only three doors, all of which were closed.

Quietly I opened the first door on the left. Aunt Bertie's room, I guessed. There was a laundry basket of folded clothes by the bed, and old-lady slippers under the nightstand.

Then I tried the door on the right. This was another bedroom, that of a girl—a quirky girl with a scientific mind. On either side of the incongruously frilly bed, floor-to-ceiling shelves stood crammed with collections of dried flowers and dead cacti, shriveled mushrooms and fuzzy twigs. A huge vase of moldering bulrushes leaned in one corner of the room, while a grungy gray bookcase, oddly empty except for a single encyclopedia, stood in the other.

Leaning closer, I realized that everything was coated in a thick film of dust. In fact, the whole place looked as though it hadn't been touched for fifty years.

I shuddered and left, closing the door behind me. It was like trespassing in a creepy graveyard at night: I wouldn't go back there unless I really had to.

At the end of the hallway was a third closed door, which I opened stealthily. This was a guest bedroom, stark and inhospitable. A single bed and dresser occupied the far wall, along with a hideous lamp the color of an overripe avocado. In a corner stood a small chest and a hard plastic chair like the one Aunt Bertie occupied downstairs. And on the opposite wall hung an empty, carved picture frame.

The skin on my arms prickled. Could it be? I looked closer. Yes!

There, etched into the corner of the frame, were the pear tree and coronet. It *had* to be one of the frames Mrs. Fealston had mentioned. But why empty? What image had it held, once upon a time?

There was no time to inspect it further. Already I could hear my mother taking leave of Aunt Bertie in the sitting room and the housekeeper's footsteps coming from the kitchen. I made a dash for the stairs and managed to reach the bottom before the two women converged by the front door.

"There you are," Mum said, wrapping her muffler around her neck. "Go back in and say goodbye."

Aunt Bertie sat where Mum had left her, hunched and wheezing, her expression peevish. For one crazy moment I thought I'd ask her: I'd steel myself and demand to know more about the frame upstairs. But one look at her sharp turquoise eyes made me pause. She motioned me to her.

"You were upstairs," she said slyly. "Oh yes, I heard your footsteps. You found her room. But just remember"—she pointed a gnarled finger at the ceiling—"they were all mad. *Mad.* Except my girl. They *tricked* her into believing all sorts of nonsense. But not you. You may look like your great-aunt, but you've got a brain in that head of yours, I can tell."

She lowered her trembling hand and drew her shawl around her shoulders. Her pinched face was no longer peevish, just sad. And very, very lonely.

"Now they're dead," she whispered. "That's all magic ever did for them. That's all it ever does for anyone."

One gray dawn, as Queen Andella hunted alone in the wooded foot-hills near the East Wilderlands, mist from the Nisnas descended swiftly and took her unawares. Darkness fell, as if morning would never come, and soon she became lost. Then wandered Andella for many long hours, till at last she sensed that she, the huntress, was being hunted.

Before she could nock an arrow, a huge wolf leapt, snarling, from the brush. Andella spun and ducked, and the beast, instead of snapping her up, snapped her bow in two with its mighty jaws. As the wolf turned to rush at her again, Andella jumped up and pulled herself onto the overhanging branch of a large pine, then clawed her way to the top.

Chapter

20

A million questions whirled through my brain as we climbed into the car. About Aunt Bertie's daughter. And the daughter's unsettling room. And the empty frame. And about Professor Kinchurch writing fairy tales. Plus a long-lost tapestry of dryads, and Clifton, and a train. Not to mention magic. Oh—and death.

In that moment I was just *tired*. Tired of other people assuming I knew everything when I didn't. Tired of being made to feel like I was nosy merely for wanting to know my own family history. Tired, especially, of Mum and her secrets.

Finally I exploded. "You know this isn't fair, right? Not knowing anything. Getting surprised by stuff people say all the time. Everyone thinking I look like Grandmother's dead sister—which is creepy, okay? You might've warned me. And all those weird things in the girl's room upstairs—"

"You went upstairs?"

"Of course I did! What *happened,* Mum? What could possibly have been so bad that no one will talk about it?"

She exhaled. "Well, where do you want to start?"

Her answer so surprised me that at first I couldn't reply. Eventually I managed, "Okay, so how about Grandmother's sister? What happened to her?"

"Fine," Mum replied. "We'll be there in an hour."

"Where?"

"The place where it happened. Or rather, where it ended."

"Wh—"

"Next question."

"Um . . ." I still couldn't get over the fact that she was willing to tell me anything at all. "What about Kinchurch? What does she have to do with anything? And what's all this about her writing fairy tales?"

"Can we pause and make note that this might be the first time you've *ever* asked to hear more about Kinchurch?" She smirked. "I'll have to tell your dad."

"Ha. Well?"

I waited impatiently as Mum negotiated a highway ramp. "For starters, Carrick Hall wasn't always owned by our family," she began. "It was originally the Kinchurch estate. For hundreds and hundreds of years."

"Really?"

"Yes, really. It's where Kinchurch herself grew up, back in the early twentieth century, before World War I. The family's wealth had dwindled significantly by then. So when she inherited the estate, as a very young woman, she had to shrink the staff. Kept only a butler and a few housemaids. Including Mrs. Fealston."

"Mrs. Fealston!" I exclaimed.

"She was quite young at the time. Barely eighteen, as I understand it. Anyway, eventually Kinchurch went off to Oxford, then
joined the faculty at Newnham College, Cambridge. A woman's
college. And one of her students was my mother's mother, Anne—
your great-grandmother, you see. The two became quite close. So
when Anne married, she and her children would visit Kinchurch in
the country, stay there on holidays and so forth."

"Grandmother vacationed at Carrick Hall? When she was a
girl?"

"Oh yes. She loved it, back then. The Professor never married,
never had children of her own. So our family was quite dear to her.
That's why, when she died, she left the estate to your grandmother."

"Ohhh . . ."

"Unfortunately, there was no money. The Professor had been
land-rich and cash-poor, as they say. But by then your grandmother
was being courted by a young man from a wealthy family. My father, of course. He'd met her at Selfridges department store, where
she worked as a shopgirl.

"But it wasn't considered respectable for a lady to work," Mum
went on grimly, "much less to serve customers in a shop. So at first
his parents wanted nothing to do with her. But then, once she inherited a vast country estate, they were very keen on her indeed."
Mum gave a caustic laugh. "His money plus her land: It was a perfect match."

She paused as we passed a rumbling lorry.

"So that's our family connection to Kinchurch," she concluded,
her voice weary. "And that's enough for now."

It wasn't enough. It'd never be enough, not till all my questions
were answered. But I knew Mum in this mood: She wouldn't budge.

For the past twenty minutes, I'd been so absorbed in these revelations that I hadn't noticed we'd left Cambridge by a different route than we'd come.

"Hey," I said as a highway sign flashed past. "Did that say London? Are we going to London?"

"You can't visit England for the first time without seeing the sights of London," Mum replied. "I thought we could stay for a bit, take in what we can. But first, a quick stop to show you something."

We looped down into the northwest suburbs and then wound our way through what seemed like endless city streets until we arrived at a plain stone church with a walled graveyard. Mum parked the Mercedes, and we stepped onto the quiet street, city air damp on our faces. The church grounds were deserted.

When we entered, I began to make my way to the church's heavy wooden door, assuming there was something inside to see. But Mum's voice said quietly behind me, "This way, Eva." She turned onto a gravel path that led through the churchyard.

Old headstones, crumbling with age, tilted at tired angles around the yard. But newer headstones stood close to the walkway. At one of these my mother stopped. It was quiet in the churchyard, all the city noises shut out by the high walls. A lone bird piped plaintively in a yew.

Mum pointed to the nearest gravestone. The markings on the stone were clear enough, so it took me only a moment to register the details:

ANNABETH MAUDE PENNINGTON
MAY 5, 1930–OCT 8, 1952

The wolf howled in frustration, deep-throated and ugly, and began pacing in circles. "By my teeth, whom have we here?" it growled, leering up at Andella on her perch atop the pine. "Not the fair queen of Ternival, surely. For what king would suffer his bride to hunt alone, save one who cares not for her?"

Andella, clinging to the branches, said nothing. Her vision swam, and she knew her hold to be precarious.

"Doth thy feckless spouse know that thou hast gone a-hunting alone, milady?" mocked the wolf, still circling. "And knoweth he that thou bearest his first child?"

At this Andella nearly fell, for it had divined her great secret.

The wolf laughed in triumph. It saw in her face that its words rang true, and it thought this made her weak. But its laughter was its undoing.

For Andella had been born fierce, and fiercer was she now as mother to queens. In a sudden rage she leapt from the pine onto the back of the wolf and, with one swift motion, broke its neck.

Hard they fell to the forest floor, Andella and the beast she had slain by her own hands. The hugeous shaggy body landed upon her as she fell, and there she lay under the trees, pinned by the heavy carcass, conscious only of the swirling mist and the waves of pain that rose and fell and rose again.

Chapter

21

A chill breeze stirred the yew in the London churchyard.

"She was only twenty-two," I observed, shivering.

"Yes. In her final year at Newnham," Mum said quietly. "So young. Too young. And she wasn't the only one that day."

"You mean . . . Aunt Bertie's daughter?"

Mum nodded. "Claire. She's buried up in Cambridge, of course. And Professor Kinchurch. Buried in Upper Wolvern."

"Wait. All on the same *day*?" I squawked.

"Some say it was the fog," Mum explained. "Especially bad that year, particularly in London. Kinchurch's cab was hit by a double-decker in the early hours. Claire's bicycle swerved off a bridge. And then the rail crash."

She continued in a sad monotone. "A local train carrying eight hundred people had stopped at the Harrow and Wealdstone station that morning. Later than usual, due to fog. And then came the overnight express from Perth. Somehow the driver missed a signal, or several signals. The express train barreled into the local at sixty miles an hour."

I gasped.

"Yes, unthinkable. Then, seconds later, another express heading the opposite direction on a different line hit the debris. Derailed instantly." She took a ragged breath. "One hundred and twelve people. Gone. Just like that."

My imagination tried to grasp the horrific scene: twisted wreckage, smoke, chaos, bodies.

"Why the three of them were in London at all," Mum added, "instead of at Cambridge or boarding school, no one ever figured out."

"Where was Grandmother?"

"Probably on her way to work. She had her own flat near the station in those days, but she was employed at Selfridges, in the city center. These are just guesses, of course. She's never spoken of it."

"Not once?" My voice squawked again. "You mean, she never told you? Never brought you here?"

"No, it was Mrs. Fealston. It was always Mrs. Fealston. And you're not to tell your grandmother we were here either."

"But—"

"The sisters had survived the war, you see," Mum said quietly. "Even the air raid that had killed their parents. So when the war ended, life was supposed to return to normal. Everyone safe again." Her voice faltered. "It breaks a person, Eva. When your grandmother got married and moved to Carrick Hall, she buried everything, even the memories."

Realization dawned slowly. "So *that's* why we don't ride trains in England . . ."

"And that's why she rarely travels more than an hour from Carrick Hall, not even by car."

More puzzle pieces were coming together. No wonder Grandmother had never visited us in the States.

A light drizzle began, brought on by the restless wind.

"Mum," I finally managed, "why haven't *you* told me before?"

She took my hand. "I'm sorry, darling. It was wrong. I know that now. At first, when you were younger, I was trying to protect you. You had such a vivid imagination, you know, and I didn't want to give you nightmares. But then, over time, it became easier not to tell you at all. You would've had a lot of questions—and the thought of answering them felt exhausting."

Nosiness, again. A warm flush of shame washed up my neck.

"Plus, it brings up a lot of painful things from my past too," Mum added.

"What things?"

"Oh, darling. I'd rather not talk about all that."

"Not ever?"

"Well, maybe someday. Just . . . not right now."

Again silence descended. The rain dissipated, leaving only soft drippings from the yew. I stared at the gravestone, at the beautiful, haunting name of the great-aunt I'd never meet.

Somewhere in my mind a bell had started ringing, very faintly. Annabeth. Claire. Their names were so much like Annabel and Claris from the tales of Ternival. Just a coincidence, right? And anyway, one name was missing: the oldest girl from the stories, Flora.

"What's Grandmother's first name?" I asked suddenly. For the life of me, I couldn't remember ever having heard it before. She was just Grandmother, or Mother, or Mrs. Torstane.

Mum glanced at me, bemused. "She goes by Bess."

"Oh." Not even close to Flora.

"Well, it's getting late," Mum said. "We'll want supper soon, and there's a guesthouse near Trafalgar Square that I want to stay at to-night."

She began to pull her hand away. But I held on.

"Thank you, Mum," I said. "For bringing me here."

She gave me a wry smile. "Well, if I didn't explain *something,* you would've driven me batty." I smiled back. "But also," she added, "I began to realize that by keeping all these secrets, I was turning into my mother."

Secrets. I was keeping some myself. I wondered, uncomfortably, if even one was too many.

ॐ ॐ

"How was your trip?" Frankie asked.

We stood in the kitchen garden after supper, waiting for his mum to finish up the last of the dishes before they headed back to the village. I'd arrived a few hours earlier, exhilarated but exhausted by the city sights. Mum had refused to explain anything further after our stop at the churchyard—so by now I had at least a hundred more questions.

"London was amazing," I said. "Although it's kind of a blur."

He dropped his voice. "Did you learn anything? In Cambridge?"

I gave him a brief summary of what I'd found at Aunt Bertie's house, and what I'd finally gotten out of Mum about Kinchurch and the tragedies that haunted my family. Frankie seemed relieved we could finally discuss everything freely. But he was most intrigued by the empty frame at Aunt Bertie's house.

"You're certain it had the same carvings as the other frame? And the box?" he asked.

"Absolutely. Which makes me wonder . . . Do you think . . . Could it be . . ."

"You mean, how is it all connected?" Frankie asked. "It's a muddle, that's for sure. The even bigger question is, What happened to whatever was inside the frame?"

We sat in silence for a while. Finches chirped drowsily among the dripping beanpoles while a pair of swallows dipped and circled overheard. The clouds broke apart, and the setting sun slanted through the wet valley.

"What about you?" I finally asked. "Did you find anything here?"

"No luck," Frankie said ruefully. "I looked everywhere I could think of outside, on the grounds, where I was less likely to get caught. But of course there must be tons of hiding places, so the box could be anywhere."

"Where does Stokes live? Could he have hidden it there?"

"He lives with us, at the cottage. While he was napping in his kitchen chair yesterday, I checked around his room. But I couldn't find anything."

"How about inside, here at the Hall?"

Frankie shook his head. "Grandad can't manage more than one flight of stairs, so really the only places worth checking are on the lower level. I hunted around in the kitchen and larder, the old dairy and storage rooms, but nothing. The only place I haven't looked—that Grandad can reach, anyway—is Mrs. Fealston's private quarters off the kitchen."

Frankie and his rule following. I would've ransacked her rooms by now.

"And anyway," he added, "it's too late to do anything about it tonight. Mum will be heading home soon. Tomorrow after chores, then?"

"I guess." Secretly I was annoyed that we'd have to wait so long. Suddenly he straightened like a soldier. "Ma'am."

I turned to see Grandmother stepping into the kitchen garden from the direction of the orchard.

"Oh, hullo there," she said faintly. "I heard you'd returned. Did you have a nice excursion?"

I nodded. It was the first I'd seen her since our arrival—she hadn't joined us for supper earlier—and all I could think of was the gravestone in the sad London churchyard. I wanted to run to her, hug her, whisper that everything was all right. But maybe it wasn't.

Meanwhile, in her expression I saw something new, something tenuous but hopeful, as if the sight of me had vanquished a consuming fear.

To Frankie she said, "I've just been to the orchard. How does Stokes think the fruit is coming along this year? The trees seem hardy."

"He's pleased, ma'am. If the weather holds, there should be a good crop this fall."

"Oh, excellent . . . Not that I enjoy pears myself." She shuddered slightly. "I was stranded once, with nothing else to eat for days. But it's good business, you know. Well, a grand evening to you both. Lovely, isn't it?" Not waiting for an answer, she strode across the kitchen garden to the archway and disappeared.

"She's glad you're back," Frankie said.

I knew he was right. That was the expression I'd seen on her face. *Relief.* Someone she loved had gone away but returned again. Whole and safe.

Then I remembered her sad face in the moonlit gardens, her wailing cry. I'd wondered what she'd been searching for, night after night. What she'd lost.

Everything, I now realized. Everything.

As Queen Andella lay on the forest floor, unmoving, there came the sound of footsteps. Something large approached out of the mist, pacing slowly. Andella turned her head, fearing yet another foul beast from the deeps. Instead, she beheld a great glowing creature with antlers like tall branches, shining with its own light.

The stag came to the queen where she lay. It lowered its antlers and swept aside the body of the wolf. Then it knelt on its forelegs and lowered its head again.

"Climb upon my back," said the stag, its voice wild and deep as the Ter in flood.

"I cannot," replied Andella, for her pain was great.

"Thou must," it said, "or thy doom is near, as is that of thy child."

She knew not whither the stag would take her, yet for the glory of its light alone would she have followed it beyond the Wilderlands to the farthest reaches of that world.

Slowly Andella rolled onto her side, then grasped hold of the thick fur on the stag's neck. Wincing with pain, she pulled herself astride its back. The stag rose gently and bore Andella the Archeress away.

Midnight it was, and the queen asleep against the great stag's back, before they arrived at the encampment on the River Ter. Andella never awoke when it laid her down in the center of the field, nor did anyone catch sight of it as it left—save one little girl who was awake with a wiggly tooth.

Chapter

22

That night I didn't wait till Grandmother appeared below my bedroom windows. I didn't wait for a glimpse of the stag. Instead, I made my way downstairs and through the French doors as soon as the moon sailed into the sky.

This time I wore jeans, sneakers, and an oversized sweatshirt. I'd snuck a small flashlight, what Mum called a torch, from a drawer in the kitchen and slipped it into my back pocket. If the stag appeared, I'd be ready. I'd follow wherever it led—and this time I wouldn't let any doors close between us. Neither would I let the night end without knowing exactly what happened. No more waking up in bed the next morning without a clue how I'd returned.

But if it was Grandmother who appeared in the gardens instead, I wasn't sure what I'd do. Silently observe, like last time? Or attempt to interact with her before Mrs. Fealston caught us?

The pavilion loomed out of the darkness. It'd be a comfortable spot to wait, commanding a view of the entire formal gardens. But it occurred to me that my greatest danger was, in fact, in being *too* comfortable, of falling asleep out there under the domed roof and missing the whole show.

I needn't have worried. Within minutes I heard footsteps. As before, Grandmother paced into view from the kitchen archway, transfigured by moonlight into an otherworldly beauty, her luxurious hair falling past her knees. She murmured to herself: "Lost again!" and "The ways are shut, alas," and "Did they mark not the danger?"

As she approached the secret garden's high hedge, she raised her hands as far as she could. "My dear!" she called in a voice choked with sadness. "Whither hast thou gone?"

To this day I don't know what compelled me. I knew the dangers. I knew that her broken mind could break further by my recklessness. Yet couldn't my presence also be a comfort?

I left the shadowed pavilion and went to her across the wet grass, quietly, so as not to frighten her. But she heard me anyway. She spun around, her face so transformed by joy that her gaze was like a blow.

"At last!" she cried.

She ran toward me and grabbed my hands. Hers were ice cold, but her eyes were warm, searching mine with tenderness and delight. It was everything I'd ever longed for in our interactions— everything and more.

Grandmother put a hand to my cheek. "So warm! Is't thou? Truly? But why hast thou stayed hidden so long? Up to thy games again?" She laughed like a girl and swung my hand in hers. "Dost thou remember how we chased thee that morning? How the light changed and we knew—ah, how we knew!—that we'd left our old world and found this realm instead?"

She touched my cheek again and then my hair. Confusion rippled across her face, and she narrowed her eyes. For a moment I thought the spell would break—she'd snap out of her strange dream, denounce me as an impostor, and send me back to the house. But then her face cleared and she smiled.

"Come!" she cried. "The moon is high, and the dryads dance. And I haven't danced in an age!"

She began to skip lightly away. Beyond the hedge, the Hall's rooftops soared to crenellated peaks, more like the palace I'd seen in the clouds than the grim old manor house. The moon seemed to have grown to twice its normal size. The dark sky glittered with huge stars, bright and close; I wanted to stretch out my fingers and pluck them. Everything felt both strange and familiar. But also somehow more . . . real.

Yet Grandmother remained herself. Her face as she glanced back at me wasn't any different—only *released*. Whatever pain gripped her on an ordinary day at Carrick Hall, whatever protective cloak she wrapped around herself, was simply gone. Like I was seeing the truest version of her, the part most fully alive. I wanted to stay here with her, beyond the veil, forever.

She broke into a run. "We shall find them in the grove, no doubt!"

I ran to keep up. She wore a kind of cape over her nightdress, and it billowed behind her in waves. Her sheer athleticism astonished me. She ran fiercely. She ran like a young woman who had danced, raced, hunted, swum, ridden, fenced, and reveled every day of her life. She ran as one who knew each stone, tree, and creature by name—who knew them and loved them and feared nothing, because they knew and loved her. She ran like a queen.

We dashed through a field toward the grove that bordered the estate. As we neared it, she slowed and raised a cautious hand.

"List," she whispered. "They sleep. But soon they shall awaken, mark thou." She pulled me into the shadow of a large beech that glowed soft and gray in the moonlight. "Mark thou," she repeated, running her hands along the bark, "how she stirs."

I pressed my hands against the beech's trunk. Sure enough, the bark seemed to sigh, like a sleeping child just starting to wake. Above us the leaves began to rustle in a light breeze. Branches swayed in shifting shadows. As we watched, I became certain they swayed to music beyond our hearing. As if the stars themselves were singing.

And then I heard the music. Or thought I did. It floated high above us in unfamiliar chords, like the haunting call of strange birds. A summons, somehow, close as our own breath but distant as deep space.

Grandmother gripped my arm, staring deeper into the grove. "There!" she whispered. My breath caught, and I felt the hair on my arms rise. As we watched, two of the trees joined branches and lifted their roots, the soil rippling around them like water as they turned in a slow, gracious, complicated dance.

The trees were coming to life. Grandmother wasn't just stuck in some weird fever dream of her broken mind. This was really happening.

More trees began to join the dance. And every minute, they looked less like trees and more like young women in long dresses and youths with flowing hair—like the topiary of the dryad, in fact. Like Grandmother herself.

Grandmother left my side and made her way into their midst. While I watched, she, too, raised her arms and began to dance. The music and movement picked up speed, and I saw the flash of her smile and heard her laughter even from across the grove. Faster and faster the queen and the dryads danced, passing one another like couples in a reel, but wilder.

I wanted to join. Truly, I did. But something held me back. Joy had become a living thing, there in the moonlight, and it smote my heart. But then, just as I'd made up my mind to join them, he appeared.

The great stag.

Larger than ever. Majestic, as always. He stood at the edge of the grove and looked on the dance with calm gladness—as if he were the magnanimous host who'd invited the revelers in the first place. As if all this moonlit realm were his and he shared it freely. I wished I were already dancing.

He made his way toward the trees. Grandmother's back remained to him as the trees parted, still whirling, and enfolded him in the reel.

But then she saw him. I could tell by the recoil of her body, the stiffness of her face. Joy fled from her, even as it emanated from every part of his being. She fell back as if struck.

"No!" I cried.

The music stopped as if someone had pulled a plug. The stag vanished. The dryads froze in place, mere trees once more. Moonlight dimmed; stars dimmed; everything dimmed. Grandmother and I stood alone in the grove amid a dreadful silence.

She turned and fled.

If she'd been fast before, she was even faster now, a silver arrow speeding across the field toward the Hall. "No, wait!" I called, stumbling behind. But she didn't stop. Though I kept up as best I could, soon she was out of sight, lost among the shadows of the formal gardens. A door shut somewhere ahead, probably one of the French doors into the drawing room, and then the only sound was a dog barking far away, down in the village.

Unlike on previous nights, I was now fully awake, aware of my own body in the cold night air, my clothes damp with dew as I hurried across the lawn. Clouds obscured the moon. I climbed the steps to the veranda and slipped into the drawing room, aware of how sad the Hall seemed now, how dark and ordinary and closed off.

I headed back to my room, changed out of my wet clothes into pajamas, and climbed into bed. A deep sadness settled in my chest. Mere nights ago I'd followed the stag myself, convinced he was good. So why did Grandmother flee from him?

Yet . . . and yet . . . Grandmother had looked on my face with joy. She'd danced with the trees. Danced!

And if it had happened once, maybe it could happen again.

The question was, Would she remember any of it? Would she remember *me*?

Though the night was calm and windless, as Andella lay senseless in the center of the encampment, there came a stirring in the nearby woods. A trio of dryads slipped into the clearing, their long hair trailing like willow branches. Silently they encircled the sleeping queen, lifted their arms, joined hands, and danced a slow healing dance around her. Then they, too, left.

In the morning, Andella was restored to herself, none the worse for wear.

At first she told no one of her wanderings, for shame of having gone alone. But soon the little girl found her (the tooth had come out in a pear fritter at breakfast) and asked, What was the great silvery creature that had borne the queen to the camp in the night? And was the wolf *very* bad? And what would the queen name the baby?

Andella laughed.

The queen named her baby Erylia, and in time she became one of the greatest queens of Ternival. And the little girl with the lost tooth grew up to be Erylia's most trusted companion, Nira, known to Ternival's children as the Tooth Pixie. (It was said that if one left a newly lost tooth in a cup on the windowsill at night, by morning the tooth would be replaced with a pear fritter.) Nira was ever a poor sleeper but wisest of all the counselors at court, for she could divine secrets. Moreover, with her own eyes had she seen the stag.

Chapter

23

Grandmother entered the dining room the next morning with a calm "Hullo." She went to the sideboard and poured herself some coffee, as if nothing had happened the night before. As if this were perfectly normal behavior for someone who occasionally danced with dryads.

She gave no sign that she remembered anything. It was like observing someone bound by a powerful enchantment, the sort of spell that deadens everything inside you. Every emotion, every memory, dulled. The good as well as the bad. But it was also the sort of spell that helps you sit down at the table, pick up the morning paper, and read with unflappable detachment.

I felt a weighty sadness again, like a heavy blanket on my chest. If she didn't remember anything from the grove, then neither did she remember me. Whatever brief closeness we'd known was gone, like it'd never been.

"Hullo," Mum replied without looking up. She was writing in a little red notebook that I recognized from home—one she always carried around when she was working on a research project. Now she tapped a pencil on her cheek and stared out the window, lost in thought, while Grandmother read the newspaper placidly, sipping coffee. Was this how they'd navigated life together, all those years ago? Like polite strangers at a coffee shop?

I glanced at the stag in the tapestry. He was frozen, as usual, in midflight: a mere image, a piece of art, hanging there unmoving as he had for hundreds of years. It was then that I noticed how Grandmother's chair at the end of the table was angled away from him. Her chair always was, I realized. She never sat with him in view.

"Three tour coaches scheduled for this afternoon already," came Mrs. Fealston's voice as she bustled in from the back hallway. "Saturdays can be mobbed, depending on the weather. And today will be rainy at first, then clear up. I hope that doesn't interrupt your plans?"

Mum groaned. "We have no plans. Maybe we should. Perhaps a trip to Hereford, Eva? Visit some bookshops?"

"But I want to stay here," I protested. I couldn't explain that Frankie and I hoped to keep searching for the box of gems. Yet if he didn't show up soon, we'd miss our window before the place was overrun by strangers.

Grandmother turned another page of the newspaper without even acknowledging my presence.

Mum shrugged. "Suits me."

I stood and grabbed my empty breakfast dishes, feeling suffocated. "Great. I'm off. See you at lunch!"

"Ev—" Mum began, but I was through the servants' door.

Downstairs, I quickly washed my dishes and headed out into the humid garden. Despite the occasional glimpse of blue sky, rain threatened the air. I knew that Frankie had turned the whole place upside down while I was away, but maybe a fresh pair of eyes would do the trick. Or maybe—and this was my secret hope—the box of gems would somehow magically choose to reveal itself to me again, like it had before.

I decided to start with the toolshed. Maybe Stokes had come back with the box, after Frankie and I had left, and stashed it there? But as soon as I stepped through the doorway, I realized what a monumental task this would be. A century's worth of gardening equipment and supplies covered almost every inch of space, and just two small windows let in light. Where on earth would I begin?

"You won't find it here," said a voice from the doorway.

I whirled around. Stokes stood silhouetted against the dim light, his wispy hair blown into a tuft on top of his head.

"Sorry, Mr. Stokes," I gasped. "I should've asked."

He came in and sat down on a stool by an ancient worktable that was piled with broken equipment. As light from the nearer window fell on his wrinkled old face, I was relieved to see that his eyes were twinkling with kindness and humor. He picked up a wrench and set to work on some sort of small engine.

"No need," Stokes said. "Not my toolshed."

"But you've been here longer than my grandmother," I countered. "And I doubt she's ever set foot in this shed."

"Well, that's true enough."

"How did you know what I was looking for?"

He gave a low chuckle. "It's what *I'd* be looking for, if I was you." Then his face grew stern. "But you mustn't. You don't know their power. Can't be trusted. The only thing that you can really trust is *him*."

"Who?" But I knew.

"Thought you might be in here," said another voice.

It was Frankie. Backlit in the doorway, his face was unreadable. How much had he heard? Was he upset that I'd been sneaking around before he arrived?

Rain began to patter outside. Frankie came into the toolshed, closed the door, and plopped down on an overturned urn next to his grandfather. "Tell her, Grandad. It's your story, after all." His glance flicked to me and then away.

Stokes laboriously turned a bolt. "Well, now . . . It was more than fifty years ago, back when I worked the grounds next door, during the war." He waved a gnarled hand in the direction of the college. "The school wasn't a good place back then. Bad management."

He picked up a different tool and spent half a minute ratcheting something or other. I bit my lip to keep from screaming with frustration.

"I was trimming shrubbery that day," he murmured, as if to himself, "along the track by the door in the wall. Heard what I thought was a hunting horn, calling, calling. But so lovely, it could break your heart. And then the door crashed wide open. And that's where he was, larger than life, like the sun. Or maybe it *was* only the sun— that's what you tell yourself later. All a dream." He looked directly at me, clear-eyed. "But it was no dream. Remember that."

I felt the usual flush of shame. Did Stokes know what I'd been doing at night? Or was he just guessing? I glanced at Frankie, who seemed unsurprised. Maybe his grandfather always talked like this, declaratively, dispensing general wisdom about magical events. It was as if such stories were as natural as rainfall or tomato vines or the earth we trod on.

Stokes began to chuckle again.

"Afterward, there was some uproar at the school about *intruders*. But when the inspector showed up, naught was amiss. Door in the wall was somehow closed and locked again, as always. And that's when they discovered the administration was up to no good. School turned around after that. A year later, I came to work here."

He closed his eyes.

"Sometimes I still see him. And that queen walking about. Can't seem to keep still, those two. But if you follow him, he'll take you there, to the door." He opened his eyes and said in an almost sing-song voice, "Into a sunlit field, beneath a summer sky. To the call of the horn from the high mountains." He looked at me, then at Frankie. "Follow that horn, wherever it leads. It's a fearful thing, but it must be done."

My heart skittered wildly. I knew, deep down, that the world beyond the door was real, but to hear Stokes speak this way, of the very things I'd seen myself . . .

Just then, the sun came out. A beam of light stabbed through the crack at the top of the toolshed door, slanting down on Stokes's wispy white hair. It lit his head like he was a saint in a stained-glass window, dust particles swirling around him. He turned his wrinkled face into the beam and smiled. It was then that I noticed how tired he seemed, how very old and tired.

"Rain's done for the day. Be off with you, now," he said to both of us with mock gruffness, "or I'll put you to work."

This was not the last sighting of the great stag. For it appeared to the people whenever the land was in peril or a wanderer was lost or whenever a Ternivali sought, for shame, to hide something of import from those they loved. For the stag not only was a guard and guide but also a counselor to the sovereigns of Ternival, coming when least expected, bestowing wisdom, then leaving again before any could detain it.

They called it the stag of Andella. And the stories of it grew—some true, some elaborations on truth, others mere fancy. It became to the people of Ternival the very symbol of their land. Its image was woven into their tapestries, stamped into their leatherworks, and etched onto the walls of their homes. And they were forbidden from hunting it—as if ever anyone would dare.

Thus was it told among the Ternivali that the East Wilderlands contained numerous portals to worlds unknown and strange, for therefrom did the stag appear, and thereto did it vanish.

And brave was the adventurer who dared follow the stag into the deeps.

Chapter

24

"It's always locked," Frankie warned. "I can't tell you how many times I've tried."

"But you've known about the door?"

"All my life. I used to beg Grandad to tell me that story at bedtime, when I was a kid. It was my favorite."

"So why haven't you told me any of this before?"

"Yeah, well, why were you looking for the gems without me?"

The two of us faced off over a row of lettuces, arms crossed. I felt unjustly uninformed about too many things—and sick of his usual excuse about these details not being "his story." Never mind that I hadn't told him anything about having gone to the door myself. And with the stag, no less.

"Mrs. Fealston said there'd be a pile of coaches today," I replied, "and I didn't want to miss our chance." My excuse sounded flimsy, even to me. "And anyway, isn't that why Stokes shared his story? Because he wants it to be our story too?"

He uncrossed his arms and reached down to yank a weed out of the nearest row.

"C'mon, Frankie," I wheedled. "You know where the door is, right? Can't you at least show me how to get there?"

"Students are still on campus for another week, at least. Even on a Saturday."

"I'm sure we could stay out of sight. It's not like the wall is right in the middle of campus . . ." As soon as I spoke, I knew my mistake.

He blinked at me. "And how do you know that?"

"W-well . . ." I stammered, "I mean, if you've tried it before, I figure it must not be very visible, right?"

He frowned. "Yes, the wall runs along the back of the school grounds, behind the cricket pitch."

"Okay, well, if you won't take me there, I'll just have to find it myself." I started toward the archway and the formal gardens.

"Wrong way," he called after me. I turned to see him heading in the opposite direction, toward the circle drive instead.

I jogged to catch up. He kept his strides long, staying just ahead of me like I was one of his annoying little siblings. I glowered at his rigid back.

We crossed the circle drive and then headed toward the grove that bordered the property, where Grandmother had taken me last night. The whole place looked decidedly unmagical in broad daylight. No sign that the trees had ever lifted their roots in dance. Even the huge beech seemed cold and aloof, nothing like the sentient being I'd seen by moonlight.

Beyond the grove ran the stream that coursed down from the hills. Beyond that, the high fence defined the edge of the estate. We hopped across the stream via some flat stones, then traipsed parallel to the fence till we came to a small opening just large enough for a person to squeeze through.

We were now on school grounds. A narrow footpath, more like a deer trail, cut through some shrubs and began to climb uphill. The slope made for slow going, but eventually we scrambled to the top—damp from the wet shrubs and hot from the climb—and found ourselves standing on a track that ran along a high stone wall.

This was it, the wall! And yes: There was the door, just as I remembered.

"Don't get your hopes up," Frankie called as I ran toward it.

I ignored him.

But he was right. Locked.

I tried again, and then Frankie tried, too, as if perhaps I hadn't twisted the handle hard enough. No luck. Finally we stepped back.

"You've used a crowbar, I suppose," I said flatly.

He nodded. "A few summers ago, when the students were on holiday. And I've tried a hammer. And a screwdriver, trying to take apart the hinges. Almost got caught by the groundskeeper that time."

"Have you ever tried to get to the door from the other side of this wall? From the hills?"

"Aye. But the way is blocked by a sheer cliff and a mess of trees. I can take you up to Table Mount so you can see for yourself."

"Table Mount?"

"The highest hilltop, or beacon, behind Carrick Hall. It's a fine view anyway, worth seeing."

We returned the way we'd come, keeping to the trees again so as not to be seen by anyone on campus. When we got back to my grandmother's estate, Frankie led me through the formal gardens and behind the pavilion, where a footpath followed the stream upward, as if someone walked this way often. We began to climb.

At a line of gorse bushes, the path rose even more steeply, and soon I was out of breath, scrambling to keep up with Frankie over rocky ledges, leaping from stone to stone in the stream itself. Within fifteen minutes we arrived at Table Mount, my shins bruised from scrabbling to the top. Winded, I flopped down on a flat outcrop to catch my breath.

Carrick Hall sprawled below, sparkling in the sunlight. It wasn't quite so imposing from this height, more like a large home than a vast mansion. The valley lay open before us, carved by the stream that flowed past the estate, through the village, and out into rolling pasturelands. On either side of us ran the ridgeline of the Wolvern Hills, rising and falling from peak to bald peak. I looked over my left shoulder and shielded my eyes. Far in the distance stretched a long, shimmering blue line. The Bristol Channel. The mouth of the sea.

I'll take you there one day, Grandmother had said. But that was before our confrontation in the churchyard, before her aloof demeanor at breakfast. Would we ever regain the camaraderie of that shopping trip to Worcester?

I turned my gaze back toward the valley as Frankie joined me.

"You can see the rooftops of the college, just there," he said, pointing. "And there's the trail we took through the trees, and a bit of the wall. But then the woods get really thick at the base of that sheer drop-off, see? If you tried to get to the backside of the wall from here, you'd fall about two hundred feet into dense shrubs. I'm guessing the college built the wall to keep students from trying to scale the cliff."

"But why can't you see anything beyond the wall when you're right next to it? No trees or clifftop or anything. From that side, it's like there's nothing beyond the wall but an open field." *A sunlit field,* I could hear Stokes saying, *beneath a summer sky.*

"It's hard to tell from here."

A rumbling from the village reached our ears. We looked down. A fleet of tour coaches snaked their way toward Carrick Hall.

"Well, that's the end of that," Frankie said. He flopped down next to me on the outcrop. "No more hunting for portals today."

I blew a lock of hair out of my eyes. "Yeah, so about that . . ." I began reluctantly. "Sorry I started looking for the gems without you. And prying in Stokes's shed. It wasn't cool."

He shrugged. "Well, it's only natural. I mean, they belong to your family, not mine. I'm sorry I didn't tell you everything Grandad knows."

"Not your story," I quipped and gave him a sideways grin. He smiled back.

The relief was like someone had lifted the smothering blanket off my chest. I'd gotten my friend back.

The coaches pulled up in front of Carrick Hall.

"Ready the battering ram!" Frankie called in a kingly tone.

"Aye, sir!" I replied. My fake accent sounded almost exactly like Paxton.

Frankie burst out laughing—the first time I'd heard him truly laugh.

And then I saw something above the distant horizon. A bank of clouds, piled in golden terraces and spires. I recognized it instantly. It was the palace I'd seen above Carrick Hall on the way to church—but now withdrawn, beyond our reach.

Frankie inhaled, and I knew he could see it too.

"We may never find the gems again," he said quietly, "or ever open the door. But we'll get *there* someday. And in that far country, all are ever queens and kings."

The turrets hovered for a moment over the world, then shifted and blurred into ordinary clouds.

In those early days of Ternival, the vale faced dangers but rarely. Giants, wolves, mountain ogres, and the occasional witch or necromancer invaded Ternival from the East Wilderlands, having come to the forests from worlds unknown.

The crown of Mesterra, which Wefan had brought thence to Ternival, offered some measure of protection from Ternival's enemies—though its strength diminished with time. Therefore did the people of Ternival think to strengthen their guard.

At the mouth of the Ter, on a clifftop overlooking the fishing village of Ter-by-the-Sea, the people built the mighty Castle Caristor. It was a wonder, wrought of golden alpine stone brought overland from the Nisnas, with windows of glass made by artists schooled in the ancient Tellusian crafts.

There did the sovereigns of Ternival make their home, and there did they train for battle, if ever such evil should befall.

But despite rare skirmishes with their enemies, the Vale of Ter knew peace for many a long age.

Chapter

25

The moon was on the wane, but it remained large and bright, winking from behind high, fast-moving clouds. I slipped the little flashlight into my back pocket and pulled up a chair to my bedroom windows to see what I could see. No more pajamas for me at bedtime: I was ready. Below me, the garden stayed quiet and still for so long that I almost fell asleep, arms on the windowsill. But then Grandmother finally appeared.

I dashed out of the room and down the stairs. Would she welcome me again, like she had last night? Or would she turn her face away, like she had at breakfast?

"Ah!" Grandmother said as soon as I joined her at the high hedge.

Her smile—that glad and glorious smile! It made my heart constrict. If only she'd look at me like that by day . . .

"Can we go to the grove?" I ventured. Perhaps she'd dance with dryads again. And perhaps I could join her. And maybe, if the stag appeared, I could persuade her not to flee.

"Nay, tonight there is something else to see. Come!"

As before, she took off at a run, her shining hair rippling behind her, the moonlight casting strange shadows in her wake. I followed her past the pavilion to the path that led up the hillside to Table Mount, then paused.

I watched, astonished, as she practically ran up it, her steps sure, her stride measured and graceful, like a deer's. It was as if the moonlight itself had become the path, drawing her inexorably higher and higher. Fearlessly, she'd hitch her nightgown and leap farther up, then jump from stone to stone in the stream, never once looking back to see if I followed.

I scrambled behind her, tentative at first, aiming for what I hoped was firm footing in the shadows. But soon her confidence became infectious. I began to race up the hillside, exhilarated, following the trail of the moon, keeping the white gown and flowing hair ever in my sight. Up and up we raced, till we reached the high table of stone where Frankie and I had surveyed the valley by day.

She waited for me there, breathless and laughing, twirling under the stars.

"Isn't it glorious?" she said. She spread her arms wide, as if to embrace the nighttime valley, the turreted Hall, the pasturelands and rolling hills.

But it was *she* who was glorious. If ever there'd been a queen worthy of fealty, it was this woman: whole and healthy and fully alive. The weight of that glory fell upon me, and it was all I could do to keep from kneeling. If I could have kept her there forever, joyous under the wheeling stars, I would've done so with my last strength.

"There!" she cried. "Dost thou see it?"

I followed her gaze over the dark pasturelands. Above them, gleaming in the starlight, towered the palace of clouds. I held my breath, afraid to move or speak lest the vision vanish.

"Long have I loved this land of mine," Grandmother murmured, gazing at the horizon, "but that distant realm is my heart's true home. Sometimes it draws near, and I swear I could climb the clouds to its very doors. And sometimes it recedes. Or vanishes altogether. But ever it calls to me."

She paused as if hearing the horn from beyond the door.

"It's where I thought thou wert, all this time," she said. "For in that far country, all are ever queens and kings." It's what Frankie had said on this very spot.

"Perhaps we could try to find it," I ventured. "Perhaps there's one who can lead us there." I didn't dare mention the stag.

The light in her face vanished, and she glared at me. "Thou knowest my counsel on this matter. Hunting that . . . *creature* hath only ever led us astray."

I kept silent. I didn't want to risk her wrath again, like in the churchyard. But she was wrong. She misunderstood the stag. His character and purpose were good, weren't they? Hadn't he—and others like him—come to the aid of many in the old fairy tales? Hadn't he shown me the land beyond the door, which she herself longed for?

But then doubt began to creep in. It was also true that after showing me the glimpse of that other world, the stag had simply abandoned me on this side of the door. Left me locked out, bereft and alone.

We stood under the stars for a long time, my heart torn between longing and doubt, before Grandmother said, simply, "Come," and led the way back down the hillside.

As we made our way through the formal gardens and up the veranda steps, one of the French doors to the drawing room suddenly opened and Mrs. Fealston peered out.

"Good gracious!" she exclaimed, looking from Grandmother to me.

"I found her at last!" Grandmother said, gesturing at me with a glad smile. "And what a glorious night! We've ventured up hill and down dale and now are in want of a hot bath and some cake." She stepped past Mrs. Fealston into the dimly lit drawing room and from there to the entrance hall. I could see her long nightgown trailing behind her as she glided up the grand staircase, head held high, hair falling in waves like a silver veil.

"What have you done, child?" whispered Mrs. Fealston, eyes wide.

"Please, Mrs. Fealston," I pleaded. "She's so happy. She . . . she talks to me, *looks* at me. She's so much more herself—so real. Please. It might help her."

The housekeeper hesitated, anger and worry deepening the creases on her ancient face. I hadn't realized till this moment what a huge burden the past forty years must've been for one so small, so slight—and yet so incredibly strong.

"Does she know it's you?" she asked. "Eva, I mean. Her granddaughter."

I swallowed. "I don't think so."

"Then this must stop! It's far too dangerous. Her mind might break even more, and then where would we be? It isn't fair to your mother."

"Please," I begged again. "She's so happy. . . . I'm so happy."

Mrs. Fealston drew herself up to her full height, which didn't even reach my nose. "Eva Joyce, if you don't stop at once, your mother will hear of it. And I have *no* doubt she'll book your flights home immediately."

I fled to my room before she could see my tears.

⟨ᚷ ᚠ⟩

Mum and Mrs. Fealston waited for me at the front doors the next morning, ready for church. I'd dressed with care again, hoping Grandmother might change her Sunday routine and join us after all. I couldn't stop hoping that our nighttime bonding would carry over into her waking, daylight hours. Maybe she'd want to maintain our closeness, even if she couldn't remember why.

But no. No Grandmother this Sunday.

I didn't dare meet Mrs. Fealston's gaze. Her reprimand still stung, and I felt trapped in a growing web of secrets.

"I thought we might cut a few flowers for your grandfather's grave on the way," Mum said, handing me a wide basket. She carried a pair of gardening gloves and shears.

The garden around the circle drive was a showpiece of late lilies and roses, and before long, the basket overflowed. As we headed down the drive under overcast skies, a warm breeze danced around us. The scent of roses enveloped me. To this day, the scent reminds me of that summer, of Mum's mousy hair wafting around her face, the brisk tap-tap of Mrs. Fealston's umbrella on the drive, the hedgerows rustling in the wind.

We arrived early for church, so after we'd arranged the flowers at Grandfather's grave, I wandered the churchyard. At first I didn't pay close attention to the many names and dates on the ancient headstones. But then it dawned on me that I was looking at the grave of a Kinchurch. Then another. And another. Kinchurches were everywhere.

Right next to me stood a modest headstone, smaller and newer than the others. I leaned closer.

AUGUSTA HARRIET WADE KINCHURCH
NOV 23, 1881–OCT 8, 1952

The Professor.

Whose initials were *A. H. W.*

My heart thudded like a drum in that quiet churchyard. But of course! It made perfect sense now. How had I not guessed it before?

Augusta Kinchurch *was* A. H. W. Clifton.

In those bright days of peace, a guild of Weavers was employed at Caristor to weave the history of all things. Of Mesterra's creation; of the comings and goings between that world and Tellus, and between other worlds entirely; and of the founding of Ternival and all that had transpired in the vale from those first days.

Intricate tapestries did they weave, depicting all the lands, peoples, and creatures of the vale. And runes did they weave into the tapestries, which told of the dooms and woes and prophecies of Ternival, including that of the crown's restoration and the return of the Children of Tellus. And into the warps did they thread the virtues of goodness and truth, the beauty of Inspiria, and the strength of Mesterra on the day of its dawning.

The famous weavings of Ternival were crafted over many generations and hung in Caristor's Hall of Tapestries. And were it not for the treachery of Mindra, there they would remain to this day.

Chapter

26

That's what Professor Rastegar had hinted in the bookshop, thinking I already knew. That's what Aunt Bertie had meant by Kinchurch writing fairy tales.

The Professor and the storyteller were the same person.

Which meant . . . that's what my dad had been trying to prove all these years! Kinchurch had published fairy tales under a pseudonym. The relatively unknown female scholar was secretly the author of my favorite children's book ever. *That* was Dad's groundbreaking theory.

Even more, Augusta Kinchurch was *that* girl. The first girl in the tales of Ternival. The one who'd stumbled into Mesterra with her friend Maggie. Which meant . . . the estate in those tales was *her* estate. The adventures were *her* adventures. And years later, the children who'd stayed at her house had been *real* children who'd had their own adventures and whose stories she must've written down.

But those children's names hadn't been Claris, Annabel, and Flora, like they were in the book. Instead, they were Claire, Annabeth, and . . .

Bess?

The church bells began their joyful clanging. Mum and Mrs. Fealston, already standing near the open doors, summoned me with a wave.

There was no time to find Frankie and reveal what I'd discovered—details he probably knew already, come to think of it. This realization raised my hackles again. Yet more information he'd kept from me. And I had no idea how to broach the subject with Mum. Why hadn't my parents ever told me? Didn't they think I could be trusted with these kinds of secrets?

By the time we'd squeezed into the Addisons' pews, I was furious with everyone—even with Tilly, who certainly didn't deserve it. She sat timidly on my left again, her shining hair falling in waves across her shoulders, while Frankie sat on my right. It felt like they were all part of the same conspiracy: to keep me in the dark as long as possible about everything, for reasons I could only guess.

Maybe my nosiness was a threat to whatever delicate equilibrium they'd all achieved at Carrick Hall. *Mustn't upset Mrs. Torstane, so best tell her granddaughter nothing.* Maybe my tendency to blather was a threat to my dad's future as a scholar. *Mustn't tell Eva about Robert's theory, or she'll blab to everyone before he can really prove it—and then he'll become the laughingstock of academia.* My shortcomings felt like a badge of shame that everyone else could see—and whisper about behind my back.

I slunk down in the pew, my face red, fighting tears.

"You okay?" Tilly whispered. Frankie glanced my way.

"Oh, just fine," I growled. Tilly shot a worried look at her brother. But before either could say anything, the opening hymn began.

I rose with the others, blinking furiously. They could keep their stupid secrets, I decided. And I'd keep mine.

ᚲᛚ

The rains began that night. They fell for more than a week, bringing a halt to my adventures. No more nighttime encounters with Grandmother. No more attempts on the door while Frankie was at school. Instead, I moped around the house, wandering the maze of rooms in hopes of finding the gems. But mostly trying to stay out of everyone else's way.

Each of my relationships was now a fraught mess. Each one required me to keep a different set of secrets. And I was too proud, too ashamed, to let any of those secrets go. I constantly worried about blathering the wrong stuff to the wrong person at the wrong time.

I tried not to think about what Mum had hinted at in the London churchyard, about the effect of secrets when you keep them too long. About what they'd done to my grandmother and even my own mum. There were good reasons for *my* secrets. Weren't there?

And anyway, it wasn't like Mum was suddenly in the mood to reveal everything. More than once I discovered her skulking about the library again, high up on the rolling ladders with her red notebook—although I took care that she didn't notice me.

It occurred to me that if this was Kinchurch's old library, then Mum was probably trying to find something that would help my father's project, some proof connecting Kinchurch and Clifton. Hence, the research notebook. Yet if that was the case, why hadn't we come to Carrick Hall before now? And why hadn't Dad joined us this summer?

Meanwhile, without tourists coming and going during the rains, Mrs. Fealston spent long hours resting in her quarters off the kitchen—the one place on the ground floor that Frankie hadn't yet looked for the gems. No good trying there. But then I learned that Mrs. Fealston often took Wednesdays off to visit her last remaining cousin in Great Wolvern. So that rainy Wednesday morning, while she was away, I sneaked into her quarters.

The housekeeper's rooms were timbered and low-ceilinged, composed chiefly of a sitting room and small bedroom tastefully furnished with antiques. A long bank of windows, their sills crowded with potted pink geraniums, overlooked the herb garden. On the opposite wall, a modest fireplace was flanked by deep corner cupboards and two antique rocking chairs. Next to the bedroom doorway hung a faded black-and-white photograph of a young officer in uniform. Somewhere a clock ticked.

It had never crossed my mind that someone like Mrs. Fealston—so attentive, so seemingly omnipresent—would need to escape from the world and its demands. But of course she did. She wasn't a robot. She was a human being, with her own needs and desires. What personal concerns had she been forced to put off, for decades on end, because she'd remained in service to my family? I glanced at the photograph of the young officer.

But there was no time to wonder. Any minute now, someone could find me here. I went to one of the corner cupboards and quickly rifled through it. Nothing but linens, tableware wrapped in felt, and a large ledger of housekeeping expenses. Then I tried the other cupboard, which contained more of the same. But on the bottom shelf, underneath a pile of lace doilies, was an old scrapbook.

I pulled it out and flipped it open to the first page.

MANY DIE AS THREE TRAINS CRASH AT HARROW, ran a newspaper

headline. It was dated October 8, 1952. Then came others like it from all over England, page after page. Each article contained black-and-white photos of smoking wreckage, crowds of bystanders, policemen carrying stretchers. A horrific nightmare.

But then came a single image of a young woman standing alone on a train platform. She wore a fashionable wool coat and jaunty hat, her gloved hands clutching an elegant handbag. Around her were smoke and chaos, debris and confusion, yet her blank gaze seemed to register none of it. She remained untouched, an icon of unperturbability.

Her eyes were deep and wistful, her lips full, expressive. Shimmering dark hair swept elegantly from a smooth white brow. Many years had come and gone, but this, undoubtedly, was my grandmother.

As I turned the pages, the headlines grew sensational: DEATH AT PLATFORM SIX; and THE LAST OF HER FAMILY, GONE; and TRAGIC BEAUTY ALL ALONE. Some articles contained the same image of her on the platform; others featured photos of her leaving a building or walking down a sidewalk, as if snapped by paparazzi. Her expression varied from stoicism to grief to barely contained wrath.

Then came wedding announcements from *The London Herald* and *The Times*. And photographs of my grandparents emerging from a chapel in their finery, flowers raining down. Other headlines followed: TRAGIC BEAUTY MARRIES WEALTHY GENT and TORSTANE TO THE RESCUE. In the accompanying photos, Grandmother didn't look particularly happy but rather . . . relieved.

I could envision my young grandparents escaping to Carrick Hall then. Hiding from the nosy press and the prying cameras. Building a new life together, away from the mess and the memories. Yet as soon as they'd gotten here, they must've realized they'd only brought the mess with them.

The last few pages were more like a traditional photo album. Faded black-and-white portraits, school pictures, and family photos, all featuring my grandmother as a younger girl, a gentle-faced middle-aged couple, and . . .

Me.

My own pert nose. My mischievous eyes. My unruly hair. Me in vintage clothing, like the statue.

But no, not me. *Annabeth.*

So this was the face my grandmother wanted to forget. And every time she looked at me, she was forced to remember.

The final page featured a larger version of Grandmother at the train station, reprinted in warm sepia. There was a caption underneath.

Florence Elizabeth Pennington.

Of course! Bess was her nickname, short for Elizabeth. But Grandmother's first name was actually Florence.

Like Flora.

High Queen of all Ternival.

Descendants of the original Weavers at Castle Caristor became known as the Writbards, storytellers who could interpret the weavings on every wall in the Hall of Tapestries. Indeed, it was rumored that when the light of the moon fell upon that Hall, the Writbards could summon the images to life, and they leapt from the walls and roamed the gardens of Caristor till moonset.

Therefore did the Writbards dwell in honor at the court of Caristor for sixteen generations.

Other artisans in Ternival became Loomkeepers, masters of the ancient arts of spinning and weaving. They formed guilds that dwelt in simplicity on the edge of the East Wilderlands, away from the bustle of castle life, and there they taught their apprentices to weave according to the patterns of Caristor. Only when the apprentices achieved mastery could they create patterns of their own.

In time their community grew to many hundreds, including the famous Hermit Igna, who communicated only through runes woven into patterns on the oldest loom in Ternival. That community became the monastery of Ignatira. And not a word was spoken there for four hundred years.

And thus the days of Ternival's peace continued.

Chapter

27

"Heavens, Paxton! You look quite drowned. Take a seat and have some coffee."

Mum rose from her spot at the crowded kitchen table that Saturday morning to grab Paxton a cup. Nearly all the staff, plus Mum and me, were crammed into that one room, trying to avoid the day-trippers who'd braved the rain and were now touring the house with Mrs. Fealston.

Paxton stood dripping in the doorway like a harbinger of doom. He wore waders, an enormous raincoat, and a battered yellow sou'wester that made him look like a deranged angler.

"Can't sit," he said grimly. "Postal clerk called from the village. Said to expect another three coaches any minute."

"Three? Oh, bother." Mum handed him a cup where he stood. "If only there was a more pleasant spot for you to distribute tickets than that abysmal little kiosk in the circle."

He didn't reply but took a sip like it was his last cup of coffee on earth.

Next to me, Frankie coughed as if to smother a laugh. We hadn't spoken all week, between the rains and his school schedule—though he'd given me several wary glances this morning, clearly remembering my mood at church last weekend. And I hadn't shaken that mood, really.

But my desire to confirm what I suspected about Kinchurch, Clifton, Grandmother, and her family threatened to eat me alive. When the grown-ups launched into complaints about the countryside becoming more and more overrun by visitors, I whispered, "Why didn't you tell me that Kinchurch and Clifton were the same person?"

He glanced at the others and then whispered back, "Took you long enough."

"Don't be smug," I retorted. "It's not my fault no one ever mentioned it."

"So how'd you figure it out?"

"In the churchyard. When I saw—"

A small bell began ringing near the ceiling—one of a row of bells, all labeled with different rooms of the house. Relics of a former era, Mum had told me, when the family would've summoned specific servants to specific locations at all hours, day or night.

Mrs. Addison jumped to her feet. "What does Her Majesty want *now*?" I couldn't tell if she meant Mrs. Fealston or my grandmother.

"And is that another coach I hear?" Mum almost wailed.

Everyone groaned.

"C'mon," Frankie whispered. "I know a place where we can talk."

In the commotion we slipped out of the room. He led me up the back staircase, up and up and up. Soon we were bumping our heads against the low, sloping ceiling of a tortuous stairwell at what felt like the top of the world.

We emerged into a narrow hallway that led to a series of tiny, chilly rooms with gable windows set in the angled roof. Several of the rooms were empty, while others contained bare shelving for storage. They were the sort of rooms where you might expect to find boxes of Christmas decorations—but probably not at Carrick Hall.

One room housed nothing but an old iron bed frame. "Did people *sleep* up here?" I asked, incredulous.

"The attic was the servants' quarters, once upon a time."

"But it's such a long way up! And so cold. Isn't it heated?"

He shrugged. "They'd take a warming pan up to bed, if they had one, I suppose."

"It seems cruel." If the attic was this cold in midsummer, what must it have been like in the winters?

"That's one reason why my dad won't go into domestic service. And why my mum hates it so. Centuries of cruelty aren't quickly forgotten."

I frowned. Were the people who owned these places—people like my family—so oblivious, so unkind?

We followed the passage's many turns, past a laundry chute, around bare brick chimneys, and along banks of gable windows. Eventually the passage ended near another narrow stairwell at the far end of the attic.

Frankie pulled a ring on the adjacent wall, and a small hidden door opened outward to reveal a crawlspace just big enough for a person to squeeze through.

"I found this one afternoon as a kid," Frankie said, climbing in. He grabbed a small torch from his back pocket, flicked it on, and turned back toward me. He was bent almost double under the sloping rafters. "C'mon."

"It's a good thing I'm not claustrophobic," I joked. But as soon as I climbed in, I felt my lungs constrict. I focused on Frankie's wavering light ahead of me and followed.

Soon he reached the end of the crawlspace, where there was a kind of cupboard door between the studs. He pushed it open and disappeared inside.

"Frankie?" My breath came in gasps.

"Lots of space in here," he called, his voice muffled. "You can stand up."

I forced myself to keep moving, then crawled through the door. Sure enough, a large space opened out under the sloping roof. It was another room with gable windows—except these had been bricked up. Frankie's flashlight flickered off the dark rafters, the shelving on the walls, the floor.

"Oh!" I exclaimed. "It's a crafting room!"

Baskets of tools, skeins of yarn, bowls of buttons, a large square frame with pegs, scraps of fabric and ribbon and thread. The shelves were bursting with supplies, long untouched. The whole place smelled of dust and wool and beeswax.

"It's more than that, I think," Frankie said. "It's a weaver's studio."

I looked around. "But shouldn't there be a loom or something? Or a spinning wheel?"

He nodded. "Odd, right? Lots of supplies, but no equipment."

"Is there a doorway to the rest of the house?"

He flicked the light at the interior wall, to a tall rectangle of bricks. "Bricked up," he said. "Like the windows."

"But whose room *was* it?"

He shrugged. "Everything in here is really, really old. Turn of the century, at least."

At one end of the room someone had used old travel trunks to set up a makeshift table and seating. There were several candles in glass jars, some oil lanterns, a deck of cards, and books. As Frankie lit the lanterns, I exhaled with relief.

"Most of this was already here," he said, gesturing at the trunks. "Maybe left by a servant trying to find a place to be alone. But these are mine."

Dozens of sketches, torn from a notebook, had been tacked to the walls. I peered closely in the flickering lantern light. The first depicted the dryad, arms raised to a star-strewn sky. Next to that was a sketch of the stag, poised in a dark wood, pursued by a distant archer obscured by shadow. Next was the statue in the secret garden, rendered in exquisite detail—or was it a drawing of me? I felt heat rise to my cheeks. The statue, surely.

"You drew these?"

He lifted a shoulder. "Yeah. It's just a hobby, really."

"You didn't tell me you're an artist!"

"I don't often have time anymore. But I come here to sketch every now and then."

I studied the pictures, drinking in the remarkable detail. Elspeth and Tilly with elfin ears and fairy wings, flying over the trees. Their middle brother, Jack, climbing a beanstalk. Baby Georgie in a miniature suit of armor, battling a dragon the size of a large dog. The images could've graced the pages of any fantasy book.

"Why haven't you brought me here before?"

He shuffled some papers out of the way and motioned for me to sit on one of the trunks. "I don't know. It's not my house, obviously, so technically I'm trespassing."

"Well, it's not my house either. Which means we're both out of bounds."

He grinned.

"So," I said, leaning in. "Kinchurch *was* Clifton, right? Augusta Harriet Wade—A. H. W.—like A. H. W. Clifton. *And* she was Augusta from the Ternival tales. I saw her gravestone in the churchyard and figured it out."

"Right."

"But why didn't my parents ever tell me? All this time I thought the Professor was just a boring old theologian—or at least, that's how my dad makes her sound."

Frankie sniffed. "Theologians aren't boring. Not all of them. Anyway, maybe your parents didn't want you to—"

"Blather about it to everyone? Spoil the big revelation?" I crossed my arms, then quickly uncrossed them. No need to look even more childish than I already sounded.

"I was going to say, maybe they didn't want you to get your hopes up. I don't have the impression your parents actually believe any of the stories, do they?"

"Mum doesn't," I conceded. "I'm not sure about Dad, but I doubt he does either. It's Grandmother. I can't figure her out." I was wandering into delicate territory now, not wanting to reveal too much. "She doesn't want anything to do with it, most of the time. . . . And yet their names are all so similar to the characters in the tales."

His eyes were bright with excitement as he nodded. "Annabeth and Annabel. Claire and Claris. Florence and Flora."

"So do you think Kinchurch was telling *their* stories as well as her own—my family's stories, my grandmother's?"

Frankie remained quiet, studying my face.

"Mum says Kinchurch was good friends with my great-grandmother Pennington," I continued, "and that my grandmother and her family used to stay here during the holidays when she was a child. What if the Professor just *based* her fictional characters off my family?"

"Eva," Frankie said with mild irritation, "after everything you've heard, after everything you've seen, is that what you really think?"

For one wild moment I thought he knew. I thought he'd somehow figured out what I'd been hiding from him about Grandmother and the stag and the world beyond the door. But then I remembered the box of gems, faintly singing, and the palace we'd glimpsed together from the top of Table Mount. No, those things were what he meant. But how badly did I wish to tell him everything!

"No," I said.

My voice wobbled with the thrill and terror of naming aloud what I wanted to be true, what I'd already known, deep down, but hadn't yet declared, even to myself.

"What I really think," I said slowly, "is that my grandmother was once a queen in another world. She was once High Queen of all Ternival."

His eyes crinkled at the corners as a smile spread across his face.

"Which means," I concluded, "that she lied."

ༀ ༀ

Grandmother had lied.

She'd stood there in the churchyard and asserted that the others, who believed the fairy tales, were mad. *There are no dryads, no giants, no great stag. There are no other worlds.*

Either that, or she'd somehow convinced herself it wasn't true.

But how could a person do such a thing? What massive power did the brain wield to erase the past, especially a past as magical and marvelous as hers? How had she been able to return to this world and live her life—survive a war, get a job, marry, bear a child, run a household, eventually welcome a granddaughter—as if the rest had never happened?

Yet part of her remembered. The Grandmother I encountered by night was still High Queen of Ternival. But the two parts of her had been sundered at some point, and it seemed as though they might never come together. Was healing even possible? Could she ever become whole again?

As Frankie and I descended from the attic and returned to the kitchen for lunch, I decided, right then and there, that I was in England for this one purpose.

To help my grandmother heal.

And I alone could do it.

PART 3

To him at least the Door in the Wall was a real door leading through a real wall to immortal realities. Of that I am now quite assured.

—"The Door in the Wall" by H. G. WELLS, 1906

MESSENGER: I see, lady, the gentleman is not in your good books.
BEATRICE: No, and if he were, I would burn my library.

—adapted from *Much Ado About Nothing*
by WILLIAM SHAKESPEARE, c. 1600

Chapter

28

The call came a few days later. Great-Aunt Bertie, her house-keeper announced with obvious relief, had fallen and would be entering a nursing home. Permanently. And according to Bertie's lawyer, the only way the old woman could afford her own care was to send her worldly goods to storage and let the house in Cambridge to university renters.

"Heavens," Grandmother said weakly, pinching the bridge of her nose.

Mum was silent for a moment. "Poor old bird."

Grandmother stared without emotion at the wainscoting. "I suppose I should see to everything. That awful house . . ."

But it was Mum who saw to everything. She spoke at length by phone with the lawyer, and the next day, she and I were back in the Mercedes, headed to Cambridge.

"I've arranged for a removal company to pick up Bertie's things," Mum said on the way, "although we'll keep some of the furnishings for renters. Might take us a few days to get it all sorted. Is that all right, darling? This isn't exactly what I'd hoped for your summer break, of course. We came to England so you could do something *other* than packing up, for a change."

"I want to help," I said. "That's why I'm coming." Which wasn't entirely true. What I really wanted was to get another good look at the frame in the guest bedroom.

After all, it wasn't as though my quest at the Hall was getting anywhere. I'd discovered nothing during all those lonely days of rain: no sign of the gems, no chance to try the door in the wall, nothing further from Mrs. Fealston or her rooms. I'd even tried visiting the bricked-up studio in the attic again, but I'd barely gone three feet down the crawlspace before claustrophobia sent me right back out again. Nope.

Meanwhile, my quest to connect with Grandmother was failing too. Night after rainy night meant there'd been no more adventures in the gardens. Morning after rainy morning, Grandmother had been her usual aloof self at breakfast, offering me the occasional half smile but otherwise keeping her distance. Her cool reserve felt calculated to ensure that I wouldn't get close enough to disappoint her.

Well, I could solve that problem. I'd simply leave for a while.

Just like Mum.

"Oh, and by the way," Mum said as we neared Cambridge, "Professor Rastegar called yesterday. He thinks he's found something for your father. So we'll stop at Warren's first."

Here was an opportunity I couldn't pass up. "You mean, something to prove that Kinchurch and Clifton were actually the same person?"

She opened her mouth and shut it again.

"Don't worry," I added, trying not to sound sulky. "Nobody

spilled the beans. I figured it out myself, at the churchyard, when I saw Kinchurch's gravestone."

"Ah."

"Why didn't you guys ever tell me, Mum? I mean, those are my favorite stories in the whole wide world. Did you think I couldn't keep a secret?"

"Oh, Eva . . . Of course not."

"It's because I blather, right? Because I could ruin Dad's career?"

She darted a surprised glance at me. "Whatever gave you that idea? No, darling. It's just . . . As I've said before, the whole thing is tangled up with some very painful family history for me—for all of us."

"So can you tell me how Dad got started, at least? Where did his theory come from?"

She paused, weighing my request. "I suppose. It was before we met, anyway. He noticed that a unique phrase of Kinchurch's was almost identical to something Clifton had written in one of the stories. And then your father began to compare their works, the way the sentences were put together. Syntax, word choice, meta-phors, themes, you know."

We were back in the usual boring academic territory. Blah, blah.

"And then he began digging into details about their lives. Turns out, other than the tales of Ternival, there's no record of an A. H. W. Clifton. No birth or death certificates, no photographs or interviews. Clifton's original publisher isn't around anymore, so that trail is cold. Meanwhile, coincidentally, there were no more Terni-val tales from Clifton after 1952."

"Oh! That explains why the collection feels so . . . unfinished."

"Right." Mum took the next exit and began to wind through the streets of Cambridge.

"After your father and I started dating," she continued, "I brought him to visit Carrick Hall. I knew Mrs. Fealston could corroborate his theory—and indeed, she did. Apparently, Kinchurch began writing the fairy tales when your grandmother and her sister visited the Hall as children. Your father thinks Kinchurch wrote to entertain them."

Or rather, I thought, Kinchurch wrote because the stories really happened. To her. To the children.

"Which is why the characters' names are so similar to theirs," Mum added. "Wouldn't it be fun to read a book by an author you know, who gave the main character a variation on your name? Eve, say. Or Joy, like our last name. Anyway, you recall that Kinchurch was good friends with your great-grandmother Pennington. And it was your great-grandmother who convinced Kinchurch to publish. But not under the surname Kinchurch, you see, or it might've ruined her career."

"Really? Why?"

"Back then, serious scholars had no business publishing fairy tales. They still don't, actually. Even worse, Kinchurch, as a female scholar, was in a precarious career to begin with. So she chose a pseudonym. And no one ever knew it except our family—and the staff at Carrick Hall, of course."

"And *that's* what Dad's been trying to prove all these years . . ."

Mum nodded. "All he needs is just one letter, one journal entry, one small reference, and his theory will be indisputable."

"And is that what *you've* been looking for this summer? In the library?"

Mum burst out laughing. "You don't miss a thing, do you? Yes, if you must know. It was once Kinchurch's library, after all. So it could contain exactly what your father needs. But after everything . . ." She halted abruptly.

"After everything?"

"Let's just say I've never had the chance to look till now. Ah! Here we are."

Mum pulled up in front of the bookshop. As we entered, a bell at the door jangled. The curtain at the far end of the shop pulled slightly aside and fell back again. Then Mrs. Rastegar emerged, carrying a tray of cream puffs.

"Welcome!" she said, placing the tray on the counter. "My husband is expecting you. Please. Eat."

"How generous! Thank you."

We both took a cream puff, then another, and for a long moment the only sound in the shop was blissful chewing.

"Mrs. Rastegar," Mum said with a contented sigh, "these are pure magic. Might I ask, What do you know about running a tea shop?"

"Tea shop?" Mrs. Rastegar echoed, puzzled.

"I wonder if you've thought about what Lord Edward said last time we were here, about opening a shop of your own."

Mrs. Rastegar hesitated. "Thank you, Mrs. Joyce. But, you see . . . when the customers come, I hide in the back. I hide and make pastries. When I was a teacher in Iran, I taught"—she waved a hand—"crowds and crowds. But after my husband was arrested . . ."

"Oh, of course," Mum said quickly. "No worries at all. Just a thought."

"What light through yonder window breaks?" came Professor Rastegar's voice. He emerged from the back room, smiling. "Is that the irrepressible Mrs. Gwendolyn Joyce and her stalwart young daughter?" He hurried toward the counter to greet us.

As he approached, I saw he carried a small book. He now placed it reverently on the counter in front of my mother as if presenting a Shakespeare folio.

"A beggar's book outworths a noble's blood," he quipped.

Mum and I leaned over the book. It was bound in black leather, lightly scuffed, with a vivid orange dragon on the cover. *The Azhdahā and Other Legends,* read the title. There was no mention of an author. Mum carefully opened the front cover and flipped through the first few pages.

"Belfry Press, same publisher as the tales of Ternival!" Her voice quavered with excitement.

"Why doesn't it mention the author?" I asked.

"This might've been the publisher's project, under their copyright. So it's entirely possible they hired Kinchurch to write it. Or a team of writers. She might've been a contributor."

Mum turned another page, revealing a handwritten inscription:

> *To Her Majesty*
> *Claire, Queen of Wildergard*
> *—From Kinchurch, 1949*

I read it again. Claire. Aunt Bertie's daughter. Not Claris, as in the tales of Ternival. But Claire. My grandmother's cousin.

Who'd once been a queen in Ternival.

I believed it, of course. But did Mum?

Generations came and went, and the years of Ternival's peace continued unbroken.

But then, one Ternivali king—Suvan the Swordhilt, as he was first known—grew fearful that his borders weren't secure enough. Rumors of marauding wolves reached his ears, and of ogres on the northern downs.

The stag of Andella had not been seen for six generations and was by this time thought to be mere myth. King Suvan became convinced that finding the lost gems of the crown—or, at least, finding a set of gems to complete it—would protect his throne forever. It became his one unswerving obsession.

All the strength of the vale was drafted to serve Suvan's end, even to the point of enslaving living things to work his cruel mines in the mountains. He became known among the Ternivali as Suvan the Mad—though none dared say so to his face.

He died without fulfilling his quest and was buried beneath the Hall of Tapestries at Caristor.

But his reign was the beginning of Ternival's undoing.

Chapter

29

"What is it, Mum? What does it mean?"

She'd grown very pale.

"Your face is as a book," said Professor Rastegar, "where men may read strange matters."

"Yes, sorry," Mum said faintly. "Do you mind telling me where this book came from, sir?"

He led the way through the maze of aisles and pointed to a shelf labeled *Persian Folklore and Other Marvels*. "I shelved it here last year but found it again yesterday. It came from a box in our storage room."

"Many, many books we found in that room when we bought the shop," his wife explained, coming up behind us.

"Oh dear," Mum said. "And I suppose you didn't keep the box?"

The shopkeeper's face fell. "Alas, no. Once we empty a box, we discard it."

"Did your predecessors keep any records? Past purchases and so forth?"

His face brightened again. "Indeed! We kept every ledger. The earliest is 1946. Shall we show you?"

"Brilliant!" Mum said. "Yes, if I could take a look. Perhaps starting with 1949 . . ."

Before long the counter was strewn with ledgers, musty with age and curling at the corners. Mum opened one of them and began scanning the entries with swift, practiced fingers.

"Here, Eva." She pushed another ledger in my direction. "We're looking for anything sold by Aunt Bertie."

"Oh!" I exclaimed. "I just remembered. There's a bookcase in her daughter's room that's totally empty except for one old encyclopedia. Which is super weird, because all the other shelves are chock full of stuff." I didn't add *gross, decomposing stuff.*

"Well, now . . ." Mum murmured.

"I shall assist you," said Mrs. Rastegar.

"Most kind. We're looking for the last name of Pennington."

For the next few minutes, the four of us bent over our respective records.

"Found it!" I cried. "December 17, 1952. Two boxes of books purchased from B. Pennington, 46 Barfield Circle."

"Yes, that's her. And just a few months after the rail crash," Mum said, studying the entry. "I wager she sold the contents of Claire's bookcase after she died."

"Do you think the rest of the books are still here?" I asked.

All four of us turned and surveyed the crowded shop.

"So many books," repeated Mrs. Rastegar in a whisper. "Thousands."

Mum exhaled slowly. "And who knows when we'll ever return . . ."

My heart sank. Did she mean to Warren's or to England altogether?

"I suppose I could always ask Bertie," Mum mused. "She seemed inclined to talk last time. We'll see if she's in the same mood today."

Mum paid for *The Azhdahā and Other Legends,* and then Professor Rastegar walked outside with us. He continued down the sidewalk, even as we paused at our car.

"Can we give you a lift somewhere?" Mum asked.

"No need, thank you," he said. "My other job isn't far."

"Your other job?"

"Must pay the bills, you know." He smiled ruefully. "Someday we shall settle where it's not so expensive. But for now . . ." He shrugged. Then he stepped closer and said in a low voice, "Is it true what your husband tells me about the bonfire, Mrs. Joyce? All those papers . . . gone?" He shook his head. "Foul deeds will rise, though all the earth o'erwhelm them, to men's eyes."

I glanced back and forth between them. Bonfire?

Mum, flustered, dropped her keys. "Er . . . ah . . . yes, I'm afraid so. Well, we'd best be going. Cheers!"

ভ ড

This time Mum was prepared. As soon as we closed the car doors, she held up her hand before I could open my mouth.

"Not now, Eva," she said, her voice wobbly.

"But—"

"I can't. I'm sorry."

We drove to the nursing home in silence. Well, if Mum wouldn't talk, maybe Aunt Bertie would. But I needed to speak with her alone.

"You're here to see Mrs. Pennington?" The nurse who met us at the entrance didn't even attempt to hide her surprise.

We followed her down the hall. The place was the opposite of

Aunt Bertie's own house: all bright pictures and floral curtains and huge potted plants. Even Bertie's room was aggressively cheerful, with a gaudy crocheted blanket on the bed and a sparkly vase of plastic daisies on the dresser.

"You've come to take me home, I hope," Bertie croaked from the corner. She huddled awkwardly in a wheelchair, her arm in a cast. Otherwise, she hadn't changed. She wore the same sack-like shawl around her shoulders, a glint of caustic humor in her eyes.

"Alas, no," said Mum, sitting down on the bed. "Seems like a lovely place, though. How's the food?"

"Horrific," Bertie snapped.

"And your arm—does it hurt?"

"Everything hurts. Can't put any weight on my hip, of course. But where is Bess? Why isn't she with you?"

"You know Mother. She doesn't travel more than an hour or two from home."

"Well, you'd think she might make an exception in this case." Bertie scowled like a petulant child.

"You'd think," Mum agreed.

This seemed to mollify Bertie, who looked at Mum with mild surprise. It was as though she wasn't accustomed to kindness.

"I've got a few questions for you about the house," Mum said. "Everything will be packed up carefully, of course. But I wondered about Claire's room. Am I to—"

"Leave it," Bertie commanded. "It's not to be touched."

"But you could use the rent from a third—"

"Do not disturb it. No one is to disturb it."

"Very well," Mum said with a gentleness she probably didn't feel. "I'll make sure it's locked. But about the bookcase in her room. You know it's empty, correct? I don't want there to be confusion later."

"Of course it's empty," Bertie said sharply. "Kinchurch kept giving Claire books. Ridiculous books full of nonsense, feeding their
mania. I got rid of the whole lot as soon as I could. Sold every last
one."

"Ah," Mum said in a noncommittal tone. "Warren's must've
taken them, I expect."

Bertie sniffed. "They'll take any sort of rubbish. I tried to talk
your mother into selling Kinchurch's library too. And those con-
founded tapestries, just like I sold the one I'd been given. But she
wouldn't touch the library—couldn't bear to look through all those
books, she said. She finally sold one of the tapestries to someone in
Hereford, years later. Old school chum of hers."

"Hereford?" Mum repeated. "You don't mean Marnie Prestwick?"

"Sounds right. Little dumpling of a woman, gone to seed. Bess
and I met up with her one day on a drive. She cried the whole time
about 'dear Annabeth.' As if I hadn't lost my daughter as well . . ."

Bertie then launched into a tirade about people's callous disre-
gard for her suffering. I tried to think of a way to interrupt her,
some excuse for Mum to leave us alone together so I could ask
about the empty frame in the guest bedroom. And what about the
books Bertie had sold? But her bitterness seemed to suck all the air
out of the room.

Bertie might've raged on and on if the nurse hadn't returned.
"I'm here to fetch you for supper, Mrs. Pennington!" the woman
announced brightly. "You've had a lovely time with your guests,
haven't you?"

Without giving Bertie the chance to reply, the nurse nodded at
Mum and me and wheeled the old woman into the hall.

I'd lost my chance.

"Marnie Prestwick," Mum muttered as we left. "Of *course*. Old friend of Annabeth's, actually."

"Do you think Marnie still has it?" I asked. "The other tapestry from Carrick Hall, the one with the dryads?"

"That's not a rabbit trail worth going down, darling. It won't lead anywhere."

"Why not?"

"Because Marnie's been dead for twenty years."

Suvan's descendants continued his evil practices, which they justified by claiming that Ternival was ever on the brink of being overrun. As tensions grew within Ternival itself and with their enemies, fortresses were erected along its borders. Ternival became ringed by watchtowers.

Then did the vale begin to tear at the seams. Some Ternivali embraced this new era, drawn to their rulers' brute force. Others spoke up but were maligned, then threatened, then imprisoned, and ultimately silenced. Ternivali everywhere spied on one another.

Yet a secret movement of resisters grew, calling themselves the Selvedges, named for the weft-edges of a woven work. They lived on the fringes of Ternivali society but deployed spies everywhere, including Castle Caristor.

And there the Selvedges soon learnt an important secret.

Kador, then king of Ternival, had begun to ally his household with the very enemies that Ternival feared: the wolves and giants and ogres from beyond the Wilderlands, who promised peace in exchange for an uneasy truce.

But in this Kador himself was deceived.

Chapter

30

Aunt Bertie's house hadn't changed much in her absence. It still was ugly, bereft of comforts, and cold. The housekeeper had shuttered it before leaving, but now Mum threw open the windows to let in the summer air.

"I'll open the upstairs windows," I said and dashed up to the second floor. At the doorway to the guest bedroom, I halted.

The walls were empty.

No frame. Nothing.

I opened the chest, which contained a stack of moldering linens, then rifled through the drawers of the dresser. More linens. I sat down glumly on the bed and stared at the opposite wall.

Had I imagined a frame? Had I wanted to believe in portals to other worlds so very badly that my imagination conjured one out of thin air?

I sat there for a long time. And maybe it was a trick of the light, but eventually I perceived a faint rectangular outline on the faded wallpaper. I stood up and peered closer, running my hand along the outline. Sure enough, there was a small hole, a nail puncture.

So something *had* hung here, at least. But it'd been taken down. Someone had stashed it away, or thrown it out, or destroyed it.

Mum's footsteps sounded on the stairs. I jumped up to wrestle the windows open, as if that's what I'd been doing all along.

"Well, this room isn't so bad," she said from the doorway. "I remember Mother saying she hated staying here as a child. She didn't particularly like Claire, who was an odd duck. Obsessed with botany, apparently. Nicer to plants than she was to humans. Claire improved, at some point, but Aunt Bertie didn't. Obviously." Mum glanced around appreciatively. "In any case, this room is downright pleasant."

"Other than that hideous green lamp," I pointed out.

Mum laughed. "Yes, well. Let's strip the bed and wash everything, and this could be where you sleep tonight. I'll sleep in Aunt Bertie's room next door."

As we made our way down the hall, Mum paused in front of Claire's room. "I know we're not supposed to touch it," she said, "but I've been longing for years to take a really good look." She flung open the door and stepped inside. "Ugh. I'd forgotten how disturbing it all is . . ."

Dust still covered the strange collections on the shelves, creating a dull fuzz on the dried flowers and spiky stalks. The empty bookcase, I realized, wasn't actually gray. It was orange, or had been, but it was so faded that the original color had dulled.

"It seems a sacrilege even to step foot in here," Mum mused. "I hate to touch anything. And yet, according to Mrs. Fealston, Claire had stored these collections away before she died. She'd grown to prefer her garden outside, with its living topiaries, to these dead things. But then, after the accidents, Aunt Bertie returned it all to the shelves, as if the new and improved Claire had never existed. So strange . . ." She glanced helplessly around the room. "It's like Claire died twice."

Mum inspected the bookcase with its lone encyclopedia, then wandered the room, peering at the dusty plants. Surreptitiously, I scanned the room for any sign of the frame. While her back was turned, I felt along the bed's duvet for anything tucked underneath, even glanced under the bed itself. Then I ran my hands between the bed frame and the mattress—and out fell a yellowed slip of paper onto the floor.

Mum hadn't seen it. I slid the paper into my back pocket.

"Well, I suppose we must lock it up," Mum said at last. She ushered me out, closed the door, and turned a small key in the lock. Then she placed a hand on the frame. "Goodbye, Claire," she murmured. "Rest in peace, poor soul."

As soon as she headed back downstairs, I pulled the slip of paper out of my pocket. At the top was a little crown and the words "Post Office Telegram." Underneath this, a cryptic string of typewritten words:

C. PENNINGTON, 46 BARFIELD CAMBRIDGE

M HAS FOUND US STOP MUST WARN B STOP K SAYS
MEET TOMORROW EIGHT THIRTY AM HARROW AND
WEALDSTONE STATION STOP I SHALL BRING GEMS = A

I rotated the paper to read the circular postmark.

October 7, 1952.

The day before the rail crash.

Later that evening we settled into our respective bedrooms for our first night in the old woman's house.

As I curled up on the guest bed, I imagined my young grandmother staying in this very room, her luggage shoved under the bed frame, a few favorite books arranged on the dresser. I pictured her lying under this same blanket while the trees outside tossed against a starlit sky. She'd gazed at whatever picture had hung in the frame and wished she was back in the magic land she loved best. And maybe somehow she *had* gotten back.

But now the frame was gone.

By the fading light from the windows, I reread the telegram. *C. Pennington.* That was Claire, of course, the telegram's recipient. And *A* stood for Annabeth, the sender. *B* was Bess, *K* was Kinchurch, and *M* was probably Marnie Prestwick, Annabeth's school friend—although how she fit into everything, I had no idea. The word *stop* took the place of a period at the end of every sentence. And Harrow and Wealdstone was the station where the rail crash had happened. But what was all this about bringing the gems? And warning Bess? Warn her about what?

Apparently, the walls were thin. Mum must've reached for the telephone by the bed, for I heard her say, "Robert? Hullo, love. . . . Yes, we're settled. . . . But listen: It's about the book Rastegar found. . . ." She went on to describe what we'd learned at Warren's, plus Bertie's explanation about selling the contents of the bookcase.

"And of course, Warren's is just the same as ever, crowded to the gills. Which means that looking for the other books Bertie sold could take months—maybe even years. . . . Yes, alas. But here's the thing: Bertie also mentioned the other tapestry, the one of the dryads that Mother sold years ago. Apparently, it ended up with Annabeth's old school chum in Hereford, Marnie Prestwick. . . . Yes, exactly! And I think Edward could help us find it."

Mum giggled in a flustered sort of way. "*Lord Heaps O'Money.* Honestly. I haven't heard you call him that in years. . . . And he wasn't my boyfriend!" I could picture her blushing furiously. "Yes, yes, I know you're just teasing. Anyway, he said he's glad to help make our case to Whitby in any way he can. And they do listen to money, of course. . . . Which isn't bribing, exactly. Is it?"

So Mum hadn't abandoned that rabbit trail, after all. She was going to try to track down the other tapestry, for reasons I couldn't quite make out. And once again, she was keeping secrets. From me.

I rolled over and pulled the covers up to my chin. Just as soon as Mum and I seemed to grow closer again—as soon as she drew me into her confidence, entrusted me with grown-up information— things fell apart.

The movers arrived the next day. They loaded box upon box of Bertie's goods into a lorry while leaving the bulk of the furnishings for university renters. Mum and I finished cleaning, spent one more night there, and then climbed into the Mercedes.

As we drove away, I looked back at Claire's old house. This was it, then. My hunt for the frame had proved fruitless. I'd scoured every closet, every cupboard, even searched for an attic entrance, to no avail. And now I'd never get another chance. I leaned my head against the window, feeling the now-familiar weight of sadness settle on my chest.

On our way out of town, we stopped by the nursing home again. Aunt Bertie was asleep.

"We don't want to rouse her," the nurse warned, eyeing us suspiciously as if we'd been sent on purpose to ruin the staff's afternoon. Bertie's expression was petulant, even in sleep.

"Oh, definitely not," Mum agreed. We stayed for a while, watching the old woman's shallow breathing.

It was the last I ever saw her.

Among the deceivers who promised peace was a powerful enchantress called Mindra. At first she masqueraded as the daughter of a nobleman from the northern downs, tall and regal and beautiful. Kador succumbed to her charms at once. One dark winter's day he pledged his troth, and they were married.

Soon Mindra became Kador's only trusted counselor at the court of Caristor, assuring him that she could find the lost gems by her divinations or manufacture new ones by her evil arts.

But the Selvedges guessed her true purpose: to find and take the gems for herself that she might rule all Ternival—and other lands besides.

Chapter

31

"Where hast thou been?" Grandmother grabbed my hand. "I feared thou wert lost again. But come: It's a glorious night for the hills!"

She'd been waiting for me at the pavilion that night, even though she hadn't joined us for supper upon our return to Carrick Hall. I'd forced myself to stay awake at my bedroom windows, just in case— and sure enough, her ghostlike figure had appeared, flitting through the flower beds, searching and searching. I'd run out to meet her, hoping she was searching for me.

Now, smiling, she released my hand and began to climb the path behind the pavilion, up to Table Mount. Moonlight flooded the stream, the gorse bushes, the boulders. It glittered from Grandmother's nightdress and cape like she was made of starshine, entire constellations winking from the folds of her robe.

As we climbed higher, the valley stretched before us under the clear night sky, serene and peaceful. When we reached the high table of stone, we stood there for what felt like hours, simply drinking in the moon-drenched view. I looked for the palace in the sky, but not a cloud could be seen.

Then came movement down in the valley. The great stag, of course, gliding majestically across the field toward the grove, shining with his own light.

"Look!" I cried. "He wants to lead us to the palace!"

Grandmother followed my gaze, and her face hardened. "Ware, beloved," she warned. "Thou knowest the danger."

"But we should follow where he leads!" I said, thinking of Stokes. "It's a fearful thing, but it must be done." Without waiting for her response, I took off down the hill.

"Stop at once!" came her commanding voice.

But I kept running, down and down, leaping over the stream, plunging past the boulders, careless in my haste. I'd missed so many chances already. I wasn't about to miss this one.

"This is madness!" she called, her voice now far behind me.

And that's when I fell.

My vision swam. My ears rang. I tried to sit up, but a dizzying wave of nausea washed over me. I tried to get my bearings: I wasn't even halfway down the hill. And in the dark, there was no way I'd be able to walk back alone. Not down this steep, rocky trail, not this far from Carrick Hall.

"Dearest?" Grandmother's voice grew closer. I could hear her scrambling across the stones.

I was tempted to keep silent out of shame. I'd ignored her warning. I'd recklessly pursued my own wishes. But I needed her help. "I'm here," I said, the sound of my voice slamming through my brain like a scream.

She appeared, leaping from boulder to boulder, then dropped onto the trail beside me.

"I'm so sorry," I whispered. "If you can help me stand, I might be able to—"

"Be still," she commanded. "Thou art wounded. Wounded and bleeding."

Grandmother knelt. With swift, sure fingers, she probed a tender spot above my right eyebrow. I could feel the blood leaking down my temple. I bit my lip, trying not to cry out with pain.

"A mighty crack to thy skull, I fear," she said. "We must wrap it."

She tore a long strip of fabric from the hem of her nightdress and wrapped it expertly around my head like a crown. Despite her gentleness, my whole head throbbed.

"You didn't tell me you were a nurse," I joked through gritted teeth.

"We learnt these tricks in wartime. Or hast thou forgotten?"

Of course. The air raids. Back then, nearly everyone in England had learned basic first aid.

But that's not what Grandmother meant. "Surely thou hast not forgotten the Battle of the Downs?" she continued. "When the giants nearly felled our cousin? We wrapped her wounds, quick as lightning, lest she perish. There. And now I fear we must wait till the pain subsides. I alone cannot bring thee down the mountainside, but I daren't leave thee to seek help."

"I'm already starting to feel better," I said. "If we wait awhile, I can probably make it." Which was true. My ears had stopped ringing. But then I began to shiver uncontrollably.

"There, dearest," Grandmother said, scooting closer to me. She pulled off her cape and drew it around my shoulders. "Foolish of thee to career down the mountainside in pursuit of that fickle beast." She took my hand and peered into my face in the gloom. "Promise me," she said imperiously, "thou shalt not trust him. Promise me *never again* to follow where he leads."

"I'm so sorry," I whispered again. I couldn't promise. I wouldn't. She made no reply.

We sat for a long time in the dark, my vision slowly steadying. I wished I could ask her questions, anything that might reveal who and where, exactly, she thought she was. Or who she thought I was. But the pain obliterated my ability to speak.

Eventually I felt well enough to rise gingerly to my feet.

"Thou art certain?" she asked.

"If I can hold on to you, we can do this."

It was a laborious half hour climbing back down the hillside. But Grandmother was gentle and knew the trail by heart. As she guided me from rock to rock, her strong arm around my waist, I realized that I'd never been this physically close to her. When I was a small child, I would've loved to crawl into her lap, feel the warmth and safety of her arms, play with the silkiness of her long hair. I would've loved to hear her tell me stories before bedtime.

But I'd missed out on all that. Plus, once I'd become a teenager, grown-ups tended to give me space. And most of the time, I did want space. Sometimes, though, I just wanted a grandmother.

When we finally arrived at the formal gardens, the tiny figure of Mrs. Fealston came hurrying toward us across the grass.

"Mercy!" she exclaimed. "Is the child all right? Whatever happened?"

"We are in need of a skilled physician, if you please," Grandmother demanded. "As swift as ever you can."

Mrs. Fealston glanced at me with a mixture of alarm and fury. I'd broken all trust now. Not only that—Mum also needed to be told about my accident. But what would happen if she encountered Grandmother in this state?

"Let's go to the kitchen," I said. "Why don't I rest there first, while you retire to your chambers to wash?" We needed to whisk Grandmother out of the picture as quickly as possible.

"Wise counsel, Your Majesty," Mrs. Fealston agreed, taking her elbow.

"Nonsense," said Grandmother, twisting her arm free. "I shall stay with her till help arrives."

Mrs. Fealston and I exchanged panicked looks.

"But if you should catch a chill, what then?" Mrs. Fealston tried again. "You shall be of no use to her if you are ill yourself. Allow me to accompany you to your chambers, and then you can return to her side."

Finally Grandmother relented, and the three of us made our way across the gardens together. As Grandmother helped me into the unlit kitchen, Mrs. Fealston hurried ahead of us and flipped a switch. Overhead electric light hit us like a bolt of lightning. I recoiled and threw my hands up to shield my eyes.

Grandmother blinked at her surroundings as if she'd never been here before. "What is this place?" Her voice came in a ragged whisper. "By what sorcery hast thou brought me hither?" Then she looked at her hands, her torn nightgown, covered in my blood.

I felt woozy again. "I think . . . I'm . . ."

"In here, child." Mrs. Fealston threw her thin arm around my waist—I had no idea how she'd catch me if I fell—and quickly opened the door to her quarters. She led me in and settled me on a small couch. "Stay here," she whispered. "Don't lie down. And try not to fall asleep. I'll just get her settled and fetch your mother."

Then she took Grandmother's arm again. "Come, Your Majesty," she said. "Up to your chambers for a good wash."

Sudden exhaustion drained all the life from Grandmother's face. She closed her eyes and shuddered. "Yes, of course."

About five minutes later, Mum rushed into the housekeeper's quarters, fully dressed and clutching her handbag. Ashen with fear, she halted at the sight of my bloody bandage.

"I think I need stitches," I blurted and burst into tears.

By her deceptions Mindra the Enchantress deepened her husband Kador's fears by insisting that he was in greater danger than ever from those who might seek to unseat him. (Which was, in fact, true, but not in the manner he thought.)

Likewise did she spin lies that the stag of Andella, if it existed at all, could not be trusted. So she encouraged King Kador to annul the law forbidding the hunting of the stag and instead to offer a bounty for its head—and, in the meantime, to erase its image from the land.

Loud echoed the hunting horns in the Wilderlands that autumn. And loud rang the hammers that were wielded against the carven stags upon the stones of Caristor. Tapestries with the stag's image were pulled down from the Hall, and if ever a Ternivali was caught with a stag depicted on their tunics, their leathern braces, or their doorposts, those loyal citizens were taken from their homes and imprisoned.

And dark was this hour for the Selvedges, for unless they hid themselves, and swiftly, their movements might be divined by the new queen. Thus, many fled into the wilds, and but few remained in secret at the court of Caristor.

Chapter

32

I did need stitches, but not many, thank goodness. Only four, over my right eyebrow, sewn indelicately by the emergency room doctor at the hospital in Great Wolvern, half an hour away. He'd ordered all kinds of tests, concluded I had a mild concussion, prescribed pain medication, then stitched up my wound like it was a rip in his trousers. He ordered Mum to keep an eye on me overnight and sent us home.

"Wandering the grounds," Mum muttered on the drive home. "Unable to sleep. Whatever gave you the idea to go outside in the first place, much less to climb the hill?"

"I told you," I said, glad the darkness hid my flush of shame. "The stars. They were so pretty."

Miraculously, Mrs. Fealston, upon fetching my mother, hadn't given me away. She'd merely told Mum to ask *me* what had happened. Which Mum did, repeatedly, all the way to Great Wolvern and back.

More secrets. Except this one I wore across my forehead like a billboard.

When I awoke late the next morning, Mum was still asleep. I made my way to the bathroom and peered, sore and hungry, into the mirror. My stitches were ugly: brown and jagged, like I'd fought a garden rake and lost. The skin underneath practically glowed orange from iodine antiseptic. Hoping the hour was late enough that Grandmother had already eaten breakfast, I went downstairs to the dining room.

But she was there. She stood alone facing the fireplace, wearing crumpled linens, her hair loosely upswept in a messy bun. Shoulders tense, hands clasping and unclasping, her face haggard: It was clear that she, too, hadn't slept well.

Grandmother didn't notice me at first. She was staring at the tapestry like it had just appeared, unwanted, out of nowhere. The stag seemed to stare back, as if daring her to speak.

"Morning," came Mum's voice as she entered the room behind me. "How are you feeling, darling?"

Grandmother spun around, startled, then blanched at the sight of my wound.

Mum inspected my forehead. "You didn't make a peep last night. I haven't counted your breaths like that since you were an infant. Does it hurt? Still have a headache?"

"A little."

"I'm told she fell while roaming the grounds last night," Mum said to Grandmother. "Still finding it hard to fall asleep, she claims."

Grandmother frowned in confusion, as if trying to remember something. But the memory of my fall, of binding my wound and helping me back down the hill, seemed to elude her. As we filled our plates and ate in silence, she kept glancing at my forehead and then up at the tapestry, brow furrowed.

"That tapestry, Gwendolyn," she finally said. "I've never liked it."

"No?" Mum said wryly.

Grandmother didn't pick up on her sarcasm. "It's the hounds. I've never been keen on a hunt."

"Yes, I remember. Father used to tease you for weeping during Old Heapworth's foxhunts. Said you were too gentlehearted." Mum studied the tapestry for a moment. "Are you saying you're going to sell it?"

"Well, it's quite ancient. Must be worth a pile."

"Edward could tell you. But Mrs. Fealston wouldn't like it to be sold, you know. It's a fixture of her tour."

I piped up without thinking. "Yeah, and she told me the frame is unique too. Made from the same rare variety of tree as the jewelry box . . ." My voice trailed off as I realized my mistake.

Grandmother blanched again.

"Jewelry box?" Mum echoed.

"Oh," I stammered, "just something . . . Mrs. Fealston mentioned on her tour. There were a few things made from the pear trees that are found only here, at Carrick Hall."

Grandmother stood abruptly. "Call Edward about it, Gwendolyn," she said. "For pity's sake, just call him."

Then she stalked out.

"Maybe someday I will understand that woman," Mum said dryly. "But not today." She appraised my stitches. "So. No more roaming. Not even in the daytime—until that wound has healed, anyway. No wandering about with Frankie, or helping in the garden, or any of the things you've been doing."

"Then what *can* I do?"

"You can come with me to Hereford. Through a bit of sleuthing, Edward thinks he's tracked down the tapestry of dryads. But he's still in London, so he wants me to confirm it's the right one."

"Whatever happened to not following that rabbit trail?"

She shrugged. "I realized it was worth a try. Although we probably shouldn't get our hopes up. Marnie's children sold it long ago. So it's quite possibly disappeared altogether. But Edward tracked them down, and they seem to think it might've ended up at this particular shop. Assuming no one has bought it, or that the shop owner keeps good records of who did, we just might be in luck."

An hour later, we pulled up at the antique shop in question. The day was warm and humid, with low, menacing clouds. But inside, the dim shop felt cool and quiet. It hushed my soul like an old church.

I followed Mum to the counter, where a youngish woman in a high-necked Victorian blouse greeted us. She flicked a curious glance at my stitches, then gave Mum her full attention. As Mum explained her quest, the shopkeeper frowned skeptically.

"Dryads, you say?" she mused. "I think I'd remember that."

But I had my own ideas of what I might find. I stepped away to look around.

Everywhere I looked, furniture was clustered and stacked in confusion, ancient pieces that smelled of must and attics and church vestries. The place had no discernible order, no helpful labels announcing *Tapestries of All Sizes*. Not every shop could be Warren's, alas. Mum glanced at me anxiously over her shoulder, but I gave a reassuring wave and continued on.

Soon I found an empty frame of light wood, its edges ornamented with gold filigree. Not the right thing at all. I turned a corner. Here was another frame of old barnwood. No good either. My explorations revealed any number of pictures, paintings, etchings, and mirrors, but their frames were too heavy, or too flimsy, or too gilded, or too commonplace.

Then, at the top of a crowded landing, I found it.

Under the false counsel of Mindra his queen, King Kador began to fear the weavings in the Hall of Tapestries. He especially feared the runes that told of the coming of the Children of Tellus and the restoration of the crown—for she whispered to him that the Children would surely unseat him, if ever they appeared.

Thus did he order the rending of all the weavings, piece by piece, and the last of the Writbards were scattered and fled into hiding. And likewise did Kador employ ogres to raid the monastery of Ignatira, sending its Loomkeepers deeper into the Wilderlands.

Worst of all, Mindra the Enchantress convinced King Kador to abandon Ternival's watchtowers, claiming it was he, not Ternival, that needed strong defense. Instead, she counseled, he should employ the very enemies that Ternival feared—giants and ogres and wolves—to defend the gates of Caristor.

Kador, by counsel of Mindra his queen, did abandon the watchtowers of Ternival. And a company of ogres and giants did he charge to stand guard at the castle.

And great was the grieving among the Selvedges when this news reached their ears, and many despaired.

Chapter

33

It was propped against the wall next to a full-length antique mirror. A large empty frame, only slightly smaller than the one in the dining room, made of dark, intricately wrought wood. It was another frame from Carrick Hall—I just knew it. The one that had once held the tapestry of the dryads. And yes! There in the corner of the frame were the carven tree and coronet.

I ran my fingers along the carvings, wondering if there was a button or panel or specific process for opening the portal. Finally, like a child, I ducked my head and climbed through.

Nothing.

It'd worked in the stories. The girls had been playing in the large manor house where they were guests one summer. And one of them suggested they pretend the world inside the tapestry was real. So they stepped forward as if they could climb through, arms outstretched, and then all of a sudden they *were* through. They found themselves in Ternival.

I crouched behind the frame, against the wall, keeping perfectly still. I held my breath and listened. Perhaps, even if I couldn't reach it, I could hear another world from this spot, on the threshold.

But all I heard were footsteps on the landing.

"Eva!" Mum exclaimed from the top step. "How on earth . . ."

Behind her came the shopkeeper. "Well, it seems you didn't need my help, madam," the woman said with a disapproving sniff. "She found the frame for you. Although if the young lady could please not climb around the furniture . . ."

"Sorry," I said and slid back through. I withdrew to the murky corner of the landing, where they couldn't see the tears caught in my eyelashes.

Mum began to inspect the frame, studying the carvings, peering around the back. "Yes, yes . . . it's just as I remember! A pity the tapestry is no longer with it. But the frame is the real treasure. If we make a down payment, will you hold it for us?"

"Certainly, madam."

"And then as soon as I hear from Lord Edward, you'll receive the rest. In the meantime, would you mind if we tag it for shipment?"

"Of course. Please keep in mind that shipping to Chicago will take several weeks."

"Chicago?" I cut in.

"Edward is purchasing it for Whitby College," Mum explained to me, "in hopes they'll hire your father."

"We're not taking it back to Carrick Hall, where it belongs?"

"Oh dear . . ." Mum paused, flustered. "No, Eva. I'm afraid not. Edward is donating it to Whitby's Kinchurch Collection, to strengthen your father's case for the position."

"The college has a Kinchurch Collection?"

She exhaled with exasperation. "We can discuss all this later."

Later. Always later. But if we waited much longer, I might never get another chance to see if the magic worked.

I was running out of time.

೮ఇ

That same afternoon Lord Edward came roaring up the drive in a shiny Rolls-Royce. He emerged from the car in a blue-and-white seersucker suit that made him look like he'd stepped out of a glamor magazine. Waving, he flashed his toothy smile.

"Family with you?" Mum called to him as Mrs. Fealston opened the great front doors.

"Alas, not yet," he said, bounding up the steps. "They'll follow from London in a few days. I've only just arrived myself."

"But you'll stay for tea."

"Honored!" Then he caught sight of my stitches. "Great Scott! I didn't know prizefighting was in your line, Eva, old girl. Whyever does your mum allow it?"

I blushed. "I fell. Up in the hills."

He tsk-tsked. "Those nasty Wolverns. I must speak to them about it."

"You remember Mrs. Fealston, of course," Mum said, deftly turning the conversation.

"Ah yes! So good to see you again, Mrs. Fealston."

Mrs. Fealston bobbed a half curtsy and murmured, "My lord," before leading us into the entrance hall.

Lord Edward followed languidly, pausing every few feet to peer at the furnishings. Sometimes he inhaled deeply, as if overcome with awe. Other times he beamed and exclaimed, "Marvelous. Simply marvelous!"

Grandmother joined us in the dining room, where Heapworth greeted her with a robust "Afternoon, Mrs. T!"

Then he stepped back to survey the tapestry. He strode around the room, viewing the scene from multiple angles while the rest of us watched in silence.

"My word," he muttered, pulling out a magnifying glass from his blazer pocket and leaning closer. "D'you know, I believe there's gold thread in here?" Then he shifted the magnifying glass to peer at the frame. "This frame, Mrs. T—reminds me of that other one, with the tapestry of the dryads, eh? It's been decades, of course, but I can remember those carvings, clear as day."

"Dryads?" Grandmother echoed faintly.

Mum tried to catch Heapworth's eye with a warning shake of her head, but he pressed on. "Gwen finding the frame was seren-dipitous, and that's a fact. I don't think the dealer has any idea of its real value. Cost more to ship it to Whitby than the actual purchase—can you believe it? But I'm glad it can help his case."

"Whitby?" Grandmother had braced herself against a chair as if her legs were made of jelly.

"You know, the college that's set to hire Robert, lucky blokes. Gwenny wanted me to—" At last Heapworth caught Mum's mean-ingful glare. "Ah, just an old thing I remember from . . . when I was a kid. . . . Something Robert can use . . . at the new job," he fin-ished lamely.

Grandmother shuddered as though a great shadow was passing over her soul. "Well, I'm afraid I have a bit of a headache and must retire. So good of you to come see us, Edward." Before he could reply, she left.

"Forgive me, Gwenny," Heapworth muttered. "I just blunder in and trample everything, don't I?"

At last: another person who knew exactly what it felt like to be me.

Soon we sat down for tea in the drawing room. Heapworth now shifted the conversation to things that could be done to increase the revenue of the estate. It could be turned into a wedding venue, he suggested, or the stables transformed into a tea shop. Or the luxury cars could be sold—he knew a fellow who'd snap 'em up like *that*.

"But back to those stables," he pressed. "They'd make a perfect tea shop. I could spot your mum a loan to get started."

"Honestly, Edward. You're relentless."

"But look—the building's got a water source, drains, the whole nine yards."

"I'll tell you what," Mum said decisively. "Invest in the Rastegars. They can relocate their bookshop to Upper Wolvern, which is long overdue for one. Maybe even start a tea shop, too, for all the tourists and students. The Rastegars have got the brains for business, not me. I'm not ever going to live here and manage things, do you understand? Not ever. When Mother's gone, all of this will be sold. All of it. You won't see me in Upper Wolvern again."

She stalked out, leaving me alone in the drawing room with Lord Edward Heapworth.

My mind was reeling. Sell Carrick Hall? Sell this amazing place, our only family home?

"Well, that went splendidly, don't you think?" Heapworth attempted to joke. "Ah, never mind. Your mother has had a beastly time—I'll give her that. Poor girl. I'll never forget the sight of that bonfire till my dying day. D'you know, we could see the glow above the trees all the way to Wolvern Court? I drove here like a madman, thinking the Hall was ablaze. Your mother had already left, of course. But the look on your grandmother's face . . ."

This was the second mention of a mysterious bonfire. As if everyone expected me to know all about it. But it didn't seem fair to beg Lord Edward to tell me what my own family wouldn't.

"That's a very long and brooding silence," he said with mock seriousness. "You get that habit from your mum, no doubt."

"Sorry," I said. "It's just . . . We don't really have any place to live right now. Not a real home. So I've always wondered about Carrick Hall. But it sounds like we'll never live here. And anyway, this whole place is . . ."

"Strange," he suggested.

"Wondrous," I said.

He chuckled. "Wondrous strange. Passing strange. Like so much of life. And what a boring world it would be otherwise, eh?"

I tried to imagine life without Carrick Hall in the background of my family story. I tried to picture the Addisons surrounded by complete strangers, or not here at all. I envisioned someday driving past the gatehouse and gazing down the winding road at what would then belong to someone else.

All of it felt wrong.

Lord Edward rose from his seat and stretched. "Well, give everyone my regards. Tell your grandmother I'll be back in a few weeks with a crew to remove the tapestry for auction. Oh, and you might give up prizefighting, you know. Bad for the old noggin." He tapped his forehead.

Just then came a frantic pounding on the door. Whoever it was didn't wait for an answer but flung the door open. It was Holly Addison, freckles stark against her wan face.

"Help me, someone!" she gasped. "It's Dad."

Then, in the deep of winter, when all the watchtowers of Ternival stood unguarded and the vale lay sluggish in its false peace, the doom of Mindra descended.

In fury did Mindra the Enchantress arise from the right hand of Kador, and crying aloud, she slew her husband the king in the throne room of Caristor. Then she took the crown and put it upon her own head and went forth in power to throw open the gates to Ternival's enemies. Within the hour the castle was overrun.

On that day Caristor fell, and the heirs of Wefan and Andella perished or were lost.

And great was the terror in the vale.

Chapter

34

One moment, Frankie's grandfather was being lifted into an ambulance parked in the circle drive. Then, what felt like mere minutes later, Mrs. Addison telephoned from the hospital in Great Wolvern.

It was over. They couldn't save him.

On the bright morning of the funeral, we hovered outside the church, Mum and Mrs. Fealston and I, in a milling crowd of black-clothed mourners. The air was so still and clear I wondered if the tolling bell could be heard all the way to the Channel.

I hadn't seen anyone in Frankie's family since the ambulance had driven away. And I wished I could catch his glance now. But he and his siblings stood surrounded by cousins I didn't know, extended family from across the United Kingdom. Frankie himself seemed like a stranger too. Cut off by relationships that had defined him long before I'd arrived, cut off by the grief that etched his face. I could only imagine how the loss of his beloved grandfather had torn a ragged hole in his heart. If he was aware of my presence in the churchyard, he made no sign.

The priest arrived. The crowd began to enter the church ahead of Frankie's family.

"Won't you sit in the family pew today, my dear?" Mrs. Fealston whispered to my mother.

"I will not," Mum whispered back. "Not today. Not any day."

Just then, an astonished murmur swept through the sanctuary.

"As I recall," came Grandmother's calm voice behind us, "the family pew is this way."

Grandmother walked steadily past us down the center aisle, long hair twisted back in a modest coil. She wore a plain tailored black dress offset by a simple posy of lavender from Stokes's herb garden, her expression placid but determined. Behind her, an entire congregation of mourners craned their necks to watch.

I glanced at my mother, who seemed paralyzed with surprise, then followed Grandmother into the family pew. Mum hesitated a moment longer before joining us.

The funeral itself was a blur. There was the priest, his words a strange combination of the grim and the exultant. And there was the sunlight, muted through stained glass, splashing color all over the sanctuary. There was the coffin, and Frankie's relatives, and Frankie's own stoic gaze fixed on the carved screen above the altar. When the church bell rang again through the still air, my thoughts flew to the golden palace that sometimes hovered over the distant horizon. Could they hear it from the battlements? Did they know what Frankie had lost? *Not lost,* came Mrs. Fealston's words to my mind. *Merely hidden.*

A sob rose in my throat. Unexpectedly Grandmother's hand clasped mine, steady and reassuring. Mum reached for my other hand. We sat linked together, the three of us, till the bell ceased.

Afterward we followed the crowd to the graveside without speaking. The only sounds were the priest's lilting voice, a wren burbling blithely on a nearby column, and Tilly's muffled sobbing, her face buried in Frankie's shoulder. Soon the coffin was lowered into the ground. The service was over.

In the fraught silence that followed, I realized that my grandmother was approaching the family. And I was expected to follow. The crowd parted for the three of us—Grandmother, Mum, and me—like waves before the prow of a ship. It occurred to me, uncomfortably, that centuries of class distinctions and empty formalities were bound up in this one moment. It wasn't merely grief that cut me off from my friend: It was an entire way of life.

Grandmother murmured a string of condolences. Mrs. Addison held herself stiffly. But Frankie's father—a solid, broad-chested man with calm eyes and a shock of red hair—defrosted the chill with a warm shake of Grandmother's extended hand.

"It's kind of you to come, Mrs. Torstane," he said. "And Mrs. Joyce, Miss Joyce. My father-in-law would've been honored."

"It was my honor to know him," Grandmother said. Then she added quietly, for only Frankie's parents to hear, "Please do visit the Hall at your convenience, Mr. Addison. I can't possibly hope to find someone like old Stokes again, but if his position is of any interest . . ."

The change that came over the Addisons was instantaneous. Mrs. Addison's face flushed. Mr. Addison likewise grew rigid and put a cautionary hand on his wife's elbow. The very air seemed to crackle with tension. Yet, as quickly as emotion had gripped him, he overmastered it, saying, "Very kind, ma'am."

Grandmother—oblivious, as always—nodded regally and continued on her way.

"Forgive us, Holly," Mum said with regret. "We manage to blunder everything. I'm so very, very sorry."

"It was kindly meant." Mrs. Addison's eyes filled with tears—whether of grief or anger, I couldn't tell.

"No harm done," Frankie's father said. "Mrs. Torstane meant it to be a comfort. And she's right. There's no one else who should fill the job." He turned to his wife. "We'll talk it over, won't we, love?"

"No, we won't," said Mrs. Addison fiercely.

"I'm so very sorry," Mum repeated. She rested a hand on her friend's arm, then slipped through the crowd as if she wished the earth would swallow her.

I hesitated. Was I expected to say something? I tried catching Frankie's eye, but he looked past me, as if I were invisible.

Painfully self-conscious about my ugly stitches, I muttered my condolences to Frankie's parents and fled.

⚜

A distant rumble of thunder woke me.

I lay there, deliberating. Ever since Stokes's funeral, whenever I'd tried to escape outside by night, Mrs. Fealston had been there. Prowling the hallways and staircases, patrolling the veranda, keeping watch for me and Grandmother, no doubt. How the old housekeeper kept up this nightly vigil while also leading daily tour groups, I'll never understand.

Would Grandmother venture out on a night like this? Or the stag? And what about Mrs. Fealston? Or would she assume that we'd stay inside with this kind of weather?

Another rumble echoed up the valley. I flung back the covers.

I couldn't see much outside my windows. No moon, no stars. Just a solid bank of clouds and the occasional flash of lightning. But the prospect of a storm in the Wolverns was weirdly exciting. Between the temporary absence of Frankie and his family, the constant invasion of tour groups, and Mum's solitary pursuits in the library, it'd been an uneventful week. Even with Stokes no longer guarding the gems, the jewelry box hadn't appeared again. And I'd been unsuccessful in trying to open the door in the wall.

But time was running short. Summer would be over soon.

I quickly changed, grabbed my flashlight, and headed downstairs, unnerved by the strange shadows of the vast house. Was that Mrs. Fealston there, on the landing? No, just a smallish suit of armor.

In the entrance hall I paused. A faint noise came from the drawing room, one of the French doors closing. Peeking in, I saw a winking light on the veranda, some sort of lantern held by a cloaked and hooded figure. The figure descended into the gardens out of view.

I switched off the flashlight and followed, slipping out the door and down the steps into the stillness. Ahead of me, lantern light bobbed away. The figure was moving swiftly. I'd have to jog to keep up.

The light came to a stop. The figure stood near the base of one of the larger topiaries—the centaur, perhaps, but I couldn't be certain in the darkness. I, too, paused.

"What news, Moongazer?" It was Grandmother's voice. Low, urgent.

As if in answer, distant lightning flashed beyond Table Mount. A rumble of thunder rolled across the highlands. In that brief flash I could see the topiary. It was indeed the centaur—except, instead of rearing, he now stood on all four legs, his torso bent toward her as if imparting state secrets.

Excitement jolted through my body.

The topiaries could *move*?

Thus did Mindra the Usurper establish herself as queen of all Ternival. She forsook the ruins of Caristor, cursed them, and took for her seat the northwestern watchtower of Marisith-over-the-Sea, which she re-built as a mighty fastness guarded by her giants and ogres. From there she ruled all the vale.

Mindra commanded that the monastery of Ignatira be razed to the ground, its looms destroyed. Every scrap of tapestry to be found any-where in Ternival was gathered in heaps. Then one dark night, atop the ruins of Caristor, did Mindra burn them all.

Flames most sinister leapt high into the clouds and were espied from the downs to the mountains, from the Wilderlands to the Path-less. And smoke from the heaps rose on the wind for seven weeks.

To this day, that great burning is remembered as the Desolate Pyre.

Chapter

35

"But whence come these monsters?" Grandmother's voice wafted across the stillness after the roll of thunder ceased. "Not from the hills, surely! Thou art certain?"

Again, the flash and the rumble. And again, the centaur, leaning down.

"With thine own eyes!" Grandmother exclaimed. "Somehow they've breached our protections. And they shall grow bolder, no doubt, with every hour. I must send messengers at once."

She swung away, then stopped as more lightning and thunder gripped the valley.

"Art thou mad?" Her voice rose. "Seek the great stag? Never, by my life. Even if thou canst find him—which I doubt, for he is as wily a creature as ever roamed the earth—his portents are not to be trusted. Seeking him has only ever led us into danger. Nay, Moongazer. We shall protect this fastness ourselves."

Grandmother fled, lantern swinging wildly. I gave chase as best I could, but it was slow going in the darkness. By the time I caught up with her, she'd begun addressing something or someone else. It was another topiary, the large rabbit, its ears twitching as if listening carefully to every word.

"Ill news, Swiftfoot," Grandmother was saying. "We must send forth messengers to the watchtowers at once—else I fear this fastness shall not hold. Now, go!"

As Grandmother turned away, the rabbit vanished into shadow, but I could've sworn it twitched its ears and gave a slight bow.

The light moved quickly again, this time back toward the veranda. And again I tried to keep up. Then Grandmother stopped and addressed yet another figure at the foot of the steps: the mastiff.

"Raise the castle, Wolfmane!" Grandmother cried. "Alert the others at once. We shall not be taken unawares. Now I must fly. Our borders must be secured."

She advanced suddenly in my direction with powerful strides, like a general. Before I could move, the light from her lantern fell on me.

"Ware, my dear!" she exclaimed. "Get thee to the castle at once!"

"But what is it? What's the matter?"

"Giants, by heaven."

"Giants!"

"Moongazer has seen them with his own eyes," she continued, "high in the hills. They plan to take us unawares. Fools." She took hold of my arm and began steering me back toward the house. "I swore to keep and protect thee, and so I shall."

"I don't *want* to be protected," I said, to my own surprise, and wrenched my arm free. "I want to *help* you."

She laughed grimly. "And with what? Art thou a sorceress now, that thou hast the power to fend off these monsters?"

"Not me. But there is one who can."

She laughed again without mirth. "Ah, so thou, too, wouldst conspire against me and take the centaur's counsel? Thou wouldst seek the great stag that pretends to guard this realm? Remember, beloved, what ill befell thee when last thou tried. Long have we hunted him, to seek his guidance, yet only ever has he eluded us and led us astray. He is not to be trusted."

"But without him we can't conquer anything—certainly not giants, anyway."

Lightning ripped across the sky overhead. Grandmother drew herself up to her full height. "I swore to protect thee—even from *him,* if I must—and so I shall!"

Just then came a flash, and thunder roared from the highlands. I turned to see the hills and trees, the gardens and hedges, lit in another blinding flash. The great stag stood mere yards away, the air around him rippling with threadlike strands, as if we all were suspended in the warp and weft of the tapestry he'd come from. His antlers crackled with blue light. I couldn't tell if he'd been struck by lightning or was the source of it.

"Away, brute!" Grandmother cried in terror. "Thou canst not protect her. Thou hast failed before, and thou wilt fail again. Begone!" She threw herself between us, spreading her cloaked arms like a great bird. Rain began to fall—not slowly, but in torrents, as though someone had ripped the low belly of the clouds from east to west.

"But he's here to help!" I yelled over the storm, already soaked to the skin.

From the hills came another sound: not thunder, but a rhythmic pounding, like monstrous footfalls. The very ground shook.

"Please!" I called to the stag. "Please, help us!"

Rain poured from the sky, streaming from the stag's antlers and down his sides. Grandmother's cloak did nothing to protect her now: She was drenched through.

The pounding grew louder, closer.

"Help us!" I screamed.

The stag lifted his face into the storm, opened his mouth, and bellowed. Then he tore away, toward the hills and the pounding, into the darkness. Seconds later, an enormous crash rent the air, then another and another, and something howled from the highlands like a wounded beast. Lightning flashed one last time, thunder rumbled down the valley, and then the storm, the rain—everything—abruptly ceased.

All was silent.

"Come inside at once, Your Majesty!" a voice behind us called. "You'll catch your death!"

Garish electric light flooded the veranda, and I realized with relief that I remained in shadow, unseen. Mrs. Fealston rushed down the steps. "Steady now, Your Majesty. All is well. Thou art safe. Just drenched through. Come with me."

Grandmother's face looked ghastly: haggard and hollowed out, her eyes like a haunted child's. She shuddered uncontrollably as Mrs. Fealston bundled her up the steps and into the house. Neither of them seemed aware of me. The light was switched off again, and I remained in the shadows for a good five minutes before I followed. I shivered uncontrollably, too, less from my sopping clothes than from the sudden relief that it was over. Whatever had happened in the hills, it was over.

I crept upstairs and showered, hoping Mrs. Fealston was too busy with Grandmother to notice. I let the warm water wash away the cold and the terror and the memory of Grandmother's helpless figure, arms outstretched, trying to save me. And from what? From the true source of her strength and safety. But no, not safety. For the great stag was wild, as wild as the storm—and just as powerful. Yet he'd conquered whatever evil had threatened us. I knew that for certain. He'd saved us, and he'd done so before, and he'd go on saving us, even to the end of the age.

But Grandmother's resistance made sense too. If the stag was so strong, so present in times of dire need, why hadn't he kept her loved ones from danger?

Why hadn't he protected her?

Under Mindra's reign, Ternival's farmlands and orchards were laid waste or left to rot. Her giants cut ugly roads across the vale, which none save Mindra's henchmen could travel without heavy tolls. Thus, the starving countryfolk flocked to the villages, now governed by ogres, or escaped deep into the Wilderlands.

As the fields lay abandoned, a foul forest crept in on all sides. The vale was overrun by vines and thorns and dense scrubby pines, and Ternival became all but impassable.

Chapter

36

"Quite a storm last night," Mum said over her coffee.

"Indeed," Grandmother replied, not meeting my gaze. She looked simply dazzling in an intricately embroidered tunic, her silvery hair coiffed, jeweled fingers sparkling.

"At one point I thought the hills were crashing down on the Hall," Mum continued. "I've never heard it rage like that."

"The Wolverns can be quite the monsters sometimes," Grandmother said. "Perhaps you've forgotten."

I glanced up sharply. Was that on purpose? *Monsters*?

Mum ignored the barb. "Eva and I can walk around the estate this morning, if you like, just to make sure everything's all right. I fear we might have lost some trees, especially in the old grove."

"Can't Addison do it? His job starts today, I believe."

"Poor man. What a wretched way to start one's career as head gardener at Carrick Hall . . ."

"Frankie's dad took the job?" I piped up. This was the last thing I'd expected to hear.

"Oh—didn't you know?"

I glared at Mum across the table. "No one tells me *anything*."

Mum ignored this barb too. "Holly decided it's preferable to him being gone for days on end, driving lorries. Anyway, we can save him the trouble on his first day by walking the grounds ourselves."

Grandmother lifted a shoulder. "If you wish."

Something about Grandmother's nonchalance troubled me deeply. I couldn't shake my sense of dread from the previous night, the feeling that some terrible doom hid among the hills, waiting to descend on us all. I couldn't shake the conviction that only by the stag's protective presence had we been preserved, safe and unharmed.

Yet here she sat, once again, as if no high drama had played out in the gardens the night before.

Mum and I donned some Wellingtons from a kitchen cupboard and headed into the drenched gardens. Stokes's herbs seemed mostly intact, but the lettuces and tomato vines had been obliterated. Debris from various plants and outbuildings littered the pathways.

"All that hard work . . ." I murmured sadly.

"It's why I'm not a gardener," Mum said. "Breaks your heart."

We continued through the archway into the formal gardens. Things weren't much better here. Broken branches and ragged leaves dotted the landscape. The blooms from numerous flower beds were scattered across the lawn like they'd been guillotined, and at least one topiary had fallen near the pavilion.

A figure appeared at the far end of the gardens. It was Frankie, wearing a raincoat, wellies, and an old tweed flatcap. I hadn't seen him since Stokes's funeral. It took all my self-control not to run over and blurt out everything I'd been holding inside for weeks. About the book at Warren's, the telegram, the lost frame at Bertie's, the found frame in Hereford, and all the questions Mum wouldn't answer.

He saw us and began to jog in our direction. At the sight of my stitches, he slowed, as if he'd never seen them before. Which, given how preoccupied he'd been at the funeral, was probably true.

"Ouch," he said, wincing.

"Mostly just itchy now," I assured him. "I'm getting them out soon. How about you? You okay?" A stupid thing to ask a friend who'd just lost his beloved grandfather.

"I've been better," he admitted. He did look exhausted, possibly even thinner. He turned to Mum. "You'll want to come and see this, Mrs. Joyce. I've been helping my dad this morning, and I found something."

"Is it the grove?" Mum asked anxiously. "Have we lost it?"

"No, ma'am. The trees are fine. It's something else." He gestured for us to follow him through the break in the hedge around the secret garden.

"I haven't been here in twenty years—maybe more," Mum said as we scrambled through. We emerged on the other side thoroughly soaked, like we'd just run through a sprinkler.

Debris littered the grass here too. Branches, leaves, even slate shingles from the Hall roof. But that wasn't the worst of it.

The statue was gone.

Or no, not gone. Rather, she'd been knocked from her pedestal backward into the pool, where she lay just under the surface, gazing up blankly through the rippling water at the cloudless sky.

"She's not damaged, as far as I can tell," Frankie assured us as we approached the pool. "The water broke her fall. But it's her feet. Shorn clear from the pedestal."

Mum and I peered down into the face of Annabeth Pennington. This wasn't a death or anything. But it felt like one.

"Heavens," Mum murmured. "I'd forgotten how alike you are. No wonder you gave Mother such a turn . . ."

"Shall we leave her here, ma'am?" Frankie asked.

"Yes," Mum said—just as I blurted, "No!"

After some discussion, I won. The three of us stepped into the shallow pool in our wellies, Mum at the statue's feet and Frankie at its head, me along the middle. We bent down and grasped hold of the stone body. On three, we lifted. It was moderately heavy but not massive—which might've been why it'd blown over so easily. But the figure was slippery and awkwardly shaped, with few handholds. Slowly we carried it, dripping, toward the hedgerow.

We laid it down carefully in the grass and then stepped back. It looked for all the world like a stone sarcophagus. Frankie even removed his cap as we stood there, silent and sad and uncertain.

"I fear we must leave her for now," Mum said at last. "Tell your father not to worry, Frankie. She's fine here. And, Eva, not a word about it to your grandmother."

Yet another secret. I was beginning to lose track.

"Dad's cleaning up the orchard," Frankie said. "I'd best go and help." He jogged back toward the break in the hedge and was gone before I could offer to help too. I watched him go, frustrated that, once again, we'd been prevented from getting caught up.

Mum and I traipsed across the ruined lawn and squeezed back through the hedge.

"Mrs. Joyce!" Mrs. Fealston was standing at the top of the veranda steps, waving vigorously. "Telephone. It's your husband."

◈ ◈

"I imagine you'll hear confirmation about the compensation package soon," Grandmother said at supper that evening. "The college will expect you to move right away, no doubt. But Eva could stay here at the Hall—"

"Mother," Mum interrupted, "we haven't told her yet."

Grandmother's eyebrows shot up. "Whyever not? She isn't a little child. Why should you keep it from her?"

Mum clasped her hands tightly in her lap. I knew from experience that this meant she was very, very angry. "We didn't 'keep' it from her. We were simply waiting to hear the final offer from Whitby. There was no point in making plans if negotiations fell through, after everything."

"Well, I suppose that's true," Grandmother said. "I imagine there are any number of highly qualified candidates. With far more experience."

Mum gripped the seat of her chair. She reminded me of rabbits I'd seen in the kitchen garden, caught between the instincts to run and to keep still. "No," she said evenly. "I'm clearly the best person for the position. We just haven't discussed the timeline with Eva yet."

"Hello," I said, annoyed. "I'm right here. So tell me now."

"Your dad has been offered the professorship at Whitby," Mum explained, flashing an angry look at Grandmother. "And I've been offered an archivist position in their special-collections library. I'll book our flights to Chicago for Monday. We can start looking for housing, and then we'll fly back to New Haven. To finish packing."

"*Monday*?" My voice rose to a squeak. "But . . . but . . . we can't leave yet!" Not with all these loose ends, all my unfinished quests. I began to breathe rapidly, almost panicky.

Grandmother sniffed.

"It all seems rather sudden."

"How about 'That's wonderful, Gwendolyn'?" Mum said sarcastically. " 'Congratulations. Sounds like your dream job.' "

Grandmother said nothing.

"It really is great, Mum," I said, trying to keep my voice steady. "Super exciting."

"But Monday?" said Grandmother.

"I'm afraid so."

I took a bite of supper while I calmed myself and pulled my thoughts together. "I wonder," I began tentatively, "do you really need me there? I mean, we're mostly packed already. Wouldn't it be cheaper if I just fly to Chicago later? Grandmother said I can stay here for now—didn't you?" I turned to Grandmother.

"You can stay as long as you like, of course." She seemed almost amused by the whole exchange.

"Mum, please?"

Mum considered for a moment. "I suppose that works. If you don't mind, Mother?"

"I'd enjoy it very much." Grandmother smiled her half smile at me.

I beamed back. This was the grandmother I remembered from our excursion to Worcester, all those weeks ago. The grandmother who enjoyed my company, who shared my love of beautiful things, who planned stuff for us to do. Together. And with Mum out of the picture, I could continue my quests in earnest.

"Well, all right," Mum relented. "As long as you've got time to settle in the new place before school starts."

"I do wish you'd consider my offer, Gwendolyn," Grandmother said with an exasperated sigh. "I wish you'd let Eva stay here for school."

I blinked. Live here? In England? Without my parents?

Mum's face flushed with anger. It was a moment before she could speak. "Very kind of you, Mother, but Eva's education is quite well in hand, thank you."

"But that's ridiculous!" Grandmother seemed at a loss. "Schools here are vastly superior. And you have no family over there."

Something finally broke in Mum. She stood abruptly, her chair rocking back on its legs before righting itself. "And who would've ever known we had family *here*?" Her voice rose. "Fourteen years, and you never wrote, never called, never inquired after your only grandchild—even after I sent letter after letter. The only reason I knew you were still alive was because of Mrs. Fealston. What sort of family is that?"

Grandmother held her gaze. "We weren't the ones who broke off a perfectly acceptable engagement—Edward was crushed, you know. And we weren't the ones who left and never returned."

Mum pushed away from the table. "A lifetime of *this*"—she motioned toward my grandmother—"and who on earth could blame me? You burned more than just the papers that day. For pity's sake, Mother. You may have lost everyone else, but you didn't have to lose *us*." She strode out of the room.

Grandmother sat without moving, her face impassive as stone.

We finished our meal in silence.

But the citizens of Ternival never forgot the Mesterran pears they had once cultivated in the vale, which they remembered now as if from a dream. Ever and anon, from some warm forgotten corner of the forest, the scent of ripe pears might waft on the air.

And, it was said, if you were very lucky, you might espy the golden fruit high on a hidden bough, take hold of it, and eat.

Then would the strength and goodness and beauty of Inspiria once again flow through your blood and strengthen your bones, and then would your heart be steadied for the next great trial.

Chapter

37

I found Mum in her room, packing furiously. She stomped back and forth between the dresser and her suitcase, flinging clothes as if she couldn't leave England fast enough. She looked for all the world like a child having a tantrum. I knew exactly how she felt.

"Mum," I said from the doorway.

She chucked a sweater at her suitcase and missed.

I sat on her bed. Eventually she slowed her frenzied pace. She walked across the room with the last of her clothes and put them carefully into her suitcase.

"Sorry, darling," she said. "It's just . . . your grandmother . . . It's a lot sometimes." She sat down on the bed next to me and exhaled. "Sometimes I just want to shake the pain out of her. Or throttle the bus driver who hit Kinchurch's cab. Or the politicians who ignored London's smog problem. Or the railman who missed that signal, forty years ago—although he didn't survive the crash, so it's silly of me. I want to blame someone, but there just isn't anyone to blame."

"I don't think she means to hurt us."

"No? I wonder." Mum frowned. "I've often thought she wants everyone else to feel the same kind of pain she does so that she doesn't have to be alone in her misery."

We sat in gloomy silence.

"You'll be okay here without me, won't you?" she asked. "I don't want you to bear the burden of this alone."

"I've got Mrs. Fealston. And Frankie. I'll be okay."

"Are you sure?"

I thought of Grandmother, arms outstretched to shield me from . . . whatever she feared most. I couldn't leave her now—not yet.

"I'm sure."

Mum rose and began to reorganize her suitcase. "I probably should've left weeks ago," she admitted, "before it came to this. You'd think I'd have learned by now."

"You'll have to tell me eventually, you know," I said, steeling my resolve. "Might as well tell me now."

Mum shook her head. "Honestly. I'd rather not relive that wretched day."

"What wretched day?"

"The day I first brought your father to Carrick Hall. The day we left and never came back."

I folded my arms and waited. She was *not* going to leave England without finally explaining everything.

Mum frowned for a moment, then heaved a sigh. "Fine," she conceded. "Since you're determined to find out one way or another, it's probably best to hear it from me." She sat down next to me again. "It goes back to about a month before your father and I met. He'd found an article mentioning Kinchurch's former estate in the Wolverns, how your grandmother had inherited it after the accidents and then married your grandfather Torstane."

I thought of the articles I'd seen in the scrapbook in Mrs. Fealston's quarters. Had the housekeeper put that scrapbook together? Or had one of my parents?

"Your dad wondered if Kinchurch's papers were still here—letters, bills, legal documents, *something* to prove the Clifton connection. He'd been trying to save up a little money and make the trek to the West Midlands."

Mum looked down at her hands and twisted her wedding ring with a faint smile.

"When your father learned that my last name was Torstane, the coincidence felt downright serendipitous. But somehow he knew to broach the subject carefully. I don't know how. Almost like he could *sense* it was painful. But his tenderness won me over, in the end."

"And the papers?" I asked. "Were they here, like you thought?"

Mum grew somber. "Once your dad explained, I knew the papers *must* be here. Mother had inherited everything of Kinchurch's, after all. I'd never seen any documents, but I figured that Mrs. Fealston would know. And if she understood why your dad needed them, she could help us."

"Did she?"

"At the end of the next term, we made the trek to Upper Wolvern together. We were dating in earnest by this time, almost engaged. And your father wanted to be introduced to your grandmother sooner rather than later. But also, he was on the cusp of receiving a very large fellowship to continue his work—if only we could find those papers. It would be a huge breakthrough in his field. Finance his work for years."

"So you came here."

She nodded wearily. "Honestly, I have to hand it to Mother. She was civil, at first. Tolerated your father, you might say. After all, for some reason she'd gotten it into her head that Edward and I were engaged—which was ridiculous, of course."

"You weren't?"

"He was a good friend, nothing more. Although I suppose I did break his heart, in a way. But obviously he's gotten over it."

I wasn't so sure about that, but I let her continue.

"While your dad and grandmother were getting acquainted, I privately asked Mrs. Fealston about the papers. And she agreed to help us."

I drew in a breath. "So Mrs. Fealston *did* know where they were!"

"Oh yes," Mum said. "In the unused servants' bedrooms, up in the attic. Box upon box. That night, Mrs. Fealston took us up there, and we began to go through them, one by one." Her eyes misted over. "My word, but they were extraordinary. The letters alone!" She shook her head. "To this day I can't believe it."

"But what happened to them?"

Her face hardened. "She found us up there, Eva. Your grandmother found us. And she was furious. She declared that they were *her* papers, not mine—the Professor had left them to *her*. That your dad had no right to touch them. That she would call the police if he set one more finger upon them."

I could picture the scene down to the minutest detail. I knew exactly what it felt like to face Grandmother's wrath.

"But what angered me most"—Mum's voice began to tremble—"was that your grandmother told me she'd suspected, all along, that your father wasn't really here for me. He was using us, she said. It couldn't possibly be love. Not with *me*."

"Oh, Mum . . . no . . ." Everything my mother had ever said—or not said—about her family made sense now. Everything. I took her hand.

But there was more.

"We left that night, of course," Mum said dully. "And that's when . . ."

I squeezed her hand. "That's when?"

"That's when my mother made Paxton take the boxes downstairs. She made him build a bonfire in the kitchen garden. And then she burned them all."

Anon, a remnant of Selvedges and Loomkeepers fled the vale and formed four secret outposts: west, east, south, and north.

To the west, on the Pathless, some escaped by night in their coracles and cutters to the mist-shrouded island of Gullcliff—so named for its sheer sides, which housed innumerable seabirds.

Long had Gullcliff been thought uninhabitable by mainland Ternivali—indeed, by Mindra herself—but the Selvedges knew better. They established a hidden port within an inlet, accessible only at high tide, and above the port they built the fastness of Islagard, in a secret valley known only to the seabirds.

From the clifftops, the Selvedges kept watch on Mindra's distant stronghold of Marisith-over-the-Sea. Never did they light fires by night, lest their fastness be discovered. And if Mindra sent her spying birds hither and yon, even over the Pathless Sea, the seabirds of Gullcliff sounded warning.

Deep blue were the tunics of Islagard, like the Pathless before a storm, and ever were the people of Gullcliff known as Islagardians.

Chapter

38

As a child, I'd watched my mother's gloved hands carefully pull materials from university shelves to assist scholars in their work. I'd followed my dad as he combed libraries, bookstores, archives, and more for precious documents. Volumes and papers, all treated like holy treasures, carefully cataloged and preserved.

A rare collection in flames would feel like the end of the world.

And it was. The end of Mum's world, anyway. She'd fled England, eloped with my father, and never returned. Until this summer.

But now she was leaving again. And this time, I doubted she'd ever come back.

"Train leaves from Lower Wolvern in a half hour," Mum said on her final morning.

The two of us stood in the entrance hall with Mrs. Fealston as Mum double-checked her passport and other papers. She'd purchased a train ticket to the airport because she didn't want to leave Mrs. Fealston without Paxton's help for the tours. That was her explanation, anyway. But I wondered if she'd done it out of spite.

"Holly will be here any minute to take me to the station," Mum continued. "She always loved driving my Mercedes."

"There she is," Mrs. Fealston said, glancing outside. "Paxton is helping her load the bags."

Mum threw a raincoat over her arm. "Well, this is it, then."

At that moment we all noticed Grandmother. She'd been standing in the doorway to the dining room, listening to every word.

Mum hesitated, then kissed my cheek. "See you soon, darling." As she headed out the doors, she added, "Goodbye, Mrs. Fealston." And then, over her shoulder, "Goodbye, Mother."

Grandmother, white as a lake of ice, said nothing.

ॐ ॐ

"Well, I suppose you're lucky it isn't worse," Mrs. Fealston said at breakfast a week later, inspecting my forehead.

My stitches were gone. But the scar wasn't. A jagged purple line tugged my right eyebrow slightly upward like I was an avowed skeptic.

Honestly, how could it have been worse? I'd permanently damaged my face. Not, say, my knee from biking or my elbow from skateboarding, like a normal teenager. Those kinds of scars could be hidden. No, I'd wrecked my forehead, the most visible part of my entire body. By chasing a magical stag in my attempts to reach another world. As one does.

"Lucky," Mrs. Fealston repeated, giving me a meaningful look before sweeping away the cutlery and leaving the dining room.

Thanks to the daily tour schedule, I'd managed to avoid Mrs. Fealston almost entirely since Mum had left. Grandmother, by contrast, had planned outings with me nearly every day. She'd drafted Paxton to take us on long drives around the countryside, where we shopped in the larger towns or visited the gardens of other estates or lingered at village inns for tea and scones. We'd even lunched up in the hills one afternoon, alone: Grandmother had insisted on carrying the heavy lunch basket herself.

It was bewildering. After spending almost a whole summer avoiding me, she now seemed hungry to make every moment count. Was I supposed to feel flattered or excited or what? And meanwhile, her focused attention kept me from my other quests. The telegram, which I'd shown to no one, practically burned a hole in my pocket.

"I was thinking," Grandmother now said as Mrs. Fealston left the dining room, "we might take some flowers to your grandfather's grave. It's a fine morning, and we could use the exercise."

We filled a basket with gladioli from the flower beds in the center of the circle drive and set out for the church. It truly was a glorious day. A flock of starlings swirled in a sky the color of cornflowers. The ancient trees in the distant grove seemed to dance in the warm breeze from the valley. Grandmother was humming—a sign, I'd learned over the past few days, that she was happy.

When we reached the churchyard, Grandmother stepped briskly toward my grandfather's gravestone, where she lowered the basket and began arranging flowers at its base. I joined her, and the two of us worked silently till the basket was empty.

I couldn't help but remember that other churchyard on the outskirts of London, the one she never visited, the one she'd never taken my mother to see. I wondered if now, after these days of companionship, I might finally touch on a subject that had been off-limits all summer. I'd be leaving soon, after all—perhaps for a very long time. What did I have to lose?

"Mum took me to the other churchyard, the one in London," I said, trying to keep my tone light. "You know, where the rest of our family is buried. You should come see it."

Grandmother was leaning forward, pulling some weeds away from the base of my grandfather's headstone. There was no sign she'd even heard me.

I pressed on. "It's a nice sort of place, quiet and peaceful. Maybe we could go together the next time I'm in England."

Grandmother didn't respond. She seemed poised on the brink of flight. For a moment I thought she'd pick up her basket and abandon me without speaking. Instead, she stood and tossed the weeds over the stone wall into the long grass beyond.

"Perhaps we might," she said. She brushed her hands on her trousers. "There. Much better. Shall we head back?"

I didn't dare push further. My small victory was enough for now. Perhaps, if I was patient and played my cards very, very carefully, Grandmother would finally come around. She'd finally acknowledge our moonlit adventures, all those memories from her years as queen.

Grand visions filled my mind: Grandmother weeping with happiness and relief, telling everyone, *It was Eva, you know. She was the one who finally reached me. I wouldn't have healed without her.* There'd be a reconciliation between her and my parents. She'd finally embrace my father as a son. The spell that had bound her for nearly half a century would finally be broken.

The next morning, as we climbed into the car for yet another day trip, Grandmother leaned forward. "You know, Paxton," she said, "I've changed my mind. Let's go to Wales. Lunch along the Wye, then on to Lavernock. Do you think the point will be crowded?"

"Not with this cool weather, madam," he replied.

After stopping at a restaurant along the River Wye, we left the main road and began winding along increasingly narrower lanes. As we climbed over the ridge of a small hill, an expanse of blue stretched across the horizon.

The Channel! The mouth of the sea.

"Roll down your window," Grandmother said. "Do you smell it?" I sensed the excitement in her; she was tense but happy.

Our journey ended roughly twenty minutes later at a car park. Nearby stood an ancient church and the entrance to a public footpath. Seagulls wheeled overhead. A cool breeze, rich with the smell of seawater, lifted the hair from my forehead.

"Tide's coming in, madam," Paxton said, settling against his seat with a newspaper. I had the impression he'd waited in this very car park for her before.

Grandmother and I headed down the stony path just as the sun burst from behind clearing clouds. The path led us along a clifftop, then down through scrubby shrubs, before emerging onto a wide shingle beach that curved away on both sides. Striated cliffs rose around us. In front of us stretched the glorious water, sparkling with sunlight, on and on to distant islands and the far side of the Channel. We were alone.

I spread out my arms, threw back my head, and spun around in circles, the sea air in my face. Then, without thinking, I ran into the surf and plunged knee-deep into the waves. I came up short with a gasp, then fled back to shore.

"Gosh, it's cold!"

Grandmother laughed. It was her laughter from the moonlit gardens, a hearty peal, untarnished, ringing off the cliffs like a bell. It was the first time I'd ever heard her laugh like that in broad daylight.

She bent and picked up a smooth, flat stone. With an expert flick of her wrist, she sent it skimming over the waves—one skip, and another, and another, then a long miraculous roll before it sank.

"How . . . how did you *do* that?" I crossed the shingle toward her. Clearly, she'd done this before.

She picked up another flat stone and handed it to me. It fit my palm perfectly. "Stand sideways, like this. Right. Now keep the stone level and your forefinger resting just so—like that. Pull back and—release!" The stone fell a few feet in front of us with a plop. She laughed again, and I laughed with her, our voices rising with the gulls along that enchanted shore.

We skipped stones for what felt like hours that afternoon. The tide slowly came in. Late afternoon found us sitting side by side on the last bit of shingle, the wind rising as a bank of clouds formed far out to sea.

And that's when I saw it. Again. The distant palace, above the blue horizon. A great pile of pinnacles and turrets, golden in the sun.

Could she see it too? I glanced her way. She gazed over the waves, her expression curiously calm, as if she'd just outridden the storm of all storms. She drew in a breath and let it out slowly. The clouds, as if in response, shifted and spread apart.

The palace was gone.

To the east lay the Selvedge stronghold of Wildergard, deep in the trackless forest. Dark green were their tunics, and white in wintertime, that they might blend into the snow. They welcomed into their fastness the last of the Loomkeepers, who had fled the razing of the monastery, and thus were the Wildergardians known as the wisest of all the Selvedge remnant.

It was from the forest that Ternival's enemies had first come, and in the forest did the Wildergardians as yet fend off strange foes, who appeared as if from nowhere. But also in the deeps had the great stag first shown himself to Andella the Archeress—and ever and anon did rumors reach their ears of his appearing.

Chapter

39

When the bright moon rose again that night, I lay wide awake in bed a long time, unsure of what to do. I now feared the hills and whatever dangers they harbored in the darkness. But I also knew that Grandmother might be waiting out there, waiting and wondering. We'd grown so close lately. I couldn't abandon her now, could I?

Finally, I decided to hold vigil in the dining room again, where I could keep an eye on the tapestry. If anything moved, I'd be ready. I grabbed the flashlight and a book from Mum's bookcase and snuck downstairs to sit at the dining room table. From here I could watch both the tapestry and the entrance hall.

But it was no use. Before long, my eyelids felt heavier and heavier. I put my head down. I'd rest for just a moment. Just one moment.

I slept, hard. I'm not sure how long nor what woke me. Everything was dark. My flashlight had run down its batteries, and I couldn't switch it on. The set of lamps that Mrs. Fealston sometimes kept lit in the entrance hall had been extinguished.

As had happened earlier this summer, the air now seemed to be moved by a great sigh. I looked up. The stag in the tapestry was gone.

I leaped from my spot and dashed into the hall—where I collided with a gowned figure moving swiftly toward the drawing room.

"Ho, beloved!" Grandmother laughed and grasped my arms. "A sleepless night for thee as well, I see. Such a moon! Shall we see if that old beech has awakened?"

She barely broke pace, so I ran with her to the veranda and down the steps. It was a calm night, gentle and peaceful. My fear of the hills melted away under the stars.

Grandmother suddenly halted.

"That scent!" she exclaimed. "Pears, by heaven!"

I inhaled. Indeed, the scent of autumn fruit floated on the air, as it had when the door stood wide open.

"Let's follow it!" I said. Surely somewhere beyond the grove the door stood open now. And perhaps the stag was waiting there. Perhaps, at long last, he would take us to the palace beyond the clouds.

"Nay, dearest." Grandmother pulled back. "Or hast thou forgotten? When we wandered the forest for days and days, with nothing but pears to sustain us? It was only by thy fortitude that we survived at all. I've not had the appetite for them since. Even the smell . . ." She shuddered.

Rebellion rose in my chest. Just because Grandmother wouldn't follow that scent, nor seek the great stag, didn't mean I was bound to her choice. I could seek him myself. This was my story too. Why should I miss out on the adventure I'd always dreamed of?

Movement in the distant grove caught my eye. Yes, it was him! Glowing, as always, a beacon made of starshine. And around him shimmered the living tapestry of rippling strands, winding up into the sky. The stag made his way deeper into the woods, then paused and looked back at me.

"There he is!" I cried. I began to run.

"Nay, dearest!" Grandmother called. "I'll not see thee hurt again!"

But I kept running. The door was open—I just knew it—and the stag wanted us to follow him. It was now or never.

Soon I could hear her footsteps behind me, light and fleet.

"Please!" she said, breathless and frightened. "Stop at once! Lest thou fall!"

Heedless, I plunged on, through the grove and beyond. Ahead of me the stag had broken into a trot, its white tail flicking. Above me the strands of light trailed across the sky, as if the entire cosmos was a loom warped with silver fire. I could've sworn I heard the stars singing again, that strange, unearthly chorus. Or maybe it was the threads themselves, taut with creative power, humming.

As the stag pressed farther into the woods, a narrow track opened, and I knew where we were. It wasn't the same route that Frankie and I had taken, but we were headed to the same place. To the door in the wall.

And now began a race I'll never forget. The three of us, stag and girl and woman, careening through the shadows along the dappled path, moonlight like a beacon, starlight and star-song filling the sky. Grandmother remained hard on my heels, not giving up. If anything, she was gaining on me, almost close enough to grasp hold of my sweatshirt. But I pushed myself to keep just out of reach, faster and faster, following the glinting light through the trees.

And then suddenly, we were there. The vast expanse of sky, the long wall, the door.

It stood wide open. Golden light from the land beyond the archway flooded the path, illuminating the stag and the shrubbery. The scent of pears grew stronger, and I could see the fair fields, the peculiar blue of that sky, the vast mountain range beyond the foothills. And atop one of those peaks, the palace.

The stag lowered its antlers and entered—and this time I refused to miss my chance. Just as Grandmother reached me, I bolted. Through the archway, onto turf that felt like velvet under my feet, dragging great drafts of clear air into my lungs.

I was finally here.

"Stay, beloved!" came Grandmother's voice, thick with sorrow and terror. It wasn't a command: It was a plea.

I turned. She stood just beyond the doorway like a queen in her long gown, arms outstretched, shuddering. In her eyes I saw the kind of love that splinters a person into a million shards.

"Please, Eva," she whispered. "Please, darling girl. Don't leave me here alone."

"Then come with me, Grandmother!" I, too, held out my arms.

At that moment, the horn sounded from the mountains. That inexorable call, full of joy and laughter and glory. It blended with the star-song and the rippling sky until my sinews sang. I wanted to leave her and run toward those hills forever.

But at the sight of Grandmother—torn with longing and fear, love and terror—I chose to remain, arms outflung.

She turned and fled.

                          ❧ ❧

The horn ceased suddenly, though its echo still rang on the air. A shadow fell across the field.

I stood alone.

Alone, again. Even the stag had vanished among the trees. Every fiber of my being yearned to follow, to explore this glorious land, to start the first chapter of *my* story, my very own adventure. But not alone. If I could only bolt back through the archway and bodily drag my grandmother over the threshold!

And that's when I understood. If Grandmother couldn't shape my story as she wished, then neither could I shape hers. It was a choice she had to make. Yet the brokenness of her mind made that decision seem impossible, wholly unfair in light of such deforming tragedy.

But even as I hesitated there, a wave of warmth billowed out from the grove, a compassion so deep that I could barely breathe for awe. No, I realized. The very presence of the stag in my grandmother's life—along with the open door, the winding horn, even my own love for her—offered glimpses of a surprising grace, an abiding and boundless mercy.

I had to return. That's what the stag's compassion was empowering me to do, there on the threshold of another world. It was the only way my grandmother would ever heal—if she'd ever heal.

A sob rose in my throat. I was really and truly here, at long last. The fulfillment of my deepest yearnings was right in front of me, and the door might not ever open for me again.

But I had to go back.

After all, she'd said my real name. She'd called me Eva.

To the north, in the boggy fens of the downs, a remnant of Selvedges built a secret stronghold called Barrowgard amongst the ancient tombs of the noblemen that once dwelt there. The fogs were so great and the fens so dangerous that any enemy attempting to find it floundered or fled in terror from what seemed to be ghosts (but which were, in fact, sentries).

Yet those loyal Ternivali who sought shelter in Barrowgard, including a small company of Writbards who had fled Caristor, were taken across the fens in safety.

Gray was the raiment of Barrowgard, its tunics like shrouds. And ever were that people known as Barrowgardians, the ghosts of the downs.

Chapter

40

Then, suddenly, it was my second-to-last day in England. My parents had packed up our apartment in New Haven and found a place for us in Chicago. So, in two days, I'd fly on my own to meet them there. But it was far too soon. There weren't enough hours left for all the unfinished things.

Lord Edward stopped by with a team of workers to remove the tapestry from the dining room. All of us stood there to watch—all but Grandmother.

"Such a shame," said Mrs. Fealston with a sigh. "The only other time I've seen that spot empty was when Mr. Torstane took the tapestry down to have it framed, years ago. It's hung there for generations."

A bland landscape, relocated from elsewhere in Carrick Hall, was installed in the same spot.

"Not quite as striking, I'm afraid," Heapworth said to my grandmother when she finally joined us. "That tapestry was a showpiece."

"Ah, but this is much better," Grandmother declared. Her entire body seemed to relax.

I accompanied Lord Edward as he followed his team out of the Hall and down the front steps. Carefully the workers loaded the tapestry into a van and drove off.

"When's the auction?" I asked him.

He grinned sheepishly and dropped his voice. "I hope Gwenny doesn't mind. But it's not going to auction."

"Oh! Where's it going?"

"To Wolvern Court." He gave me a conspiratorial wink. "I'm afraid I just couldn't let it go. I'll give your grandmother a tidy sum for it, of course, as if it went through the whole auction scene and came out a winner. But you won't breathe a word, will you?"

Secrets upon secrets.

The moon returned that night. I slipped into my usual garb and made my way downstairs to wander the gardens, my mind restless.

I'd be leaving soon, just like Mum. And there was still so much unresolved. Even worse, the tapestry was gone. Did that mean the stag was gone too? Or was it now wandering Lord Edward's estate instead?

Nothing moved in the garden. No Grandmother. No stag.

After half an hour I returned to the Hall, shivering with cold and damp and disappointment, and climbed into bed.

స్ చ

"Where on earth have you *been*?"

I was barreling down the back staircase the next morning in search of Frankie—who, apparently, was barreling up the same staircase in search of me. I should've been packing, but by now I felt permanently panic-stricken. Like everything I'd gained or learned or sought was slipping away, never to return.

"I've been helping my dad all morning," Frankie said. His usually pale face was flushed, his eyes bright. "And I just found something. We need to go upstairs. A pile of coaches just pulled up. Campers this time. The worst."

"And I've got so much to tell you!" I said. After weeks in my back pocket, the telegram had practically begun to disintegrate.

We clattered up the staircase. From the windows in the servants' hallway near the dining room, we could see about six tour coaches pulling up the drive. Ever since schools had gotten out for the summer holidays, camp programs everywhere had been sending their students on field trips all over England, touring heritage sites. Carrick Hall was no exception. If we'd felt besieged by tourists before, August was a veritable onslaught.

Now herds of squawking, shoving, misbehaving summer campers spilled out of the coaches. Paxton, his long face visible inside the kiosk where he distributed tickets, clearly wasn't amused. After much shouting and threats from their leaders, the swarming masses collected themselves into the semblance of a line. Mrs. Fealston's stalwart figure began marching up the front steps.

"Stick close to me, if you please." Her voice wafted down the entrance hall from the open front door, her umbrella tapping smartly against the flagstones. "Stragglers will be sent back to the coaches immediately."

We continued up and up the back staircase and down the length of the attic. Frankie pulled open the hidden door to the crawlspace, and we scrambled through. I closed it behind us.

It was dark as pitch. Next to me, Frankie sighed with exasperation.

"I forgot my torch," he said. "Stay here." He shuffled through the crawlspace, and I could hear him push open the small door to the studio. More shuffling, a loud bump, muffled exclamations, then the sound of a match striking repeatedly.

"You okay?" I asked nervously. My throat was beginning to tighten, my breath becoming shallow.

"Fine," came his irritated voice.

Finally, a flame. A wick hissed and sputtered, growing just bright enough to see by. I climbed through the door. Flickering shadows from a single candle danced across the room.

As I steadied my breath, Frankie sat down on one of the travel trunks and gestured for me to do the same.

"Okay. You first," I said. "What did you find?"

He hesitated, then reached into the large pocket of his jacket. From it he drew the wooden box.

"Oh!" It was just as I remembered: the carven tree and crown at one corner and a great slash across the lid. But someone had fitted the box with a new clasp.

Frankie set it on the trunk between us.

"I found it just now, in the secret garden," he said, the old excitement returning to his voice. "Grandad had hidden it at the base of the statue. Clever, really. I'm not sure anyone ever would've found it if the storm hadn't knocked the statue over."

"Is there a key?"

He reached into his shirt and pulled from around his neck a loop of twine on which dangled a small key. "Mum found this when Grandad died. She didn't know what it was for, but I have my guess." He lifted it over his head.

"Haven't you tried it yet?"

"I wanted to wait for you."

It was a gesture so generous, so unlike what I myself would've done, that I fell silent.

He studied my face. "Are you ready?"

I nodded. I was so focused on the box that I'd completely forgotten about the telegram.

He handed me the key. I placed it in the lock and gave it a turn. There was a light click, and the clasp jumped open. Slowly, reverently, I lifted the lid.

A faint ringing, like distant bells, filled the space between us. There lay the gems on their bed of velvet. Six of them. To this day, I find them hard to describe. They seemed to glow with their own light, mysterious and beckoning. And yet their beauty was not in their luminescence but, rather, in their effect on the viewer: You wanted to snatch them up and hold them forever.

I reached out a hand.

"Don't!" Frankie shouted, yanking the box away.

He was right, of course. Just as Stokes had been. It was a foolish thing I'd almost done. Depending on which fairy tales you believed, anything could happen. One touch, and the magic gems might transform you into a hideous wraith. Or render you invisible. Or transport you right out of this world, never to return. Even so, I felt a stab of annoyance. *I'd* been the first one to find the box, after all. Stokes had taken it from *me*. And besides, hadn't he said they were *my* grandmother's?

"Sorry," Frankie said, pushing the box back toward me. "But we don't yet know their power. And we should probably try them together." I looked up to see him staring at me. The candle guttered on a nearby trunk. "It's like this," he whispered. "If the gems truly are magic, then we should never try them alone. It's far too dangerous. They could send us suddenly, when we're not prepared. And we don't know what we might find once we get there. Foul creatures, kingdoms at war, darkness . . ."

"But can't we use them to return if need be?"

"If that's really how they work." He continued staring at me earnestly. "Promise me, Eva."

"Promise what?"

"That you won't ever go alone."

"I . . ." My voice faltered. Frankie knew me. He knew my faults and weaknesses. But somehow that didn't stop him from being my friend. I glanced away, overwhelmed by a confusing mix of gratitude and shame. Apparently, I hadn't been as good at keeping secrets as I'd thought. "I promise."

"Well, then." His tone grew lighter. "What's to stop us from trying right now?"

Excitement bubbled up in me again. "Yes, let's!"

"Right. Why don't we say that gem is yours? And this one will be mine. We'll want to grab them at the same time, since we're not sure exactly how they work. Oh," he added, "and we should probably hold hands."

It only made sense, given how little we knew about whatever awaited. All the same, it felt awkward. He took my hand in his lean, rough one. Again I looked away.

"Ready?" he said. "On three . . ."

I'm not sure what came over me. Embarrassment at our closeness. Shame that he knew my shortcomings. Awareness that anyone who found us would think we were crazy—or up to something inappropriate. Probably all those things. Whatever the case, as Frankie began to count, I shifted position nervously.

"One, two, thr—"

Several things happened at once.

I lost my balance, yanking my hand from his.

The candle tipped, plunging the studio into darkness.

And Frankie disappeared.

The mountain caves of Nisnagard were the southernmost outpost of the Selvedges. Deep into the Nisna Alps did this remnant delve, and there they discovered a network of ancient mines which they fortified into an underground fastness found only by secret entrances. Loyal Ternivali dwarves made their way to Nisnagard, and there have they dwelt ever since.

Fell were the Nisnagardians, and mighty were their forges in the mines. White-gold was their raiment when on the mountainsides, that they might disappear into the snow or blend in with the marbled rocks. But in the depths of the mines did their Weavers fashion tunics of rich black, burnt red, and orange the color of flame, that from the deeps they might pour forth upon their enemies like living fire.

And they became known as the terror of the mountains.

Chapter

41

I screamed. I couldn't help it. The studio was so completely dark, I couldn't see my own outstretched hands. Frankie could've been there, keeping perfectly still. Or he could've snuck away, back into the crawlspace. But—do you know that feeling when you enter an empty apartment and you can tell, somehow, that you're alone? No rustlings or stirrings, not even a draft. That's how the studio felt in that moment.

Frankie was gone. He'd vanished right out of this world.

"Frankie?" My voice wobbled.

No answer.

I groped for the open doorway, then stumbled along the crawlspace till I found the door to the attic hallway and pushed it open. I climbed out, trembling. Frankie wasn't there. I peered around the corner down the passage. No one. I glanced back into the crawlspace. Darkness. Worry gripped my stomach. Was he okay?

Footsteps sounded on the stairs. I spun around and nudged the door shut behind me just as Mrs. Addison stepped into the attic, eyes wide.

"Miss Eva! Everything all right?"

I was just working up an answer when the door opened behind me again and Frankie emerged. He looked like a man waking from a nightmare.

"Hullo, Frankie," Mrs. Addison said slowly, raising one eyebrow. "What on earth?"

I was the first to recover. "Oh, we were just playing a game. Frankie hid in the crawlspace and then jumped out and scared me. That's all."

She glanced back and forth between us. "Well, whatever you were doing, your scream could've stripped the hide off those campers. Not that they would've heard you, with all their racket. Anyway, I was coming to find you. Your mum is on the phone."

I glanced at Frankie, who still looked stunned. "Okay," I said and reluctantly began to follow her. As she descended, I looked back at him. *The gems,* I wanted to say. *Go back and get the gems.*

But he was staring at his open palm.

It was empty.

The gem he'd been holding was gone.

 ॐ

"Frankie, what *happened*?"

He sat across from me at the kitchen table, eating lunch distractedly. Next to him, Paxton wolfed down a tuna sandwich, complaining to Mrs. Fealston and the Addisons about the shortage of good tuna these days. When a kettle on the range began to wail, I took advantage of the general chaos.

"Well?"

"I could ask you the same," he said stiffly, avoiding my eyes.

I drew back. "What do you mean?"

"I said we should never try the gems alone. But you let go of my hand."

"No! I lost my balance! How could you think I just . . . *left* you to go alone?"

He was silent as he took another bite.

"Frankie, please, just tell me what happened. It was so dark, I couldn't see a thing. You weren't just playing a game, right? You weren't hiding on me?"

"Hiding?" He looked up. His face seemed older somehow, the lines more set. "Would I do that? Play games?"

"Fine." Did he always have to be so darned *earnest*? "I messed up. But I wasn't the only one, *was I*?"

He blanched.

"You lost it," I said hotly. "The gem. It's gone."

A gasp made us jump. Mrs. Fealston stood stock still at the range, staring at us in horror.

"It's all that *mercury* poisoning and whatnot," Paxton droned on.

"And the cost of petrol," Frankie's dad added. "Can't run those fishing boats like they used to . . ."

Everything inside me froze. We were caught. It was over.

Trembling, the tiny old woman brushed her hands across her apron and whispered severely, "Come with me, both of you."

The other grown-ups continued chatting, oblivious, as Frankie and I got to our feet like inmates on death row. She led us into her quarters, motioned for us to sit, and closed the door.

"If this is what I think it is," said Mrs. Fealston, "I'd better hear everything."

❧

So we told her. Not everything, of course—not even Frankie knew everything. But we told her about digging up the box, Stokes whisking it away, and the two of us trying to find it again. We told her about our attempts to open the door in the wall, plus everything I'd learned about Kinchurch and Clifton and my grandmother's family. I explained to both of them about the book at Warren's, the frame at the antique shop, and how the other frame at Aunt Bertie's house had gone missing. But I left out the telegram for now, unsure of how to broach the subject without hurting Frankie's feelings all over again.

And then Frankie shared the story of finding the box that morning. When he got to the part about the two of us retreating into the studio, Mrs. Fealston drew in her breath.

"You found her weaving room, did you? And here I thought it was all bricked up . . ."

"Whose weaving room?" I asked.

"Kinchurch's, of course. She wasn't only a storyteller, you know. Or a theologian. She was a Loomkeeper. As was Annabeth. And your grandmother."

"Grandmother!" I exclaimed.

"Haven't you guessed? Her love of fashion, of color and fabric . . . She learnt it on her adventures. But then, after 1952 . . ."

Of course. After 1952, Grandmother had bricked up everything. Even her heart.

"But what happened to the loom?" Frankie asked.

"Gone. Dismantled, I imagine. I never saw it again. But back to your story. You took Eva to the studio. And then?"

He grimaced. "After that, it's a bit of a blur. I remember counting to three and grabbing the gem, and then everything started spinning. I felt myself shoved forward, shot through what looked like a tunnel of threads, endless strands of them."

"Oh!" I said. "Like in the Ternival tales!"

"Hush, child," said Mrs. Fealston.

"I kept hoping they'd twine together, somehow, and catch me," Frankie continued. "But they seemed to go on forever. Then I crashed, hard. Thrown onto my back—got the wind knocked out of me. And it was dark. I remember lying there for a while, sort of numb, wondering if maybe I'd fallen through some shaft in the attic, an old laundry chute or something. But then I realized I was outside. At night."

"At night!" Mrs. Fealston echoed.

"I'm pretty sure there were stars, and the silhouettes of trees against the sky. And that rustling sound a forest makes after dark. Not from animals or anything. Just air, moving in the branches. I looked over and realized I was lying near the mouth of a tunnel, almost as if that's what I'd fallen out of. And then . . ."

His eyes took on a haunted expression—so unusual for Frankie, and so alarming, that I almost reached out to take his hand.

"Then I heard a voice, hissing and whispering, from a few yards away. Some kind of Thing, talking to itself. I don't recall exactly what the Thing said, but it kept muttering about how I wouldn't last long in the Night Wood."

"Good heavens!" Mrs. Fealston exclaimed with a start.

My stomach twisted. "You don't mean—"

"Keep going," the housekeeper interrupted. "What then?"

"And then . . . I remembered the gem in my hand. So I opened my palm. And all of a sudden the Thing sort of shrieked—from pain or excitement, I couldn't really tell. And it started hissing, 'It sings! It sings like the others!' And I heard it scrabbling toward me in the dark."

He shuddered.

"All I remember is thinking, *It wants the gem, or hates it—and either way, it's going to kill me for it.* So I shot up and out of there, back into the tunnel. Then the spinning started again, and I felt myself being shoved forward, into the arching threads, on and on. And next thing I knew, I was back in the crawlspace, in the dark, and I could hear my mum's voice on the other side of the door."

"But the gem . . ." I prompted.

"Lost," he admitted. "Somewhere between the tunnel and the Night Wood, I'm guessing."

He looked at each of us in turn.

"And I'm pretty sure that *Thing* has got it."

For the creatures yet loyal to Ternival, Mindra the Enchantress held an especial hatred, fearing that they plotted to overthrow her—which was, perchance, true. A bounty was placed upon their heads, particularly upon the dryads, wisest and most unyielding of all.

And so it was that Ternival's loyal citizens lived in hiding, or attempted to flee over the Nisnas, or found their way to the four secret outposts of the Selvedges.

Chapter

42

The gems had worked. Frankie had grasped one of them in his bare hand and found himself transported right out of this world.

To the Night Wood, no less. That in-between place, deep in the Wilderlands beyond Ternival, a kind of way station where many roads meet. Except, in this case, the roads were a tangle of tunnels containing portals to other worlds.

If the gems had worked once, they could work again. But what was this Thing that Frankie had encountered? And would the Thing now be able to encounter *us*? Could it use the lost gem and travel *here*?

Frankie must've had the same idea, because he said, "I went back into the studio and grabbed the box with the rest of the gems. Then I left the crawlspace. I dragged the biggest chest of drawers I could find in the attic and pushed it up against the door. Nothing's going in there." He shuddered again. "And nothing's coming out."

272272 SARAH ARTHUR

"You have the box?" Mrs. Fealston asked.

Frankie slid a finger into his shirt, lifted the twine with the key over his head, and handed it to Mrs. Fealston. Then he reached into his pocket and set the box between us on a tea tray.

Mrs. Fealston sat down in a nearby rocking chair and drew in a long breath. "My word," she whispered. "Forty years." She traced a trembling finger over the carvings, brushed her thumb along the slash on the lid. "Annabeth's weaving box. It's just as I remember. She used to keep her bobbins and shuttles in here."

I waited for her to open it, my eyes fixed on her face. But instead, she looped the twine over her neck and tucked the key inside her blouse.

"We've seen what happens when the box is opened," she said crisply. "So it will remain closed. For now. Well, I suppose it's my turn. But this will take some explaining."

Frankie and I exchanged glances. Was this it, finally? Would we learn everything at last?

"You've heard, no doubt, how this was the Kinchurch estate," she began. "And how I worked here, as a young woman, for the Professor. But by 1952, Professor Kinchurch had joined the faculty at Newnham, you see, so she rented out the Hall to wealthy families and took her own modest lodgings at Cambridge. I'd moved there, too, into a nearby flat so I could keep house for her as a daily, plus pick up other work as well. And that's when the gatherings began. At her place in Cambridge, in the evenings.

"They called themselves the Loomkeepers. The girls were all grown, by then, of course—or nearly. Annabeth was in her final year at Newnham. Claire would make the trek from boarding school, where she was a sixth year. So the Loomkeepers would gather, and they'd stay long after the fire burned low in the grate, telling stories and singing strange songs. I never joined them, since it was not my place. But I'd listen at the door and wonder."

"Where was Grandmother?" I asked. "Why wasn't she there?"

"Oh, she was living in London by then. They'd invite her, but she wouldn't come. Over the years she'd tried to go back to Ternival, you see, many times. But every attempt had failed. So rather than break her heart again, she began to shut out the memories. When the others gathered in Cambridge, she always made some excuse that she had other, more important things to do."

I didn't know what I'd hoped Mrs. Fealston would say. Maybe that Grandmother had wanted to be there but couldn't. Or that Grandmother's family had pleaded, reasoned, and cajoled, because they loved her and couldn't bear for her to miss out. I felt the suffocating sadness creep in again.

"Then came an evening in September when the conversation took a sudden turn. I'd stepped outside to shake out the coffee grounds. Roses love them, you see. And when I returned, the Loomkeepers had grown just as grave as if someone had died. They spoke so quietly and urgently that I couldn't make out a thing. But *something* had happened. Some dreadful news had reached them, some awful vision. From then on, I could tell they were making plans. But I never discovered the details. Just a few weeks later, they were all gone."

She rocked in her chair, lost in thought.

"But of course . . . they had no business being in London at that time of year. Everyone should've been in Cambridge or Upper Wolvern for the new term."

This was the perfect moment to finally pull the telegram out of my pocket. Perhaps Mrs. Fealston would be able to decipher the contents. But again I held back. I could confess to Frankie later. And maybe *he* could make sense of it.

"I received a wire from young Mr. Torstane, your grandfather, later that evening," Mrs. Fealston continued. "He and your grandmother were engaged by that time, although he hadn't yet told his parents. The wire said that your grandmother's sister had been involved in the terrible crash that'd been all over the news.

"I knew that Professor Kinchurch had also gone to London that morning—she'd left quite early, though she hadn't told me why. My heart was in my throat, I can tell you. So the next morning, I took the earliest train from Cambridge that I could. But as I got closer to the city, the rail lines were all snarled up. Finally I had to take a cab. When I got to your grandmother's flat, Mr. Torstane confirmed the worst. Not only was Annabeth gone, but Claire and the Professor too."

Mrs. Fealston's eyes closed with fatigue, and I was reminded of how old she was.

"Your grandmother was catatonic on her bed. Wouldn't speak, wouldn't move. But on her bedside table was this." She reached out and touched the box again, reverently. "I knew it instantly. And I noticed that this slash was new—bright and raw, like the box had been damaged recently. The police at the train station had given your grandmother the few personal effects they could find. And I realized this must've been one of them."

Frankie sat up straight. "What?" he exclaimed. "Annabeth had brought the gems with her, on the train?"

The telegram was practically burning a hole in my pocket again. My mind was working furiously. What had the Loomkeepers been planning? And what were they going to warn my grandmother about?

"I took the box," Mrs. Fealston confessed to me. "Your grandmother's mind was already wounded, you see. So once your grandparents were married and settled at Carrick Hall—and once I'd rejoined the staff here—I buried the box in the garden. At the time, I hid it deep under a birdbath, where it couldn't be dug up. But years later the bath was removed. I lost track of where the box was."

Mrs. Fealston turned to Frankie. "I told Stokes to be on the lookout, in case it turned up again. But wouldn't you know? After forty long years, it was Eva who found it." She gave me a brief smile, as if the past was in the past and all was forgiven.

"Stokes told me right away, of course," she continued. "We agreed it should be hidden again, where you would never find it. But it seems as though the gems were determined to be found."

The clock ticked in the quiet. A bee blundered into a geranium by the open windows and blundered out again.

"What I don't understand," I said, "is why Grandmother was so angry when Elspeth asked her about the stories—why Grandmother was so furious with *me*. It doesn't feel like she just *outgrew* the stories. It's more like she . . . hates them. Hates everyone." *Even me,* I wanted to add.

"Oh, my dear," Mrs. Fealston said helplessly, "you must understand. Those memories aren't merely painful to her: They're dangerous. Because if the others hadn't kept longing for other worlds, they wouldn't have been making plans. And if they hadn't been making plans, they wouldn't have been in London that day. And if they hadn't been doing any of that, they wouldn't have died. So any hint that you, her own granddaughter, might get caught up in the same kind of thing must frighten her terribly, you see? She'd rather you believed a lie than lose you."

"But . . . but . . . wasn't it a wonderful thing to be queen? Doesn't she want to remember the good things, the lovely things?"

"That's the terrible bit about tragedy. It takes what was once good and makes it seem horrible and cruel. She must wonder why she was allowed to experience all the joy if it was only going to be snatched away in the end. It must seem frightfully unfair." Mrs. Fealston thought for a moment. "And I suppose she feels guilty too."

"But the accidents weren't her fault," Frankie said.

"No, but she could've been there. She could've chosen to join them on those evenings when they gathered to remember and tell stories. But she didn't. And because she wasn't there, she survived when the rest did not. Survivor's guilt, as they say."

Mrs. Fealston then seemed to snap out of her reverie and pull herself together.

"Unfortunately, she's right to be afraid. A mere chest of drawers won't stop the Thing, whatever it is. And yet we don't know for certain that the Thing has the gem to begin with."

Frankie looked like he wanted to bolt right out of there, as far from Carrick Hall as possible.

"No," Mrs. Fealston said with conviction, "the only thing to do is return. We must get back that gem."

As the years of Mindra's reign lengthened, unbroken, the enchantress never seemed to age, nor weaken, nor grow lazy in her watch from her stronghold of Marisith. Instead, her units of ogres and giants grew into vast armies, fashioned cruel weapons, and strengthened their defenses.

And the Selvedges despaired of ever overthrowing her.

Chapter

43

"Return?" Frankie said faintly, as if he'd just been told that nightmares can come true.

"Not you," said Mrs. Fealston. "Me."

"But that's crazy!" I cried. "You can't do that, not at your age. And anyway, I thought grown-ups were too old for magic adventures."

She gave me a bemused look. "Too old, am I? And how old were Stokes's aunt and uncle when they traveled with Augusta all those years ago? Or the governess?" She had a point.

"No. Eva's right," Frankie said determinedly. "I'll go. It's my fault the gem is lost, after all."

"Don't be a fool—" she began, but at that moment someone knocked on the door.

"Another tour group, Mrs. Fealston," called Mrs. Addison.

The housekeeper rose. She glanced at the box and then patted the key under her blouse.

"Till I return, don't you dare touch that box, either of you," she commanded. "Now, out you go."

We followed her into the kitchen. She locked the door to her quarters, then left.

"But this is awful!" I hissed to Frankie. "We can't let her do this!"

Frankie's dad stood by the back door, hauling on a pair of Wellingtons. "There you are, lad," he called. "I need you in the orchard this afternoon."

"Later!" Frankie mouthed to me and left with his father.

✧✧

Agitated, I attempted to pack for my trip but gave up. Then I roamed the grounds, tracking the progress of Mrs. Fealston and her tour groups—which, mercifully, were legion. Coach after coach roared up the drive, keeping the housekeeper far too busy to deal with the box.

At teatime I headed back to the kitchen, where I found Mrs. Addison picking lavender by the back stoop.

She handed me a slip of paper. "From Frankie. You just missed him." She gave me a wan smile.

I took the paper, blushing, and fled into the empty kitchen.

The paper had been carefully taped shut along one edge. I peeled it open to find a tidy, precise scrawl: *Meet me at the reflection pool after tea.*

At last!

Distractedly, I helped Mrs. Addison with the tea service and the washing up afterward, which seemed to take forever. I slopped dishwater in a rush, unmoved by the scent of lavender wafting through the open back door. I didn't know then how I'd miss that scent, months—years—later, when it was too late to undo the events of that afternoon.

Then I made my escape, cut through the formal gardens till I came to the high hedge, and climbed through.

The statue lay on the ground near the far hedgerow where we'd left her, as if napping in the shade. And Frankie was there, pacing around the pool. He didn't see me at first, so I paused to observe him. How old he seemed! So grown up, the way he walked: steady and confident, almost a man.

It struck me that time might be running out for him—although if what Mrs. Fealston had suggested was true, one was never too old to visit other worlds. But still, at a certain point you grew up. You had to make your own way in life with only the memory of your favorite stories rather than the promise that you'd ever relive them.

Nostalgia, like the twang of a bow, quivered through my body. I, too, was growing older. Would it soon be too late for me as well?

Frankie turned and waved. My face must have reflected my sadness, because he took a step toward me. "You okay?"

"I was just thinking it might be our last chance . . ."

"I know." He kicked at the lip of the pool. "You leave in the morning."

"I mean, before we're too old. I keep thinking . . . what if Mrs. Fealston's wrong? What if growing older means giving up all this?"

His face grew even more grave. "Yes, I thought of that."

He reached into his pocket and drew out Annabeth's box.

I couldn't help it: I finally released the shriek I'd been holding in all summer.

"Shh!" Frankie said, half laughing. "The last thing we need is for someone to find us here."

"How'd you get it?" I asked. "I thought her room was locked."

He shrugged. "She left the windows open, remember? Took me about thirty seconds to pop in and out."

"Brilliant! Could we break the clasp? Like we did the first time?"

He grinned mischievously and pulled a key from his pocket. "Grandad had two of them."

I grinned back. "Well, look at you, breaking the rules for once."

His smile broadened. Then we both knelt, and he set the box gently on the ground between us. He held up the key, his expression now solemn, and handed it to me. I unlocked the box and lifted the lid.

Again, a faint ringing, as of distant music, wafted in the air. There the gems lay, nestled together, glimmering in the late-afternoon sun. Even outdoors they seemed to hold their own light, like the first stars born at the dawn of a new world.

Once again, Frankie took my hand. It felt natural this time, like we were meant to do this.

"Ready?" I asked him.

He nodded grimly, his face set. "Just like before. That one is yours, and this is mine. We each take one in our free hand and hold tight. On three—"

Footsteps. A sharp gasp.

Grandmother stood just inside the hedge, frozen like a statue. But she wasn't looking at us. She stared at the box.

"Oh . . ." Her lovely face hardened. A sneer lifted the corner of her lip. Even on that awful day in the churchyard, she'd never looked less beautiful—or more terrible.

Before we could rise, she advanced, snatched the box from between us, and slammed the lid. Then she backed away.

"I should've known," she said, as if to herself. "I should've destroyed it at the station. Burned it or thrown it in the wreckage—*anything*. If only they'd told me their plans! I would've stopped them. The madness . . ."

She looked at each of us in turn, every inch of her stately body radiating scorn.

"I suppose you've been told these are magic. But it's just costume jewelry, no doubt. Do you know, they probably laughed at you behind your backs? *Children.*" She nearly spat the word. "You're far too old for this."

Frankie rose to his feet, his face blotchy. I stood beside him, trembling like a moth caught in a web.

"I would've thought you were smarter than this, Eva. And you, young man. You're old enough to know better. But I suppose such foolishness runs in the family. Queen of another world, indeed!"

Frankie blinked.

"Oh, I know all about it," she continued with another sneer. "I've known for years how your grandfather cooked up lies and spoon-fed them to you at bedtime. But never forget. We are, none of us, queens and kings. None of us. Just lonely wretches who work the earth and die and are forgotten."

Frankie grew still. His shame vanished: It was all grief now. But he squared his shoulders and looked her full in the eye.

"You're wrong, ma'am," he said, his voice trembling. "I know, because I've been there. I've seen the Night Wood."

She laughed, a caustic, graceless sound. "Fascinating how our minds play tricks like that, isn't it? Especially when we're so very *sad.*"

Frankie winced as though he'd been slapped.

Righteous indignation filled my chest, anger on behalf of my best, most honest friend.

"You don't mean it," I retorted. "You know it's all true. You know because you lived it; you've been there. You were called. And you became a queen, and those were the loveliest days of your life." My voice began to break. "And *I* know, because I've seen you. I've watched you dance with dryads. And defend your castle from the threat of giants. You've seen the stag, and breathed the sweet air from beyond the door, and heard the horn from the high mountains. I know you remember—or you could if you tried. Why won't you admit it's true? Why won't you believe anymore?"

"Dryads?" Frankie said beside me. "The stag?"

Grandmother laughed again, cruelly. "Ah, the secrets we keep from those who love us, eh, Eva?"

"No, it's not like that!" I cried. "I was going to tell you, Frankie, really."

His expression hardened. "Ma'am," he said to Grandmother with a curt nod. Then he exited the garden without looking at me. I wanted to chase him down, explain everything. But I couldn't leave Grandmother, not when there was even the slightest chance of persuading her. Not if I could get the gems back.

Desperate, I pulled the telegram out of my pocket. "You're wrong," I said, thrusting it at her. "They were coming to warn you. Because they *loved* you. Do you understand? *They loved you.*"

In that moment, everything seemed to freeze, suspended, like we'd been turned to ice. She stared, unblinking, at my outstretched hand. I stared back, barely breathing.

Suddenly she snatched the telegram from me, tucked the box under her arm, and tore the yellowed paper to pieces. She didn't even read it. Then she swung around, strode to the break in the hedge, and pushed through.

I stood rooted to the spot, unable to think or move. Scraps from the telegram lay scattered around me on that jewel-green grass.

Was there a way to feel nothing at all? I wanted the memory of this horrible moment to vanish forever. I wanted the years to pass, lichen to cover me, new generations to come and go without anyone ever knowing how deeply my grandmother had wounded me.

Then, with a great shuddering breath, I ran. I pushed through the hedge into the formal gardens and pelted across the field, into the grove, and across the stream. I slipped through the opening in the fence and scrambled up through the shrubs. Finally, I emerged at the wall, my vision blurred with tears.

There stood the door, closed, as always. Locked, of course.

I tried, desperately. Nothing. I began to pound.

"Please! Please, let me in!" I pounded harder. "I believe. I really do. She doesn't mean it. I know she doesn't. Please . . ."

There was no answer.

Then, one gray afternoon in early fall, three maidens stumbled out of the forest into Wildergard.

They were not magicians, nor witches, nor even Mesterrans. They were Children of Tellus.

And their names were Flora, Claris, and Annabel.

Chapter

44

The next thing I remember was hearing the sound of wood scraping against stone. I'd collapsed on the ground, sobbing, and then . . . had I fallen asleep? It was all a muddle. But now a warm breath of air, sweet as pears, wafted over me. I raised my head.

The door stood open. Golden light streamed from it, flooding the shrubbery. I glimpsed undulating fields, trees laden with fruit, and a radiant sky that rippled with glimmering strands like a living tapestry. I rose to my knees.

Just then, a young woman peered out. She was short and stocky, with auburn hair and intelligent turquoise-blue eyes. "Oh, there you are," she said with a grin. "My, you *are* grubby. But there's no mistaking: You're as like her as two peas in a pod." She squinted at the track and the shrubs, then wrinkled her nose. "I'd forgotten how gray it all is. Well, hurry up, then! You're wanted. She's been waiting for *ages.*"

The girl emerged from the doorway in a blaze of color. A hooded burgundy robe cascaded over an orange doublet and breeches as she extended her hand. It was warm and sturdy: She was utterly real.

Who was she? I had my guesses, but I was too overwhelmed to string words together. And what did she mean, I was wanted? *Who* was waiting?

She helped me to my feet and led me through the door. Before me stretched the golden fields, riven by a clear stream bordered by a grove of pear trees. Farther up, the rolling blue foothills began, and above those rose the familiar turrets of the distant palace, solid as the high mountains. Light that didn't seem to come from any sun washed over me. My sorrow fell away.

I looked back. The wall was gone. The doorway stood alone, a stone arch rising unaccountably in the sparkling field. Through the arch I glimpsed the world I'd just come from, all grays and browns, like a dull dream. *This* was real.

The girl headed away from it all, toward the stream and the mountains. Somehow I knew, without being told, that my questions weren't necessary here. I would learn what I needed to soon enough. In the meantime, it was my honor to observe and be glad.

I turned my back on the doorway and followed.

We reached the stream and began trekking along it, farther up the valley. While at first I struggled to keep pace, I found new strength with every breath. Even so, I lagged behind. The girl paused and waited for me.

"The air is so clear, isn't it?" she said. "A bit of a shock, at first."

She said nothing else for a long time. We followed the stream, the mountaintop palace now hidden by the blue foothills. And all the while I grew stronger.

Finally a large avenue appeared under the trees ahead. It was the beginning of a road, a grand promenade lined with tall beeches that climbed the foothills. There, a vast crowd had gathered.

I halted, astonished. The crowd was composed of creatures of all kinds. Some appeared to be safe, ordinary animals like horses and dogs, while others had no business in the company of the rest: leopards, bears, the occasional wild boar. And then—was it possible?—creatures I'd only ever read about in fairy tales: nymphs and sprites and dwarves. And others I didn't have names for, whose tales I didn't know at all. Noise from the crowd reached us, a chattering, snorting, roaring din.

The girl made for the avenue, stepping along paving stones of white marble. But I hesitated. I wasn't afraid—it was impossible to taste fear in such a country. It was something else, closer to what I'd felt in the studio with Frankie just before he disappeared. Shame, unworthiness. The girl glanced back at me.

"Don't worry," she said, as if reading my mind. "We all felt that way at first. If only you knew what the rest of us have done at one point or another! Don't you see? None of that matters here."

I took a breath and followed.

As we entered the avenue, the company gradually grew quiet and parted for us. All bowed deeply as we passed. Then, unexpectedly, among the creatures appeared a face I recognized: the oversized rabbit from my grandmother's topiaries. But here in this glad country, it was soft and brown. It twitched its nostrils, then nodded and bowed as if it, too, recognized me.

Next to the rabbit stood another familiar figure: the mastiff who guarded the veranda steps at Carrick Hall, alive here as if released from an enchantment. And next to him, the centaur. Everywhere I looked, the Hall's topiaries, transformed, gazed back at me. Something or someone had set them free from their roots, breathed life into their lungs, given them their proper raiment of skin and hair, fur, or feathers.

I now noticed that two rows of thrones lined the avenue, all facing the center. Humans in elegant but simple garb sat upon them, each crowned with a plain circlet of gold. Dignified, gentle-faced folk, royals at their ease. Above them, high standards rippled. As we advanced between the rows, the faces on the thrones grew more and more noble, more and more radiant in their piercing joy, till I could hardly bear to look at them.

Silence descended. The creatures fell back, and now I saw, at the far end of the grove, a dais lined with yet more thrones. One of them was empty.

The girl stopped. Not a sound could be heard in all that royal glade. Every creature waited.

"She's here," the girl called.

The three maidens were strangely clad, filthy, and bewildered, and they spoke in accents that none before had heard in Wildergard. Through brief questioning, it was discovered that they knew not how they'd arrived thither, save that one moment they'd been playing in a large manor house somewhere called England and the next moment they'd found themselves in a dense wood.

("Annabel had gotten in trouble," explained Claris, the youngest and cousin to the other two, "so we were sent upstairs. We pretended the tapestry of the dryads was real and tried to climb inside it. Which, of course, it wasn't, because there's no such thing as dryads." Clearly the poor lass was raving.)

Annabel, the middle girl, told of how they'd wandered the forest for days, until at last, almost despairing, they saw light through the trees. It shewed forth from a mighty creature, a stag of impossible size, glowing like the moon. And despite their fear, they'd trusted the light. They'd followed the stag through the trees till it vanished amidst a circle of ancient cedars, and thus had they found the secret entrance to Wildergard.

At this the Selvedges hushed and drew back. For the maidens had seen the great stag of Andella.

("Oh, and we ate nothing but pears for days and days," Claris added. "Nice pears, really, for a wilderness. A little hard to reach. But nothing else for *days*.")

Chapter

45

A company of sovereigns rose from their thrones on the dais and made their way down the steps. First came a kindly couple in simple tunics of vibrant green. The woman reminded me of Holly Addison, only more amiable. Then followed a grandmotherly matron with a purple robe and a long silvery-blond braid, whose laughing face brought to mind, of all people, Lord Edward. Then came a scholarly older woman in a wine-red jerkin and spectacles, carrying a book under one arm. And last, a youngish woman with ginger-blond hair.

She moved gracefully in a kirtle the color of white-gold, a matching circlet atop her unruly curls. As she drew near, I found myself gazing upon the face I knew best.

My own.

And yet not my own. It was the photo from the scrapbook. It was the statue in the secret garden, breathed to life. It was my grand-mother's own sister, long dead.

Annabeth.

The company drew near and bowed. I did the same, my knees trembling. It was like meeting the gods of Mount Olympus, living legends from the old tales. Real. In the flesh. Except here they bowed to *me*, even as I bowed to them. And then I recalled what both Frankie and my grandmother had said after we glimpsed the palace in the clouds from Table Mount: *In that far country, all are ever queens and kings.* Well, I was here now. This was the far country.

Without thinking, I knelt. Annabeth laughed, the same ringing peal as my grandmother's laughter on the shore, filled with the sun's warmth and the earth's joy. She approached and knelt before me, face-to-face.

"If you kneel," she teased, "then so shall I. For we are royal kins-women. And here you are, at long last! Let me look at you."

Annabeth rested a hand on each of my shoulders and peered into my face. We weren't identical, after all. I had a fresh purple scar above my right eyebrow, for one thing. Her nose had freckles. And her irises were flecked with gray, reminding me of my mother.

My eyes began to burn. It wasn't fair. Mum should've grown up with an aunt like this. She should've had such moments of loving regard, keen glances from one who knew her every fault yet loved her anyway.

But this aunt *had* been there, hadn't she? She'd watched from her stone pedestal as my mother had grown from a child toddling among the flower beds into a young woman who couldn't bear to stay. Annabeth herself wouldn't leave Carrick Hall, even as lichen covered her neck and chin and cheeks till it reached her eyes and she could see no longer.

"You never left her," I said. "You never left Grandmother."

"No, not ever."

"But she thinks you're lost for good."

"Not lost, beloved. Have you learned nothing? Merely hidden. Beneath the stone is breath—see, this very breath I draw into my lungs—and a warm beating heart and a body that awaits the restoration of all things. Nothing is ever lost that doesn't want to be."

A sob grew in my throat. "I fear *she* wants to be lost."

Sadness flickered across her face, and a shadow seemed to fall upon the whole company. "Her throne awaits her, if she would only claim it again. But that is her story, not ours. Alas, many thrones shall remain empty beyond the world's last night."

"But she is so broken. Can't I choose it for her?"

"Ah, my dear. That is the gift and the burden of it. The only story we're given is our own."

"But why did her story have to be so sad? She didn't choose to lose you."

"That I cannot answer. I can only offer myself—and even my own story is not yet full-told. When a star sets below the hills, its fire hasn't gone out: We simply can't see it. Yet it rises again. What we thought was the final chapter is merely the prologue. Think of all the chapters you have yet to tell, both before your own fire sets below the rim of the world and long after!"

"Please," I whispered, "are other ways still open? I keep trying, but nothing has worked till now."

"Many ways are now shut that once were open. *This* glad country, however, is the realm of all realms, which shall never be shaken. But there are yet other worlds, worlds upon worlds, and portals yet to be discovered."

She rose and helped me to my feet. We turned to greet the rest of the company. The gentle couple was Stokes's aunt and uncle, who'd disappeared and then returned. The girl who'd greeted me at the door in the wall was exactly who I'd guessed: Claire Pennington, Aunt Bertie's daughter. And the matron with the braid was known as Lady Margaret. And the scholarly woman? Augusta Kinchurch.

The Professor. My literary hero. The one who'd started it all.

Kinchurch peered back at me through her round spectacles, a wry smile at the corners of her mouth. She was standing right here in front of me. The one who'd traveled beyond our world to realms unknown. Who'd treasured my family enough to give us Carrick Hall. Whose work my father had spent decades studying. I could finally ask her everything.

But instead, I just stared. It was as if all my questions had turned into starlings and lifted away in a cloud.

Movement from the trees drew our attention. The beeches had begun to sway and bow like the trees in the grove back at Carrick Hall. Gliding toward us, down the avenue, came one of the dryads. Her hair cascaded to the ground and whispered around her feet like a bubbling stream.

I knew her at once. This was *the* dryad, the topiary from my grandmother's garden, warm and alive on this side of the door.

"She hath been summoned," said the dryad to Annabeth. Her voice sounded like rustling leaves in a warm wind. "He awaits further up. Moongazer shall take you both."

The centaur stepped forward from the crowd of creatures and bent his forelegs till his shoulders bowed low. "Climb upon my back," said Moongazer, his voice so deep and wild that for a moment I thought the earth itself was speaking.

"Fare forward, Queen's Beloved," said Professor Kinchurch, bowing. "We shall meet again." The others did the same.

Claire drew me aside. "You'll tell Mum I'm all right, won't you?" she said. "Poor old bird . . ."

Remembering where Aunt Bertie was now, the state of her mind and body, I couldn't bring myself to reply.

Annabeth climbed lightly onto the centaur's back and reached out a hand to me, eyes sparkling.

"Come, Eva, Queen's Beloved. It's time."

Then Rifka, one of the last remaining Loomkeepers of Ternival, rose from her place by the cooking fires, whereat she had been stirring a savory soup. Rifka alone remembered the prophecy about the coming of the Children of Tellus and the restoration of the crown. Rifka alone perceived the import of these guests arriving, in this very hour, when all hope seemed lost.

She approached the maidens and peered at them closely. They did not seem particularly strong, nor wise, nor over-virtuous. The middle girl's eyes danced with mischief. The youngest girl talked too much. But the oldest girl . . . A beauty, to be sure, but also courageous. And yet a haunted expression flickered across her face. This girl trusted no one and nothing.

But the stag had sent them, and that was enough for Rifka.

"Feed them," she commanded her fellow Selvedges, "and clothe them in the raiment of Wildergard. For they must be strengthened ere they learn of their mission here."

Thus were the maidens clothed in green tunics and feasted at last. And a trio of dryads danced a healing dance, to Claris's everlasting astonishment. And all Wildergard joined in, the revelry lasting long into the night. Then did the maidens lie down to sleep so as to strengthen themselves for whatever the days ahead might hold.

Chapter

46

How long we traveled into the foothills, I cannot say. An hour, at least. Annabeth and Moongazer spoke little as the high peaks drew nearer. Despite our climb into the heights, the palace remained hidden from view—though I could sense its presence, calling me further upward.

Eventually we climbed above the tree line and followed a cleft between rocks, craggy peaks on every side. Then the cleft opened up, and we entered a bowl-shaped valley carpeted in moss the color of emeralds. In the middle stood the great stag.

For the first time in that glad country, fear gripped me. Not the bad kind, like in a nightmare, but the good kind: the awe you feel when standing near a mighty waterfall or watching a thunderstorm.

Moongazer knelt, and we dismounted. Annabeth gave me a gentle push toward the stag.

"You're coming too?" I whispered anxiously.

"Shortly. But you'll have your own audience with him first. As did I, long ago. As do we all."

This wasn't exactly comforting. I inhaled tremulously and walked forward. My legs felt weird, like they weren't attached to my body. I thought of all the ways I'd messed up, how I'd failed to be a good friend and daughter and granddaughter. But then I remembered the compassion that had enveloped me after Grandmother fled the door. The compassion hadn't been for her alone. It had been for me too.

I stopped a few yards from the stag.

He surveyed me in silence, eyes glimmering, impassive, mysterious. What did he see? A girl familiar yet strange. A child, really, still full of wonder, still clinging to hope. As in the garden of Grandmother's estate, I wished he would speak yet feared what he would say.

Then he spoke.

"Long have thy kindred hunted me," said the stag. His voice echoed in a full, clear baritone, even richer than the centaur's. I couldn't tell if this was a reprimand or a simple statement of truth. Yes, my family had chased him, yearned for him—but also feared him, fled from him. I thought of the tapestry in the dining room and of my grandfather's portrait in the gallery, longbow at the ready. There was a fine line between yearning to draw near to a mystery and desiring to conquer it.

"Long have you evaded us, my lord," I replied, my voice quavering. "And yet you remain my grandmother's protective guard. Why? And why does she fear you? And why lead me to the door, only to close it? And why am I here? Are we going to the palace?" Nosiness, blathering—all my faults were on display, as usual. Even here. But I didn't know when I'd get another chance to ask.

A low rumble came from the stag. His eyes crinkled. Was he laughing? Yes. But not *at* me, in derision. He was laughing in delight.

"The family inquisitiveness is strong in thee, I see," he said. "That is good. Very good. But all in its proper time, Queen's Beloved. For not everything is thine to know. Nor hast the time yet come to make thy dwelling in the Palace Beyond the World's End. Even so, many things will be revealed. Come."

He nodded to Annabeth, and together she and I fell into step behind the stag.

We passed through another cleft between high ridges. To my surprise, this one opened into a calm garden under sheltering pines. Not far off, a cliff dropped away—with nothing beyond it but sky. It felt like the rim of the world. My legs grew wobbly again.

The stag paused near a clear shallow pool in the middle of the garden. Water bubbled up and spilled from the pool, forming a narrow, chattering stream that wound to the cliff's edge. Silently the stream slipped over it. I listened for the plashing of a waterfall far below but heard nothing. If the sun (such as it was in that country) ever set there, I had the distinct impression I'd see nothing beyond the cliff but stars. No horizon, just stars dropping away below us like clouds beneath an airplane.

"The spring at the world's edge," whispered Annabeth with awe. "I've heard about this place, but I've never been here."

"Come closer," said the stag. "Now we shall look into the spring to see what we can see."

Annabeth and I drew near. We leaned over the water. A murky cloud began swirling in the middle of it. The cloud separated into strands that wove over and under one another until they began to coalesce into flickering, moving shapes. Then one of the shapes took on color and became a human figure.

Before I got a good look, Annabeth cried out, "Bess!"

It was Grandmother. Standing on a platform, exactly like her photo in the scrapbook. She stared off into a muddled mass of other moving shapes, clutching a handbag, mist rising around her.

Some of the shapes now coalesced into people wearing old-fashioned uniforms—nurses and policemen and military personnel—all rushing about with grim faces. Then the murky background became piles of wreckage, men carrying stretchers, columns of smoke, a crowd of helpers straining to wrench the doors off an overturned train car.

"Heavens!" whispered Annabeth. Her face had turned almost green. I gripped her hand.

On the platform, a police officer approached Grandmother, took off his hat, and handed her something. She looked down at it dully. It was Annabeth's box, a bright raw slash across the lid. Slowly Grandmother placed the box in her handbag as if she hadn't even registered what it was.

A young man shoved through the crowd toward her. My grandfather, young and tall and lean, like his portrait. "There you are, darling!" he exclaimed. "Let's leave this ghastly place. They've said they'll call if they hear anything more." He took her by the elbow. "Bess?" She didn't look up but allowed him to lead her mutely away, her face expressionless.

As they left, another figure appeared, stepping carefully over the wreckage. It wore a long cape of darkest red, its face partly obscured by the cape's hood. But I could tell the face was pale, eerily pale, like a specter. It followed the couple till all three vanished in the crowd.

"No . . ." said Annabeth in horror. "It can't be . . ."

Just then, the murky strands shifted and re-formed, and another scene appeared: a foggy city street, wet and gray in the early-morning light. Suddenly a red double-decker bus careened toward us at top speed. We ducked instinctively, but it swerved at the last minute and crashed into oncoming traffic, pushing a cab into a nearby shop front. Glass and brickwork exploded.

A man hollered, "Help me get her out!" to a crowd of bystanders, who rushed forward. With a mighty tug, the side door of the cab fell open. Out tumbled a body.

Kinchurch. I knew by the broken spectacles on her face, the books scattered across the sidewalk.

Then a hideous white hand reached down from among the bystanders. It pulled away the Professor's glasses and closed her staring eyes. The hand retracted, and the person it belonged to stood up. It was the red-cloaked figure. Next to me, Annabeth clutched my hand.

"Who *is* that?" I gasped.

The scene shifted again: another wet, foggy city street, lamplight reflecting off the railing of a bridge.

"No!" I cried. This time, I knew what was coming. And sure enough, a young woman on a bicycle appeared, pedaling urgently, moving far too quickly through the mist. But before she reached the bridge, out stepped the hooded figure, white arms raised as if to strike. The girl ducked, the bicycle swerved, and then both sailed silently, horrifically, into the fog. There wasn't even a splash.

Beside me, Annabeth gave a strangled cry.

It didn't seem possible that there could be more. But there was.

The strands collapsed and re-formed. A tiny middle-aged woman in a pillbox hat was storming through a surging crowd of reporters. She beat back their cameras with an unopened umbrella till she reached what looked like a boardinghouse, entered swiftly, and slammed the door in their faces.

"Mrs. Fealston!" It was my young grandfather, gaunt and unshaven, standing in the hallway.

"The beasts," Mrs. Fealston said fiercely. She stripped off her gloves and hat. The housekeeper was much younger, of course, but unmistakable. "Now. Where is she?"

"Upstairs."

"Tell your man to pull up the car."

"He'll never get through. They're crowded forty deep in the street."

"The back alley, of course. We'll bring her out that way."

"She won't move."

Mrs. Fealston glanced up the stairwell, her lips a firm line. "Leave that to me." She marched up the stairs and entered the first bedroom on the left. Inside, the shades were drawn. She made her way to a figure sprawled on the bed. It was Grandmother.

"My dear," said Mrs. Fealston gently, "I've come. It's time to get up now."

There was no reply. Grandmother lay still as a stone, one white arm curled over long dark hair.

"The driver is bringing Mr. Torstane's car around now," Mrs. Fealston continued in the same calm tone. "You'll want to leave at once."

Just then, she gave a start. Annabeth's box rested on the bedside table. It seemed to jolt her into action. She turned and shook Grandmother with all her tiny might.

"Rise, Your Majesty," she bellowed. "Giants are upon us!"

In one startled motion, Grandmother sat up.

"Your Majesty must fly at once," said Mrs. Fealston desperately. "The bridge hath been secured, but should they ford the moat, the gates will not hold."

Grandmother blinked twice. "What of the sentries?" she said in a commanding tone. She rose swiftly and gathered a shawl from a nearby chair.

"Standing fast," Mrs. Fealston replied. "The tall one awaits at the back gate with the carriage."

Grandmother strode from the room, swinging the shawl around her shoulders. Unnoticed, Mrs. Fealston reached for the wooden box and tucked it under her arm.

"And where are my kin?" Grandmother asked from the top of the stairs.

Mrs. Fealston hesitated, struggling for composure. "They tarry, Your Majesty," she said faintly, "in a far country."

There was the slightest pause on the stairs before Grandmother plunged on. "Then let us hasten," she said, striding past my grandfather, who stood at the bottom, stricken. "The day is far gone, and we have many leagues to ride."

Grandfather Torstane looked wide-eyed at Mrs. Fealston. She shook her head, and the two of them hurried after Grandmother, out the back door. They climbed into a waiting car and drove off.

I felt suddenly cold. There, hidden in the shadows of the alley, waiting, watching, was the red-cloaked figure.

Once again, the strands pulled apart and re-formed into a moving image. And now we saw the car making its way through the English countryside, driven by a man I didn't recognize. Young Grandfather sat next to him in the front seat, Grandmother and Mrs. Fealston in the back. After imperiously surveying the passing scenery for a few moments, Grandmother's shoulders sagged. The bold light in her eyes went out.

"Is it a dream?" she whispered.

"No, dearest," Mrs. Fealston replied.

"Then it is a nightmare," Grandmother said. "And I'll never wake up."

That night, as Wildergard slept, Rifka the Loomkeeper did warp the ancient loom of Igna the Hermit, which she had saved from the monastery. She wove three tiny tapestries that she then tied off, furled like scrolls, and attached to three falcons of Ternival.

Before daybreak, the falcons took flight—north, south, and west—and soared aloft beyond the view of any below, and thus did the tidings of Wildergard reach the three other Selvedge outposts.

Of all that transpired the next fateful morn, much is recorded in *The Writ of Queens*. How the maidens learnt from Rifka of the stag's purpose in bringing them to Wildergard—indeed, why they were summoned to Ternival at all. How their hearts sang when they learnt of the prophecy, and raged at Mindra's treachery, and longed to see the crown restored. And how the Selvedge armies from the four outposts were to muster in secret on the northern downs, near Marisith, and there make ready to storm Mindra's stronghold at last.

And so the maidens rode forth with the secret host from Wildergard.

When all the armies had arrived by stealth at the downs, hope swelled further: For mere days before, deep in the mines of Nisnagard, the lost gems of Mesterra had been found. And they were brought therefrom with the Nisnagardians to the mustering place, and great was the rejoicing among the Selvedges.

For the downfall of Mindra was at hand.

Chapter

47

Next to me came the sound of muffled weeping. "Oh, Bess," whispered Annabeth raggedly. "Oh, my dear . . ."

One last time, the strands pulled apart, wove over and under one another. And now their shifting seemed to happen inside the scene itself. A figure came hurtling through a tunnel of threads.

"Frankie!" I cried. But of course, he couldn't hear me. It was the scene he'd described to Mrs. Fealston and me. He was shuttling between worlds—from the studio into the Night Wood.

He landed, hard, on his back, just as he'd described. He struggled to take a breath. Around him stood tall trees silhouetted against the night sky, and next to him, the yawning mouth of the tunnel.

Then came the whispering, hissing, sinister voice, far worse than I'd imagined.

Frankie took a breath and opened his palm. Suddenly the voice shrieked, and we heard a horrible scrabbling through the dark. Terror-stricken, Frankie launched back into the tunnel and vanished.

The scrabbling stopped. All was still in the Night Wood. But there, glittering in the dark grass before the mouth of the tunnel, lay the gem.

"Oh, no, no, no . . ." moaned Annabeth.

From the trees emerged the red-cloaked figure, hissing excitedly. "At last!" it whispered to itself.

"Stop her!" I cried, reaching toward the pool. For I knew now who this was.

Annabeth held me back. We watched, horrified, as the figure snatched up the gem in a gloved hand. It stifled another shriek, as if the gem burned through the glove like fire. Then it stashed the gem somewhere inside the folds of its cloak.

"Shall we follow him now?" it hissed to itself. "No, no, best grow stronger first. Build up our army once more, take the Children of Tellus unaware, in their own world. Yes, that's what we shall do."

And the figure vanished into the Night Wood.

The scene's woven threads pulled apart and spun away, and we could see clear to the bottom of the pool.

Shaking, I turned to Annabeth. "The *M* in the telegram you sent to Claire. *M HAS FOUND US.* It wasn't Marnie, was it?"

"No," she whispered. "It was Mindra."

༼ ༽

"But what shall we *do*?" I cried. "She has the gem, and she'll try to use it. She might be using it even now!"

"Peace, Queen's Beloved," said the stag. "For many long years hath Mindra sought, with her evil arts, to track down the Children of Tellus and find the gems they took back to thy world. And many times hath she failed. Even now, she has but one of the gems, and she knows it does not make her strong enough. Not yet."

"Then let's get the box from Grandmother and track Mindra

down in the Night Wood. Let's take the gem back! It's not too late, is it?"

"Peace," he reiterated, more sternly. "The greater danger is that Mindra might take the other gems from *thee*—and then all would be lost indeed. Nay, there is no grave urgency yet. Thine own adventures are drawing near their end. But when the time comes, thou shalt help other Children of Tellus hear the call and fight the fell enchantress of old."

My heart sank. My own adventures, ending? But they'd only just begun. Annabeth squeezed my hand, as if she, too, rued the brevity of my time beyond the door.

"Now," he continued. "Thy task is to return. Thou must confess to Frankie all that thou hast seen—not only here, but also what thou didst witness, night after night, in the gardens of your grandmother's house. But it will not be easy. He bears the wounds of thy secrets, and your grandmother's words cut him deeper than anyone knows. Indeed, he is farther than ever from the door."

Tears blurred my vision. As always, it felt like I'd ruined everything.

The stag's countenance softened. "But take heart, Queen's Beloved. It is never too late to make wrong things right—or to try. Thy story cannot be taken from thee. Tell it to him so that he, too, might be ready to help the others when the time comes."

I took a shaky breath. "I will, sir. But please, how will we know when it's their time?"

"When thy heart is again pierced by a longing greater than joy or grief, thou shalt know. Now, thou must return before the way is shut."

Moongazer stepped forward and bent his forelegs again.

I turned to Annabeth and grabbed her hands. "I'm ready. Let's go."

Her face had grown very grave. "Only you shall return," she said

solemnly. "I shall stay. The stag will take me back to the Grove of
Thrones. But take heart. Be valiant. Now, go."

"But—"

She pulled me into a fierce embrace. "Not lost," she whispered,
then released me. I could sense by her resolve that our time together
was finished.

I scrambled awkwardly onto Moongazer's back.

"Hold fast," said the centaur, "for this shall be a swift and har-
rowing race. Shouldst thou fall, I cannot save thee."

"Fare forward, Queen's Beloved," called the great stag, just like
Kinchurch. "We shall meet again, a long time hence."

Nothing prepared me for what happened next. Moongazer
leaped forward like a cataract, racing with such power, I felt my
stomach drop. I clung to his back, unable to even look back at the
others, much less wave goodbye.

Moongazer crested the nearest ridge and then nimbly vaulted
down, down, down the mountains, crossing chasms of unimagina-
ble depth, leaping from cliffside to cliffside, racing at the speed of a
plunging falcon. I could hardly breathe or raise my head.

His pace didn't slow in the gentler foothills but instead increased
until he sped like an arrow fired from a longbow. As the stream
flashed past, he kept to the trees till we reached the open fields and
the pear grove. When I finally dared to raise my head, he was closing in on the archway to my world, which stood gray and forlorn
against the golden fields.

At the edge of the grove, Moongazer slowed to a stop, blowing.
He bent his forelegs again, and I fell gracelessly to the ground.

ॐ ॐ

"Well, that was a near miss, and no mistake!" exclaimed a muffled
voice, practically in my ear.

"Got to keep your wits about you, this close to the door," said another voice close by. It sounded like the speaker had a bad cold.

Through the tall grass of the grove two whiskered brown faces appeared, nosing blindly along the ground. Their bodies were about the size of squirrels in our world, so at first I couldn't tell what manner of creature they were. But after a moment it struck me: They were large moles. *Magic moles.* And each carried a tiny spade in its long-fingered paws.

"Over here, fellows," called a third voice, much higher off the ground. This was a human, a man who sounded strangely familiar. I lurched to my feet. Striding cheerfully through the grove came Frankie—or no, not Frankie, but a man who looked like Frankie in another twenty years. It was Stokes. A younger version, to be sure, but with something of the old maturity about his wise eyes. A thin circlet of gold rested on his head.

"Stokes!" I cried.

He hesitated, mild confusion on his face. Then he nodded in recognition. "Just in time to watch the first of the cultivars go in," he said. "We've grafted some cuttings, see?" Stokes pointed to a series of potted saplings not far from where the moles were now digging. His face broke into a broad grin. "What I wouldn't have given for a pair of Mesterran moles to help me back at the Hall! But there's no toil in working the earth now. It's the birthright of the world's first queens and kings. It's what we were made to do."

As the moles kept digging, Stokes reached up into the branches of one of the trees and twisted off a golden pear. It shimmered in his hand like it was alive.

"Ever seen such beauty?" he said in wonder, holding out the pear to me. For the first time on this side of the door, I was suddenly ravenous. I reached out to take it.

"Stay thy hand!" commanded the centaur.

We froze.

"The fruit of this country is not for them that dwell beyond the door," Moongazer warned, circling us. "Only those who face grave peril shall take of it and eat. Now, Queen's Beloved, thou must bid farewell to this fair vale. Thou must take thy leave before the way is shut."

I turned reluctantly. Beyond the arch, the track and shrubs were barely visible, every bit as gray as Claire had said. Everything in me rebelled against going back.

Just then, a sound pierced the grove, the high call of the horn ringing from the distant mountains. It smote my ears like a lightning bolt, sending a charge through my bones. As before, I wanted nothing more than to heed that call, to chase its echoes unceasingly, even to the farthest rim of that world.

Moongazer lifted his head, nostrils flaring. "Farewell, Queen's Beloved," he said. "That is the summons, but not for thee. Thou knowest thy task." He bolted through the grove back toward the foothills.

Young Stokes, too, faced the mountains, his usually calm face quivering. "I'd best be going," he said without regret. "That's what you've got to do. Follow where the horn leads. It's a fearful thing, but it must be done." And he, too, took off at a run, the moles at his heels, the golden pear in his hand.

I thought I'd be torn to pieces between my ache to follow the horn and my instructions to return to Frankie on the far side of the door. But I knew what was required of me. I was being asked to do the hardest thing of all: return from a realm beyond the walls of my world, a place I'd been longing to find my whole life, back to an ordinary afternoon, on an ordinary day, in the ordinary world where I'd been born. Where I had to try to make things right.

I stepped toward the archway, paused for a moment, then leaped.

Then did the Children of Tellus take their place amongst the captains of the remnant. For in their brief sojourn amongst the Selvedges had they grown wiser, stronger, and more like Andella of old.

Early in the morning did the silent Selvedge armies amass, unseen in the fogs. Then, at Rifka's signal, they poured forth against the watchtower of Marisith-over-the-Sea. They descended upon the giants and ogres and took them unawares, and within minutes they'd breached the gates. The captains fought their way over the threshold as their enemies fell before them, then pressed forward into the great hall.

But the hall was empty—save for the crown on a little pedestal near the throne.

For the enchantress, startled from slumber in her upper bedchamber, had fled, crownless, toward the topmost battlement. Even now they could hear her footsteps on the stairs. But just as the captains rushed the stairwell, she broke out alone upon the battlement.

Then uttered Mindra her most powerful enchantment of all. And in that moment, every living thing in Ternival froze.

Silent and still stood the Selvedge armies. Lifeless as dead branches were the captains upon the stairs. Frozen in place were Mindra's own hordes, the prisoners in her dungeons, and the children and grandfathers still at home across the vale.

And alone stood Mindra, laughing on the battlement, victorious.

Chapter

48

I stumbled past the shrubs. I had to find Frankie at once. But I wanted to stop and embrace the trees, call to the birds that flitted through the underbrush. I had thought that after such an adventure I'd despise the very ground of our everyday, fog-shrouded old planet. But my time spent beyond the door hadn't made me love this world less. It had re-enchanted the world. I loved it more than ever.

Yet I'd been told to hurry, and I didn't know where to find Frankie. I'd been gone for hours, and he very well could've left for home.

I pelted down the hill to the opening in the fence, then back across the stream, through the grove, over the field and the drive. As I entered the kitchen garden, I noticed the door of Stokes's toolshed propped open. I peeked inside, eyes adjusting slowly to the dusty gloom.

"Frankie?"

A figure sat hunched on an overturned urn.

"Frankie!" I wanted to blurt out the whole story at once. But the stag was right. This wouldn't be easy.

"Can't I be left alone for ten minutes?" Frankie's voice was unusually sharp.

"Ten minutes? But—" I began to protest that I'd been gone for hours and hours. But, no, time must move differently beyond the door, as in so many of the fairy tales.

"Please," he said wearily. "Please don't. I couldn't bear to play games now."

I felt the breath leave my lungs. "It's no game," I said. "Listen: It's all true. I've been there. On the other side. And I'm sorry I never told you. I'm not sure why I didn't. I think I wanted a story that was just mine . . . but I know now that I was wrong."

This was awful. I was making things worse. But I had to keep trying.

"All this summer, I've been with Grandmother in the gardens at night, when she thinks she's still a queen. And I've seen the stag, and I've followed him to the door. And just now, after you and I . . . after my grandmother . . . I went to the door again. And this time it opened, and a girl led me into that golden land, and I realized it was Claire—"

Frankie stood abruptly. "Enough."

"But it's true!" I protested. "I saw it myself. I was there!"

Even in the shed's gloom, I could see the stern lines on his face. He wasn't swayed.

"You must believe me," I begged.

He made for the toolshed doorway.

"The stag said it might be like this, but you can't just walk away," I pleaded. "There *are* other worlds, Frankie. You know there are. You've been to one yourself."

He laughed as I'd never heard him laugh before: mocking, almost cruel. "Oh yes. I see it all now. We *wanted* it to be true. I would've believed almost anything."

Hadn't I wished he would laugh more often? Well, I didn't want that now. I wanted the old earnestness back. "But you said . . ." The tears came fast now. "I . . . you . . . It was real. They were all real. Everyone was there. All the people from the stories. The creatures, and my family . . ." I stepped closer. "Even your grandfather."

He flinched. If I hadn't known him better, I would've thought he was about to smash his hand through the nearest window. Instead, he said in a controlled voice, "You don't get it, do you? She sacked my parents, Eva. Your grandmother. She said she couldn't have the staff interfering in her affairs. That I couldn't be trusted. So she sacked them. We're leaving Carrick Hall. We'll probably have to leave the Wolverns."

He pushed past me out of the shed.

It was as if the ground had started to sink below my feet: the shed, the garden, the estate, the earth, crumbling away. I followed as far as the threshold, but at the sight of his stiff figure marching past the tomato vines, I knew.

It was over. I'd failed my friend and his family, ruined everything. For good.

I stared numbly at the vegetable rows. Frankie and I had worked this good earth. I'd poured so much of my time, myself, into this place that if someone had taken a spade and dug me up and tossed me aside, I wouldn't have felt greater uprooting than in this moment.

I wished I could hide in the toolshed for the rest of my stay at Carrick Hall. But eventually I threaded my way back through the formal gardens, pausing at the topiaries. Now that I'd seen their warm, breathing bodies on the other side of the door, their leafy silence drove my despair deeper still.

I sneaked into the house through the drawing room, hoping to avoid everyone, even Mrs. Fealston. I decided to slip into the servant's passageway from the dining room, where I could take the back stairs up to my room. But once I reached the passageway, the sound of raised voices wafted up from the kitchen.

"But this is ridiculous!" came Mrs. Fealston's voice. "She can't do this."

"She can, and she did." It was Mrs. Addison. Her voice was shrill, strained.

"There, now, Holly," Mr. Addison said. "Paxton's offered to drive us home. I've loaded the boxes with our things. It's time."

That's when I remembered what the stag had told me by the spring at the world's edge: *It is never too late to make wrong things right—or to try.*

I tore down the stairs and burst into the kitchen.

"It's all my fault!" I cried. "Not Frankie's. I was the one who found the gems. I suggested we try to use them. Don't leave yet. I'll talk to her. I'll make her see the truth."

Five pairs of eyes turned toward me. Mrs. Fealston, the Addisons, Paxton, and Frankie all stood in the kitchen as if poised for flight. Mrs. Addison's pinched lips told me everything I needed to know about her opinion of me now. Frankie dropped his gaze.

Mrs. Fealston was the first to speak. "Peace, child. It's valiant of you, but not necessary. I've been trying to tell everyone. Your grandmother *cannot* do this."

"Well, it's too late—" Mrs. Addison began spitefully, but the housekeeper held up her hand.

"She can't do this, Holly, because *she is not your employer.*"

Everyone stared.

"Listen, all of you, if you please," said Mrs. Fealston, exasperated.

"When Mr. Torstane died, Gwendolyn inherited the bulk of his fortune. She's held it in trust all this time so that Mrs. Torstane can live peacefully here at the Hall, so her condition doesn't worsen. Do you hear? *All* the estate's affairs, including the hiring and firing of staff, are Gwendolyn's responsibility."

A stunned silence met this announcement.

"So you're saying Gwen's my boss?" said Mrs. Addison. "And she never told me?"

"Think, for a moment, of all the reasons why she might not have done so," said Mrs. Fealston.

Mrs. Addison's scowl deepened. "Well, she might be my boss, but she can't force me to work for *that woman*. You can do what you like, Jim, but I'm leaving."

"Please—" I began, but one look from Mrs. Addison silenced me.

I dashed back up the staircase to my room. I couldn't bear to watch them leave. After locking the door, I climbed into my canopied bed for the last time and wept myself to sleep.

ఌ ಝ

Very early the next morning, Mrs. Fealston knocked to say Paxton was waiting. She'd tried several times the night before to speak to me—even left a supper tray of my favorite soup outside the door. But eventually she'd given up. Now she waited at the door till I emerged, my hair combed and face washed, brand-new luggage carefully packed. I didn't meet her gaze but mumbled an apology about a headache.

"Your grandmother claims to feel poorly too," Mrs. Fealston said, studying my face. "Well, she said for me to see you off, though it breaks my heart. And after you two had such a lovely time together!" She led the way down the stairs to the front doors.

She paused there and studied me again. "Never forget who you are," she said gently, "nor who your grandmother is. Just you wait: One day it will all come right. She'll come around. She always does."

"Does she?" I sounded just like Mum.

"You wait. You'll see." Mrs. Fealston's eyes glittered as she gave me a brisk hug and then sent me down the steps to Paxton and the waiting car. "Come back soon!"

I watched her through the rear window as the Bentley began the long journey away from Carrick Hall. She stood unmoving like one of the topiaries, arm raised, until a bend in the drive hid her and the house from view.

PART 4

As I am always telling you, the most wonderful things happen to all sorts of people, only you never hear about them because the people think that no one will believe their stories, and so they don't tell them to any one except me. And they tell me, because they know that I can believe anything.

—*The Enchanted Castle* by E. NESBIT, 1907

These things . . . are only the scent of a flower we have not found, the echo of a tune we have not heard, news from a country we have never yet visited. Do you think I am trying to weave a spell? Perhaps I am; but remember your fairy tales. Spells are used for breaking enchantments as well as for inducing them.

—"The Weight of Glory" by C. S. LEWIS, 1941

Chapter

49

I sit at the end of the portrait gallery near the wing where my grandmother lies dying. In the wintry gloom, my ancestors' faces are obscured. Yet even from here I can see it: the white creature in the background of my grandfather's portrait, glimmering like a star.

I'm alone yet not alone, for light slants down the hallway from my grandmother's rooms. Mum's voice rises and falls as she talks on the phone. I can't hear what she says, but her tone is plaintive and sad. She misses my dad. She wants him to come to England as soon as possible. Time is short. There are decisions to be made.

I, too, feel an ache in my stomach, though not just from missing Dad. I miss everything suddenly. I miss being a child tucked in by my mother, begging her to whisper a fairy tale by lamplight. I miss the summer evenings at Carrick Hall five years ago, watching the swallows in the gloaming. I miss Stokes, too, with his gardener's hands and wise, solid face. And I miss Frankie—or, at least, the friendship we once had. He's due any moment from Cambridge, having caught the first train home now that the term is over.

Here in the gallery I can escape the strange gurgling Grandmother makes as she breathes. Pneumonia speaks its own language. Yet she's improved since yesterday. An hour ago, when last I passed through the hallway outside her rooms, I glanced in to see her thin face framed by a purple turban. Her eyes, alert yet infantile, gazed up at Mrs. Fealston, who hovered, as always, nearby.

"The window," my grandmother rasped, her first coherent words in days. "Leave it open. I wish to hear the sea."

"Yes, Your Majesty," Mrs. Fealston replied.

The sea is many miles away, of course. Grandmother thinks she's in a castle—a castle in another world.

Where she was once a queen.

෴

Holly Addison greeted us when we arrived yesterday. Paxton drove us through the rain—always rain—which fell most of the way from the airport. But as the car climbed through the valley toward the hills, the rain turned to sleet, and the crest of the hills disappeared behind swirling clouds. We were well up the drive before Carrick Hall became visible, the faint outline of its peaks and towers like a half-remembered dream.

Mrs. Addison stood shivering at the top of the front steps while we exited the car. "Welcome home," she called. "Mrs. Fealston is upstairs with your mother just now, but tea is in the drawing room. Jim built up the fire."

Mum climbed the steps with a faint smile. "Where we're from, this doesn't count as winter." Her smile faded as she faced her child-hood friend. "How are things here?"

Mrs. Addison's glance flitted to me, then back to Mum. "The doctor says pneumonia at this stage of cancer is a hard thing, I'm afraid. Prepare yourselves for a big change. She's thin as a child. She's delirious most of the time—the morphine does that. She's lost her hair . . ."

Mrs. Fealston had warned us about that on the phone. It was impossible to imagine. All those beautiful, silvery locks . . . gone.

In the five years since that eventful summer, we'd heard nothing from Grandmother. Mrs. Fealston was the one who'd sent cards and letters, who'd called on each of our birthdays. She was the one who'd told us that the Addisons had agreed to resume working at the Hall, after Mum smoothed things over. Yet the news Mrs. Fealston had delivered a few days ago, just one hour after I took my last exam of the college semester, hit us like a blow.

The end was soon.

Grandmother hadn't wanted us to know—not through all the grueling weeks of doctor's visits and treatments and nausea and hair loss. But as things worsened, Mrs. Fealston wouldn't obey Grandmother any longer. The housekeeper called us.

Mum had booked our flights immediately.

"The doctor just left," Mrs. Addison continued, leading the way to the drawing room. "He comes daily. But other than morphine, there's not much to be done." She glanced at me over her shoulder. "Looking more and more like your mum now, Miss Eva! Fairly grown up. Frankie will be home tomorrow. He'll be glad to see you."

I smiled weakly. Apparently, Mrs. Addison no longer carried a grudge against me, thank goodness. Maybe she wasn't the kind of person who could carry one for five long years. But Frankie . . . Of all the reunions I dreaded in England, I dreaded seeing Frankie the most—after Grandmother, that is. *Would* he be glad to see me, or was Mrs. Addison just making conversation?

The manor house was darker than I remembered. Entire rooms remained unlit, their furnishings shrouded in sheets, the high ceilings in shadow. Even on the gloomiest summer days, the Hall had never been as grim or silent as it was now. Like it had fallen under an even deeper spell, one that began in the corners and worked its way into the soul.

"And how is Frankie?" Mum asked, helping herself to tea.

Mrs. Addison beamed. "Well, as you know, he received that scholarship from Lord Edward's foundation—beat out hundreds of other applicants." I could tell it was a much-recited speech by a very proud mother. "Loves it at Magdalene, of course. I'd feel out of place, myself, but not Frankie."

"I'm so glad!" Mum said. "There's a lot of pressure at university. It can take a toll. You'll want to keep an eye on him, if he starts to turn thin and wan."

Mrs. Addison didn't exactly scoff, but she seemed amused by the suggestion. "He's found himself there. It's far and away the best place for him."

"And your other children? What are they up to?"

"They're on holiday already. In fact," she turned to me, "if it ever gets too quiet here, Miss Eva, the cottage is a regular rugby pitch. Georgie, now! Six years old and heavier than his brothers and sisters put together. Built like his father, that one."

I could picture the Addisons' cottage down in the village, brimming with laughter and light. Carrick Hall, on the other hand, was cold as death. The mantel definitely needed something: candles, holly branches, white lights—anything. The fire's warmth was a comfort, though. Tea, scones, even the familiarity of Mrs. Addison's freckled face, which hadn't aged a day. It was good to be back.

But eventually we had to set down our teacups. We had to follow Mrs. Addison up the grand staircase to the second floor and enter the gilded wing that now smelled like a hospital. We greeted Mrs. Fealston, whose tiny body seemed bowed with a burden twice her weight.

The housekeeper started at the sight of me, as if she'd seen a ghost. To my mother she said, "So good to have you home, Mrs. Joyce. You're welcome to go in to her now. She's sleeping, but if she happens to wake, she'll be glad to see you." She looked again at me. "Ah, my dear, you'll have a trickier time of it, I'm afraid. I didn't realize . . . You see . . . you're just the age . . . Her sister . . ."

Of course. Grandmother's sister, Annabeth, had died not much older than I was now. After five years I looked more than ever like her statue in the secret garden. Tall, willowy, my curls tamed in a pixie cut. No longer a child.

"I want to try," I said, "no matter what happens."

"That's right, love," Mrs. Fealston agreed. "On her better days she asks for you. It's the right thing."

Did she ask for *me*? Or for Annabeth? I couldn't bring myself to ask.

We entered quietly. I'd never been in this suite of rooms. The shades were drawn, but even so, I could make out the rich cream and gold of the walls, the tapestried curtains, the French baroque furnishings. Someone had expended a fortune here. And in the center of it all, on a massive canopied bed, lay my grandmother.

Her thin body, like that of a young girl, barely made a bump under the bedclothes. Her turbaned head rested on the pillow, mouth slightly open in a gurgling snore. She made no movements, but her face wasn't peaceful. It was deeply lined, her brows drawn together. Concentrating on not feeling the pain, maybe. On not feeling her body at all.

Mum sat down on the edge of the bed, neither speaking nor reaching out her hand. She seemed numb, lost in one of those bad dreams where you remember none of the plot, only a grief so real you wake with tears on your face. I hung back, giving her a moment to reckon with the fact that this was no dream. Her mother was dying. There would be no re-scripting of any scene that had ever passed between them. Not now. Not ever.

Then it was my turn. I sat awkwardly, afraid to inflict further pain by drawing too near. But I couldn't help taking Grandmother's hand. It was light as a bird.

"I'm sorry," I whispered. I wasn't even sure what for. That she'd had to endure so much tragedy so long ago. That my mother had chosen to disappoint her. That I'd persisted in pursuing the thing she feared the most. That she suffered so greatly now. All those things.

Her eyes opened, just tiny slits. But I knew she saw me. Her hand tightened on mine. Her brow cleared. Then she sighed deeply and fell into a peaceful sleep.

But faulty were Mindra's plans. For among all the living things in Ternival was one person upon whom the spell had no power. Indeed, when the captains of the remnant had rushed the stairs, one alone stayed behind in the throne room of Marisith.

One alone drew near the crown. For to this one had Rifka the Loomkeeper given the gems of Mesterra, to safeguard with gloved hands until just such a moment.

Swiftly had this one grasped the crown.

Deftly had this one restored the gems to their settings.

And then had Flora, eldest of the Children of Tellus, placed the crown upon her brow.

Chapter

50

Frankie's letters began during my junior year of high school. Just postcards, at first, with his own sketches on the front. The bridge in Upper Wolvern. The top of Table Mount. The view from the kitchen stoop of Carrick Hall. On the back, his tight, elegant script: *Cambridge is magical in the fall. My studies are going well, although there's one lecturer whose voice is like heavy anesthesia.* Or, *Autumn is when I miss the smell of the pear orchard at the Hall. Sometimes I catch a whiff, just beyond the cloisters, like I'm almost home.* Frankie never made mention of our last conversation in the toolshed, but his tone was conciliatory.

I was unsure how to reply. I sent occasional postcards in return, mostly banal updates about life in Chicago: *I've joined the swim team, made some new friends. Please say hi to Tilly for me when you see her.*

Then his correspondence turned lengthy, journal-like in detail: *Did you know the halls here were nearly empty during WWI? Young men drifted through these echoing buildings, waiting their turn, learning about the deaths of their classmates at the front, one after another. Almost an entire generation, gone . . .*

And then a few months later: *I've been doing some thinking, beginning to climb up and out of grief.* He seemed to think I'd know what he meant by this. Grief at losing Stokes? At losing our friendship? Both? And meanwhile, I still couldn't tell whether or not he believed me about my adventure beyond the door. And what about his own adventure with the gem—did he still deny it?

Doubts of my own began to creep in. Had any of it really happened? Or had we been foolish dreamers, confused by emotion, ready to believe just about anything?

But then came his most recent letter, just last week. He and some classmates had begun to rent Aunt Bertie's house in Cambridge. The old woman was gone by now, of course. The house was still cold, ugly, and sparsely furnished—and, thus, cheap. Plus, Frankie got a discount as a friend of the family. *The avocado lamp is our favorite,* he joked, *and we've fought bitterly over the plastic chairs (!). By the way, I found the hidden entrance to the attic. And you'll never guess what was up there. More soon, Frankie.*

I felt the old thrill of excitement, like I was fourteen again. Had he found it? The missing frame?

Now, Mum tells me, his train has arrived. He's here.

The kitchen is warm when I enter, still the warmest place in the entire house. It's the only room that's just as I remember. Mrs. Addison stands in Mrs. Fealston's place at the range. She's stirring the same soup—there's the scent of sage, and potato peelings litter a nearby cutting board. And in Stokes's old spot at the long table sits Frankie's father, large work-worn hands cupped around a mug of something hot. Seated across from him—at least a head taller, an easy confidence in his bearing—is a lean young man with dark hair and a pale, freckled face.

Over his father's shoulder he catches sight of me. Both men rise. "Hey," I say.

There's an awkward silence. Then Frankie's mother steps forward with a bowl of soup and motions toward the stool at the table's end, between Frankie and his father. "Frankie remembered it was your favorite," she says as I take my seat. "He reminded me this morning to get the soup going."

I smile. I can't help it. I might've come to England because my grandmother is dying. I might've felt hurt and ashamed after my last interactions with everyone here. But it's good to sit at this table with my old friend, enjoying the warmth of the dearest place I've ever known.

And Frankie smiles back.

&

A mutual shyness makes conversation difficult at first, but we take tentative forays into safe topics: classes and dormitory life, favorite books lately, our plans for the upcoming semester. Already I know a great deal more about him than he does about me. His letters have given me a window into his thoughts. But it's his physical presence that takes getting used to: his height, his confidence, his unpretentious maturity. It's odd that someone I know so well also feels like a total stranger.

Meanwhile, everything I *really* want to discuss is too fraught, too painful. What happened on my last day in England. How foolish I was. How sorry I was—and still am, even now. And what he found at Aunt Bertie's house. No, I'll let him broach those things when he's ready. After all, I was the one who wounded *him*. And right now he's sitting comfortably beside me at the kitchen table in Carrick Hall, chatting, and I don't want to mess up everything all over again.

Eventually I'm invited to visit the Addisons' cottage. Tilly is now a bold teenager, laughing easily. Nine-year-old Elspeth hangs back, but I can see her mind working behind those intense dark eyes. She's trying to discern something about me—I'm not sure what. Maybe whether or not I still believe in fairy tales. Or maybe she doesn't remember me at all.

The other two boys—Jack, now twelve, and Georgie, age six—are a blur of chaos and motion, especially Georgie.

"Oi, it's Frankie's girlfriend!" Georgie shouts, his red hair sticking up all over the place. Jack starts pelting him with socks from a nearby laundry basket while Tilly chases them, scolding. The two boys clatter up the stairs out of reach, their footfalls like a herd of rhinos. Frankie pretends he hasn't heard while I turn my flaming face away.

"Have you seen the Rastegars yet?" Elspeth asks.

"No—but I want to. Shall we?"

Elspeth throws on a coat, and she, Frankie, and I make our way up High Street.

Mrs. Fealston has kept Mum updated on how the Rastegars finally took the plunge two years ago. They packed up their bookshop in Cambridge and relocated to Upper Wolvern, where New Warren's, as it's now called, is a favorite haunt of faculty and students from Wolvern College. It looks much like the old shop in Cambridge, with its bow window and maze of bookshelves. But it's the Rastegars' other business that I really want to see.

There, in a quaint half-timbered storefront next to New Warren's, is a little tea shop called Much Ado About Cream Puffs.

The Rastegars opened it within a year of moving here, and it was an instantaneous success. Customers from all over the West Midlands make the trek to Upper Wolvern for the pastries alone. In fact, the Rastegars' grown daughter and her young son have joined them from London to help run everything. Now, to see the place in person, nestled among the shops of High Street, brings me a rush of joy.

"She did it!" I exclaim with a grin. "Mrs. Rastegar did it!"

We push open the door.

Instantly from the crown burst music like none heard in Ternival before or since. Bright glowed the gems, flaming like suns. Golden light poured from the crown, out upon the hosts frozen in their charge, up to the highest battlement, and forth into all the vale.

And any Selvedges that the light touched were restored to life and motion. But Mindra's armies melted into mist and vanished.

Mindra herself, crying aloud in terror, leapt from the battlement, but by her magic arts, she landed safely on her feet and began to flee.

Then suddenly another light shewed forth, a silvery beam from the heart of the vale, which sought and held the golden light of Flora's crown. Between them grew an even brighter light, like the making of stars. Mindra shrieked and hid her face, for she was caught between them, and there was nowhere to hide.

Then out of the silvery beam came the great stag.

Chapter

51

Behind the tea shop counter sits a striking dark-haired woman, maybe in her midthirties, reading a book. She looks up as we enter and sets the book down slowly, as if she's on the last paragraph of the very last page and our timing is terrible.

"Hullo, Frankie," she says, managing to smile anyway. Then to me, "And you must be Miss Joyce. We heard you were coming."

"Yes. I'm Eva," I say. "And you must be the Rastegars' daughter."

"I'm Mahsa," she says.

A curtain in the back of the shop twitches aside.

"Is it a coach?" comes Mrs. Rastegar's wary voice.

"No, just special guests," Mahsa reassures her. "Frankie and Eva."

"One moment!"

I take the opportunity to look around. Unlike the old Warren's in Cambridge, with its baffling maze of random inventory, this tea shop is pristine. Comfortable seating, a gleaming counter, the aroma of chocolate and powdered sugar and spices, and shelves upon shelves of daintily packaged pastries. Leaning in, I realize that every shelf is carefully labeled in the same elegant handwriting as the bookcases in old Warren's. *Chocolate with a Hint of Rose Water. Persian Delectables for Which There Is No Good Translation.* And *Mrs. R's Attempt at Dairy-Free—Please Tell Us What You Think.*

Mrs. Rastegar appears, carrying a tray of pastries and wearing the frilliest apron I've ever seen.

"So good to see you, Miss Eva." The tiny woman is smiling, as usual.

"Congratulations, Mrs. Rastegar! Your tea shop is just perfect."

She nods as if this is a fact of nature, like the sunrise, indisputable and universally pleasing. Then her smile fades. "She is okay, your grandmother?"

"I'm afraid not, Mrs. Rastegar. She's very sick."

"Oh dear. So sorry. I will send you with pastries."

"That's terribly kind, but I'm not sure she can eat much of anything."

"No, not for her. For you. For your mother." She busies herself behind the counter, piling an assortment of confections into a white paper bag.

"Arash!" Mahsa calls. "Come meet our guests."

A boy about Jack's age—eleven or twelve—emerges from the back room. He's gawky and shy, blinking at us from behind thick spectacles. Elspeth stares at him in much the same way that she once looked at me, like she's meeting royalty.

"Yes, yes, grandson, come here!" Mrs. Rastegar brightens and beckons to the boy. "Arash was just accepted at Wolvern," she says proudly. The boy ducks his head.

"Congratulations," Frankie says with an affirming nod. "Well done."

The shop door opens, and in walks none other than Lord Ed-

ward Heapworth. Behind him trails a teenage boy wearing a sullen
scowl, followed by a pre-teen girl with a long braid so blond it's
almost white. She waves shyly at Elspeth, as if they've met before.

"Miss Eva, is it?" Heapworth exclaims. "Grown into an absolute
goddess, by heaven!"

I can sense Frankie's amused smirk without seeing it. Heapworth
himself is simply stunning in a tan cashmere coat that looks impos-
sibly soft, with a tartan scarf effortlessly flung around his neck. He
hasn't changed a hair.

Introductions are made. The boy is Heapworth's younger son,
Charlie, and the girl is his only daughter, Aurora. She smiles a
toothy smile, just like her father, and a faint memory stirs in me.
Who else does she remind me of?

"Charlie's on his Christmas hols from Wolvern. Desperate to
escape the village, aren't you, lad?" Heapworth slaps his son cheerfully on the back. Charlie's scowl deepens.

"Arash here will attend Wolvern next year," Frankie says.

"Brilliant!" Heapworth exclaims. "Perhaps you can show him
the ropes, eh, Charlie?"

Charlie is silent while Arash looks as though he wishes the floor
would swallow him whole.

"And how is Mrs. T?" Lord Edward asks me, dropping the breezy
tone. "Your mum holding up?"

"Not well."

He shakes his head. "Such a shame. I'll have to come see Gwenny
soon, but I've got to get these two to London first, for Christmas
with their mum. I'm here to pick up my order before we fly the
coop. What have you got for me today, Mrs. Rastegar? The usual?"

As Mahsa reaches behind the counter and hands Lord Edward an
enormous pastry box, the voice of Professor Rastegar floats from
the back room.

"Greetings! We are well met."

He emerges from behind the curtain and joins us at the counter. The shopkeeper's hair has thinned, and his back stoops a little, but otherwise he's unchanged.

"Hi, Professor Rastegar," I say, shaking his hand heartily.

"Now I am reminded," he says. "I found a box, unopened. From our storage room in Cambridge. The name was Pennington, yes?"

"Yes, actually. Have you found something?"

"Perhaps. I'll ring the Hall if I have. And your grandmother— how is she?"

"Not well," I say again.

"Ah," he sighs sadly, "but sweet are the uses of adversity, which, like the toad, ugly and venomous, wears yet a precious jewel in his head."

"Especially when it's other people's adversity," mutters Mahsa dryly. I give her a sidelong glance. Is that a little dig at her dad, or at Shakespeare?

"And this our life," quips Frankie, "exempt from public haunt, finds tongues in trees, books in the running brooks . . ."

"Sermons in stones," continues the shopkeeper, beaming, "and good in everything."

"Brilliant!" says Lord Edward. "*Much Ado About Nothing.* I'd wager my Rolls."

"*As You Like It,*" the others correct him.

"I *knew* it was one of the comedies, eh?" Heapworth cries, inordinately pleased with himself. "Alas, no more Rolls for me. Charlie, Aurora, how do you feel about trains? Well, I fear we must be going." Heapworth hands the pastry box to Charlie and sweeps open the shop door. "Cheerio!"

As Aurora follows her dad toward the door, Elspeth stops her and the two begin whispering fiercely.

"Have you seen him yet?" I can hear Elspeth asking. "Enormous, with antlers like trees. I'm pretty sure he glows."

I feel a jolt, like I've just been yanked back through time into the moonlit gardens of Carrick Hall. Has Elspeth merely *heard* about the stag or actually *seen* him?

Aurora shakes her head. "Not yet. I'll let you know!" Then she waves goodbye and dashes out the door after her father.

And that's when I realize who Aurora looks like.

Lady Margaret, the grandmotherly woman from beyond the door.

Maggie, from the tales of Ternival.

ध ध

On the afternoon of Christmas Eve, at the Addisons' cottage, I announce my decision. "I'm going to decorate the Hall."

Everything stops. Everyone stares.

"I'm sick of the gloom," I say. "And the cold. And feeling like everyone's given up. I'm going to decorate the Hall for Christmas. Anyone want to help?"

Frankie grins. "Is this the part where we say, 'Yes, madam'?"

I grimace. "This is the part where you can help a friend."

"There's holly by the gatehouse!" Georgie shouts. "I'll get Dad's clippers from the toolshed." He starts pulling on a pair of Wellingtons.

"You will *not*," Frankie says sternly. "*I'll* get the clippers. You get some twine. And doesn't Mum have a box of lights and bows somewhere? From the women's tea?"

"I know where they are!" Elspeth disappears upstairs.

The two youngest boys bolt out the door and down the street, shouting and pelting each other with pine cones. Tilly follows, bellowing for them to be quiet. Frankie studies my face, his head nearly brushing the low timbered ceiling.

"Your grandmother mightn't like it," he warns.

I shrug. "She might not."

We leave for the Hall together.

As Frankie and I make our way up the drive toward Carrick Hall, he clears his throat. "Has your grandmother ever mentioned the gems?"

It occurs to me that this is the first time we've been alone since he arrived from Cambridge. Has he been waiting, all this time, for a good moment?

"Not once."

"So," he continues slowly, "you two haven't talked about . . . You haven't addressed what happened . . . that last day . . ."

"No, never."

"I'm sorry."

"Oh, well. Nothing new." I sound cynical, even to myself.

"No, I mean, I'm sorry for shutting you down that day. In the toolshed." He halts and faces me, the old earnest expression on his face. "It was unfair of me to assume you were just telling stories, trying to make me feel better."

I open my mouth to interject, but he keeps going.

"Wait, Eva. Listen. I've thought a lot about it. I began to realize that you couldn't have been lying—there's no *way* you would've expected me to fall for something so outrageous. And you obviously weren't crazy. If anything, *I* was the one who wasn't thinking straight, from grief. Which really leaves only one choice, which is that you were telling the truth. And I just want to say . . ." He pauses, his gaze ranging over the fields, the orchard, the house, then returning to me. "I believe you. I was wrong."

It feels like a massive mountain has been lifted off my chest. I could almost float into the sky.

"Well," I say, "*I* was wrong not to tell you about my adventures with Grandmother. And about the stag. And the land beyond the door. It was petty and selfish and unreasonable." Again, that floaty feeling, like I've been wearing shoes made of lead and finally took them off.

He seems to be holding back a smile. "Come to think of it, yes, it was," he says in a teasing tone.

"Frankie! I'm serious."

"Of course. Sorry." He grows solemn again. "You confessed all this before, you know. In the toolshed. And I've forgiven you." He holds out his hand. "Friends?"

I shake it. His hand is warm and solid and comforting. "Friends."

"There must be a thousand lights in here, Frankie." Elspeth stumbles up the drive behind us, lugging a heavy box. "You couldn't have waited for me?"

We turn reluctantly to help her, and the three of us make our way toward the Hall together.

Frankie's right, of course. There's so much left unsaid between Grandmother and me.

But I might never get to speak with her again.

"Mindra, enchantress of old," proclaimed the stag, "thou art defeated."

Mindra lowered her hands from her face. But her features remained proud, unyielding, and she trembled with rage.

"Into the Wilderlands art thou banished," the stag continued, "ever to wander the forest alone whilst the crown and its gems remain upon the heads of Ternival's sovereigns. For from this day forth shall the gems' music be torturous to thine ears, and the closer they be, the greater thy torment. But likewise, ever shall thine hunger for the gems and crown grow, and ever shalt thou seek them, though many worlds might lie between them and thee, to the end of all ages."

From that hour was Mindra banished deep into the Wilderlands, nevermore to be seen by any Ternivali who that day witnessed her undoing. Long did she haunt that corner of the forest, which grew darker and darker from her fell presence, till it became known as the Night Wood.

And none dared enter it, lest they never return.

Chapter

52

The rest of the day is a happy blur. The younger boys run pell-mell up and down the grand staircase as Frankie and his father bring in armfuls of greenery. After initially urging them to keep quiet, even Mrs. Addison joins in, stringing ribbons and lights. Someone finds a wireless and turns up "A Festival of Nine Lessons and Carols" from King's College, and soon we're all humming along. Between the lights and some white tulle from Mrs. Addison's box, I turn the drawing room mantel into a snowy, starlit wonderland.

Then Mum appears in the doorway.

Everyone halts, watching her. I know it's the first time she's seen this room decorated for anything, much less for Christmas. At first her expression is unreadable.

"It was my idea," I say quickly, fearing that she's displeased.

Her face relaxes into a smile. "And a good one too. It's marvelous."

"Oh, bother—I almost forgot supper!" Mrs. Addison exclaims, glancing at the mantel clock. "Is just a simple soup acceptable for tonight? I'll leave it on the range. That way you can eat whenever you're ready. I'm saving the pheasants for tomorrow."

"That's more than acceptable, thank you," Mum replies. "And really, feel free to spend the rest of today and tomorrow as a family. It's Christmas Eve, after all. Eva and I can attend to the pheasants. You spend far more time here than we deserve."

"But you *will* come to the church, won't you?" says Elspeth from the window where she's arranging holly on the sill. "Midnight mass?"

"And stop by the cottage beforehand for wassail?" Tilly adds. "It's village tradition."

My introverted mother pauses indecisively.

"I'll be there," I assure them. "Mum will want to stay here with Grandmother. But I'll join you."

Mum looks at me gratefully. "It's not as though you'll be missing any Christmas Eve traditions around here, darling. But yes, I think a quiet evening is what I need."

Someone gasps from the doorway. Mrs. Fealston stands just behind my mother, hands clasped, eyes wide. For a moment she looks like a young girl who's just stepped into a wintry fairy tale. "It's beautiful!"

Mum steps aside, smiling. "It was Eva's idea."

Tilly and Elspeth each take one of the housekeeper's elbows and guide her into the room. Someone turns off the overhead lights, leaving just the mantel twinkling in the December gloom.

The housekeeper observes for a long moment, then nods. "Just as it should be." She turns to me. "I hate to interrupt the festivities, but I was sent to fetch you, Miss Eva. Your grandmother is awake. She's asking for you."

The spell is broken. Elspeth stares at me in horror, like I've just been summoned to the throne room of a sorceress.

"No need to fear." Mrs. Fealston pats my arm. "Just be yourself."

I don't dare ask aloud, *But what if myself is exactly the wrong thing to be?*

ᚳ ᚹ

Grandmother is sitting up in bed, teacup in hand. She's cheerfully alert in her purple turban and an embroidered robe, her fingers glittering with rings. A fire burns in the enormous marble fireplace. The tapestried curtains are open. The whole suite feels downright pleasant.

"There you are!" she wheezes. Her face lights up with that summer smile, the one that can raise kingdoms and tear them down. For five long years I've been aching to see that smile turned toward me once again. And here it is, so effortless, as if nothing terrible ever passed between us.

I approach the bed, uncertain who she thinks I am. Annabeth? Or me? And if she knows it's me, does she remember anything about my last day in England?

I decide to be myself, as Mrs. Fealston suggested. "Hello, Grandmother."

To my relief, she smiles again and pats the coverlet next to her. I sit. "It's been too long," she says. "And how is university? Do you like your classes? Have you made any friends?"

It's a safe cluster of subjects, and I answer at some length, just to keep that smile on her thin face. What I don't tell her, because I'm assuming she knows, is that I'm attending Whitby, the same college where Dad is a professor and Mum is an archivist. Shortly after my dad took the job, they purchased a cozy, rambling, bookshelf-lined house just a few blocks from campus. I remember the night he came through the door with his first paycheck, a bottle of wine, and a huge vase of flowers for Mum, who cried. For the first time in my life, I've had a real home.

I avoid telling Grandmother that my parents have expanded Whitby's Kinchurch Collection, drawing scholars from all over the world. Nor do I mention the large painted portrait of Augusta that hangs just inside the library entrance, which sends a quiver of longing through me every time I see its carven frame.

Grandmother listens avidly at first, her breath coming in measured rasps. Then she lowers the teacup to the saucer on her lap, eyes drooping. I slow my narration to a halt.

"I'm so very sorry, my dear," she says as a mighty shudder overtakes her. She rests her turbaned head on the pillows behind her. "Sometimes I just feel so sleepy."

"I should go and let you rest," I say, gently moving the teacup to the bedside table. I pat her hand and begin to rise.

She grips my fingers, eyes still closed, brow furrowed. "No, no, please don't leave me. Please, Eva."

"Of course, Grandmother." I sit closer, stroking her hand. "I'm here. I won't leave."

She nods imperiously and turns her face away with a rattling sigh. Then suddenly her eyes fly open.

"Dost thou hear it?" she whispers, half in hope, half in terror. Her gaze is now fixed on something beyond my shoulder.

"Hear what?"

"The horn winding from the mountains. Surely thou dost hear it!"

Despite the intervening years, every sinew in my body remembers the pure, piercing call of the horn beyond the door. I strain my ears. Ash settles in the grate. A clock ticks on the mantel. These, and my grandmother's rasping breaths, are the only sounds I hear.

She grips my hand harder and peers into my eyes. "Ah, beloved, but it shall rend me in two!"

"Then follow it," I whisper, leaning closer. "It's a fearful thing, but it must be done."

"Nay," she gasps. "He cannot be trusted." I know she means the stag. "If he had been there, my dear ones would not have died."

"But they are safe with him now, Grandmother. In that fair country beyond the door. You know that, don't you? Safe and whole and waiting. For you."

"But I daren't go! For it would mean leaving thee."

"I'll be okay," I try to reassure her. "I promise. It's okay."

Eventually she closes her eyes again and draws the slow, deep breaths of sleep.

That very day were the Children of Tellus established as the three queens of the vale.

Annabel was established as Queen of Nisnagard in the south, where her cheerful countenance drew strength from the mountain's inner fires, and her endless curiosity meant even deeper explorations of the ancient mines. For this the dwarves loved her and pledged fealty forever.

Claris became Queen of Wildergard in the east, a fierce friend of trees and protector of the vale against its enemies from the forest. Under her reign were the Wilderlands charted as far as could be reached, and the known portals marked, and her sentries stationed as far as the edge of the Night Wood.

As for Flora, she dwelt at Caristor, which was rebuilt in glory, and there was she established as Queen of the West, High Queen over all Ternival. During her reign she commissioned the building of great ships, charted the unknown islands in the western seas, and built a summer palace at Islagard. For the sea was her home.

Barrowgard they kept as a northern watchtower, ever vigilant against enemies that might appear in the wastelands beyond the downs. For they knew not how many of Mindra's hosts were indeed vanquished, or if some yet lingered.

And theirs was a realm of peace for many a long year.

Chapter

53

Heavy frost crunches under my feet as I make my way down the darkened drive, lantern light bobbing. At some point earlier in the evening, the clouds must've cleared, and now the winter sky is strewn with stars. I'm reminded of those summer nights with Grandmother—except tonight the stars are distant and piercing, like diamonds, instead of close and comforting. Table Mount is a dark smudge behind the Hall, which would look vacant but for two lit windows. I've never felt more alone.

Perhaps that's why, when I arrive at the Addisons' bright cottage, I find myself holding back. If this is to be my last visit, then no need to wade in too deep. It'll just make the goodbyes that much more painful. As if losing my grandmother and Carrick Hall aren't hard enough, I'll be losing all of them too—just when I've found them again. I can't bring myself to look at Frankie.

But soon Tilly hands me a cup of wassail, Elspeth drapes me in some sort of garland, and Georgie begs me to pull the other end of the world's loudest cracker. Jack starts bellowing, "Gifts, gifts, gifts! What are we waiting for?" No one seems to notice or care that I brought no gifts myself.

They pass around a pile of tissue-wrapped parcels, which everyone opens at once, and soon we're comparing hand-knitted mufflers ("Oh, well done, Tilly!") and ugly pot holders ("Quite the weaver, aren't you, Elspeth?") and sticky pine cones covered in birdseed ("Georgie, what on earth is that *smell*?").

Into the mess wades Frankie, balancing a large, flat, rectangular parcel. He sets it down on the table and motions for everyone to be quiet.

"You lot," he says, indicating his four siblings, "come here. This gift is for all of you. But Elspeth gets to open it."

As the others draw near, his gaze remains fixed on me, those old points of light, like stars, glinting from the depths. And I understand. He means the gift is for me too.

Elspeth, in her careful, quiet way, slides a finger under the tape and slowly loosens the paper.

"Do come *on*, Bethie!" Georgie whines as she pulls the paper back one side at a time. As the last fold falls away, everyone leans forward.

I gasp. Frankie found it! The missing frame from Aunt Bertie's house. But now, instead of being empty, it displays one of Frankie's drawings—a more intricate, mature piece than any I've yet seen.

"Oooh, it's the dryad!" Tilly exclaims.

"And the stag!" Georgie says. "Look, there, in the woods."

"I like the frame," Jack announces, running his finger along the carven tree and crown.

"It's your best yet, Frankie," Elspeth says quietly.

The dryad, in a dark wood, is just morphing back into a beech tree (or is it vice versa?) while, far behind her, the great stag emerges from the forest. Craggy mountains rise above the trees, and above those, the towers of a high palace. Beauty and adventure and deep magic infuse every line.

The children speculate at top volume. "She's changing into a tree to escape some kind of danger—see the branches in her hair?"

"No, she *was* a tree, and now she's changing back into a human."

"I think she's going to meet the stag."

"Or maybe she's running away from him!"

"Something isn't right." Elspeth's soft voice is barely audible. "She isn't safe. The stag is coming to warn her. If only she can reach the towers . . ."

I ask Frankie over the din, "And you're studying theology rather than art because . . ."

He shrugs, but I can tell by his grin that he's pleased. "No reason why I can't study both. Truth *and* beauty. I hope it's okay that I took the frame from the Cambridge house?"

"Take anything you like," I say. "But I want the avocado lamp."

He laughs. Then he says with his old earnestness, "The frame was empty, of course, just like you described. Which made me wonder . . . All this time we've thought the tapestries were magic, you know? That somehow the tapestries themselves were the portals to other worlds. But what if that's not it at all? What if it's the *frames*?"

"You mean . . . that whatever picture one installs in the frame can become a kind of portal?"

"Something like that."

"Do we tell them?" I gesture toward the four younger ones, their heads bent together over the table.

"When it's time, they'll know."

The church is hot and crowded after the cold walk along High Street. Dozens of lit candles add to the closeness, but there's no time to peel off our coats and mufflers before we find ourselves crammed into the usual pews. And either the church has gotten smaller, or we've all gotten bigger, but once again I'm crushed between Tilly and Frankie, our shoulders pressed together.

Frankie's gaze is fixed on the carved screen behind the altar. I lean into him. "So you still believe all those old stories?" I whisper one last time. "Those fairy tales about other worlds?"

His expression as he turns to me—bold, dignified, fierce—holds all the hope it once did. More, even. It's the expression of a king. "And why not?"

As the bells clamor overhead, I shift position, and my hand accidentally brushes his. But this time neither of us jumps with embarrassment. Instead, I slip my hand into his, and he holds it.

He doesn't let go till we say good night at the kitchen door of Carrick Hall.

And now our tale draws to a close. Elsewhere much is told of how, one day in midwinter, Queen Flora and Queen Annabel went to the aid of Queen Claris in the Wilderlands during a skirmish with wolves; and how, whilst in the forest deeps, they once more met the stag—and were not heard of again in Ternival.

Elsewhere much is also told of how they found themselves back in Tellus, in the very manor house where they'd been staying as guests for the summer holidays, still dressed in their royal garb. Indeed, Flora still wore the crown and gems.

And it seemed to the queens as if no time had passed. Annabel was still in trouble with the head gardener for picking flowers, which is why she and the others had tried to enter the tapestry to begin with (it was through this frame that they'd first found themselves in the East Wilderlands). But their hostess, a perceptive older woman whom Annabel and Flora's mother referred to as a theologian ("a philosopher who goes to church," Mother explained), seemed far less interested in the flowers than in their adventures.

For their hostess was Augusta, all grown up, and she knew quite a lot about these things. And it was she who first wrote down the tales of Ternival.

She wrote many other things as well, including how the queens safeguarded the crown and gems by separating them and keeping them well hidden, lest Mindra find her way to Tellus. That tale and more did Augusta record in *The Writ of Queens*, which you may yet be able to find in Tellus if you seek it with all your heart.

Chapter

54

Christmas morning. I'm awake early in the gray dawn. Snow fell sometime in the night—not the heavy midwestern blizzards I've gotten used to, but a light dusting that drapes the hedgerows like lace. It traces the branches in the orchard and rests on the statue of Annabeth in the secret garden, her eyes frozen, unseeing.

I throw on my coat and boots and exit the French doors into the formal gardens. There I walk among the motionless figures. The dryad. The centaur. The rabbit and mastiff. I want to breathe on them, rub their leafy hands or paws between my warm palms, whisper that it will be all right. One day. Everything will be all right. Won't it?

When I reach the high hedge of the secret garden, I'm grateful that the entrance is no longer hidden. Someone has widened this opening, like the gateway to a maze, and it's now large enough for a grown person to enter comfortably.

The white lawn is trackless, pristine. Snow dusts every branch and twig. A film of ice covers the pool, which holds nothing but an empty pedestal. And there, along the far hedge, lies the stone statue where we left her five years ago, as if asleep under a blanket.

Silently I make my way to her, loath to mar the snow with my dirty boots. I reach down and brush the cold flakes from her face. The last time I saw her, she was real and alive in the world beyond the door. I can't forget Annabeth's searching gaze, the warmth of her breath as she whispered, *Take heart. Be valiant.*

We look more alike than ever.

"Eva?"

It's Frankie, rushing toward me in a navy wool coat and red muffler. His cheeks are flushed; something gold glitters in his hand. He's practically running to greet me.

"I saw your footprints in the snow and figured you were here," he says, breathless.

He draws near, holds out the object. A golden pear, shimmering in the gloom, pulses with light.

"Wh—where in the world?" I gasp. "How did you come by this in the middle of winter?"

"It was on the track behind the school, by the door in the wall."

I try to speak but can't. We stand staring down like it's a living creature, indescribably beautiful.

"It's just as I remember," I whisper. "That day, beyond the door. But here, in this world, it's even more glorious."

"I think it's for your grandmother," he says.

I glance up at him quickly, my heart thundering. He's right, of course.

"But I'd like to give it to her myself," he adds, "if you don't mind."

We exit the garden and head for the steps to the veranda. At that moment my mother hails us from the French doors. "Oh, there you are! Merry Christmas, of course. She's awake again and calling for you."

Frankie slips the pear into his coat pocket and takes my hand while Mum appraises us with a quizzical smile. We head up the steps together.

"I'll be in the kitchen," Frankie says as I head toward the entrance hall. "I'll join you later."

"Oh, but she's calling for both of you," Mum says.

Wordless, he and I climb the grand staircase, apprehension filling the space between us.

Mrs. Fealston greets us at the door to Grandmother's rooms. "Merry Christmas, my dears. Are you ready for an audience with Her Majesty?"

"*Her Majesty*, is she?" Frankie echoes, wary.

"She's not in our world right now, you see," Mrs. Fealston warns. "But you'll know what to do."

Once again, Grandmother is awake and alert—although I'm not certain she knows either of us. A smile plays on her face as she looks first at Frankie, then at me.

"For shame, to keep thy sovereign waiting on this, of all mornings!" Her voice is light and teasing. "Now, then. Gifts are the custom, I believe."

Grandmother passes something to Frankie. It's wrapped in tissue, which he carefully peels back. It's the wooden box from the garden.

"'Twas crafted by thy grandfather's uncle," Grandmother says, "from the pear trees he planted. So 'tis thine by right. Do with it what thou wilt." I can't be sure, but I think there's an apology in her eyes.

Frankie bows: a natural, grace-filled gesture. "An honor, Your Majesty. As it happens, I likewise have a gift for you."

From his coat pocket he draws out the golden pear and places it in her lap.

She smiles her half smile and says in a more normal voice, "Oh dear. I wish I liked pears. I was stranded once, with nothing else to eat. I'm afraid I haven't had much appetite for them since."

"You'll like this one," he assures her.

She shifts her gaze to me. "And now for thy gift."

I open my mouth, then close it again.

"Nay," she says with a laugh. "Not *thy* gift for *me*. Rather, mine for thee. But I fear I must send thee on a journey to retrieve it, as I have not the strength."

She takes my hand.

"Listen well. Knowest thou the staircase that climbs to the top-most battlement?"

The only staircases I can think of lead to the attic, but I assume that's what she means. "I think so, Your Majesty."

"At the northwest corner, underneath the eaves, is a hidden door. Knowest it?"

The door to the crawlspace. Beside me, Frankie grows very still.

Grandmother tightens her grip on my hand. "Long ago, I did possess a treasure. But before thy birth, in a fit of rage, I ordered it to be burned." She closes her eyes and frowns. "Alas, 'twas an evil thing I did. I rue it. Yea, I rue it every hour." She tugs at my hand and drags her eyelids open.

"You're tired," I say. "Better rest now."

"No!" she exclaims and attempts to sit up straighter. "Mark thy sovereign well. Some treasure yet remains, I tell thee. Still un-touched. It is *thy* treasure, dost thou hear? I give it thee. It is thine to do with as thou pleasest."

With a start, I recall those summer days in the lamplit studio, Frankie and me dreaming of adventures—while sitting on heavy wooden trunks. The papers! She means the Professor's papers. Trunks of them, still there. Paxton didn't burn everything after all. And they've been in the studio ever since.

I want to dash up the stairs to the top of Carrick Hall and yank open the door. But Grandmother still grasps my hand. I glance at Frankie. His eyes say everything.

Grandmother then reaches under the coverlet and pulls out an old bound notebook. It's a journal, for I can see words scribbled in longhand on the cover. And sticking out of the book is what looks like a yellowed bookmark.

"And this is for thy mother. 'Tis what she sought, all those summers ago, but I kept it hidden. Out of spite." Again Grandmother frowns. "I rue that as well. Do you suppose she shall ever forgive me?"

"It's never too late to make wrong things right," I say. "Or to try."

She hands me the book. Scrawled across the cover are the words *The Writ of Queens.*

The lost, unpublished tales of Ternival.

I open it reverently, and out falls the bookmark onto Grandmother's bed. But it isn't a bookmark: It's the telegram, carefully pieced back together with clear tape. She picks it up with a trembling hand.

"All those years," she whispers, "I thought they'd left me behind. As though I wasn't worth the trouble. As though my story wasn't worth telling. And then they were lost, and so was I."

Grandmother lies back against her pillows, exhausted. Her eyes find mine.

"But no. Not lost, beloved Eva, my heart. Not lost. Merely hidden."

We remain by her bedside until she drifts off to sleep, the pear, still untouched, on her lap.

ᚳ ᛒ

In all the old stories, in those fairy tales I still believe, this is how it happens.

Ordinary kids return from their adventures in other worlds. Wiser. Braver. And humbler, too, for they've had to reckon with their faults—and face fell enemies, whose strength surpassed theirs, and thus call upon a strength greater still to save them.

But what the stories don't tell is what happens next. How those travelers must make their way in this ordinary world, grow older, learn to love, attempt to thrive, face their worst fears, fail, and help other young ones have their own adventures someday. And those stories are also worth telling.

I don't know what Grandmother will do with the golden pear. I don't know whether she'll choose to join the others at last, to claim her throne beyond the door. I can't make that choice for her.

What I *can* do is stay by her side, here in this quiet room on Christmas Day. I can hold her hand, admire the embroidery on her robe, and run my finger along the lovely rings she still wears. I can try to love her, regardless of what she chooses.

For this is my story too.

Author Q&A
with Sarah Arthur

What's the story behind the story of this book?

About twenty years ago, I stumbled across an obscure article about the British rail crash of October 8, 1952, which killed 112 people and wounded 340—to this day, the worst peacetime rail accident in British history. I began to think about the victims. Where were they going? Who did they leave behind? How did the survivors feel, knowing they'd lived through World War II only to suffer tremendous loss in peacetime?

As often happens with me, a story began to take shape in my head. Let's suppose a young woman experienced a series of tragedies, including losing someone in that crash. What would it do to her as a survivor? It became clear that this kind of trauma likely would have a profound effect on her mental health, on her trust in a good and just universe, and on her relationships with family and friends—including her children and grandchildren—for the rest of her life.

I began writing. And along the way I realized that the story was partly about my own grandmother, who died of cancer when I was fourteen. Born in 1913, she had a tough childhood. She lost her father to the flu epidemic of 1918. Her mother remarried not once but twice—and one of those marriages ended in divorce. The family relocated to land in northern Michigan that was supposedly good for farming—but it wasn't. She grew to hate farming. Later, my grandmother's husband died of a heart attack when my mom was seventeen.

My grandmother carried those wounds, including a refusal to believe in a good God, into my own childhood, when she went into rehab for alcohol addiction and suicidal ideation. Then, after her cancer diagnosis, she came to live with us during the last weeks of her life. Her medically-induced psychic breaks gave us a window into even more pain, which was both scary and heartbreaking. But in the end, there was a moment when she seemed to turn back to faith in a very childlike way, which gave me hope that the trauma she'd experienced wouldn't have the last word in her story—or ours.

In *Once a Queen,* the fallout of generational trauma continues into the summer of 1995, when my story begins and the survivor's only granddaughter—American teenager Eva Joyce—travels to England to meet her grandmother for the first time. But generational trauma doesn't get the last word in this story either. We can trust that the Author is ultimately good and just.

Tell us about the influences on your writing.

I grew up reading authors like Frances Hodgson Burnett (*The Secret Garden*), George MacDonald (*At the Back of the North Wind*), C. S.

Lewis (The Chronicles of Narnia), Elizabeth Goudge (*The Little White Horse*), and Madeleine L'Engle (*A Wrinkle in Time*), among others. I suppose all my fiction echoes these stories in some way. *Once a Queen,* in particular, echoes classic fairy tales, so I decided to invent my own fictional world with its own origin story.

The key metaphor in my tales is that of weaving: There's a World-Weaver, who creates worlds on a cosmic loom, and the storytellers of those worlds are known as Loomkeepers, who weave the stories into tapestries with images that sometimes come to life. For the weaving imagery and terminology, I've relied on the incredible artistry of my sister, Abigail Deloria, who is a master weaver based in northern Michigan.

What's your purpose in writing this book?

I once heard Newbery-winning author Katherine Paterson deliver a keynote in which she said, "I want to be a spy for hope." That's the purpose of all my writing: to inspire young people like my main character, Eva, to hold on to the hopes, dreams, stories, creative play, and imaginative worlds they inhabited as children, even as they turn their faces toward adulthood with all its pain. What if those childhood things actually are glimpses of the true joy, the true hope, that holds up the world?

I want to show how joy is a living thread that runs through the warp and weft of the universe. That's the hope I've built into this book.

Acknowledgments

The idea for this story came twenty years ago, when I was under a publishing deadline for something else. That's when all my best ideas hit me, when I'm least able to give them my full attention. I typed out three terrible chapters and a synopsis, which I then inflicted on some generous friends and colleagues. Their feedback is the reason I felt brave enough to cut the awful stuff and keep going.

In particular, many thanks to the 45th Parallel Writers' Group in northern Michigan—especially Jami and Mark Blaauw-Hara—for asking the hard questions. To the little group of romance writers in my hometown, who let me bring my non-romance chapters to our monthly dinners, thank you for teaching me how to love my main characters. To Drs. Peter Schakel, Michael Ward, and the late Dabney Hart: I have no idea why world-class scholars would agree to read the scribblings of an amateur, but the fact that you took it seriously pushed me to do the same.

Other drafts were inflicted on Tracy Tooley, Amy Scott, Erin Wasinger, Ashlee Cowles, Ami McConnell Abston, Charlotte Jones

Voiklis, Candy Bryant, Stephanie Rische, and many more (I should've made a list!). And of course, Sarah Rubio, whose history with this project eventually came full circle in ways I never could've guessed or even hoped. Your enthusiasm is the reason I kept going.

If the book is any good, it's thanks to Marjorie Lamp Mead of the Wade Center at Wheaton College, who told me ten years ago to make the story stand on its own feet. Also to novelist Laura Weymouth, who introduced me to the "Save the Cat!" resources (which I've since dubbed "Save My Tail!"), and especially to author Carey Wallace, who gave me eleventh-hour line edits and plotting tips that helped me become more than a mere dabbler—and who has become a dear friend, besides.

Twenty years—including long pauses to publish twelve nonfiction books, earn a master's degree in theology, move numerous times, raise two sons, and fight breast cancer—and then a serendipitous reunion with Alice Fugate, one of my undeserved superfans. She's now the Best Literary Agent Ever. By the time the book reached Sarah Rubio's hands again at WaterBrook, I was surprised at nothing anymore.

Through it all, my family has been unswervingly supportive, even when it was unclear whether this book would ever happen. *Especially* when it was unclear.

To Mom and Dad: Thank you for a happy, unpressured childhood full of books, for encouraging my creativity, and for babysitting the boys so I could write.

To my in-laws, who asserted I could do this: Your prayers were everything.

To my sister, Abbie, a master fiber artist: Your insights about weaving made the story smarter than I am.

To my sons, Micah and Sam, who let me read it aloud during the dog days of COVID-19: Your exclamations of "More! Please, Mommy? Just one more chapter?" made it all worth it.

Above all, extra *super-duper* thanks to my husband, Tom, who's the main reason this book exists at all. Thank you for clearing your schedule so I could take writing retreats, for believing in me 1,000 percent, and for weeping after you read the final page. It's all for you.

Lastly, this book honors the memory of two women.

Marta Arthur, my late stepmother-in-law, who loved fiction and told me, "You were born to do this." My biggest regret is that I didn't finish this, my first novel, before we lost you to cancer.

And my maternal grandmother, Flora Elizabeth, who died of cancer when I was fourteen. When your mind broke during those final, morphine-laced weeks, the childhood faith that had eluded you somehow returned in strange and beautiful ways. We glimpsed the girl you must've been—before trauma, or doubts, or both, took hold. But your love for us never wavered, and neither did the deep and abiding Mercy that buoys us all.

May we meet again one day on the far side of the door.

About the Author

Sarah Arthur is a fun-loving speaker and the author of a dozen books for teens and adults, including the bestselling *Walking with Frodo: A Devotional Journey Through The Lord of the Rings*. After more than twenty-five years working with teens, she plays a wicked game of four square, but don't ask her to eat cold pizza from a box, ever. Among other nerdy adventures, she has served as preliminary fiction judge for *Christianity Today*'s Book Awards, was a founding board member of the annual C. S. Lewis Festival in northern Michigan, and co-directs the Madeleine L'Engle Writing Retreats. Her preteen sons have Very Important Things to Say About Books, and apparently this one passed muster.

Sneak Preview of Book 2,

Once a Castle

The castle had appeared out of nowhere.

Jack Addison had hunted for geodes in this valley before, at least a hundred times. Normally the place contained only some scrubby underbrush and one small lake fed by a burbling stream, all encircled by stony bluffs. But today, at the far end of the lake stood a castle.

And not just any castle. A really, really old one. Boxy and un-adorned, with sheer stone walls rising to high battlements, it had the same weathered look as a ruin he'd visited on a class trip last term. Six hundred years old, at least.

But this was no ruin. A thin wisp of smoke spiraled lazily from the highest battlement. A strange rumble echoed across the water, like someone rolling a cart across a stone courtyard. Back and forth, back and forth.

Jack began to edge around the lake toward the castle, following what looked like the familiar path. He felt slightly dizzy, like maybe he'd cracked his head harder while rock climbing yesterday than he'd realized. This couldn't be the same valley. He'd taken a wrong turn somewhere.

But no. There was the scree of fallen rocks where he'd found that simply spectacular geode last summer. There was the boulder where he'd eaten leftover fish-and-chips on Sunday. He'd chucked the newspaper into the shrubs, he remembered now. If it was the same valley, wouldn't it still be there?

It was. After a brief scramble, he found the newspaper balled up nearby. Another wave of dizziness swept over him. He glanced back and forth between the smoke curling from the battlement and the paper in his palm.

Same newspaper. Same valley. But castles didn't just grow from the ground.

One lone arrow-slit toward the topmost battlement seemed to stare at him like an unblinking reptilian eye. It made him feel small and vulnerable, which he didn't often feel these days—a mighty growth spurt after his thirteenth birthday had taken care of that. But now he felt tiny as an insect, easily crushed.

The rumble grew louder for a moment, paused, then resumed, a little deeper now. Jack stayed put, watching warily, until curiosity drove him forward again.

Now he was in the castle's very shadow, its grim exterior rising to an impossible height. As he drew nearer, a nauseating smell hit him: an organic, almost animal sourness that reminded him of wet dog and sweaty gym clothes, but worse. The rumble shook the ground beneath him, with more pauses filled by a strange whooshing like enormous bellows.

For about ten seconds he considered retreating up the trail that had brought him here. He could climb back to the ridgeline that connected the high summit of Giant's Beacon to Table Mount and descend from there to Carrick Hall, his parents' workplace. He'd enter the normal chaos of the kitchen, study his maps at the table, and regain his bearings over tea and scones.

But the castle wall was almost within reach now: Just a few more steps, and he could confirm whether or not it was real. Plus, he was beyond range of the arrow-slit, which gave him a sudden boldness. He reached out.

Real. He could feel the grit under his fingers, the clammy coolness. He could feel the rumble, too, vibrating through the rock, and smell the stench. The sound, at least, was coming from somewhere on the other side of the castle.

Jack stepped gingerly through the rubble at the base of the wall and made his way around the building, deep in shadow from the bluffs. As he turned the corner, he expected to find a portcullis or some other entrance, but instead, the route was blocked by what looked like massive lumpy earthworks, or like a section of bluff had crashed down against the castle wall maybe five hundred years ago. He could see no way around it either: The shadowed mound extended from the castle wall all the way to the bluff. He'd have to climb over it or take the long way around.

He decided to climb. But as he approached the mound, the stench grew so strong that he nearly retched. The rumble increased, like the earth itself was moving.

And then it was.

Right before his eyes, the top of the mound rose like an inflating zeppelin, with a thunderous rumble, and fell with a mighty whoosh. Then up and down again, up and down. For all the world as if the ground was snoring.

Jack froze. Heart racing, he scanned the mound from one end to the other. It couldn't be.

But it was.

Stretched out full-length on the valley floor, next to a castle that had appeared out of nowhere, lay a sleeping giant.